MAY THE TWEL

MASS-OBSERVATION
DAY-SURVEYS 1937
by over two hundred observers

Edited by

Humphrey Jennings
Charles Madge

and

T. O. Beachcroft
Julian Blackburn
William Empson
Stuart Legg
Kathleen Raine

With a new Afterword by David Pocock,
Director of the Tom Harrisson
Mass-Observation Archive

faber and faber
LONDON · BOSTON

First published in 1937
by Faber and Faber Limited
3 Queen Square London WC1N 3AU
This paperback edition first published in 1987

Printed in Great Britain by
Mackays of Chatham Ltd, Kent
All rights reserved

British Library Cataloguing in Publication Data

[Mass-Observation day-survey]. May the twelfth:
    Mass-Observation day-survey.
    1. Great Britain——Social life and customs——
    20th century——Sources
    I.Jennings, Humphrey   II. Madge, Charles
    941.084   DA566.4

    ISBN 0-571-14872-7

Preface

Early in 1937, fifty people in different parts of the country agreed to co-operate in making observations on how they and other people spend their daily lives. These fifty Observers were the vanguard of a developing movement, aiming to apply the methods of science to the complexity of a modern culture. In June 1937, a pamphlet called *Mass-Observation* was published (Muller, price 1s.), outlining this experiment in its theory and practice, and stressing the need for a large number of Observers. This pamphlet, which is the fullest statement so far, was given astonishing publicity in the Press. Within a few weeks more than a thousand people had applied to be Observers and the number is steadily rising.

The Observers by this time cover the whole country. They are in the industrial centres, in rural and urban areas, in country towns, suburbs and villages. They include coalminers, factory hands, shopkeepers, salesmen, housewives, hospital nurses, bank clerks, business men, doctors and schoolmasters, scientists and technicians. A large proportion of them have already shown themselves able to write really useful reports. Prof. Julian Huxley has written of some of these that they 'would put many orthodox scientists to shame in their simplicity, clearness and objectivity.'

Since February, these Observers have been making reports about what happened to them on a given day, namely the twelfth of each month. They have concentrated on normal routine events. The survey of May 12 which takes up most of this book was therefore exceptional: it is almost wholly concerned with one event, which affected the whole country. This gives a unity to the reports which is an advantage in the first published example of the method in action. It also gives scope for the study of crowd behaviour, to which the method is well suited. As a rule, however, Mass-Observation will be dealing with everyday things rather than special occasions.

It seems to us that the organisation gives a meeting point between many fields. The results that should be obtainable when the method is fully developed should be of interest to the social worker, the field anthropologist, the politician, the historian, the advertising agent, the realistic novelist and indeed any person who is concerned to know what people really want and think. We propose to hold our files open to any serious worker. But in addition to special scientific uses, we believe that observing is itself of real value to the Observer. It heightens his power of seeing what is around him and gives him new interest in and understanding of it. He also benefits by seeing specimens of others' reports. Results must be issued in a form that will be available and interesting to the non-specialist. Moreover Mass-Observation depends for its vitality on the criticisms and suggestions of the whole body of its Observers, who must be more than mere recording instruments.

The main development of Mass-Observation has been two-fold, firstly the network of Observers all over the country; secondly an intensive survey of a single town. Charles Madge runs the former, Tom Harrisson the latter. Humphrey Jennings is responsible for the business of presenting results. These three activities are closely linked. The local survey starts with whole-time research workers studying a place from the outside and working inwards, getting into the society, and so coming to the individual. The national plan starts from the

individual Observers and works outwards from them
into their social surroundings. One aim of Mass-
Observation is to see how, and how far, the individual
is linked up with society and its institutions. The third
important task is that of issuing our reports and find-
ings in a form which will be of interest and value to
Observers, the general public, and scientists.

The final responsibility for presenting the material
must in the case of this book rest on the whole-time
editors, Charles Madge and Humphrey Jennings.
Many others worked hard over shorter periods and on
special problems. They include T. O. Beachcroft,
Julian Blackburn, William Empson, Stuart Legg and
Kathleen Raine. Ruthven Todd compiled the index.
The real authors of the book are the Observers, who
must be anonymous, but without whose help nothing
could have been done.

August 1937.

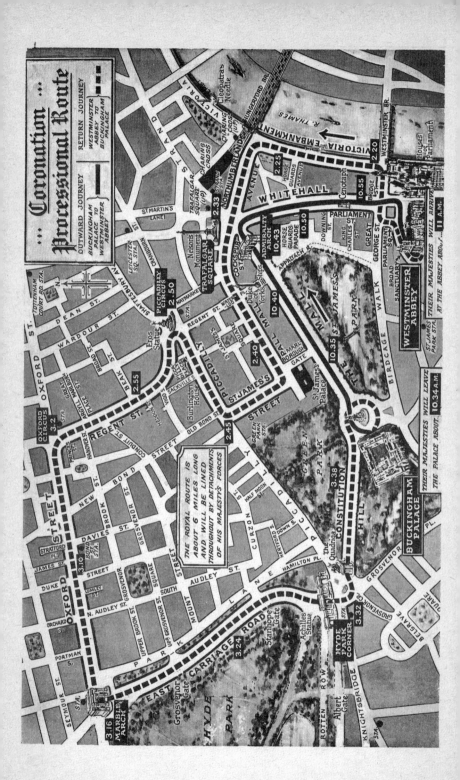

Contents

vii

Illustrations

Chapter I

PREPARATION FOR MAY 12

'The Eight Means of Government are: Food, Goods, Sacrifices, Labour, Instruction, Protection against Crime, Entertainment of Guests, and the Army.' (*The Book of Records* edited by CONFUCIUS.)

1. When surveys were made by Mass-Observation of three normal working days, February 12, March 12 and April 12, 1937, it was found that each day had been carefully prepared beforehand. For example, newspapers, which play such a part in the life of a day, were produced on the preceding day, while a great part of their contents dated from earlier still. The day's big advertisements were planned months ahead, and so were B.B.C. programmes, films, plays, books, lectures, conferences, sporting events, religious services, etc. A detailed study was made by Mass-Observation of the relation of these preparations to ordinary human lives on February 12. This study was to have formed part of the present book, but for reasons of space it was decided to devote the whole volume to May 12, with a final section on the normal day survey.

In the case of May 12, preparations were infinitely greater and more protracted. To understand the day, it is essential to devote some time to them. This chapter deals entirely with events leading up to May 12. The reader who wants to see at once the more dramatic effects of Mass-Observation in action should therefore turn on fairly rapidly to the second chapter, but he will probably find himself turning back to the earlier pages for the light they cast on subsequent events. A library of press-cuttings was built up during the three months

3

preceding the day; about 5,000 cuttings were taken from national and provincial newspapers and periodicals. Even then the collection was very far from being exhaustive, and it could profitably have been begun several months earlier. In making this collection, the Observers themselves played an essential part; they made cuttings from their own local newspapers, and were able to keep us posted as to the preparations and incidents they observed in the pre-Coronation months in their own localities. All this gave us a mass of data, which had to be sorted, indexed and filed. The material presented is intended to represent in outline the various types of preparatory activity, from the most solid and official to the most popular and hysterical. In this chapter the bulk of the quotations are from the press, which played the double role of both describing the preparations which were made and also of being itself one of the main instruments for preparing the people. In the remaining chapters the people themselves will say what the day was like for them.*

Preparations (i)

2. The Coronation of King George and Queen Elizabeth in May will cost the Treasury £454,000, a far greater sum than has been spent on any previous Coronation. In the estimates published yesterday it is disclosed that £524,000 will be required altogether, but towards this £70,000 will be realized from the sale of seats along the route of the procession.

*The following abbreviations are used in this chapter: *D.E.*, for *Daily Express*; *D.H.*, for *Daily Herald*; *D.T.*, for *Daily Telegraph*; *E.N.*, for *Evening News*; *E.S.*, for *Evening Standard*; *M.G.*, for *Manchester Guardian*; *N.C.*, for *News Chronicle*.

The last five Coronations have cost:

George IV. 1821 - - -	£238,238
William IV. 1831 - - -	£42,298
Victoria. 1838 - - -	£69,421
Edward VII. 1902 - - -	£193,000
George V. 1911 - - -	£185,000

Comparing the estimates with those for the Coronation of King George V, the greatest part of the increased cost is in the estimate of the Office of Works for the preparation of Westminster Abbey and annexe and the erection of stands along the route. This has increased from £33,000 to £354,000 —less the £70,000 for the sale of seats.* (*D.T.* 4.3.37.)

3. The 7,700 invitations to attend the Coronation which are now being issued take the form of cards 10½ in. by 8¾ in., printed in black, and headed: 'Coronation of Their Majesties King George VI. and Queen Elizabeth.' The wording is:

'By Command of the King, the Earl Marshal is directed to invite......to be present at the Abbey Church of Westminster on the 12th day of May, 1937.'

Then follow the signature, 'Norfolk, Earl Marshal', and the arms of the Earl Marshal. Round the words of the invitation are the arms of the British Isles and the Commonwealth. The King's arms are in the top left corner, and the Queen's new arms, with the uncrowned lion of the Bowes-Lyon family, occupy the top right corner of the card. Between them are the arms of England and Scotland, with the Rose and the Thistle. Then, running right round the edges of the card, follow:

The arms and shamrock of Ireland;
The arms, oak leaves and acorns of the Union;
The arms and maple-leaf of Canada;
The arms and fern-frond of New Zealand;

*The £454,000 did not, however, cover the cost of the troops present, for which £218,000 was allotted from the Defence Vote, or include £17,400 from the vote on account (current running expenses).

The King's cypher, 'G.R. VI.';
The arms and protea evergreen leaf of South Africa;
The arms and wattle of Australia;
The arms and lotus of India; and
The arms and leek of Wales. (*D. T.* 6.4.37.)

4. The delegations from overseas to the Coronation will include 34 Royal personages, 29 Indian Princes, 9 Foreign Ministers, 7 Prime Ministers and several Commanders-in-Chief.

Among the Royal visitors will be the Count of Flanders, the Crown Prince and Princess of Denmark, Princess Juliana and Prince Bernhard of the Netherlands, and Crown Prince Michael of Rumania, the Crown Prince Olaf of Norway, the Crown Prince and Princess of Sweden, and Prince Chichibu, brother of the Emperor of Japan.

The United States delegation will include Gen. Pershing and Mr. James Gerard, former U.S. Ambassador in Berlin, M. Litvinoff will represent Soviet Russia, and Turkey will be represented by her Prime Minister, Gen. Ismel Inonu.

Australia, Canada, New Zealand, South Africa, and Southern Rhodesia are sending their Prime Ministers. The official Indian delegation includes the Maharaja Gaekwar of Baroda and the Aga Khan. (*D. T.* 30.3.37.)

5. The King has surprised and delighted four workpeople by personally inviting them to be present at the Coronation service in Westminster Abbey on May 12. One is a Scotch woman weaver, another a South Wales steel works foreman. Then there is a girl employed at the Birmingham electricity works and a young pit worker at Chesterfield.

The King issued the invitation through the Industrial Welfare Society of which he was President for some years, as a mark of his close connection with industry. (*N.C.* 6.4.37.)

6. Peers and their wives, peeresses in their own right and dowager peeresses have now received the Royal Summons to the Coronation. (*D. T.* 13.4.37.)

The form of the Summons to a peer and his wife is as follows:

Right Trusty and Well-beloved—We greet you well.

Whereas the twelfth day of May next is appointed for the Solemnity of our Royal Coronation.

These are to Will and Command you and the Lady your wife (all excuses set apart) to make your personal attendance on Us at the times above-mentioned, furnished and appointed as to your Rank and Quality appertaineth, there to do and perform all such Services as shall be required and belong unto you respectively.

Whereof you and she are not to fail. And so We bid you most heartily farewell.

Given at our Court of St. James's this twelfth day of April in the first year of Our Reign.* (*D.T.* 14.4.37.)

7. In the House of Commons yesterday Sir A. Sinclair, (Caithness and Sutherland, Liberal) asked the Lord President of the Council whether he was in a position to make a statement regarding the representatives of the forces taking part in the Coronation procession and lining the streets, and what arrangements had been made for the accommodation of those troops in London.

Mr. Ramsay MacDonald (Scottish Universities, Nat. Lab.) replied: The number of officers and men from home and overseas in the procession and the lining of the streets at the forthcoming Coronation will amount to approximately 32,500. In the procession will be detachments from the Royal Navy and

*It is of scientific interest to note the antiquated language of this summons, corresponding roughly to fifteenth-century usage.

A similar tendency to use obsolete or unusual language is evident in much of the writing about the Coronation, in official statements, in newspapers and in advertisements. One may compare a dictum of the Archbishop of Canterbury on the Coronation Service: 'It is no mere paradox to say that the very merit and meaning of these rites is precisely that they are in a sense "out of date".'

the Naval Reserves, from all corps and units of the Regular and Territorial Armies, and from the Royal Air Force and the Auxiliary Air Force, the Navy providing 4,000 and the Air Force 3,000 respectively out of the total. (*Times*, 17.3.37.)

8. When the last of the Empire troops arrives in London about May 8, the total strength of the Dominion and Colonial Coronation contingents will be brought up to 1,641 men.

Practically every section of the armed forces of the Empire will be represented, and their picturesque uniforms will add considerably to the brightness of the London Coronation scene.

The scarlet coats of the Royal Canadian Mounted Police, the blue and khaki of the askaris from the King's African Rifles, the Indian turbans and the colour patches of the Colonial Militia forces will make a fine show when all the men are assembled. (*D.T.* 9.3.37.)

9. Personnel required in connection with the Coronation will be housed or encamped in London from May 10 to 13. The camps will be in Kensington Gardens (processional army troops and Royal Air Force), Regent's Park, Primrose Hill, and Olympia (Royal Navy, the Dominions contingents, and three Guards battalions), and at Hampton Court (Indian and Burmese contingents). The Colonial contingent will be accommodated in barracks in London. (*Times*, 17.3.37.)

10. The final cost of building the temporary annexe to Westminster Abbey and preparing the Abbey for the Coronation will be about £100,000. The annexe, where the procession will form and where the robing rooms will be situated, will cost nearly £24,000, but the major part of the £100,000 will be spent on the erection of 7,700 seats in the Abbey. 'The structural work is similar to that in a theatre,' said an Office of Works official. 'Three separate tiers of rising seats will be put up in the transept and two elsewhere. The tremendous weight will be carried on great steel girders.' (*D.T.* 24.2.37.)

11. Five hundred and seventy miles of steel tubing, enough to reach out from London to Basle, in Switzerland, are now in place. The figure is a sober calculation. Thus: contractors reckon that an average of twenty foot of tubing is needed for each seat in a properly made stand. The number of seats which the Office of Works is providing is known to be about 90,000. Unknown is the total seating capacity of stands on the parts of the route which the Office of Works does not control, but there is a guide in the fact that about six steel scaffolding firms have supplied materials for an average of 10,000 seats each.

The total comes to three million feet.

Office of Works contractors are using also 850 tons of timber (Columbian pine, 3 in. by 9 in.) as decking. When the proportionate amount of timber in other stands is added, the weight reaches 1,400 tons. (*N.C.* 22.4.37.)

12. Mr. Attlee (Limehouse, Labour) asked the Lord President of the Council whether he had any statement to make regarding the price of seats on the Government stands to view the Coronation procession.

Mr. Macdonald (Scottish Universities, Nat. Lab.)—Yes, sir. This is a question which has given rise to prolonged consideration. (Laughter.) The subject was approached with the idea of using these stands to accommodate representatives of the many-sided life of the nation. Obviously if this was to be done prices had to be fixed which would not be a bar to anyone invited to attend. The net cost of the seats on the uncovered Government stands is about 30s., and on stands covered £2 5s.

It is clear, however, that such charges would be beyond the means of many people whose presence should be made

9

possible. We examined very carefully various proposals involving differentiation of charges, but came to the conclusion that any scheme based upon differentiation was unworkable; and accordingly the Government have felt justified in fixing the price for uncovered seats at 15s., and for covered seats at £1 2s. 6d.—the Treasury finding the balance. These seats are not to be sold to the general public but only to persons chosen by the groups among which the representation is to be allotted. (*Times*, 18.2.37.)

13. All the 85,000 seats in the Government stands to view the Coronation procession have now been allotted. I learn that they include the following:

Dominions - - - - -	20,000
Colonies - - - - -	5,700
India - - - - -	5,500
Houses of Parliament - - -	2,500
Pensioners and veterans of the Defence Forces, including the British Legion and Old Comrades Association - - -	2,500
Co-operative Movement - -	1,800
Foreign Office - - - -	1,500
London County Council - -	700
City Corporation - - -	500
Federation of British Industries -	500
Boys' Organizations - - -	500

More than 5,000 seats have been allocated to the Royal Household. Seats have also been allotted to the Navy, Army and Air Force. The Home Civil Service, trade unions and other organizations representative of labour, the Diplomatic Corps, associations of people engaged in professional occupations, associations of people representing science, art, letters and teaching, women's institutes, religious organizations, public utility corporations, etc. (*E.N.* 15.3.37.)

14. Schemes for the decoration of nearly four and a half miles of streets for the Coronation, including most of the route of the procession on May 12, were announced by Westminster City Council yesterday. Altogether they will cost £23,000, or £3,000 more than was spent at the Silver Jubilee of King George V and Queen Mary in 1935.

In Regent Street there will be white, blue and gold islands, and red, gold and white masts. Buildings will be decorated in blue, red and gold with white, blue and red and pink flowers.

For Piccadilly the colours will be blue, white, gold and red for the islands, and red, white and gold for the pavement masts, the building scheme being in blue and white.

Red, white, gold and blue have been selected for Whitehall itself, the buildings being dealt with according to the colours recommended by the Office of Works.

In the Strand the colours will be red, white, gold and green for islands, red, white, gold and blue for pavement masts, and blue, red and gold for the buildings.

At night in a number of streets there will be gas flambeaux or electric floodlighting to illuminate the decorations. These will be placed on the islands along the centre of the roads, and the naked flames of the torches will rise from specially fireproofed pylons 13 feet high.

Along every pavement there will be decorated masts 28 feet high, topped with a crown of gold and bearing a banner with the initials of the King and Queen, 'G-E' (*D.T.* 11.3.37.)

15. Plans representing six months' unceasing work by experts of Scotland Yard and London Transport were finished this week-end. Now the traffic planners are confident they have done their best to deal with the 36-hour Coronation rush on May 11-12-13. The whole traffic scheme will be available to the public to-morrow as a souvenir booklet.

Underground trains will run all through the night of May 11-12, key stations remaining open. Twelve of the less important stations will not open at all on Coronation Day, to avoid delays. Four stations will be closed on May 12 until after the Royal Procession has passed—Westminster, Trafalgar Square, Hyde Park Corner and Bond Street. At six of the key stations on the Procession route, restrictions will have to be imposed. (*D.H.* 5.4.37.)

16. Police constables with an aptitude for draughtsmanship have turned cartographers to assist in Scotland Yard's preparations for the Coronation. Their crowning achievement is the production of a map, drawn to scale, measuring 12 ft. by 10 ft. This now occupies the entire side of a room at Scotland Yard, where it will be available for the chiefs of every department concerned with the Coronation. It shows the whole ceremonial area in detail, and the route of the Coronation procession is indicated by red tape.

The route, with vantage points along it, is dotted with coloured drawing pins, different colours representing barriers, 'staggered' barriers, ambulance stations, points where crowds can safely assemble and temporary refreshment places. (*D.T.* 30.3.37.)

17. The Coronation procession is to be led by a Scotland Yard wireless van.

It will just be one of the sixty which will be on duty during the day, but its task will be of far greater importance than the others.

It will supply Scotland Yard with a running commentary of the procession's progress and it will at the same time notify the authorities of points along the route where police reinforcements may be needed. (*E.S.* 26.4.37.)

18. An elaborate network of telephones to link up every important point on Coronation Day has been installed by the

Post Office. Through this private network Buckingham Palace will be in direct touch with the Abbey, the Earl Marshal's Office with all stands on the route, and Scotland Yard and the fire brigades with every point at which mishaps might cause need for their services.

The heart of the system will be a special exchange, Whitehall 4422, in St. James's Palace. Here the procession itself will be controlled. (*E.S.* 12.3.37.)

19. The Coronation procession on May 12 will be—

> 3,500 yards long (about 2 miles),
> And take 40 minutes to pass a given point.
>
> (*D. Mail*, 17.3.37.)

On the way to the Abbey, six processions will precede that of the King and Queen, who will leave Buckingham Palace at 10.30 a.m. and arrive at the Abbey at 11 o'clock.

Following the Lord Mayor of London's procession will be that of the Speaker of the House of Commons. Then will come a procession of carriages carrying Mr. Baldwin, the Dominion Premiers, and other Empire representatives, and later the carriage processions of the Royal Family and Queen Mary. Princess Elizabeth and Princess Margaret will drive to the Abbey in a glass coach with the Princess Royal and a Captain's escort.

The King and Queen will be in the State Coach drawn by Windsor Greys. The Standard will be carried immediately behind the coach, and will be followed by the Duke of Gloucester and the Duke of Kent riding side by side. (*D.T.* 28.4.37.)

20. Sir John Reith spent an hour at Buckingham Palace yesterday discussing with the King arrangements made for broadcasting Coronation ceremonies.

The King wanted to hear how technical and other difficulties will be overcome, particularly as it was feared that it might not be possible to give a true representation of the Abbey service.* (*D.H.* 24.2.37.)

21. Seven observers will tell to home and Empire listeners the story of the procession from Buckingham Palace to the Abbey.

Fifty-eight microphones will be used, 32 in and near the Abbey itself.

It is hoped that listeners will even hear the King's voice during part of the service.

The total weight of equipment installed is 12 tons, and the total length of wire used approximately 472 miles. (*D. Dispatch*, 16.4.37.)

22. Inside the annexe Michael Standing will tell of the marshalling of the procession;

Of the memorable scene as the 'great Proceeding' moves slowly up the carpeted aisle through the organ screen and on towards the High Altar;

As the King himself passes through the West Door to the inspiring sound of the opening anthem.

*Each person meets in the course of his daily life a large number of people. Some he meets every day, or most days: such as his family and people living in the same house; tradesmen and roundsmen who call at the house every day; people working in the same office, shop, factory or wherever he spends his working day; regular cronies and acquaintances, etc. All these we propose to call people in area 1. In area 2 come all strangers and people met for the first time. In area 3 are all those people like prime ministers, film stars, celebrities of all kinds, historical figures, mythical figures, collections of people like the Conservative Party, the Church, etc.—whom you probably do not meet in the flesh, but whose faces, actions, words, etc., you may know as well as you know your best friend, and which may have just as great an influence on you.

The King is the archetype of all the personages of area 3. On the great public occasion of his Coronation he exhibits himself *in the flesh* to thousands of his subjects. This is obviously of the greatest importance as a means of establishing his position at the centre of the entire social system. Hence it is that broadcasting plays so vital a role, in enabling the contact between areas 1 and 3 to be effected on a far wider scale than has ever been possible hitherto. It is this too which gives potential significance to the added use of television, by whose agency the King is not only heard but actually seen in the process of exhibiting himself to the masses.

During the service the B.B.C. Director of Religion, the Rev. F. A. Iremonger, chaplain to the King, will offer guidance for the thoughts and prayers of listeners during that part of the Abbey service which will not be broadcast. (*Ibid.*)

23. The culminating point in the Coronation Ceremony, when Dr. Lang, the Archbishop of Canterbury, places the crown on the King's head, will be reached, I understand, shortly after noon on May 12. This is the time indicated by the preliminary rehearsals in Westminster Abbey. Further rehearsals and tests with stop watches are expected to fix the time within two or three minutes.

The fact that the King has been crowned will be proclaimed officially by the firing of guns. Elaborate arrangements are being made to ensure that the firing synchronizes with the ceremony. Direct telephone lines are being installed from the Abbey to artillery batteries in St. James's Park, the Tower and Windsor, the three chief firing points. An observer stationed in a box in the Abbey will be watching the ceremony, and the moment the Archbishop places the crown on the King's head he will give the signal to fire simultaneously to the batteries.

The authorities are not relying on the telephone alone. Wireless will be used to ensure that the firing takes place at the precise moment. A special signalling set is being installed on which the observer will flash a message to the batteries. (*D.T.* 1.5.37.)

24. It is anticipated that Their Majesties' drive in state from Westminster Abbey to Buckingham Palace will begin at approximately 1.40 p.m.

George Blake again will continue the story as the waiting crowds acclaim their newly-crowned King and Queen, and there will be the sounds of pealing bells, gun-fire, and cheering. Then, instead of the voices of observers, four special

'atmosphere' microphones will tell their own story by repro-
ducing the sounds—the martial music, the cheers—as the
procession passes. (*D. Dispatch*, 16.4.37.)

25. The arrangements being made promise that tele-
viewers will see on their screens more than a great many spectators will see in the crowded streets. The transmission will be
made early in the afternoon during the return procession
from Westminster Abbey.

Three television cameras will be placed at the Apsley
Gate, Hyde Park Corner. One on the plinth will give over-
head views of the advancing procession down East Carriage
Drive, and a second immediately to the north of the gate
will provide telescopic close-ups, including pictures of the
King and Queen, as the procession passes. (*D.T.* 7.4.37.)

26. The largest telephoto lens in the world will be used by
Paramount in filming the Coronation.

By the use of this lens a distant object, which would normally appear so small as to be hardly discernible, can be
made large enough to fill the entire screen with full definition
and thus will permit close-up views to be taken from distant
camera positions.

British Paramount News will use it in taking pictures of the
Royal Family when they appear on the balcony of Buckingham Palace after their return from the Abbey. (*The Cinema*,
5.5.37.)

27. After crowning King George VI at Westminster Abbey
on May 12, Dr. Lang, Archbishop of Canterbury, will go
to a dark room in the West End to play a new role—film
censor.

His Grace, ever vigilant of public interest and good taste,
will carefully scan the films of the Coronation made by the
news reels. With him will be the Earl Marshal the Duke of
Norfolk. The Primate and the Duke will have a free hand to

cut from the film records anything which may be considered unsuitable for the public at large to see. (*D. Mirror*, 6.3.37.)

28. The *Daily Telegraph* learns that King George's address to his peoples which will be broadcast on the evening of Coronation Day, May 12, has been fixed approximately for 8 p.m.

The King's speech is expected to last about ten minutes. It will come as the climax to a programme of Empire homage in which five Premiers and the Viceroy of India, the Marquess of Linlithgow, will take part.

The programme will begin at 7.20 p.m. Mr. Baldwin, the last Premier to broadcast, will speak a few introductory sentences which will bring the King to the microphone at Buckingham Palace.

The entire programme will be recorded and re-broadcast from the Empire station at Daventry during the following 24 hours. (*D.T.* 24.4.37.)

One Big Family

29. An appeal to Londoners and English people generally to make an effort to throw off 'standoffishness' and reserve during this Coronation year was made last night by Sir Archibald Weigall.

He was speaking at a dinner of the Royal Empire Society, over which he presides as chairman of the Council, held in honour of the Lord Mayor of London and the Lady Mayoress, Sir George and Lady Broadbridge.

Tributes to the warmheartedness of the peoples of Australia and New Zealand, founded on experiences during his recent tour, were paid by the Marquess of Hartington, M.P., Parliamentary Under-secretary for the Dominions. 'Out there', he said, 'the people make the visitor feel that he is one of the family. I hope we will do the same this year.'

London, the Lord Mayor said, belongs to inhabitants of distant parts of the Empire as well as to people of this country. 'London has beauty and dignity, peace and tranquillity to set off against the thunder of her traffic, her dirt, her grime. She is London, whichever way it is—England's old sweetheart, loved by her sons for 2,000 years.'* (*D.T.* 2.3.37.)

30. Arrangements for the accommodation of the official guests of the Court and of the Government are fast nearing completion.

Already the West End hotels are preparing their royal suites and most spacious rooms, though most of them do not yet know who will occupy these apartments.

At the Ritz Hotel, where the Aga Khan is expected to stay, 25 suites, including six royal suites, have been reserved for official guests. At the Dorchester about 40 rooms have been set aside, and at the Mayfair Hotel 20. Four royal suites overlooking Green Park have been reserved at the Splendide.

Similar preparations are being made at Brown's Hotel, at Grosvenor House—where 70 suites will be occupied by delegates to the Imperial ·Conference—the Carlton, Claridge's, the Berkeley and the Savoy.

The arrangements are mainly in the hands of the Lord Chamberlain and of the Government Hospitality Board. The

*This type of utterance is of interest in showing that another social function of the Coronation is to break down the barriers between areas 1 and 2, temporarily at least (v. para. 20, footnote). Not only do people in the crowd 'mix' with total strangers, but there is intended to be a fraternisation *between groups; e.g.*, between upper and lower classes, between the home country and the visitors from abroad, especially from the Dominions and Colonies. At such a time, the 'One Big Family' concept is applied in numerous ways, and produces abstract 'Sweethearts' and 'Mothers', such as the personification of London in this speech by the Lord Mayor; he is treating a figure from area 3 in terms of area 1, in order to stimulate a mixing of areas 1 and 2.

Government's invitation extends to a week's stay, but in most cases the individuals will stay on much longer. (*D.T.* 1.4.37.)

31.   Bombay, Sunday.

Gen. Sir Kaiser Shum Shere Jung, ruling Minister in Nepal, land of the Gurkhas, has sailed for England for the Coronation festivities as head of the Nepalese delegation. He has with him an ancient Order of Nepal which is being conferred on the King-Emperor. He also carries with him a diamond said to be worth £100,000, which he will wear during the festivities.

The official Indian service contingent sails to-morrow in the troopship *Neuralia* and arrives at Southampton on May 3. It comprises units of the Indian Army, the R.A.F., auxiliary and territorial forces, police and native troops from 42 States. (*Times*, 12.4.37.)

32.   Bulawayo, *April* 4.

Paramount Chief Yeta III arrived at Bulawayo from Barotseland on Saturday *en route* to England for the Coronation. He received an enthusiastic reception from the Barotse employed in Southern Rhodesia, who asked their chief to convey the humble duty and devotion of the Barotse to his Majesty, with the assurance of their abiding loyalty and affection for the Throne.

Addressing his people, Yeta urged them to conduct themselves respectfully to the Government and expressed his gratification at going to the Coronation. On the departure of the train for Capetown the assembled natives sang the Barotse National Anthem and 'God Save the King'.* (*Times*, 5.4.37.)

*'N'KOSI, N'KOSI, BAYETE! This is the Royal Salute of the Zulus, and it means "Mightiest Chief of Chiefs, all hail!" With a single voice on Coronation day the myriad tongues of Africa will unite in thunderous homage to the King-Emperor. Then warriors will be at one with workers—the men, for instance, whose toil in the plantations of Rhodesia and Nyasaland helps to bring your Three Nuns Empire Blend to its perfection. 10½d. an oz.' (Advt. in *Radio Times*. 7.5.37.)

33.   S.S. *Arawa*, Caribbean Sea, Monday.

Pitcairn, the volcanic island in the South Pacific, is sending a delegate to the Coronation.

He is Mr. David Young, 61, a great-great-grandson of Edward Young, midshipman in Captain Bligh's ship, the *Bounty*, and one of the mutineers who landed on Pitcairn and populated the island. (*D.T.* 20.4.37.)

34. The most envied girl in Australia to-day is Miss Sheila Martin, of Wagga Wagga, New South Wales.

She has been chosen to come to London for the Coronation as the best representative of Australian girlhood, and plans are being made to give her a queen's reception in Britain.

An influential committee has been set up in London, including representatives of every state in the Commonwealth and prominent English people interested in Empire affairs, to arrange an itinerary for her, and to see that she will get the opportunities of taking part in some of the important functions at Coronation time. (*Sunday Express*, 7.3.37.)

35. I learn that Mr. Mackenzie King, the Prime Minister of Canada and the Dominion's chief representative for the Coronation, has invited Mr. R. B. Bennett, the leader of the Opposition, to be a member of the Coronation delegation.

Mr. Bennett, I understand, has accepted the invitation and will sail with the other delegates for England in the *Empress of Australia* next Saturday.

This fine gesture of Mr. Mackenzie King will enhance his reputation as an Empire statesman. (*E.S.* 21.4.37.)

36. Hundreds of family parties will be among the 150,000 Americans coming to Britain for the Coronation. 'Seventy "Coronation ships" will leave the U.S.A. from April 1 onwards,' Mr. R. E. Towle, representative of the American Express Company, told me. 'These ships alone will bring about 50,000 people. The American is deeply interested in Europe and particularly in Great Britain. We look upon it as

our home in spirit, because nearly all Americans can claim European descent.' (*D. Mirror*, 29.3.37.)

37. Two hundred thousand Coronation visitors from Overseas threaten to swamp completely the accommodation that London is preparing.

With all hotels booked up, the newly-established Coronation Accommodation Committee talks of the need for another 50,000 rooms!

Figures of probable arrivals already gathered by the *News Chronicle* are likely to be far below the actual number. Here they are:

Europe - - - -	100,000
United States - -	23,000
Australia - - -	19,000
Canada - - - -	19,000
India - - - -	9,000
South Africa - - -	8,000
New Zealand - - -	5,000

To these must be added foreign visitors from other parts of the world, the tens of thousands who will flock to London from Great Britain itself. (*N.C.* 20.2.37.)

38. 'We want more offers still from Greater London,' Mr. Hugh Wontner, secretary of the Coronation Accommodation Committee, told an *Evening News* representative to-day.

'We have had them from as far away as Leeds, but we want to exhaust every possible London offer before going even as far as Brighton. London has already been amazingly hospitable. I have masses of letters here from people, obviously in quite humble circumstances, offering accommodation purely from a public-spirited point of view, and asking me how much I think they ought to charge. I have here every sort of offer, from bed at 3s. 6d. a night to a castle at a thousand guineas for a period.' (*E.N.* 20.2.37.)

39. In the advertisement columns of the New York newspapers that have just reached here the Coronation is already casting its shadows before. A leading tourist agency 'invites' readers to it and presents for their choice a great variety of ways and means, with every detail arranged in advance. One of its schemes provides seats in a 'covered reviewing stand for the Coronation procession in Hyde Park.' This stand is 'ideally situated in the garden of Apsley House, home of Dukes of Wellington since Waterloo, adjacent to the present Royal residence, commanding a long view of the processional route.' Seats in it are offered at from fifteen to twenty-five guineas. (*M.G.* 18.2.37.)

40. 'We have already done four times more Coronation business than we did right up to the day King George was crowned in 1911.' This was said to *The Star* by Mr. Herbert Smith, managing director of Keith Prowse. He was talking of the seats for seeing the procession.

'We happen to have got hold of accommodation running into many thousands,' he went on. 'The top price so far is 600 guineas each for two balconies on the premises of Dickens and Jones.' (*Star*, 19.2.37.)

41. Beauty is to be enthroned and comfort have its coronation at Olympia on Easter Tuesday, when the Duke and Duchess of Gloucester open the Ideal Home Exhibition for its 21st anniversary.*

First of all the spectacular events in the Coronation season, it will be the proud coming-of-age festival of a vast display that has for a long time been a national institution. From a primitive thatched, mud-and-wattle hut to the splendour of the Golden Hall of Homage, it will tell the story of Home and of England's loyalty to her monarch.

*This is one of several examples quoted in which the symbolic language of the Coronation is adapted to suit the needs of advertising and trade; in fact, not only the King and Queen, but everyone else, is to be 'crowned' in one way or another.

A hall of golden, misty light, over which reigns a majestic golden statue of the King, is to greet those who enter from Addison Road. They will walk through the broadways of this Golden Hall of Homage while music by Alfredo and his picturesque gipsy orchestra or Sidney Baynes and his broadcasting orchestra floats to them from unseen sources. High under the vault of gold they will see, group by group, the peoples of the Empire, bearing rich tribute from each land in a pageant of homage. (*Croydon Times*, 27.3.37.)

42. Australia's Coronation Contingent—150 tall, bronzed men representative of the Commonwealth Navy, Army and Air Force—were given a rousing reception when they arrived at St. Pancras from Tilbury on Thursday and marched behind the band of the Scots Guards and the Coldstream Guards drum and fife band to Wellington Barracks.* (*D.T.* 27.3.37.)

43. Four long white banners swung in Bond Street yesterday afternoon, the first rehearsal there of Coronation decorations. (*Times*, 18.2.37.)

44. The Southern Rhodesian contingent to attend the Coronation were given a great welcome when they reached England yesterday, disembarking at Southampton from the Union-Castle liner *Winchester Castle*. They comprise members of the military forces, the old Rhodes Pioneer Column, and Rhodesian Girl Guides.

Eleven veterans of the early settler days average 70½ years of age, and Mr. A. Tulloch, the oldest, is 78. Three of them were in the Shanghai patrol which was almost annihilated by

*One function of the contingents from the Dominions and Colonies was to serve as part of the display, so they had to arrive in good time, just as the street decorations had to be put up in good time, in order to give people something to look at while they waited for the day itself to arrive. But the Colonials also came in the capacity of visitors and guests, and therefore the decorations were partly by way of a welcome for them.

the Matabele in 1893, and two of them were in the Jameson
Raid. (*Times*, 30.3.37.)

45. With yesterday's sunshine came new splashes of colour
on the route of the Coronation procession.

Hints of the pageantry to come are creeping into the scene
outside Westminster Abbey and in Parliament Square.

The huge central stands in the square were being draped
with red, gold and blue cloth, the overhanging edges of the
canopies having a pattern of red and gold. (*D.T.* 20.4.37.)

46. It was New Zealand's day in London yesterday. With
cheering crowds to voice the Mother Country's welcome, a
further contingent of bronzed, slouch-hatted troops marched
into the Empire's capital to represent the Dominion at the
Coronation.

Arriving at Tilbury in the liner *Rangitiki* in the early
morning, the troops travelled to London by train. At St.
Pancras the band and drums of the Grenadier Guards welcomed them with the strains of the 'Distant Greeting'
march. (*D.T.* 20.4.37.)

47. 'I come from Heilbron, a quiet little town in the
Orange River Colony, where nothing ever happens.

The huge volume of traffic in the streets of English cities
bewilders me, but the magnificent shops and stores with their
wonderful displays of jewellery, wearing apparel, furniture,
etc., hold me fascinated beyond measure.' (Quoted in *D.E.*
13.4.37.)

48. Eighteen sculptors have been working for twelve
months on the Coronation decorations scheme for Messrs.
Selfridge's store in Oxford and Orchard Streets, and eighteen
panels, representing episodes in Britain's history, from the
time of the Druids to Armistice Day, will be shown.

In outlining the scheme, which is nearly complete, Mr.
Gordon Selfridge said that Sir William Reid Dick, R.A., who

has designed the great central piece of sculpture entitled 'The Empire's Homage to the Throne', has supervised the decorative sculpture, with Mr. Albert Millar as controller of the entire scheme.

The great pelmet of scarlet and gold, edged with silver fringe, is 17 feet long and 19 feet across. The top of the figure of Peace which towers above the 12-foot medallion of the King and Queen is 150 feet from the pavement.

Two women sculptors have executed work for the scheme. An enormous picture showing the great ports of the British Empire—100 feet long and 35 feet wide—has been done by Clara Fargo Thomas, and a panel representing Boadicea is the work of Clare Sheridan.

The whole scheme will be flood-lit. (*E.N.* 12.4.37.)

49. Drages are among the first of the great stores to welcome the Coronation—with Music, Pageantry, Colour, and Souvenir Gifts to all customers.

The Bells of famous Cathedrals ring throughout the gaily decorated store. In the windows are striking life-size models of the King and Queen in Coronation Robes, and pictorial panoramas of Royal Homes. (*Advert.*)

50. From head to heel and from skin to skirt they are now clothing themselves with Union Jacks, Royal Standards, and portraits of the King and Queen. Had I not viewed the actual goods with my own eyes I would never have believed that girls would wear red, white and blue 'undies', and go to bed in dainty sleeping suits bespattered with Imperial Crowns and Royal Monograms. But apparently they do.* (*Reynolds News*, 2.5.37.)

*Also mentioned in the newspapers were red, white and blue goldfish (*Star*, 20.3.37), mice (*Star*, 24.2.37), pianos (*Daily Dispatch*, 21.4.37), while hostesses were said to be dressing their maids in the Coronation colours: 'Lady Knollys' maids wear light blue dresses and white mob caps threaded with cherry-red ribbons and their big white aprons are tied with cherry-red sashes.' (*D.T.* 17.3.37.)

'Hearth rugs and bathroom mats, bicycles and bedsteads, carpets and

51. Crown Yourself With Glorious Hair FREE. Harlene-Hair-Drill Coronation Offer. This morning comes news of a magnificent gift. It is a Gift which can pave the way to lasting Beauty! It is a CROWN for every man and woman! A Crown more beautiful than gold or jewels!—a CROWN OF GLORIOUS HAIR! (*Advert.*)

52. . . . And long after the cavalcade of Coronation Year is but a faded memory, the Dorchester Silver-plate Pastry Server will grace your table to remind you and your children of a great occasion. (*Advert. for* Sylvan Flakes.)

53. The plans for entertaining overseas visitors to the Coronation have advanced so far as the quality is concerned, and the immediate problem that now faces the societies, the Dominions Office, and the High Commissioners' offices, is one of co-ordination and transport to functions outside London. This applies particularly to the garden parties, of which several more are announced. The Archbishop of Canterbury is giving one, and there will be others at Denham, Hurstmonceaux, Nuneham, Warren House, Stanmore, and Wycombe.

cushions, dinner services and toilet ware, coal-scuttles and linoleums, all are on sale in Coronation colours.' (*Reynolds' News*, 2.5.37.)

Not only were houses covered with flags and bunting, and even painted red, white and blue all over, but the three symbols, House, Flag, Empire, became confused in the popular imagination, as in the advertisement reproduced in FIG. I. 'Commemorate the Coronation by buying your own "Empire" at Perivale Park, Western Avenue, Perivale. A solid and lasting semi-detached modern home. . . . Cliffords Estates.'

The symbolism did not always have the desired effect, however, as in the following example, from a letter to the *Birmingham Mail* (28.4.37):

'As an Englishman I was disgusted to see displayed in the shop window of a furnishing stores in this town a Union Jack in the form of a rug, and I would like to appeal to those who have fought for our flag in the past and to those who may fight for it in the future, to remonstrate against this desecration of our national emblem. It is not a pleasant thought for those of us who are proud of the flag that it is being offered for treading underfoot!'

There will be organized visits to the Mint, the Bank of England, the Royal Stud at Newmarket, the halls of City Companies, newspaper offices, the Law Courts, a film studio, the Post Office, dress shows, and ships for the Naval Review. Cocktail parties, luncheons, dinners, theatre parties, and week-end invitations are also available in reasonable quantities. (*Times*, 12.3.37.)

54. The London Zoological Gardens will be open on Coronation Day from 9 a.m. to 7 p.m. and such summer attractions as the Pets' Corner and the chimpanzees' tea-party, which are usually started at Whitsun, will be in full swing. The chimpanzees will drink their milk from Coronation mugs and their table will be decorated with a Union Jack. The elephants will have their nails gilded as do the elephants used in processions in India. (*D.T.* 5.4.37.)

55. Plans are being considered for presenting Sheffield to Coronation visitors. It is hoped that facilities may be obtained for showing them the city's industrial advances in conjunction with the many beauty spots of North Derbyshire, which are close to the boundaries of Sheffield. (*E.N.* 24.2.37.)

56. That rural England at her loveliest may welcome our Coronation visitors could we not compact with one another, and with the parties we take to or join in the country, that we will this year at any rate refrain from picking the wild flowers in any place to which the public have access? For the most ardent among our visitors will have come from families in which our English wild flowers are a cherished remembrance from the talk of parents and grandparents—the early settlers. (Letter to *Times*, 31.3.37.)

57. Coronation visitors arriving at Liverpool will be greeted with a huge floral Union Jack which is to occupy the centre bed at the Pier-head. (Manchester *Daily Dispatch*, 17.4.37.)

58. Twelve sun-burned young men from Rhodesia are travelling around Britain with only a few shillings in their pockets, but as happy as millionaires.

They will wake up in Manchester this morning, after being two days on the road and travelling 250 miles, to count their loose change and find that each has spent exactly two shillings.

That is the way the Boy Scouts' Association are making sure that Colonial Scouts over for the Coronation see Britain without having to break into the few shillings they have brought over as pocket-money.

For nine days the Rhodesian Scouts are 'seeing things'— Cumberland and Chester, Wales and Winchester—travelling in a luxury motor-coach, and being fêted wherever they go by the local Scout troops. (*D. Mirror*, 3.5.37.)

59. CORONATION—An occasion which affords untold opportunities for the GROCER and PROVISION MERCHANT, the BAKER and CONFECTIONER, the WINE and SPIRIT MERCHANT, the BREWER and the MINERAL WATER MANU-FACTURER.

Huge sums of money will be spent on eatables and drink to celebrate this auspicious occasion, and local gatherings will undoubtedly buy locally.

·YOU cannot afford to miss this opportunity of a lifetime by failing to make known your GOODS and SERVICE.

The cheapest and most effective local advertising medium is

THE ANDOVER ADVERTISER

which is read in over 6,600 homes in Andover and District and covers an area of over 600 square miles. (10.4.37.)

60. Coronation trees were planted in the public park, Prestwick, by Lieut.-Colonel T. C. R. Moore, M.P. for Ayr Burghs, Provost Govan, and others, and were dedicated by the Rev. Luke M'Quitty, Prestwick.

In this Coronation year, Colonel Moore said, the people of this country had kept their heads and weathered the storm of the greatest constitutional crisis in their history, and he believed that, with their great traditions behind them and their unswerving stability of character to help them, they would go forward quietly, determinedly and confidently to even greater glories and a more prosperous future.* (*Glasgow Citizen*, 22.3.37.)

61. Birmingham is to be artistically decorated for the Coronation. Its municipal buildings and the chief streets in the city centre will be adorned with shields and banners of historical importance.

Upon the Council House the shields represent the arms of the Lords of the Manor of Birmingham from 1166 to 1824 and in addition to various members of the de Bermingham family, include the arms of St. Liz, Someri, Marrow, Key, Archer, Windsor, and Musgrave.

Over the main entrance of the Council House under the great arch will be displayed a banner mounted with the arms of England, with the Royal Cipher and powderings below and the Crown above. The quartered arms of the King will not be displayed, as this is only correct where the King is in residence.

The column which is now being erected in Victoria Square will be thirty-five feet high to the top of the capital and carries a gilt equestrian group of St. George, eight feet high, in which the saint presents the Crown with outstretched arm. Grouped about the foot of the column are to be four beds of rhododendrons. (*Birmingham Mail*, 21.4.37.)

62. The arrangements for the big military parade and march past, on the morning of Coronation Day, May 12,

*In local items such as this we begin to see the variety of uses to which the Coronation can be put—it can be used to advertise hair oil, or a political party, or the beauty of England's countryside, or in many other ways all producing their own special shift of emphasis, all contributing to the total transformation of scene.

which is being organized by Colonel O. D. Smallwood, the
O.C. Troops, at the request of the Lord Mayor, are now
nearing completion. All units of the Territorial Army will
participate, and it is hoped that all ex-service men's organizations will be strongly represented. (*Birmingham Mail*, 6.4.37.)

The 45th R.E. Battalion from Thorp Street will have with
it some of its big lorries, carrying searchlights, while with the
69th Brigade there will be two mobile anti-aircraft guns
which will be sure to attract much attention. The 68th Field
Brigade R.A. will have four mechanized 18-pounders, the
R.A.M.C. will have one of its ambulances, while with the
Signals contingent will be cable-wagons and wireless lorries,
and 24 motor-cyclist dispatch-riders. While the parade is
in progress, nine machines from the 605th Squadron at
Castle Bromwich will be flying overhead. (*Birmingham Mail*,
29.4.37.)

63. Coventry is now well set to commemorate the Coronation and to enjoy itself in so doing. The five special committees of the City Council, collaborating with the Coventry
Hospital Carnival Committee and other organizations, have
drawn up a comprehensive programme, embracing all
classes and ages, for Coronation Week. The whole of the
centre of the city will be gay with bunting, flags and streamers
in a decorative scheme carried out by the Corporation.

There will be three main events on Coronation Day itself:
A fair on the usual Hospital Carnival lines on the Memorial
Park, with football and baseball matches, ox-roasting, open-
air dancing, variety performance and firework display in
addition;
A sports meeting at the Butts Stadium in the afternoon;
A Coronation Ball at the Drill Hall in the evening.
(Midland *Daily Telegraph*, 1.4.37.)

64. *Croydon*: There will be plentiful illuminations and
decorations in well-selected centres, not to mention a special

firework display, to delight the eyes of the public, and band performances in the parks. The young, the old, and the unfortunate are not forgotten. As is most befitting to the occasion special shows of Coronation pictures for children will be arranged in several theatres and cinemas and every boy and girl in the elementary, day central and special schools in the Borough will receive a gift book about the King. A special tea with entertainment is to be arranged for crippled and physically defective children. About 3,000 old age pensioners are to be invited as guests to tea and entertainment, and the unemployed and their wives will receive similar hospitality. The blind, too, are to be invited to supper and entertainment in the Large Public Hall, whilst the deaf and dumb will also be entertained together over a cup of tea and refreshments. A civic banquet and ball will be held, whilst the solemnity attendant upon the occasion will be duly expressed at the civic and thanksgiving services. (*Croydon Times*, 3.4.37.)

65. Coronation celebrations are to be on an elaborate scale at Liverpool. Nearly 2,000 people have some special role to play in the week's activities.

On Coronation Day contingents of his Majesty's forces will march past the Lord Mayor, and the Corporations of Bootle, Birkenhead, and Wallasey, together with the Dock Board, are co-operating with the Lord Mayor and the city shipowners to present a river spectacle. A long line of ships extending from New Brighton to Eastham will fly their flags, and at night their myriad lights will illuminate the river. (*Times*, 12.3.37.)

66. A daylight fireworks display is to be one of the attractions at the athletic carnivals which are to be held at Hampden Park, Glasgow, on Coronation Day. This display will be primarily for the entertainment of spectators and the 1,300 children taking part in the afternoon's programme which will consist of a 'keep fit' and athletic display. (*Glasgow Evening Citizen*, 19.3.37.)

67. In Bishop's Waltham, Hampshire, there will be dancing in the High Street on Coronation night. Coloured electric lights will illuminate the scene from end to end of the street and one of the older councillors, with the prettiest girl in the town as partner, will lead off the dancing, which will go on to midnight.

An ingenious and quite decorous version of the strip-tease act will be part of the all-day Coronation sports in the old town of Hastings. Couples—men and girls—wearing ordinary clothes over bathing costumes, have to undress and then dress in each other's clothes. Prizes go to those who do the change-over in the shortest time.* (*Sunday Referee*, 9.5.37.)

68. Children and old folks are being specially catered for in the plans for Coronation Day in the Black Country.

At Bilston additional arrangements are being made in the form of town grants to the unemployed, the blind ex-service men, and old age pensioners. These grants will be spent on providing a tea and entertainment. A total of 7,000 medals for distribution to scholars of the town are being purchased at a cost of £102, and will be presented at the schools by the Mayor (Ald. Walter M. Hughes) the day before the Coronation.

A service in the Parish Church opens the day at Willenhall. This will be in the morning, and early in the afternoon school children will assemble for the presentation of Coronation mugs. (*Birmingham Evening Dispatch*, 12.3.37.)

*In many savage tribes people wear the clothes of the other sex on occasions of public importance. The Hastings undressing competition was a 'version of strip-tease' all right. But it is also a fine spontaneous example of what anthropologists call 'transvesticism', a practice about which there are various conflicting theories. Observers reports give many examples of it during the celebrations.

69. The Coronation shilling allowance for school children is to be used in the Arbroath landward district to provide a souvenir money box filled with sweets, a souvenir medal, and a propelling pencil for each child.

This was the decision reached by Arbroath Landward S.M.C. on Saturday. (*Dundee Courier*, 8.3.37.)

70. At a cost of 11d. each, Coronation 'tuck boxes' will be presented to about 23,000 scholars in the schools of Poplar.

Each will contain an apple and orange, a bar of chocolate, a buttered bun, a packet of biscuits, a piece of cake, serviette with medallion, and a paper cap. (*D.H.* 22.4.37.)

71. The Mayor of Dover, Alderman Norman, has announced that he will make personal gifts of a 15s. savings certificate and a silver spoon to babies born in Dover on Coronation Day, provided the parents have lived in the borough for twelve months. Twins or triplets will each receive a gift, and if any member of the town council qualifies the gift is to be doubled. (*Observer*, 28.2.37.)

Troubles

72. For all the careful preparations which were made, it was inevitable that human fallibility and unforeseen accident should intervene. This sub-section will illustrate some of the ways in which this happened; it will include samples of the problems which had to be solved, and of breakdowns and difficulties. Right at the end of the preparation period came the most formidable breakdown of all, when the London busmen went on strike and it was feared up to the last moment that they would be joined by the other London transport workers. This sequence of events is narrated in a final sub-section giving the history of the last eleven days before May 12.

c

73. Mr. Ernest Brown, Minister of Labour, announced in the House of Commons this afternoon that it is proposed that the Unemployed Assistance Board should be authorized to make a special Coronation payment of 2s. 6d., with 1s. to each dependent child. (*E.N.* 4.3.37.)

Mr. Thurtle (Shoreditch, Lab.)—Will this 2s. 6d. be paid by instalments or in a lump sum? (Laughter.)

Mr. Brown—It will be paid in a lump sum and will be cheerfully welcomed by those who receive it. (*Times,* 5.3.37.)

74. Mr. Geoffrey Mander, Liberal M.P. for Wolverhampton East, asked the Secretary to the Treasury in the Commons to-day whether it is proposed that the 2s. 6d. Coronation allowance shall be paid to all old-age pensioners.

Colonel Colville replied that the cost of an allowance of 2s. 6d. per adult and 1s. per child to recipients of old-age widows and orphans pensions in connection with the Coronation would be £450,000. As it was stated on January 19 the Government regretted that they could not see their way to promote the legislation necessary to authorize such grants. The making of a grant to persons in receipt of public assistance was a matter for the local authorities. Mr. Denville said his question referred to old-age pensions and he had a petition—(cries of 'Order!'). Every other body of persons in the country was receiving something extra.

Colonel Colville: That is not quite correct. Many people in the community would be glad to receive a grant. The line must be drawn somewhere. (*Express and Star,* 11.3.37.)

75. The Coronation is not to be made an occasion for granting special clemency to prisoners. This is stated in a letter from the Home Office to the Rev. C. Ashlin West of Girvan, Ayrshire, who made representations on behalf of the three members of the Welsh Nationalist party sentenced in January to nine months in the second division. (*Star,* 3.3.37.)

76. Many of us think that the Coronation season would be a fitting time for a special effort to gladden the hearts of British dogs. For thousands of these the 'festivities' may be just another succession of drab days like all the rest—chained to a leaky, draughty apology for a kennel; left alone all day with a pannikin of muddy water, and only given scraps of unsuitable food in a haphazard way. Will dog-lovers please co-operate in securing an amnesty for these canine prisoners? (Letter to *Wallingford and Carshalton Times*, 8.4.37.)

77. Imperial Chemical Industries Ltd. so far as is practicable will give all employees a day's holiday on Coronation Day, and under the company's existing agreements with the trades unions, this day will be paid for at normal rates to those not working, while those who are required to work will be paid overtime at the agreed rates. The company will also give 10s. to every employee on the pay-roll of its various offices and factories throughout the United Kingdom on May 12. (*D. Mirror*, 31.3.37.)

78. Lancashire weaving operatives will, subject to the approval of employers' local associations, have a holiday on Coronation Day and receive 5s. for it. This is less than an ordinary day's wage. Operatives under 18 will receive 2s. 6d. Some operatives will lose several shillings on the day under these terms. (*Manchester Evening News*, 15.4.37.)

79. Two thousand workmen of the Ocean Colliery, Treharris, decided to-day that as the coal-owners were not prepared to give a day's holiday with pay on Coronation Day they would go to work as usual. The men stated that they would be idling their time by taking the day as holiday insomuch as there were no local celebrations. (*D.E.* 27.4.37.)

80. We are going to burn £200 in a fire on Leith Links. In a few moments it goes up in flame and smoke. Do we expect

the disabled and unemployed ex-Service men of Leith and
Edinburgh to gather round with their wives and children and
throw up their caps in jubilation at the beginning of a new
reign when the debts of the last have not been paid? (Letter
to *Edinburgh Evening News*, 5.3.37.)

81. *Surrey:* 'There are times', said Coun. Russell Pickering,
'when we as a local authority should give a lead in the display of loyalty and civic spirit, something for the younger
generation to recall in years to come.' He emphasized that
what he proposed was not an attempt by the traders to foster
extra trade in the district but an endeavour to bring into the
borough an atmosphere of celebration. It was said that it
would be very difficult to determine what roads should be
decorated and that people in the side roads would feel
slighted because decorations would be impracticable there.
The decorations could be concentrated in the main roads and
people in the side roads should not be aggrieved. They would
realize that it was quite impossible to decorate every road.
What would the borough look like on Coronation Day if
nothing was done? Absolutely dead.

Why was the Council trying to rebuff the traders? He had
received a letter from the Tooting Chamber of Commerce
stating that promises for £100 had been received from
traders towards the cost of decorations in the main road at
Tooting. The Town Clerk informed the Council that seven
London boroughs had decided to decorate, while twenty-one
had decided not to do so or were still considering the matter.
(*Wallingford and Carshalton Advertiser*, 25.1.37.)

82. *Ayrshire:* Mr. T. Paterson moved an amendment that
the hall be granted free of charge as it was the duty of the
Council to help the Committee so far as possible. Mr. David-
son seconded.

Bailie Sandilands protested they had made regulations to
the effect that the Town Hall was never to be granted free.

They had no right to do it. Mr. Paterson said that at a recent meeting of the Coronation Committee Bailie Sandilands had said any and all means fair or foul were to be adopted to raise money. This he thought was one of the fair means. Bailie Gibson said he could not see anything wrong with it. Bailie Sandilands still protested the procedure was incompetent. Bailie Gibson—I am going to take a vote on it at least. Only the mover and seconder supported the motion so that the hall will be granted free of charge. (*Ayrshire Post*, 5.3.37.)

83. At a meeting on Wednesday, the Coronation Committee received a report from the Souvenir and Entertainments Committee recommending that an ox and sheep roasting display be given, all proceeds from the sale of meat sandwiches to be allocated to the local hospitals.

Councillor C. L. S. Weedon pointed out that there would be many difficulties in the way and not a little expense. Councillor R. D. Reeve, chairman of the Entertainments Committee, agreed that there would be difficulties. Since the committee met he had spoken to many who objected to the idea of roasting. They did not object because it was a pagan custom, but because they do not favour such a celebration. There would be great difficulty in making sufficient arrangement and, personally, he hoped the idea would be abandoned. Councillor Weedon: In the wilds of Australia, yes. In a civilized country I move this be deleted. Councillor Reeve stated that at the cinema that week he saw pictures of a calf-roasting ceremony, and it did not look very nice. (*Kentish Mail*, —.4.37.)

84. Protests against proposed ox-roasting in Midland towns as part of the local Coronation celebrations have been sent by the London Vegetarian Society. Telegrams were sent last night to:

> The Lord Mayor of Birmingham;
> The Mayor of Halesowen;

The chairman of Bromsgrove Council;

The Lord Mayor of Coventry; and

The chairman of Brewood Council,

in all of which areas ox-roasting is to form part of the Coronation programme. (*Express and Star*, 21.4.37.)

85.   Bombay, *April* 5.

A resolution appealing to Mr. Baldwin to intervene in order to prevent the public ox-roasting ceremonies proposed in various parts of Great Britain during the Coronation festivities was passed by a public meeting held in the Corporation Hall to-day. The resolution stated that such ceremonies were viewed by millions of his Majesty's subjects with horror and pain and were regarded as unworthy of a civilized nation. (*Times*, 6.4.37.)

86. Invitations to the Coronation have been sent to Abyssinia and Spain. Lord Cranborne, Under Secretary for Foreign Affairs, disclosed this in supplementary replies to the House of Commons this afternoon, but he could not give the names of the countries' representatives. Miss Wilkinson (Soc., Jarrow) asked whether any intimation had been received as to who would be the chief representative of Germany to the ceremony. When Lord Cranborne said there was no information, Miss Wilkinson added, 'Can we have some guarantee that we shall not be insulted by the presence of General Goering?' There were cries of 'Order' and 'Shame'. (*E.S.* 22.2.37.)

87. Angered by the British invitation to Haile Selassie to send a representative to the Coronation, a crowd of 200 people gathered round the British Consulate at Messina. Stones were thrown and one window was broken. (*E.N.* 8.3.37.)

88. The Scottish Protestant League will be the only Protestant society in Scotland making definite arrangements for

celebrating the Coronation of the King and Queen on
12th May.

On Coronation Day a Service will be held in the Forum at
11 a.m., when Mr. Ratcliffe will preach. This service will last
an hour. At 7 p.m. a Great Social Gathering of rejoicing will
take place. After the Social Leaguers and other good Pro-
testants will make their way to a certain place (the name of
which will be intimated later on) where *the Pope in effigy will be
burned*. This is our reply to the British Government in sending
a representative to the Vatican and in asking the Pope to send
a representative to be present at the Coronation. (*The Vanguard*, May 1937.)

89. Surprise and indignation has been caused among the
cotton workers of Mossley by the action of the Town Council
in turning down, early in the week, a suggestion that they
should grant one of their Coronation stand tickets to a local
mill girl to enable her to view the procession as the representative of the Mossley cotton workers. The suggestion was
made by Alderman M. B. Farr (Socialist), who offered to pay
for the ticket himself. Only one other member of the Council,
Councillor Martin, supported his proposal, however, and it
was heavily defeated.

The Mayor (Alderman H. Laming) ruled that members of
the Council must have the first refusal. The two tickets were
alloted to Councillor L. Rawson, who, it was stated, wished
to take his daughter. (Manchester *Daily Dispatch*, 24.4.37.)

90. I wonder whether the officials dealing with the Coronation seating arrangements are aware of the growing dissatisfac-
tion at the manner in which the matter is being handled? Do
they realize, that while visitors from the Dominions are being
catered for extensively, and foreigners offered every facility,
the large majority of tax-paying British subjects are being
practically excluded from viewing the procession by the
enormous prices asked for seats? (Letter to *D.T.* 12.4.37.)

91. 'A householder on the route was showing me how the official stands obscure the view of the procession from her particular house, and said that about eighty people could get a brief glimpse through the trees. I suggested she should advertise seats at 10s. 6d. or £1 1s. for Coronation Day.

'She laughed. A syndicate, she said, had been canvassing all houses on the route, and had offered her £400 if she would let 120 people stand in the windows of the house.

'Later, I phoned the syndicate. "Yes—just a few seats available," they said. "And the price?" "Well, the positions vary—between £20 and £30 each" ...' (Letter printed in *N.C.* 19.2.37.)

92. Will anyone who reads this visualize for a few moments what a small child must suffer when hemmed in by a terrific mass of human beings towering above its head, quite unable to move, terrified of being crushed to death, and no matter how deadly tired, how frantically hungry and thirsty, how desperately frightened, how agonizingly it craves to go home, having to endure this ghastly torture for many hours probably. (Letter to *Times*, 27.3.37.)

93. Catering workers in the London area state that unless they are given guarantees of a living wage within the next two weeks, there will be many 'Walks out' during the Coronation week. Trade union membership among catering workers in London has increased 75 per cent. during the past twelve months. (*D. Worker*, 8.4.37.)

Mr. A. G. Parker, a district officer of the union, said yesterday: It is a national disgrace that some workers in this trade have to work 60 to 80 hours a week for 14s. a week "house money", and in some instances, for no wages at all. There are platemen, kitchen porters and similar grades that get no tips, and work for 60 to 70 hours a week for 40s. Conditions of food and accommodation are often primitive. Some food served goes, instead, into the pigs' tubs.' (*D.H.* 25.3.37.)

94. Protests against the manner in which those responsible for choosing the Coronation Orchestra of 60 players for the Abbey service on May 12 have ignored the great Northern orchestras were made during the week-end. 'It is the usual old story,' said Mr. R. J. Forbes, Principal of the Royal Manchester College of Music. 'Anything in London is regarded as national—in London.' (Manchester *Daily Dispatch*, 12.4.37.)

A number of leading London musicians are refusing to play in the special orchestra to be conducted in Westminster Abbey at the Coronation service, on account of the terms offered. Players are not only being asked to forgo their normal union rates of pay, but will run the very considerable risk of losing a great deal of their regular livelihood, because of having to attend unpaid rehearsals. (*D.H.* 9.3.37.)

95. I visited the mother of three little girls who had worked on the pot banks. One little girl, 14 years old, got out of bed to see me. Six months she has worked in the pottery, and this is her third time ill. Her main job is burnishing the gold bands of saucers. 8s. a week she gets. Very often she is in the factory at 7.15 a.m. working until 5.30 p.m., with a half-hour break for breakfast and one hour for dinner. . . .

Everyone admires the many-coloured decorated beakers and cups for their fine craftsmanship. George and Elizabeth look well in royal blue, gold and rose red. Lithography is a highly-skilled job, done under continually cramped and wet conditions. This girl, 17 years old, gets 13s. for a 47-hour week, plus time squeezed out of her dinner hours, for lithographing these goods. (*D. Worker*, 10.3.37.)

96. Having failed to pay in money he had collected for a Coronation street tea party in Frederic Street, Walthamstow, Lewis Dowling, aged 28, married, of Amberley Road, Leyton, hanged himself in stables in Station Road, Walthamstow. (*E.N.* 6.4.37.)

Henry Sullivan, of Arthur Road, Brixton, was a journeyman tailor. He worked so hard and worried so much over the increased work due to the Coronation that his reason gave way and he committed suicide. (*D. Worker*, 25.3.37.)

97. The contrast between the Coronation spirit evinced by people living in cheerless slums and those in comfortable upper middle-class houses in, say, St. John's Wood, is extraordinary. In the East End practically every house is gaily decorated. Families with little to spare have saved up to express their feelings of loyalty in a burst of colour. The emotion aroused in richer homes by the Coronation is surely no less profound— but it is apparently 'bad form' to express it openly.

The nearer one gets to the West End the more meagre are the decorations on the larger private houses. Whenever one sees extensive decorations in this area they almost invariably prove to be on the premises of a small shopkeeper. At such a time cannot Englishmen forget their dread of giving vent to their feelings in public?* (Letter to *D. T.* 7.5.37.)

98. A sheet of cardboard in the front parlour window announced the present total collected as £163.

'And that', added Mrs. Gould, the secretary's wife, 'doesn't count the £7 for the band we're having in the evening—rhythm aces from Clapham!'

Henley Street, Battersea, has had a committee running the Coronation collection ever since last July. They meet every week in Mr. Gould's house and the secretary reads the minutes and the chairman proceeds to further business, all in slap up style.

'There are going to be barricades at the end of the street', said Mrs. Gould, 'so that only the people living in the street take part. Young Mr. Guymer, the decorator and plumber up the road, has painted two lovely banners on ordinary

*This letter calls for a loosening of the normal restrictions in the behaviour of one social group towards another, and of individuals to those in area 2.

white sheets, and we're going to hang one at each end. Real pictures, those banners are, you'd never think.'* (*E.S.* 1.4.37.)

99. And then there is Trinity Street in Islington, where each child is to be given the following special certificates:

THE GREAT CORONATION
This is to certify that

.   .   .   .

did take part in the Great Celebrations & Function given at Trinity-
street
to commemorate the
CORONATION
of
Their Most Gracious Majesties
King George VI and Queen Elizabeth.
LONG MAY THEY REIGN.

This street is more elaborately decorated than any other in this part of London. Red, white and blue flags stretch from one side of the road to the other. There is a cardboard crown and shield over the doorway of each house. I saw it on a windy, dark, and grey evening. The young men were walking along in their best clothes, girls hanging on their arms. The wind sent pieces of dirty paper bowling along after them. The flags fluttered and wavered. The coloured lights, placed so that they formed patterns of red, white and blue, were lighted up. And all about you was the sound of rustling paper.† (*Observer*, 9.5.37.)

*In this and the following instance, a difficult problem has been successfully surmounted: namely, how to get the maximum of enjoyment of the Coronation with the minimum of means. It is interesting too to note the barricades isolating the street, and basing each set of celebrations on the local street grouping.

†The style employed in the newspapers for describing local celebrations in the East End is simple and effective, perhaps because those who reported it were genuinely surprised at what they saw; more important still, because they really saw it, and did not invent it for purposes of fiction.

Rumours and Adaptations

100. The preceding sections show an attempt to arrange a big occasion from above, and troubles arising from below. It is clear that the next question is the process of adaptation on both sides. In order to adapt the whole of a society for such an occasion, it was necessary to take certain risks, and these risks had to be insured against. 'At Lloyd's, one gathers,' to quote the *Daily Record* (8.3.37), 'rather surprisingly high rates are being quoted for insurance against postponement of the Coronation, but there is no suggestion, of course, of any further sensational developments. The volume of the insurance business itself accounts, in part at least, for the rising rate. The only other consideration is that the King, who, as has been mentioned before, is rather highly strung, might conceivably break down under the increasing strain as the ceremony draws nearer. But the week's rest he proposes to take beforehand should be sufficient safeguard.'

This suggests an economic reason for the rumours that the Coronation would not take place; these were usually rationalized as a fear that the King himself might fail to adapt himself to the strain of the occasion.

Observers' reports illustrate this rumour, and also the individual adaptations that were made; while two Observers in Africa raise the wider problems of adaptation affecting other races in the Empire.

101. 'There won't be no Coronation. The King will be dead by then. He's dying on his feet. They're keeping him alive artificially.' (Newspaper man at Lewisham, April 29.)

Daily woman reported in course of normal conversation that she had been told there would be no Coronation. She would at first give no reason but when pressed said it was be-

44

cause everybody wanted the Duke of Windsor back. (Black-heath, May 3.)

102. April 30. Told by a friend from the North that Bradford business men are betting against the Coronation taking place.

May 1. Told the following story by another friend. Two people she knew were coming up from Brighton by road a night or so ago, when they got into a traffic jam. An old gipsy woman jumped on the footboard and clamoured to tell their fortunes. They refused. She went on clamouring. As the traffic started, they gave her a shilling and asked her to get off. She did so, saying, 'I can tell you two things. One is, there will be death in your car before night. The other is, there won't be any Coronation.' Half an hour later they were held up by a policeman, who said, 'There has been an accident and a man is seriously injured. Could you take him to hospital in your car?' They agreed, and the injured man was hoisted in. He died in the car before reaching hospital. Now what about the Coronation?

May 6. A young man repeated the story about the gipsy as follows: 'An Indian friend of mine was told on going out of London in a car that there would be a dead man in the seat of his car before night (this happened) and that there would be no Coronation.'

103. A rumour was current in the town (Northern Ireland) about a fortnight ago, and is still heard, that there would be no Coronation (not that it would be postponed), because—if any reason was given—of the King's illness. (April 30.)

104. Elderly traveller for bird's seed has a 'feeling' about Coronation. 'It may not come off.'

Daily help (superior charwoman) says that there 'won't be no Coronation!'

Middle-aged tobacconist indifferent. Does not seem unduly concerned about rumours that King is in poor health. (Ayrshire, April 14.)

105. I said to the proprietress of the stationer's shop from which I was telephoning, 'Have you heard any of these rumours that there will be no Coronation?'

She said, 'Oh yes, a good many people are saying so. I'm sure I don't know why. I expect they must be Communists.' (London, May 6.)

106. I have heard twice to-day—once from woman friend and once from someone now forgotten—that 'Lloyds are betting heavily against the Coronation'.

My charwoman said 'They are beginning to say that there won't be one—that we won't have a King to crown. It's in all the Monument Road shops—that the gipsies prophesied that he'll have a fit and choke. . . . But they didn't ought to say such a thing after all the money that's been spent.' (Birmingham, May 1.)

107. A friend had told my mother that someone they knew had been stopped along the Dymchurch–New Romney road one evening the previous week by a gipsy who had asked him for a lift. He complied with the request and she told him that the Coronation would not take place.

My mother then said that that morning another friend had said that a woman friend had told her that she had picked up a gipsy the previous week along the Dymchurch–New Romney road. This gipsy had apparently asked her for a lift. This gipsy had told her that the Coronation would not take place. My mother's comment to this was 'Oh, it's a woman this time.'

10.30. Somebody else came in and said 'What do you think I've just heard—some people had put a flag of Mrs. Simpson and the Duke of Windsor outside their house, and the 'pyksies' (originally gipsies who had migrated into the town some years ago) had torn it down.' (Ashford, Kent, May 5).

108. The most amusing incident of which I heard occurred a day or so before the Coronation. My family were seated together in the sitting-room and somebody switched on the wireless. To everyone's horror and astonishment an announcement came to the effect that the Coronation had been postponed owing to the serious indisposition of the King, who was to have an operation. The prayers of the people were asked for his safety. At the end of the announcement they switched the wireless off and it was not until the evening that they discovered it to be a broadcast of King Edward VII's reign, in which this actually happened. (Isle of Man.)

109. A student returned to England from Rumania, where he had been studying at a university, told the following story:

Travelling through Germany he gave himself out to be not English but Rumanian. During a train journey he got into conversation with some young German Nazis, and the forthcoming English Coronation was discussed. The Nazis said what a splendid opportunity it would be for an air attack on London by Germany. The English student said that he had read an English novel in which a similar idea was suggested. One German was very much annoyed at hearing that the idea had been put forward in England, and said that it was a great mistake to give the enemy warning. (Blackheath, May 5).

110. It is part of the history of England that whenever a decision of the Government has to be adapted to the people, the work has to be done by innumerable committees. Their function is to adapt the official view to the individuals concerned, usually the important individuals of the district before the others. It is inter-

esting to compare newspaper accounts of a Scottish committee quoted in **82**, which arrived at frank disagreement, the two English committees in **81** and **83**, which apparently reached an agreement, and the following account by an observer who was present at one such meeting. Here the mechanism of successful compromise is made clear, since the economic motives and prejudices are also recorded.

III. *Meeting of the Coronation Committee of a Local Authority on April 26, 1937, at 7.30 p.m.*

The meeting was to consider the Souvenir Coronation Programme, which is being prepared by a local printer who in consideration for the advertisement fees is printing it free. The charge is to be threepence, to go to the Coronation funds, but the price is to be printed on the inside of the back page so as not to deface the front of the programme and detract from its value as a souvenir.

The printer had submitted a proof copy and the business of the committee was to consider its suitability. The first page contained a foreword by the Chairman and his photo; on subsequent pages there were short biographies of the King, the Queen, and the Royal Family. The Town Clerk advised the Committee that in certain particulars the information was inaccurate; even with his rather scanty knowledge of the subject he could draw attention to one or two errors, he thought also that the biography proceeded too rapidly to the marriage; he feared that the whole thing had been 'lifted' from somewhere, and that there might be an infringement of copyright.

The chairman moved that the biographies should be deleted because he thought that the less that was said about the Royal Family's private life the better.

The main objection was that there had to be something in the programme besides advertisements, there had to be a certain amount of 'padding', but finally it was agreed to delete the biographies and maintain the proclamation, the King's address on his accession, and three full page photos of the King, the Queen, and the Royal Family.

Some discussion also took place upon the question of the inclusion of a genealogical table, the Town Clerk again pointed out that the table was inaccurate, for it showed Edward VIII as having married somebody, but it was certainly not Mrs. Simpson. Councillor X said that he thought it interesting to trace back the descent of the King, he could himself trace his ancestors back to 1730 in the local church registers. Councillor Y saw no reason for including the pedigree, and it was finally agreed to delete it. Having determined the main layout of the programme the order of the actual celebrations was the next matter for consideration.

On the Sunday preceding Coronation Day there is to be a Girl Guides parade to All Saints Church. The Chairman explained that they were meeting outside the station and were marching to church, the question for the Committee to decide was whether it should be included in the programme, he personally thought that it should be, it was a Coronation event and therefore should receive their support. Councillor Z said that he thought the Guides were going to church by train for it was some three miles away, and in any case nobody was very interested in them, therefore he proposed that it should be left out. This was agreed to.

On the Sunday evening the local dramatic society is giving a patriotic play and some discussion arose as to whether this item should be included in the programme. Councillor Z pointed out that it was nothing to do with the Council's activities, that the society had declined to give the proceeds to the Council funds, and that in fact they were giving them to a charity with which he did not wholly agree. The argument on this subject was lengthy, but it was finally agreed by a narrow margin to mention the dramatic society's effort.

About the actual programme on Coronation Day there was

D

little difference of opinion; the day is to commence with the opening of a fountain; Councillor P making the frivolous suggestion that the chairman should arrange for it to flow with champagne on that day and that they should all go along with their Coronation mugs. There is to follow a United Service. The main part of the day is to be occupied with sports in the various school playing fields; while a band is to enliven the proceedings in the largest park where children's sports will also be in progress and where it is anticipated that most people will congregate. There is to be an old people's tea, the planting of oak trees by the Chairman and his wife, a torchlight procession by Boy Scouts and a bonfire in the park, and finally a Coronation Ball.

While minor arrangements were being made for the allocation of duties between the various councillors, Councillor Y, in the course of an aside conversation with his neighbour, suddenly discovered that there was to be a running buffet at the Coronation Ball; unable to control his indignation he butted in on the proceedings: 'Mr. Chairman, am I correct in understanding that intoxicating liquor is to be on sale at the ball?' 'That is so.' 'Then I must disassociate myself with it entirely. I have never been so shocked in all my life, to think that we, as a Council, are sponsoring a Ball at which intoxicating liquor is to be sold. I am greatly upset, there is too much of that sort of thing in the public halls to-day. I have seen young girls reeling about under the influence of drink at dances where there has been no buffet, where, I believe, drink is brought in from outside.'

'That shows', retaliated Councillor Q, 'that it makes little difference, people will drink whether there is a buffet or not.'

'It will be much worse if drink is easily obtainable at a bar,' answered Councillor Y, 'and what also I have the greatest objection to is the fact that the —— Hotel will be profiting from this Dance; we are running a Dance for our own funds and much of the profit is going to the —— Hotel.'

The rest of the Councillors received this peroration in silence. They knew nothing would be done in the matter, and so when calm had been restored the correspondence was considered. There was a letter from a local bowling club asking the Council whether they would give three trophies to be awarded in connection with a Coronation Tournament. It was objected by Councillor X that by doing so they would be creating a precedent, and probably every club in the district would be asking for a cup. Councillor R pointed out that this indeed was a special occasion, they ought to be magnanimous this year, there would not be a Coronation every year, at least he hoped not. The request however was turned down.

It was ten minutes past nine and the Councillors had become impatient, as the Town Clerk was explaining a few minor matters he wished settled, some of the Councillors stood with hats and coats on, assenting apparently without consideration and gradually edging towards the door.

112. Wednesday last there was a village meeting to decide what should be done for the Coronation. About fifty people were there including the vicar, two other local farmers and myself. One of the farmers was put in the chair, at the vicar's suggestion, and he suggested that the procedure at the Jubilee should be repeated. This had consisted of a tea and sports. . . .

A day or two after this my wife went into the post office. The postmaster did not seem to approve of the tea. (Incidentally tea here means meat and beer.) He said to her, 'If you will pardon the vulgarity, all they want is a gluttonous feast.' (Norfolk, 12.4.37.)

113. Miss D. a young woman of 22 who is employed as a clerical assistant at the Admiralty Research Station at West Drayton, asked me if I could help her to get 'Coronation seats'. I replied that I hadn't applied for any as I couldn't see myself paying 15/- for the sake of sitting as many hours. 'That's what Dad says, that's what all the men say, I think.' I

asked how the ballot went. They had had two seats allocated
between 7 of them. 'Unlucky as usual,' she replied with a
shrug, 'but I had just hoped I might get just one. The
typist was ever so excited when she got one. She waved her
arms in the air and danced up and down on her toes.'
(12.4.37.)

114. *Chesterton Road, Sparkbrook, Birmingham*, 12. Over £50
collected on April 6, out of which the children have already
been treated to seats at a pantomime. The street will be
barricaded at 7 o'clock a.m. and the men and boys will sweep
and water the road and wash down the pavements. (The
informant added: 'You could eat off the ground at the Jubilee.') In the morning races for prizes will be run by the
children. In the afternoon there will be a sit-down tea for the
children and an open-air whist drive for adults. The street
will be divided—half for children, half for adults. A group of
mothers will be in charge of the children during the morning
and will be relieved by another group in the afternoon.
Twelve pianos will be on the street—six each side. In the
evening there will be bonfires, fireworks, singing, dancing and
drinking. (Information supplied by woman whose house
backs on to this street.)

115. 20.4.37. An elderly woman who owns a small coffee
house near the Birmingham markets, where she and her
daughters serve. She also has a large house in one of the residential districts. When asked if she is going to London for the
Coronation, she laughed and said—'Do you know what I'm
going to do on Coronation Day? Me and the girls are going
to cut the bottoms off the blinds at home, where they've got
dirty, and then sew them up again.' She went on to say that
she was going to lose a lot of trade because the market would
not open again that week and would be closed for the whole
of the following Whit week.

20.4.37. My husband, who is thoroughly bored with the

whole business, says he is going to spend his day opening his hives. (His hobby is bee-keeping.)

20.4.37. After buying a pair of shoes at a large shop in Birmingham, I said to the middle-aged assistant, 'Are you closing for the Coronation?' She looked horrified—'Of course,' she replied, 'EVERYONE is having a holiday. It's a great day for us all—everyone will have the day off!' 'Let's hope they will, anyway,' I said.

21.4.37. 'I suppose you will be taking the family out on Coronation Day?' I asked the greengrocer, a man of about 40. 'Oh, we shall be busy gardening,' he replied. 'I've got a load of earth coming in for the greenhouse, and all the plants are still waiting to be put out—we've got a lot to do.'

24.4.37. The window cleaner says he would love to see the Coronation, but doesn't think the effort worth it. He and a number of friends are having a party on Coronation Day, and are spending the following day going round Birmingham on 'buses to see the decorations.

116. Young man in Devon (22) remarked to me while building a hut that his brother in London on being asked if he was going to see the Coronation procession, said emphatically—'Not if I have eighteenpence for a cinema show.'

117. I have asked several people what they planned to do on May 12. All these people had made no plans whatever for this particular day. They had no interest in it except that it was to be a holiday. They were glad of that part of it. Two boys, 17 years of age, were going out, one on his push-bike, the other tramping on the moors. But no one else had any plans prepared. (In a Bolton cotton mill, 27.4.37.)

118. As our West End branch is on the Coronation route, a certain number of people are going there on Coronation Day. They have to be there by 7 a.m. One man said he was going. 'Just think of all the silly b——s who are paying £10 to see it and we shall see it for nothing.' He changed his tune con-

siderably when he heard he had got to pay 17/6 for the meals which were to be provided. (A London bank.)

119. Man of about 35, Conservative Political Agent—over the Coronation leaflet which I was showing to a third person— 'Well, I shall probably play tennis all day.' (Birmingham.)

120. My wife had this from the village 'help' (*i.e.* midwife). Mrs. X and her husband came to see Mrs. D the village 'help', to engage her to attend Mrs. X in her confinement. 'But I feel rather vexed' said Mrs. D 'because it is to come on Coronation day, and they did it on purpose. They counted up and found that they had to commit the act on their little girl's birthday.' (Norfolk.)

121. Observer asked a dining-car attendant (young) (Derby-Manchester route) whether he was free on the 12th.

He replied, 'Unfortunately, not. There was not much going on, but we had to be on duty.' He said he did not think they would get extra time off, but did not appear to mind.

122. A railway porter (Newcastle L.N.E.R.)—

'I'm not looking forward to it. It means a lot of extra work. Besides, it seems as though there's going to be a general strike, and all the railway chaps will be in a worse position than ever if they have to come out. If we *do* come out, I think we can blame the Duke of Windsor. If he hadn't gone off with that woman there wouldn't have been any of this.'

(Said to a middle-class woman a week before the Coronation, and reported to me soon after.)

123. A schoolboy was out in the warehouse. His father had sent him for a piece of steel. He was wearing an old pair of trousers much too large round the waist, and the cloth was folded over and safety-pinned. His tie was a bleary rag which showed traces of red and blue stripes.

'Getting ready in your street for the Coronation?' I asked.

'Ah,' he said, turning away shyly and grinning.

'Having a feed?'

'Ah,' he said, looking on the ground, 'we ain't having no cake though.'

'How's that?'

'There's a fat old woman in charge and she's getting legs of chicken and wine and beer. Us kids don't like it.'

'Don't you drink beer?' asked Henry, who was swinging his can of tea round.

The boy giggled and said: 'Nee-ow.'

'Your father'll see your lot off for you,' said Henry.

'I know he will,' said the boy. (Birmingham.)

124. Boy. 'I'd like to draw a Union Jack.'

Observer. 'Why?'

Boy. 'It's hard.'

Obs. 'What made you think of drawing it?'

Boy. 'We did it in school on Friday and mine was the best.'*

*Compare the following letter in a competition organized by the *Leeds Mercury* (1.5.37):

24 Fairfield Street,
Moorend, Cleckheaton.

Dear Editor. When I get up on Coronation day I shall be very excited. (I am excited now.) I shall have a good wash and my breakfast and put on my new red and white dress which I have got for the day. Also I have a red white and blue hairband and a belt. I shall be decorated like a coronation dolly.

Then I shall play my new coronation songs on the piano and my friend will come for me and we shall go round and look at the streets which are decorated. After dinner I shall get ready to go to the school treat which we are having in the sports field. We shall sing some patriotic songs, it will sound very nice because there are over 300 children.

Then we shall start the sports and games and finally have tea. After tea we shall be presented with souvenir spoons. When we have dismissed from the field I shall go to the Park and listen to the Band play.

I am sure it will be a very happy day for all people to know that our King and Queen have been crowned.

KATHLEEN PARKER (13),
South Parade Modern School.

All details of Kathleen Parker's day are settled well in advance. Will all the arrangements go off perfectly according to plan?

125. One of the Observers, whose job involved travelling in different parts of the country, sent in a diary from March 5 to May 5, in which were noted all incidents bearing on the preparations for the Coronation. This diary follows in full.

Scotland

March 5. I notice (for the first time) a tradesman's van flying a small Union Jack on its bonnet. Woolworth's full of Coronation wares. Big business man says: 'Well, they'll get a big welcome when they come here after the Coronation. Especially the Queen. She's a commoner like ourselves.'

March 6. I notice (for the first time) allusions on the screen. Film News: 'Coronation coiffures', 'Coronation Throne'.

March 9. Woolworth's decorated. Wares include Coronation powder puffs, rattles, bags, balls, souvenirs and a pile of comic papers still on the corner of one stand. News film 'Changing face of London', announced very impressively and in a tone of compelling enthusiasm. Stands seen going up. Cleaning of 'Big Tom'. Postilions. Observer misreads 'Corporation St.' for Coronation St. On station large poster (Travel Agency): Coronation Year—The Golden Year for Travel.

March 10. Parson's family show me a piece of the Duchess of York's wedding cake sent from Buckingham Palace to them. This was recently on show at their Parish Exhibition.

March 11. Window dressed with mackintoshes grouped round an Imperial Crown, with a little crown on each buttonhole. 'Be the first in Dundee to wear a Coronation mackintosh.'

I notice the *Strand* and *Illustrated London News* Coronation Souvenir numbers on sale at the Station bookstalls.

March 12. Shop girl of 18 recounts enthusiastically Coronation Day festivities: 'There'll be great doings—bonfire on the hill. Torchlight procession and games and sports.'

Midlands

March 15. Smaller shops are using 'patriotic' decorations already. Rather poor localities. One very white powder puff lying in the middle of a Union Jack in the centre of a hairdresser's window. Curate's wife writes to say she has bought a £5 5s. seat to see the procession.

March 16. Large draper's shop has enormous lettering round the back of its shop front: 'Burst into colour for a Coronation Spring.'

March 17. Trade journal announcing a special display stand says: 'Cash in on the Coronation. Give your shop a patriotic effect.' Well-off spinster (elderly) at boarding house announces she has applied to Westminster Hospital but there are no seats available under £50. Says it is dreadful to think (*a*) how they are knocking about the Abbey with all those seats and doubts whether they will stand it. (*b*) What a lot depends on those two lives. Staff canteen waitress is wearing a red, white and blue jumper under her overall. Is pleased when this is commented on.

March 18. See the 'Coronation Song' on the bookstalls (Station).

March 19. *Bolton (Lancs.)*. A notice 'Join our Coronation Club' in a shop (poor district).

Farnworth (Lancs.), known as a Lancs. depressed area. Farnworth C.W.S. bottom floor completely hung with large flags, banners and photos of the King.

March 20. Met girl on the moors (*Yorkshire*) with dogs, and wearing red white and blue gloves.

March 23. *Nottingham*. 'Bring the children to moving procession of the Coronation: proceeds to the hospital.' (Big store notice on barrows drawn thro' the streets.)

London

April 2. Small child outside Euston stops me and asks, 'Please spare a halfpenny or a farthing for the Coronation party.' Observer feeling mean, doesn't. (This happens often since.)

April 10. Waitress at a quiet solid London hotel says they were booked up months ago by them 'regulars'. They are only charging £6 6s. od. a week (this is not much in excess of usual charges), tea not included. Says they will have to be up early to serve breakfasts at 5 a.m.

April 11. Communist (non-gossiper) asks if I have heard that the workmen in Westminster Abbey gave the communist salute when the Queen visited there. Says no official notice was taken as (a) it was desired to keep it quiet (b) they could not afford to hold the work up.

April 12. Many people announce their intention of going into the country for the Day. Many want to see the Coronation. I cannot analyse these people into any particular classes, except perhaps Socialist and non-Socialist.

April 30. New Bond St. shop announces this is the worst season it has had for fifteen years. Trade generally in the non-special shops seems poor. S. Moulton St. dressmaker complains also. Says all the trade is going to the 'big four'— Molyneux, Hartnell, Handley, Seymour, etc. Her type of customer is going into the country.

A small typical street in Battersea has collected 6d. a week from the families in the street for the past six months, formed a committee and is having a children's tea and (we think) free beer for the grown-ups. My informant (a simple fellow of 23) says: one street has collected as much as £500.

Notice outside St. Paul's Church N.: 'An honoured Sunday means an exalted Empire.' (A crown and a British flag on top of the world decorates the poster.)

Notice outside Friends' Meeting House, Clapham:

'May 12th. Strong drink is dangerous. Let your celebrations be sober.'

May 3. An elderly woman clerk: 'I think this strike is disgusting. It's not British.'

May 5. Boarding house breakfast conversation. Woman Doctor (youngish): 'Well, there seems all these rumours that the King's to be assassinated two days before the Coronation.' Elderly widow: 'No wonder he stutters. But perhaps they get used to it.'

Girl of 23: 'I shall be glad when this Coronation is over. I hate red, white and blue.'

126. Notes on preparations in Africa come from observers in Nigeria and Rhodesia. While we have not been able to cover all parts of the world affected by the Coronation, or even to give a balanced estimate of the reactions in the British Empire, yet we feel what we have to be interesting and worth inclusion. It was part of the theory of the Coronation that all members of the British Empire, of whatever class or creed, belong to one big family. The consequent exchange and confusion of cultures led to many troubles not only of psychology but simply of climate; *e.g.* our Observer with prickly heat, and the African chiefs with colds.

127. *Report from Nigeria*

Lagos. 120,000 people.
    1,000 Europeans, mostly paid from £300 to £1000 p.a.
    Masses are Yoruba, Mohammedan and pagan.
    Christianity is 'Yanga'—sign of education and culture.
    Other tribes are 'Foreigners'.

Collection raised for children and poor—feasting and other celebrations—£1,000. United Africa Co. (Levers') gave £400. Some social competition among Africans, who gave up to £10 when senior European officers gave only £2.

Africans—illiterate—offer to take part in celebrations— *e.g.* organize Native dancing, canoe regattas, etc.—but expect substantial Government contributions to costs of arrangements and subsequent refreshments. Officials repel these claims on Subs. or Govt. allocations.

Muslim Koranic 'piazza', 'hedge' or verandah school children (4,000) represented by heads of seven sects, ask for share in school children's feast money (£500) and for place in school children's parade (8,000 present—addressed by His Excellency—march past, 5 p.m. 12th May on Race Course).

Levers' £400 is for Lagos area (Illorin, Oyo, Ijebu, Abeokuta provinces and Colay Districts outside Lagos Municipal area, a total of some millions of people, as well as for L.M. area itself). Educated African opinion, *pro* and *anti* government, considered the £400 a very smart move.

Sidelight: H. E. sends to Lagos Coronation Committee (represents Administrator, Police, Town Council, Education, P. W. D., P. & T., African Community—educated, pagan, Christian, Muslim—Missions (Catholic, C.M.S., Salvation Army, etc.)) to say he will play polo on Race Course to entertain people. Committee states people not interested in polo. H. E. reported very angry. Sorry he offered instead of instructing committee to make arrangements. Polo on Race Course an old sore point—people regard it as public open space (football, etc.: but Africans on board of management say 'except on Saturdays').

Suffering from prickly heat, boils and nerves, too much Coronation palaver, self, 2 clerks, 2 messengers, have to distribute to schools: 14,400 plates

12,000 flags

9,000 bars chocolate (given by Cadbury and Fry)

and organize parade and march past for 8,000 of the 12,750 *school* children in Lagos Municipal Area. (Schools mostly very undisciplined, most of teachers barely of 'Standard Six' education.)

African reactions:

(i). Conventional loyalty, not so much *insincere* as *inculcated*.

(ii). Joy in a 'show'.

(iii). What can I get out of it?

(iv). Keep an eye to trip foot on *Minor* points.

(v). No criticism on *Major* points to be heard or read even among 'opposition'—or very difficult to come by.

European opinion far more sceptical and disillusioned than African—in spite of Abyssinia which left its mark here.

128. With the prickly heat compare *D.T.* 14.5.37:

Because of the English climate, only four out of the fifteen of the West African representatives in England for the Coronation were able to visit Portsmouth Dockyard and Tangmere Aerodrome to-day, while a garden party arranged by Mr. H. S. Goldsmith, former Lieutenant-Governor of Northern Nigeria, at Eastergate, near Bognor Regis, resolved itself into a homely tea party in front of a blazing fire. . . .

'Ademola II, Alake of Abeokuta, and Sheikh Omar Fye, of Gambia, were ill in bed with fever. Others, suffering from colds, did not think it wise to brave the English weather.'

129. African chiefs found difficulties with the weather; other coloured subjects of the King met with another type of trouble, illustrated in the *Daily Herald*, 12.3.37, which says under the headline 'No Coronation Colour Bar in Hotels':

Several London hotels are putting on a 'colour bar' for the Coronation. This allegation is made in a letter written to the *Daily Herald* by a man who tried to find accommodation for an Indian friend. 'Several hotels gave me prices for that period, but when I said that the visitor was an Indian, they became embarrassed and informed me that they are "full up"' he writes.

Here is what hotel managers and others said on the subject yesterday:

Colonial Office. 'We have had nothing brought to our notice of a colour ban.'

Dorchester Hotel. 'We use our discretion as far as all our visitors are concerned, but the position of having to refuse accommodation to coloured people because of their colour has never arisen.'

It is easy to understand the discretion of the Dorchester Hotel, but what was in question was whether the ordinary non-wealthy coloured visitor will be able to find tolerably civil accommodation at moderate prices. Under its bold headline the *Daily Herald* makes no attempt to deal with this question, contenting itself wholly with the above interview with the Dorchester Hotel.

130.   Capetown, Sunday.

Direct from the Kalahari Desert, 800 miles away, 55 bushmen, strangest of all King George's subjects, arrived in Capetown yesterday. Naked but for buckskin loincloths, they scurried and pranced through the city streets, returning as out of a pre-historic age, and stamping on the ground which belonged to their ancestors centuries ago. They came to a city beflagged in honour of the Coronation of a King of whose existence they had vaguely heard. When they saw for the first time a portrait of His Majesty in a shop window they gave an impressive demonstration of loyalty. This was the 'Chief of Chiefs', their Great Master, so they knelt and kissed the window-pane. They also kissed their hands to the picture.* (*D.T.* 10.5.37.)

131.   *Report from Rhodesia*

Bulawayo. This report was written up on May 9th 1937 from notes made at various times during the previous fortnight. The notes were always made as soon after the observation as possible, up to about one hour after.

*Another account of this incident, in the *Evening Standard* of the same date, described the bushmen as 'Demonstrating for their rights'.

Press. The newspaper placards often referred to the Rhodesian Coronation Contingent, *e.g.* on the 31st March, 'Rhodesians Go Down the Strand' and on 2nd April, 'Rhodesians get warm reception in London'.

Decorations. Decoration of the town was commenced on May 1. The street decorations consist of poles and drums of gravel, the poles draped with red white and blue bunting. Between the poles and across the street are strings of multi-coloured pennants. The poles are placed at intervals of 20 yards from the kerb. A letter to the *Bulawayo Chronicle* complained of the obstruction caused by these poles and advocated an alteration scheme of making temporary flower beds in the middle of the streets (which are very wide) in the area usually reserved for parking cars.

Several buildings are floodlit, the Post Office, War Memorial, Town Offices and the Bulawayo Club. The Municipality has offered supplies of electric current at very cheap rates to all shop-owners who wish to use it for floodlighting or decorating. This offer has been accepted by about half of the possible consumers. 'Kaffir Stores' (stores owned usually by Jews for native trade) are very lavishly decorated with Union Jacks, noticeably more so than the higher class stores.

Effects on Work, etc.

The general effect of the Coronation activities on the work of the town is probably not as great as in most large English towns, certainly London. I was not able to obtain many definite instances of speeding up, etc., though most people have the impression that it has caused a general increase in business activity. These people are usually unable to quote any concrete instances. The Post Office are offering cheap cable rates, selling silver and bronze Coronation Medals and issuing special Coronation stamps (information obtained from a Post Office telegraphist). Hardware stores are selling very large numbers of coloured electric lights (from an assistant in such a store). Stationers are selling large numbers of pictures of the Royal Family and novelty pencils, envelopes, etc. (from an assistant). On these articles they are making about twice the usual profit. A reporter on the *Bulawayo Chronicle* told me that the amount of extra work for him was very great, he has had to work about fifteen hours a day for the last four days. There are a few instances of overtime being worked by shop assistants, but in no case has this extra work been paid.

The Coronation Memorial in Bulawayo is to be a Children's Clinic. A door to door collection has been organized for this by the Mayoress.

Opinions. A Mrs. R. said, 'we have to do something for the Coronation, and anyway it's good for trade.' Asked if she did not think the energy could be put to some more useful purpose, she said, 'Yes.' I asked for an example. After thinking for some time she said, 'Well, what would you suggest?' Mr. R., her husband, said, referring to the decorations, 'Well, it makes Bulawayo look quite gay for a change.'

Mrs. M., a landlady, lower middle class, 'I'm not going to put up *one* flag.'

A Town Council workman who came to put up decorations said on being questioned, 'If I had my way I'd decorate the whole town in pure white, what we want is peace.' Also, 'I'm sick and tired of these decorations.' He complained of being severely overworked. He is Afrikaaner (South African Dutch).

I have so far been able to obtain no direct information about the natives' opinions, not being able to speak the language fluently, but J. (who was a missionary) told me they did not think about it, or if they did they considered it as just another of the white man's peculiar stunts. I have seen several natives with Union Jacks on their bicycles.*

*Paramount Chief Yeta III, ruler of the Barotse, had an enthusiastic reception in Bulawayo on his way to the Coronation in London (para. 32).

Preparations (ii)

132. In this sub-section we return to newspaper accounts of the practical arrangements for the Day itself: how people were going to be fed, how they were going to dress, how they were to follow the day's events by means of the official programme, how they were to reach the route, and finally how the Royal procession itself was to reach its destination.

133. The breakfast that will be served to the Gold Staff officers in the House of Lords at 5.30 on Coronation Day has had to be carefully planned to ensure that the dishes will be—or at least look—hot after their journey of 250 yards from the kitchens to the Royal Gallery. The meal will consist of:

> Grapefruit
> Finnan haddock
> Grilled sausages
> Preserves and
> Tea or Coffee

Both the fish and the sausages have been chosen for their heat-retaining qualities. The grapefruit has been added in acknowledgment of the changing fashion in English breakfasts. (*D.T.* 19.3.37.)

134. Biscuits, chocolate and thirst-quenching tablets will be served out as emergency rations to 20,000 London police officers when they begin duty on Coronation Day. (*D. Mirror*, 24.4.37.)

135. The Milk Board has decided to distribute milk free to the 40,000 London school-children who will watch the Coronation procession from the Victoria Embankment. (*D.T.* 27.3.37.)
Five and a half tons of potatoes will be used by the Potato

Marketing Board to provide each child with a packet of potato crisps. (*D. Mirror*, 11.5.37.)

136. Peers and peeresses who attend the Coronation ceremony in Westminster Abbey on May 12 will be supplied with a fork luncheon in the Royal Gallery of the House of Lords at a cost of 10s. 6d. a head. The fork luncheon—as distinct from a sit-down meal—will consist of light dishes, sandwiches, cakes and coffee and lemonade. Wines, spirits and minerals will also be available, 'for which cash payment will be taken at the time of ordering.' (*D.T.* 2.3.37.)

'It is a crowning insult', added another M.P., 'that with our meagre pay, we should be asked to pay 10s. 6d., exclusive of wine, for luncheon in the House of Commons on Coronation Day.' (*News Review*, 1.4.37.)

137. Catering for the large numbers of troops now assembling in and near London for the Coronation is being arranged by the Navy, Army and Air Force Institutes.

Two large messing stores are being erected for feeding about 26,000 men. The diet to be provided for them on Coronation Day will be as follows:

Breakfast: A pint of tea.
           Bread and butter, marmalade.
           3 oz. fried bacon, two sausages and mashed potatoes.

A haversack ration will be supplied, consisting of:
           A bread roll, cheese.
           A rock cake, two apples.
           Marching chocolate.

When the troops return to camp, they will be given a meal consisting of:
           Thick tomato stew, dumplings.
           Boiled potatoes and peas.
           Boiled jam roll with jam sauce.

Supper will consist of tea, bread and butter and saveloys. (*D.T.* 19.4.37.)

138. All records for street eating and drinking will be well and truly broken on Coronation Day. Some of the figures would make the housewife reel. Stock for buffets on the route alone will cost £20,000.

Assuming 90,000 people in the stands and about 1,000,000 along the route, this stock will include—

    100,000 sandwiches,
      50,000 meat pies and veal and ham pies,
    100,000 assorted buns and cakes,
      1,000 slabs of fruit cake,
    £1,000 worth of 2d. packets of assorted biscuits,
    £3,000 worth of chocolate,
    250,000 cups of tea—requiring 2,800 lbs. of tea, 1,500
              gallons of milk, and five tons of sugar—
    150,000 half-pint cartons of milk,
      2,500 lbs. of fruit essences to produce 250,000 glasses
              of orangeade and lemonade,
    And £3,000 worth of cigarettes.

                              (*Evening Dispatch,* 14.4.37.)

139. ' Say, your gelatines of pork pressed into coronet shapes and cased in crimson jelly, just give me the creeps!' (American quoted in *Reynolds News,* 2.5.37.)

140. Americans, says the *News Chronicle* New York correspondent, are very interested in the knee breeches to be worn at the Coronation by U.S. representatives. Mr. James G. Gerard announced that he would have his made in London. 'I wouldn't dare trust an American tailor,' he said. 'He would make me plus four knickers.'

This so annoyed Congressman Dirksen, of Illinois, that he hopes 'those silk pants will split down the seams when they have to genuflect'. To which Mr. Gerard retorts: 'I had that possibility in mind in avoiding an American tailor.' (*N.C.* 22.4.37.)

141. A British missionary is now travelling post haste to London via Siberia, bringing with him the elaborate gold-braided Coronation suit left behind by Mr. H. H. Kung, China's Vice-Premier and Finance Minister. Mr. Kung spent two weeks in being fitted before he was satisfied with the suit. (*N.C.* 23.4.37.)

142. Colonial visitors can entrust their laundry to us with confidence. (*Advt. D.T.* 12.4.37.)

143. We sent our Easter Rabbits to Siberia to grow special Ermine Coats in honour of the Coronation. They went with open minds but have returned convinced anti-bolshies—so there! (*Fortnum and Mason Advt.*)

144. On the first day of Coronation Week, May 10, Mary Adams will present Pearl Binder and Margaret Leona, the dancer, in a review of women's clothes through the ages. The scene will be an artist's studio. Pearl Binder will be the artist and Margaret Leona will be her débutante friend, proud of her summer trousseau. A wager about the up-to-dateness of the outfit will result in revelations, in several senses. Margaret Leona will begin by shedding a flower coronet, and then follow it up with cloak, dress, silk stockings, and so on, finally appearing in a modern bathing suit.

All this will be entertaining and educational. The coronet, you might hear, was worn by primitive West African tribes; the cloak was worn in Chaucer's day; the dress in the early nineteenth century; the silk stockings by Queen Elizabeth herself; lacquered toe nails by Cleopatra. Only the bathing-suit apparently has no precedent. (*Radio Times*, 30.4.37. Television Supplement.)

145. Mr. Ramsay MacDonald, Lord President of the Council, answering a question in the House of Commons

yesterday, denied that an order had been given that men
with seats on the stands around the Queen Victoria Memorial
must wear frock or tail coats. (*D.T.* 5.5.37.)

146. How a peeress will be able to wear both her tiara and
coronet, as the regulations insist, without detriment to the
arrangement of her hairdressing is still a problem. But by
leaving the greater part of the back of the head very simply
dressed, there is less chance of complete disorder such as
might occur with an intricate arrangement of curls. It rests
with the owner of the coronet to find an easy way of putting
it on and taking it off with the best results. Each coronet is
supplied with a forked metal pin, resembling a large hairpin,
which can be drawn in or out at each side. (*E.S.* 20.2.37.)

147.   Even if your stockings won't be seen much,
        it would seem right, don't you think, to wear
    the loveliest possible. And on that day, of all days,
                they ought to
        be British made. The name is Aristoc.
                                (Advert. in *Vogue*, 28.4.37.)

148. The gown to be worn by the Queen when she is
crowned in Westminster Abbey on Wednesday next is a
triumph of symbolism, a creation of sheer artistic beauty
combined with the magnificence that the occasion calls for.
It is a gown worthy of the high place it must take in the history of Costume.

English satin of soft texture and ivory tint is the material
used, the embroidery on which skilled workers have spent so
many days and weeks is carried out in various shades of gold
with light touches of diamante. . . .

The rich embroidery of the gown follows, by Royal command, a strictly traditional form. There are the emblems of
the British Isles, the rose, thistle, shamrock and leek. To
symbolize the new spirit of unity with the Crown of the

Dominions overseas—the emblems of the maple leaf of Canada, the wattle for Australia, the fern frond for New Zealand, and the protea flower for South Africa, together with the lotus flower for India, have all been introduced. Lastly the typical English oak leaf and acorn have been used as border all round the gown.* (*D.T.* 7.5.37.)

149. To enable British subjects in the most isolated parts of the Empire to participate, 'in spirit if not in person' in the Coronation service, the official souvenir programme, issued by the Jubilee Trust, has been dispatched from London by land, sea and air.

This—Britain's message to its Empire—was blessed by the Duke of Gloucester, speaking at a London luncheon yesterday to celebrate publication.

The Duke, chairman of the Trust, concluded: 'It is our object that this programme shall reach every British subject, wherever they may be—in city, waste or wilderness.' (*D. Mirror*, 28.4.37.)

150. 'You can loosen the tightest purse-strings if you just use a smile,' declares Lord Baden-Powell in a message to Scouts on the sale of Coronation programmes. 'Put on a grin and worm the money out of them. Even if they've already got a copy, persuade them to buy a second copy of this historic document for Granny at home.' (*D. Mail*, 5.5.37.)

151. Orders for many thousands of copies of the Official Souvenir Coronation Programme have been received by King George's Jubilee Trust Fund from business houses. Many other firms will distribute copies to their customers in England and oversea before Coronation Day, and orders for thousands of programmes wrapped with printed presentation bands have been received. Banking, insurance, chemi-

*The Queen dresses herself as a flag (*cf.* 1: para. 50) and she has a peculiar right to do so. It is interesting to see that the Statute of Westminster modifies not only the King's Oath but also the Queen's dress.

cal, wireless, and many other firms and institutions are among those whose orders have been received to date.

Every patient in English and Welsh voluntary hospitals on Coronation day will be able to follow the Coronation ceremonies in his or her copy of the Official Programme. This has been made possible by the generosity of the Philco Radio and Television Corporation of Great Britain, who are meeting the entire cost. (*Times*, 8.3.37.)

152.   *Listeners in the Kraals*

It was revealed in London yesterday that the General Electric Company had received an order to instal apparatus that will enable hundreds of thousands of West African natives to hear the Coronation.

The equipment, which includes 5,250 loud-speakers served from seven centres, will furnish a permanent radio relay service. This the British Government can maintain for propaganda among the native peoples. (*N.C.* 10.4.37.)

153.   *Coronation Weather*

It is much too early yet to make any definite forecast based on scientific principles. All that can be done is to assess the probabilities in the light of past records. These make cheerful reading.

On the average of a long period, there is sunshine in London for at least half of every hour from 9 a.m. to 3 p.m. on a day in the middle of May. The statistical odds are nearly 4 to 1 against any rain between 7 a.m. and 7 p.m. on May 12, and about 9 to 1 against a substantial fall.

It is true that Buchan's third cold spell is scheduled for May 9 to 14, but, as most people know by now, these dates are mere approximations, and the parting kick which winter usually gives us during the first half of that month may well be over before the twelfth. (*Star*, 6.4.37.)

154. Trains will run all night on the Underground for the Coronation. This will be the first time there has been an all-night service since the Underground was electrified. Police expect a million visitors to London on the day. The main line railway services are arranging services, and the Underground will run the longest trains that the stations will take. (*Star*, 9.3.37.)

155. From midnight on May 11 there will be a police-guarded ring around Central London to check the entry of cars which would otherwise create appalling traffic confusion as the hour for the Coronation procession approaches. But cars will be able to enter the Coronation area with passengers, drop them at or near the viewing places, and escape out of the ring again—if they go the right way about it. This, announced Scotland Yard during the week-end, is the right way:

Spectators who are going to use cars must first consult the map of the royal route and find the colour under which they have been classified. Thus:

For places in the Mall, Whitehall, Parliament Street, the Sanctuary, Bridge Street and Victoria Embankment the colour is GREEN;

Northumberland Avenue, Trafalgar Square, Pall Mall and St. James's Street are BROWN;

Piccadilly (and Park Lane), Piccadilly Circus and Regent Street are BLUE;

Oxford Circus, Oxford Street and Marble Arch are RED;

East Carriage Road, Hyde Park, are YELLOW;

Hyde Park Corner, Constitution Hill and Queen's Gardens are MAROON.

At a date to be announced later the appropriate coloured labels for car windscreens will be issued on application for cars making for various points on the route.* (*N.C.* 15.3.37.)

*Compare the following NOTE in a folder-map issued free by the L.P.T.B.:

'The restrictions described below may seem to complicate travel: they

156. Those who have the energy to get up early and be in the streets of London by 6 a.m. next Sunday may see a rehearsal of the Coronation procession. . . .

Will you be there? Have you the energy to get up in the mornings? Or do you feel drowsy and heavy, and find it's a hard job to get out of bed?

If so, the remedy is in your own hands. For over sixty years, wherever Englishmen have had to be 'on parade' bright and early, their one daily rule of health has been 'Eno first thing every morning'.

Life to-day calls for Eno's!* (*Advert.* 13.4.37.)

157. In the grey light of dawn, with the night mists still clinging to the wind-whipped waters of the Thames, troops and carriages mustered near Westminster Abbey yesterday for a rehearsal of the Coronation procession.

Despite unpromising weather and the loss of an hour's sleep in the change-over to summer time, tens of thousands of people lined the route from 3 a.m. onwards for this 'preview' of the procession. (*D.T.* 9.4.37.)

158. A shrill, early-morning cheer was evoked by the sight of the newly regilded Coronation coach, drawn by eight 'creams' with fawn-coated postilions in top-hats. The coach swayed a little because it was empty. Red blinds were drawn above its doors. Its ornate carving and panels cast a temporary glow over the procession.

In this 4-ton coach, which cost £7,000 when it was built in 1761, George III, George IV, William IV, Victoria, Edward VII and George V drove to their coronations; and it will go forth again on May 12.

are in fact designed to simplify it. . . . Without these restrictions, movement would be seriously impeded or even blocked. They are, therefore, necessary.'

*This firm makes use not only of the Coronation itself, but of one of the numerous rehearsals held in preparation for it, to advertise its product.

The crowds pressed forward to examine the massive gilt tritons from whose backs the coach is slung on broad leather braces. They saw that while the leading tritons were blowing shell horns to announce the advent of the monarch of the seas, the two behind carried fasces—Imperial Fasces topped with tridents. (Fasces had a less distinctive association in the time of George III.)

The panels, allegorical paintings—one of Mars, Minerva and Mercury supporting the Imperial crown; another of Peace burning the implements of war—shone as they passed. After the first welcoming cheer the crowds watched the coach go by in awed silence. (*N.C.* 19.4.37.)

Eleven Days to the Coronation

Saturday, May 1

159. Royal May, which is to be packed so full of moving spectacle, was ushered in yesterday with the auspices of a rising barometer and every prospect of 'King's weather.' The day saw the activities in London in connection with the Coronation rapidly approaching a climax. . . .

The first day of the strike of London's 25,500 busmen, which began at midnight on Friday, passed quietly yesterday, without any display of ill-will by strikers or public, and without any sign of sympathetic action by other transport workers. Not one of the 5,000 buses, which daily cover 600,000 miles, left the garages. The strike was thus complete. . . .

The King and Queen saw Sunderland win the Association Football Cup at Wembley by three goals to one. Their Majesties were given an enthusiastic reception by the crowd of 93,000. . . .

The London May Day procession was on a larger scale than usual. Observers agreed that this was the biggest May

Day procession ever seen in this country. The procession was about four miles long, and by the time it reached Hyde Park the busmen's contingent numbered several thousands.

The demonstrators marched into the park under a forest of red flags, maypoles and banners, singing *The Red Flag* and giving the Communist salute of the clenched fist. Among the marchers was a group of strikers from the Harworth Colliery area, Nottinghamshire. (*Observer*, 2.5.37.)

Scenes of chaos without parallel were witnessed in the West End last night. The synchronization of the bus strike with the cup-tie led to a congestion in the Underground, between 11 p.m. and midnight, which cannot be described.

Scores of women—and men—fainted in the crush, but they had to recover without medical assistance. (*Reynolds News*, 2.5.37.)

Sunday, May 2

160. King George, wearing for the first time the khaki service uniform of a Field-Marshal, was present at the dedication of the completed Royal Military College chapel at Sandhurst. . . .

During the address of the Archbishop of Canterbury, as his Grace referred to the 'same spirit of willing service and sacrifice that would be aroused again', those outside heard distant but very distinct rattle of machine-gun fire. (*D. Mirror*, 3.5.37.)

Monday, May 3

161. The Duke of Windsor sped through Austria and Switzerland to-night on his way to France—and Mrs. Simpson.

His departure from St. Wolfgang was so sudden that he did not even have time to shave before he left his villa. A telephone call from Mrs. Simpson was the cause of all the hurry. The moment she heard soon after half-past ten this morning that her decree *nisi* had been made absolute, she rang up the

Duke. They spoke for eight minutes. Then things began to happen. The Duke, flushed with excitement, called his equerry, Captain Greenacre, and asked him to have all his bags packed and everything cleared up so that he could catch the express at Salzburg at 4.50.* (*D.E.* 4.5.37.)

Throughout Monday King George studied the bus strike, conferred with experts and on Monday night had a discussion with Mr. Stanley Baldwin at Buckingham Palace. Turning from his heavy and urgent programme of Coronation affairs early in the day, the King sent for Mr. Ernest Brown (Minister of Labour) and gave him a long audience at Buckingham Palace. (*D. Mirror*, 4.5.37.)

Wednesday, May 5

162. 'This day week our young King and Queen, who were called suddenly and unexpectedly to the most tremendous position on earth, will dedicate themselves to a service which can only be ended by death.

'I appeal to that handful of men on whom rests peace or war to give the best present to the country that could be given at this moment, to do the one thing that would rejoice the hearts of all who love this country, and that is to rend and dissipate this dark cloud that has gathered over us and show the people of the world that this democracy at least can still practise the art of peace in a world of strife.'

In these words Mr. Baldwin concluded his farewell speech in the House of Commons this evening. He was answering Mr. Attlee, who had opened a debate on the coal crisis.

Cf. D.E. 10.5.37, where William Hickey writes:

'Talking of sacrosanctity, I see that some foolish people are deploring the publication of those happy pictures of the Duke of Windsor and his duchess-to-be; they even suggest that he's chosen this moment to muscle in on the Coronation limelight.

'What nonsense! As in the case of the busmen it's pure coincidence; it is simply because the legal process of the divorce happened to be completed at this time.'

While Mr. Baldwin was speaking, the London tramway and trolley-bus men decided to send a deputation to Mr. Ernest Bevin, general secretary of their Union, to ask for Union permission for them to join the London bus strike. (*E.S.* 5.5.37.)

After the Premier had spoken, delegates of London's 12,000 tram and trolley-bus workers decided not to join the busmen now on strike. (*D.E.* 6.5.37.)

The King and Queen held their first Court at Buckingham Palace, a week before their Coronation. (*D.T.* 6.5.37.)

Thursday, May 6

163. Lakehurst (New Jersey), Thursday Night. *Hindenburg*, world's greatest airship, burst into flames and was destroyed as she prepared to moor here at 7.20 p.m. at the end of her first flight of the season over the Atlantic. It is feared that nearly 100 people aboard—passengers and crew—have all been killed. *Hindenburg* was due to rush the last of the American visitors to the Coronation—a trip which would have brought in £10,800 for seventy passengers who had booked seats to Europe many weeks ago. (*D.E.* 7.5.37.)

One of the most critical Stock Exchange Settlements of recent years was carried through without a casualty. . . . The fact that no fresh trouble came to the surface relieves markets from immediate anxiety. Any liquidation that might now take place need not occasion disturbance. . . . With next week devoted to the Coronation, followed by the Whitsuntide holiday, these influences would prevent any quick return to pre-slump conditions. . . . (*D.T.* 7.5.37.)

Friday, May 7

164. With only four days to go before the Coronation, hopes of an early settlement of the London 'bus strike were disappointed. Unexpected difficulties arose, and there is now little prospect of the 'buses running during the week-end. (*D.T.* 8.5.37.)

Amid all the Coronation ceremonies—most of them rooted in long tradition—the luncheon to the KING in Westminster Hall is unique. This was the first occasion, as His Majesty himself said, upon which the Sovereign has been present at a luncheon in Westminster Hall to meet those who represent the Legislatures of the Empire. (Leading article, *D.T.* 8.5.37.)

Thousands went decoration-gazing in the West End on Friday night, gave London police an idea of what to expect in Coronation Week. Pavements were blocked. Traffic jams were so great cars stood still while traffic lights went on flashing 'Stop—Caution—Go'. (*D.E.* 8.5.37.)

Saturday, May 8

165. Only three more days, and the great event on which the attention of the Empire has been focussed for weeks will be an accomplished fact—King George VI will have been crowned. . . .

Three hundred thousand oversea visitors from all parts of the world will by Wednesday have been joined in the invasion of London by people from every corner of the British Isles. . . .

There were wonderful scenes in Central London last night when crowds, estimated by an experienced official at not far short of a million, crowded the route along which the Procession will pass, to see the decorations. Progress was necessarily very slow, and motorists were no better off in respect of speed than pedestrians; but the utmost good humour prevailed, and everybody was happy. . . .

There is little prospect of the buses returning to the streets of London until Tuesday morning at the earliest—if then. (*Observer*, 9.5.37.)

London Transport Board offered to negotiate on all matters in dispute with the Busmen—except on the vital principle of the $7\frac{1}{2}$ hours day. (*Reynolds News*, 9.5.37.)

Sunday, May 9

166. After spending the night in the rain, half a million people saw the final rehearsal of the Coronation pageant crawl from Buckingham Palace gates to Westminster Abbey —seventeen minutes late, its colour and glory hidden by mackintoshes and horse blankets. . . .

Nothing was amazing about this mufti show except the number of people who would face a cold, wintry night to see a golden coach. Even they were disappointed.

'Now cheer, cheer,' cried Sir Arthur Erskine, royal equerry, dancing down the carriage way, umbrella in the air, trying to stir some enthusiasm. Instead the crowd laughed. (*D.E.* 10.5.37.)

London experienced the greatest traffic congestion it has ever known on a Sunday. An experienced police official expressed the view that at least 1,000,000 people must have gone to the West End during the day. . . .

Peace efforts by the Ministry of Labour in the strike of 25,600 London 'busmen were abandoned last night.

Five thousand 'busmen from every London garage assembled on the Embankment and marched in the rain to Trafalgar Square for a mass meeting. (*D.T.* 10.5.37.)

Fifty thousand cheering people besieged Buckingham Palace late last night. All night the throng had grown since the moment when 10,000 men and women mobbed the King's car outside the Palace as he returned with Queen Elizabeth and the Princesses from their week-end rest at Royal Lodge, Windsor. King George raised his hat. The Queen waved her hand, as the car moved inch by inch along a path forced by a small army of police.

Queen Mary's car, too, was marooned in the centre of a great crowd. . . . Shortly afterwards the Duke and Duchess of Gloucester drove in, followed by the Duke and Duchess of Kent. There was a wild rush to the railings, and police had great difficulties in keeping the entrances to the gates clear. At last officers cleared all pavements, forcing thousands into the road. (*D. Mirror*, 10.5.37.)

167. Sunday was a day of preparation in the churches for the Coronation. The service broadcast from all transmitters of the B.B.C. was impressive in the way it called to mind the religious significance of the Coronation. The Archbishop of Canterbury naturally dwelt on this theme in his address. . . .

The Archbishop said:

The long expected day of the Coronation is at hand. In two ways this Coronation will be distinguished from any that have gone before it. In the first place and for the first time the ceremony as it unfolds itself in Westminster Abbey will be actually heard by millions of people in every part of the world. It is scarcely an exaggeration to say that the whole world will be the audience.

In the second place . . . in the Oath which the King will take he will promise to rule according to their respective laws and customs, not as in 1911 the people 'of the United Kingdom and Great Britain and Ireland and the Dominions thereto belonging', but of the peoples 'of Great Britain, Ireland, Canada, Australia, New Zealand, and the Union of South Africa, of his possessions and the other territories to any of them belonging or pertaining, and of his Empire of India.' Each of the great Dominions will thus be mentioned by name so that its people hearing the name will realize that it is their own King who is to be consecrated and crowned. (*Times*, 10.5.37.)

Monday, May 10

168. Whatever the weather to-morrow, Coronation Day, the procession will take place without modification, it was officially stated last night.

Latest forecast for to-morrow—Unsettled.

(*D.E.* 11.5.37.)

London faces its greatest traffic hold-up since the general strike of 1926. A lightning strike of West End hotel waiters planned for to-night may add to the confusion. Busmen are continuing their strike indefinitely. Tramway and trolley-bus men are asking their executive for permission to join them. Taximen are making a similar plea. Underground men may be forced to stop work by sheer physical incapacity to carry on under the terrific strain that will fall on them. (*D.E.* 11.5.37.)

169. The Coronation Honours List, published to-day, is the most widespread list within living memory. It is a real 'all ranks' list. The Queen and Queen Mary and Lord Wigram receive the Victorian Chain, one of the rarest of all decorations. . . .

Among the new knights are Mr. Hugh Walpole, the novelist, Mr. Arnold Bax, the musician, and Mr. P. F. (Plum) Warner, famous cricketer. Those awarded the Medal of the Order of the British Empire include bus and railway workers, a greaser on a Channel steamer, and a porter and housemaid at the British Embassy in Madrid. A Gold Coast chief, Nana Agyeman Prempeh II, of Asantahene, has been made a Knight of the Order of the British Empire, and a Maori princess, Te Pui Horangi, of Ngakuawahia, New Zealand, a Commander of the Order. . . .

'I don't know why they picked on me. . . .'
'I hope it will fit in with my war medals.'
So said two busmen yesterday. They have been honoured by the King in the Coronation Honours List. (*D. Mirror*, 11.5.37.)

Tuesday, May 11

170. The enthusiasm of the Coronation crowds in the West End remained undamped by the almost continuous rain in the morning and afternoon. (*D.T.* 12.5.37.)

Rain the spoiler left its mark on Coronation Eve. Decorations in some of the side streets and on houses—schemes on which poor people had spent hard-earned savings and lavished time and care—suffered badly. (*D. Mirror*, 12.5.37.)

The Executive Council of the Transport and General Workers' Union, after an all-day sitting at Transport House, rejected an application from the tram and trolley-bus section for plenary powers to call a strike and also refused a request from the 'bus section that the strike should be extended. (*D.T.* 12.5.37.)

171. The Duke and Duchess of Kent attended the Coronation 'day of united intercession and conference' at Queen's Hall, London. The Duke, in an address to the audience of 3,000, said:

'We can all see how the hand of God guided the King and Queen from 1911. I hope the same God will guide and protect our new King and Queen. . . .' (*D. Mirror*, 12.5.37.)

'TO-DAY I STAND ON THE THRESHOLD OF A NEW LIFE. . . . I SHALL DO MY UTMOST TO CARRY ON MY FATHER'S WORK FOR THE WELFARE OF OUR GREAT EMPIRE.'

The King, speaking at Buckingham Palace, made this pledge. He was replying—the Queen an intent listener—to nine loyal addresses presented by his Dominion Prime Ministers and representatives of India and the Colonies. (*D. Mirror*, 12.5.37.)

172. Shots were fired in Dublin on Tuesday night when Civic Guards clashed with men attempting to hold a Republican parade which had been banned. The police made baton charges and many people were injured and taken to hospital. The avowed object of the parade was to 'repudiate the Coronation of an English King as King of Ireland'. The disturbance spread, and by 10 p.m. the whole centre of the city was seething with excitement. (*D.T.* 12.5.37.)

Insurgent aircraft carried out to-day what the Basque Government regard as a full-dress rehearsal for the Coronation

Day destruction of Bilbao. . . . Twelve times between 6.30 a.m. and noon Junker bombers and Heinkel III pursuit planes flew over the city and dropped tons of high explosive on its outskirts and surrounding suburbs. (*D.E.* 12.5.37.)

Insurgent batteries began a furious bombardment of Madrid at 4 a.m. to-day . . . and kept it up for seven hours. Again the Gran Via, the 'Piccadilly of Madrid', was littered with bricks, mortar and broken glass, and pocked with new shell holes. Tramway services were suspended, the trams being abandoned in the streets by the drivers, and people could be seen running panic stricken in all directions. (*D.T.* 12.5.37.)

173. Lights in the royal private apartments at Buckingham Palace went out last night at 9.30. The King and Queen had dinner quietly alone, then retired to rest in preparation for to-day. (*D. Mirror*, 12.5.37.)

Shortly before midnight Mr. Thomas Coke, equerry to the King, drove from Buckingham Palace to Westminster Abbey and laid a wreath of crimson roses on the Tomb of the Unknown Warrior. The wreath was tied with a ribbon in His Majesty's personal colours of crimson and blue, edged with gold, and bore a card with the words: 'To the Empire's Dead —GEORGE R.I., ELIZABETH R.' (*D.T.* 12.5.37.)

174. *Ecce felix hora gaudiorum!*

This Coronation Day breaks upon the world like some sublime chord that is the climax of a long crescendo. It has been expected, awaited, counted upon; yet when it comes it stirs the blood like a sudden revelation. The preparation has been long—so long that some few have felt, and some few more have affected, boredom with the whole affair. In the people as a whole, week after week, the excitement has increased. A horrible internecine war in a foreign country and a sudden outburst of industrial unrest at home have ceased to exist for the general consciousness, except in their possible and actual effects upon the Coronation.

Let the few feel as they may, the appetite of the many for Coronation news and for Coronation preliminaries has grown from day to day; and no observer of it could believe that it was confined to any one rank or sort of people. The grocer's paper bag has been gay with flags, and the portraits of Their Majesties; the schoolchild's button-hole has borne a red, white and blue ribbon, the houses and flats of the workmen are all aflutter with 'baby bunting'; but at the other end of the social and the financial scale the enthusiasm has been just as hot. . . .

The monarchy has become so truly democratic nowadays that nothing which the Royal House either does or does not can be counted alien to the welfare of the people. The Crown is the necessary centre, not of political life only, but of all life!* (*Times*, 12.5.37. Leading article.)

175. Coronation Day. The day of royal pomp and circumstance. The day of purple and gold. Of sanded streets and gilded carriageway.

London, the capital of the Empire upon which the sun never sets and into whose slums the sun never shines, is agog with excitement and gay with lights and decorations.

And all for what? To add to the happiness and well-being of the Empire's teeming millions? No! To crown a King and Queen around whom the powerful engines of imperialist propaganda can weave an atmosphere of royal patriotism, that can enable the institutions of Monarchy to be more effectively used to uphold British imperialism.

*The remarkable thing about these assertions in the newspapers, and above all in *The Times*, is that they rely on a peculiar kind of literary skill. A reasonable interpretation for the remark can be found if it is challenged and under this cover the remark makes a direct statement of primitive animism. It will be noticed that *all* life, animal and vegetable too presumably, has its necessary centre in the crown. However, these methods are much used in poetry as well as in propaganda, and the writers have probably not decided whether they mean their statements literally or not.

The London that visitors will see, and crowds come up to gaze upon, is not representative of the real Britain. For a day or so in the working-class streets, cheap bunting and flags may strike a note of glamour and brightness, but only for a day or so.

We remember these things on Coronation Day because we are loyal and devoted to the real interests of the people and their true happiness. When the shouting and tumult have died down, when the garish display is all over, and tawdry and soiled decorations still hang about our streets, they will symbolize the contrast between the two Britains.

The Britain of a tiny handful, who own its factories, banks, land and rivers, who out of working-class exploitation lead lives of luxury and idleness.

And the Britain of working men and women who have nothing but their power to labour, and millions have not even the opportunity to exercise that. It is this Britain that we best serve by remembering it when its class enemies seek to gild its chains.

It is this Britain which will yet conquer. And on that day, the workers in all their majesty, dignity, and power, will so organize the resources of this country that in fraternal alliance with the freed peoples of present subject colonial countries, they will transform it into a paradise in which the sun of joy will never set. (Harry Pollitt's Message. *D. Worker*, 12.5.37.)

Chapter 2

LONDON ON MAY 12

King Henry V

Upon the King, let us our lives, our souls,
Our debts, our careful wives,
Our children, and our sins, lay on the King:
We must bear all. O hard condition,
Twin-born with greatness, subject to the breath
Of every fool, whose sense no more can feel,
But his own wringing. What infinite heart's-ease
Must Kings neglect, that private men enjoy?
And what have Kings, that privates have not too,
Save ceremony, save general ceremony?
And what art thou, thou idol ceremony?
What kind of god art thou? that suffer'st more
Of mortal griefs, than do thy worshippers.
What are thy rents? what are thy comings in?
O ceremony, show me but thy worth.
What! is thy soul of adoration?
Art thou aught else but place, degree, and form,
Creating awe and fear in other men?
Wherein thou art less happy, being fear'd,
Than they in fearing.
What drink'st thou oft, instead of homage sweet,

87

But poison'd flattery? O, be sick, great greatness,
And bid thy ceremony give thee cure.
Think'st thou the fiery fever will go out
With titles blown from adulation?
Will it give place to flexure and low bending?
Canst thou, when thou command'st the beggar's knee,
Command the health of it? No, thou proud dream,
That play'st so subtly with a King's repose.
I am a King that find thee: and I know,
'Tis not the balm, the sceptre, and the ball,
The sword, the mace, the crown imperial,
The intertissued robe of gold and pearl,
The farced title running 'fore the King,
The throne he sits on; nor the tide of pomp,
That beats upon the high shore of the world:
No, not all these, thrice-gorgeous ceremony; ·
Not all these, laid in bed majestical,
Can sleep so soundly, as the wretched slave:
Who with a body fill'd, and vacant mind,
Gets him to rest, cramm'd with distressful bread,
Never sees horrid night, the child of Hell:
But like a lackey, from the rise to set,
Sweats in the eye of Phoebus; and all night
Sleeps in Elysium: next day after dawn,
Doth rise and help Hyperion to his horse,
And follows so the ever-running year
With profitable labour to his grave:
And but for ceremony, such a wretch,
Winding up days with toil, and nights with sleep,
Had the fore-hand and vantage of a King.
The slave, a member of the country's peace,
Enjoys it; but in gross brain little wots,
What watch the King keeps, to maintain the peace;
Whose hours the peasant best advantages.

SHAKESPEARE: *Henry V*, IV, I.

1. In making a survey of May 12, Coronation Day, various kinds of phenomena had to be observed. There was the life of the streets, existing for that day only, called into being by an exceptional occasion. There was life at home, and in routine environments, disturbed and modified by the demands of the day. More difficult to grasp and define, there was the mass reaction to the events, the floating opinions and counter-opinions which they provoked, and the interactions of opinion among individuals and among groups. Such was the varied field to be explored, and in order to make as round a picture as the forces of Mass-Observation would allow, three distinct lines of attack were adopted.

2. Firstly there were the Observers, who having made surveys on the twelfth of February, March and April, could now bring most useful experience to bear on the peculiar problems of the twelfth of May. 43 of them sent in reports, many of them of 10,000 words or more, showing a marked increase in accuracy and control of the subjective elements over their earlier efforts. These are numbered CO.1—CO.43 when quoted in the text.

Secondly, several thousand leaflets were issued, headed

WHERE WERE YOU ON MAY 12?

MASS-OBSERVATION WANTS YOUR STORY

and asking for answers to the following questions:

1. Name, address, age, sex, occupation? Married or single Religious or political views if any?

2. Did you yourself see, or did you want to see, the Coronation procession?

3. What did you do on May 12? Give a *short* hour by hour description of your day.

4. Do you think it benefits the country to have a Coronation?

5. What was the most stirring incident, the most peculiar incident and the funniest incident that you saw or that you heard of during the day? (Say whether you saw it, or heard of it; and if you heard of it, from whom.)

6. Were your neighbours mostly keen on the Coronation? What did they say to you about it?

To this questionnaire 77 answers were received, a return of about 3% plus a certain amount of material on other people's opinions and days collected by Observers. Some of the answers were several thousand words in length, and the opinions represented were of all kinds, from 'Conservative and Church of England' to 'Communist and Atheist', though the bulk of them lay between these two extremes. They are numbered CL.1— CL.109.

Thirdly, a Mobile Squad of 12 Observers was set to work to cover happenings in the streets of London from midnight on May 11 till after midnight on May 12. They worked in shifts, and kept in touch with the Mass-Observation headquarters by telephone, like reporters and a newspaper office. During the time they were working they took notes almost continuously, and from their notes wrote up lengthy reports, numbered CM.1—12.

3. By these three methods, three kinds of focus were obtained, not to mention the individual differences of focus between each of the Observers. Close-up and long shot, detail and ensemble, were all provided. Some recorded just what reaches the threshold of a normal consciousness, others by concentrated effort saw and heard far more than they were normally accustomed

to. On the whole, the excitement of the day seems to have stimulated most people's powers of observation to an unusual degree.

The survey of May 12 is divided into three parts. The first, Chapter 2, is based mainly on the work done by the Mobile Squad, with additions from CO and CL. It gives a panorama of London, and especially of the route of the Coronation procession, the area in which took place those events which gave the day its exceptional character over large parts of the world.

4. Some general points can be made about the celebrations, points which are well illustrated by the Observers but might have been expected anyway. They were unescapable; people who tried to avoid them found themselves going back to the radio on one ground or another, or showed a sense of guilt, or found themselves interested after all. However, in many ways it was treated as a public holiday and festival like any other, to be enjoyed in the usual ways, carrying the emotional weight natural to the special days of a large society, but no extreme interest in what the function of a King may be or the significance of his Coronation. Even when people find themselves suddenly and powerfully moved by the sight of one of the processions they may not be clear *what* has moved them—the symbolism of a procession and a crowd and a band, in themselves; a patriotic feeling about the country as a whole; or some feeling that refers to this particular Coronation.

5. It is notable that any break-up of the routine of life is satisfactory to most people; thus they forgot to be angry with the busmen for being on strike—they added somehow to the drama of the occasion by making it more unusual, or even more inconvenient. A curious record-hunting ascetic feeling always appears on such days, as in the people who sat for 25 hours, though it must have been obvious that there was no need to. This may be connected with the idea that you have a duty

to enjoy yourself on a public holiday very thoroughly. However the curiously sinister effect of the reports of the night before the Coronation seems to show feelings of a more special kind. The Observers note a revival of war-time atmosphere and the *Evening Standard* ran a 'Coronation Camp Fire' which printed stories of the war. This is partly because the war gave a great deal of companionship and change of routine, so that people swap war-stories whenever these conditions hold. The feeling about war, if present, is however passive; nobody seems to conceive the troops so prominent in the day as doing any actual fighting. And so far as the King himself becomes an object of emotion he is conceived in family or 'Freudian' relations, not as a person who might do anything and hardly even as representing a country or a class. The performance in fact was viewed very largely in an aesthetic way, and this was the way which involved least strain and was for the majority the best social adaptation to the circumstances.

What Central London was like from midnight to 5 a.m.

6. (CM.7.) 11.45 p.m. Euston full of people staying the night on waiting-room benches. Refreshment room and Enquiry Hall full. In waiting room drunk man knocks chair over, sits on floor, policeman says 'Hey, sit up,' but leaves him to lie there. Man drinking beer and eating sandwiches in a telephone box. Rush of excursionists arriving from Macclesfield to engage seats for their return journey.

Accidentally met a friend from Cambridge come up with his mother, 'A great show' he says.

'This is what London is,' says North countrywoman jostled by crowd.

People waiting to meet friends on Liverpool excursion.

'A lot of soldiers,' says one and his wife goes on to talk about Willy, whose regiment has been drafted to Malta.

Young men go by shouting, old lady says: 'Somebody lit', apparently talking to herself, or rather to the world in general for everybody here is talking to nobody in particular—the effect perhaps of having to shout so much to make oneself heard.

Refreshment room, man and fiancée talk over Coronation Gold Cup runners, they go on to play This year, Next year, Sometime, Never, with the rolls arranged along the counter. Later the fiancée says that it is a prejudice that one should always sleep at night time. He begins to sing 'Night and Day you are the one.'

Train departure platforms silent except for porters loading mail-bags.

Outside the station thick fog. Euston Road very quiet, only a few drunks on the running boards of taxis.

7. 12.40 a.m. Baker Street. Scouts selling programmes, worried about their collecting boxes being full. One small pale scout with glasses complaining that he has lost his collecting box, his chief helps him to look for it.

Welshman from Aberystwyth asks me the way to Paddington. 'Very handy these tubes' he says. I mention the bus strike, he looks blank. Curious nobody mentions the bus strike.*

Regent's Park. Cars on wrong side of road because of fog. Man earning coppers at gate by directing fog-bound cars.

I try to enter park and find it locked on west side. Get into Bedford College for Women by mistake, porter stops me, I say I thought people were allowed to sleep in the park, he says there are some sleeping in there (indicating the College) but I am not allowed in. The east side of the park is apparently occupied entirely by soldiers and I am not allowed in there either.

*There is no discussion of the bus-strike in the reports, and only a few casual mentions that it was going on at all.

Very few people on the circular drive because of the fog and damp.

At top Baker Street drunk man goes to sleep in sand and gravel box. Policeman observes to passers-by that he is safer there than in the road.

Traffic jam at Marylebone Circus. People leaning out of taxis shouting at each other; people on top of car roofs; one taxi with about ten people on it singing 'Hallelujah, I'm a bum.' Man standing by traffic lights offers to chaperone (*sic*) girls leaning out of back of taxi, they answer that they are going home. He says 'Where?' They answer their home is on the streets and laugh, of course their home is obviously, from their dress and accent, not on the streets.

Evening News placard 'All about it', It being understood.

Marylebone Station deserted, L.N.E.R. excursions apparently all arriving at King's Cross.

Immense motor van passes bearing sign 'Bladen Milk for 4,500 Children at Coronation of King George VI. Long May He Reign.'

Edgware Road, two closed buses full of Scottish soldiers. Groups pass singing *Alone on this night of romance* and *A bicycle made for Two*.

Two sailors, Edgware Road Station, chaffed with *Popeye, The Sailor Man*.

8. 1.45. Paddington. All seats crowded, people eating, sleeping, reading, on seats and porters' trucks. Looking at Arrival Indicator, woman says 'Trains not a bit late yet, the organization's wonderful!' People generally not talking about the Coronation but about trains, food, drinks, relatives, etc.

Boy in tube: 'The train's going this way.'

Father nods and grins.

Boy: 'I thought it was going the other way.'

Father: 'No, it's going this way,' etc.

Outside snack bar near Paddington, man says 'Not going home, are you?' Girl: 'No fear, just a walk.'

Restaurant nearby with notice 'Breakfast served now'—time about 2.15.

9. Lancaster Gate. 2.20. Kensington Gardens shut, full of soldiers, girls leaning over park railings calling to them, soldiers indicate guards at gate despairingly.

Indians arguing in tube about the necessity of the Bakerloo extension to Stanmore, one says 'People in suburbs are scarcely human, they should be kept as far out of London as possible.' Every time train enters tunnel people make animal noises. Others unscrew light-bulbs; they are all doing the sort of things Undergraduates do when canned, but they are not Undergraduates, they seem to be aged between about 25 and 35 and they look like clerks, typists, etc.

Terrific jam at Oxford Circus, takes about 15 minutes to get up escalators. Singing coming from every part of Oxford Street. Fruit barrows, sellers of rosettes and newspapers, no motors. People camping on the pavement all the way down Regent Street, four deep from the pavement edge.

Young man to girls 'Hey, have you got to go home to-night?'—This seems to be the most frequent question asked, answer always in the negative; apparently even in moments of great excitement people are still thinking of their homes as their centres of life.

10. Continual processions of 20-50 people all the way down Regent Street, one going round Oxford Circus till leader with Union Jack gets dizzy and stumbles, someone else snatches the flag and carries on exactly as in boys' story-books of pre-trench-warfare days.

Old lady in red, white and blue trousers selling rosettes.

Police appear to be acting as entertainers to the crowd, chatting with pavement-sleepers.

Black Maria full of police goes slowly up the street, crowd hoots and jeers at it, policemen's heads grinning through grille. Well-dressed people, upper middle class, elderly, sitting in shop-windows, watch antics of crowd. Some of crowd make faces at them from outside, everybody laughs.

Man with very large mouth singing 'Aaaaah, I kinda make you laugh', and selling pamphlets full of jokes.

Groups singing *Shoe-Shine Boy* and *Annie Laurie* next to each other.

Three fire engines in street off Regent Street, fireman asleep on pavement.

Band—trumpets, saxophone, drums—players dressed as negroes, marches by. Two real negresses on pavement mistaken for part of the band by crowd, which gathers round waiting for negresses to perform. One negress just stares back, the other combs her hair, back-chatting. Police approach, doubting their sexual intentions, but retire reassured when one negress points out her husband.

11. 3 a.m. Piccadilly Circus. Several bands, people dancing, playing 'Nuts and May'. *Pennies from Heaven* the most audible song. Man and girl begin to undress in front of Regent Palace, man has taken off his shirt and girl pulled up dress when police stop them, they protest they are doing a strip-tease act and point to flash-light photograper who has camera ready to shoot them. Police make them put on their clothes and leads the photographer away. Hard luck on him, says someone.

40 policemen marching down Shaftesbury Avenue, they look as if they would be happier if they could burst into song like everyone else.

3.15. Cambridge Circus. I am accosted. I say 'You look as if you've done enough for to-night.' Reply: 'None of your sauce, me lad.'*

More crowds at Leicester Square. By this time I am a little canned and can't hear much.

In tube: 'Funny how you don't mind waiting when there's something to look at.' (Midlander speaking.)

Argument as to whether the train is going to Edgware or

Cf. para. **16**.

Kennington only settled by our arrival at Euston where the arguers hurry out, apparently wanting to go to Charing Cross.

'Aren't some of these girls' faces awful?' says middle-aged Northern woman, jerking her head at very red-lipped revellers.

3.45. Belsize Park. People sleeping in train, apparently being carried from one terminus to the other continually.

12. (CO.38.)* (About 12.40 a.m.) In Shaftesbury Avenue, a file of about 30 policemen marching to take up position in Piccadilly Circus are greeted with spontaneous cheers, bottles of beer are offered them from a taxi and two hatless youths carrying a crate of beer fall in behind police, in step, to get safe conduct through crowd. Crowd knows that police are instructed to be more than usually 'blind-eyed' for the occasion, and crossing Piccadilly Circus the outburst of cheers and clapping is heavy and quite sincere—probably a few in the crowd realize that these men are to take up position with little chance of break or rest, until 4 or 5 p.m. and sympathize. The steps around Eros statue are filled with an excited crowd, coster's barrows stand around selling fruit, chocolate, etc. Hot chestnuts, roasted potatoes and peanuts are selling fast. It is 1 a.m. and most of the roadway is filled with people who read aloud the slowly spelled news reports on the running electric signboard over the end of Glasshouse Street. When the rain is indicated in the report, a few hoots and derisive cheers occur. At 1.15 a.m. walk slowly westward in Piccadilly, in roadway. Kerb edge is filled already, almost all people sitting. A coster is selling empty apple boxes at 1s. each; but most people have folding stools, rugs, raincoats and groundsheets.

13. Walk through the temporary gateway across Piccadilly near the Ritz Hotel and at about 2 a.m. am in Berkeley

*M: agent: now out of work: lived in East End.

Street watching four semi-drunken sailors dancing with untidily-dressed and well-drunk poor factory-girl types, to music of bagpipes played by 6 ft. 3 in. immaculate Guardee in tails, who has borrowed pipes from one of a taxi-party. Sellers of flags, whistles, etc., are doing brisk trade but no foodstuffs being sold here. Look at crowd on pavement, and decide it's because they are 'good' near-middle-class people who have brought plenty of food from home. The women are mostly sensibly dressed—heavy shoes and tweeds, or big tweed or leather coats, quite a few in breeches and rubber boots; very few hats, most women wearing scarves of bright colours on heads giving scene an odd reference to a Russian occasion. The males are already mostly lying down, on coats, newspapers, rubber sheets and women are using *them* as mattresses. Whole of kerb both sides of St. James Street full at 2.15 a.m.

Find policeman acquaintance on a corner who tells me that groups of about 24 or 30 have already been turned out from most stations within five miles, and have been in position since 11.30 p.m. They had been called only during the evening, most of them expecting to start not before 3.30 a.m. or 5 a.m. from their respective stations. I ask him how long he is there for, and if they have any special instructions. He expects to be relieved shortly, and many of them get food and drink in marquee in Green Park, and can rest until 5.30 a.m., when certainly *all* of them will be out amongst the crowd for the rest of the day. They have been instructed that the crowd is being mostly well-behaved, so that they must be lenient about everything. No interference for mere drunkenness, they must only intervene in case of fighting or bad disorder or very obstructional crowds. All the policemen have pockets full of iron rations (biscuits, chocolate, and thirst-quenching tablets); as they are wearing ceremonial dress (tunic, leather belt, white gloves, etc.) they are feeling the cold already—not much chance to move about very

freely—many of the crowd are already establishing good relations with them, and an occasional one is seen accepting a
sandwich or a cup from a thermos, hiding in the crowd from
the eyes of inquisitive superiors.

14. Just after 2.40 a.m. I have walked down Piccadilly
and through the Circus into Regent Street. Crowd filling footways, but very few arriving; no one walks on footways, we all
progress along the road, pedestrians in a hurry, slow-moving
groups who've come to see the fun almost all accompanied by
a trumpeter or piano-accordionist who plays continuously.
Sellers of hot pies, buttered rolls and other substantial foods
doing well here; people now beginning to feel the cold, fog
almost entirely gone. Oxford Circus much quieter than
Piccadilly (time now about 3 a.m.). Along Oxford Street
westward I meet groups of revellers, obviously from poor
quarters (overdressed factory operatives, good-looking partly-
drunken girls, youths about twenty, all hatless) and most of
them have picked up sailors or soldiers revelling who have
all lent hats to girls. Everybody sings and here and there an
accordion or even a four-part good band (trumpet, saxophone, accordion and banjo) stands under one of the island
lamp-posts playing for a group who dance in the midst of a
knot of a hundred or so persons. Selfridge's rather vulgar
décor scheme attracts a fringe along the opposite pavement,
who crane necks, and one knowledgeable youth recites subject matter of each panel to group of girls, one of whom says
repeatedly in a dazed way, 'Lovely, lovely—but what a lot
of money' and 'How do they build all them things up there?'
—the young man apparently can't answer this. Outside
Mount Royal residential flats, notice that women much
superior numerically to men. Very few standing, and everything that can keep cold out is in use. Most people seem to be
here in couples, or groups of 8 or 10, etc.—not many small
parties noticeable. Newest foodstuff venture is the sale of cups
of tea from a complete apparatus (spirit stove, enormous

teapot, jugs, sugar box, etc.) carried in shallow box by one man, whilst other has converted orange-box with about 40 cups slung on shoulders. How—and if—the cups are washed doesn't seem to have occurred to anyone. Reach Marble Arch at 3.40 a.m.

15. People thronging towards route from Edgware Road, carrying parcels, boxes, rugs, children, flags, rucksacks, etc. Lots of shocked comments on discovering that they are not the first on the scene. I walk very quickly through Hyde Park section of route—identical scenes as Oxford Street—and here, in addition, the crowds are camping on the grass-verge as well as the footway, so a few may sleep in a little comfort. By now a pathetic and sordid spectacle: everyone's weariness is apparent, couples mutter in each other's ears, close-folded in one another's arms under rugs and coats, children weep or mutter sleepily, young girls of 12 or so run about to keep warm and shout irritably to one another.

16. The clock at Hyde Park Corner shows 4.8 a.m. as I turn away from the route and go east along Piccadilly. Arrivals now pouring in, having walked possibly miles, some being decanted from cars or motor coaches. In St. James's Street police are combing crowd to seize all boxes, stools or other devices for standing clear of the kerb: a motor van crammed full of them is being more tightly packed by three men—and many of the crowd have only bought the stools an hour or so ago from hawkers.* At 4.35 a.m. I cross Piccadilly Circus and am swept some yards back by a crowd rushing from the Underground, which has now begun to disgorge arrivals; I cannot board a train here, have to walk to Leicester Square Tube Station. On way push against somebody, say 'Sorry' and hear 'That's all right, dearie, don't be in such a hurry.' Look round and think it possibly someone who knows me and whom I can't place—in spite of lack of make-up and neat well-cut coat, I realize that I am being quite

*Cf. para. 21.

nicely accosted by a prostitute, quiet-voiced, good accent, etc. Ask her why she's out so late—or so early? and she says business is not so good as it might be. Before she can decide whether I'm a potential client or not, I cut across the road and into Underground station.

17. (CL.65.)* I am in the employ of a large firm of chemists, and was sent by them to do special duties in London during Coronation week. My station was their 'Oxford Street' branch, five minutes' walk from Tottenham Court Road and I had to work there from seven o'clock on Coronation eve to six o'clock Coronation morning, the shop being kept open specially all night. After six I was free till twelve midnight the next night.

The first two hours of Coronation Day, 12-2, were my turn to rest and were occupied in sleep in the cellar.

Between two and three we had four people in the shop, three to buy aspirins and one, a Cambridge undergraduate, to buy a draught for his friend outside who had just swallowed two bottles of sherry. By this time there was a steady tramp of people towards the Marble Arch. They were quiet but looked happy. A few carried camp stools, but most of them just food and overcoats. Outside the shop three young people were selling the *Daily Worker*. They seemed to treat the situation as rather a joke.

Between three and four I got someone from Manchester who had twisted a knee, but who was still determined to hobble along to see the procession. Another girl had the skin taken from her heels by walking, but after patching up said she was still going to try to see the show. The most popular sale now was films. Few of the people seemed to think preventative medicines necessary and all were very optimistic about the weather.

*M: 24: single.

Between four and five two 'St. John's Ambulance' nurses came in. They said they would be glad when it was over but were rather looking forward to it all the same. My two colleagues in the shop differed in their plans for the day. One said he was going to go home to bed and the other said he was going to come to town at two o'clock and 'chance his luck'. Both disapproved of long waits.

All the time the tramp of people got louder and between five and six a veritable army were marching towards the Marble Arch and Oxford Circus. All were quiet, however.

18. (CL.25.)* On Wednesday, May 12, 1937, I was awakened at 2.10 a.m. by a newsboy yelling *Daily Mail*. I crawled out of bed and was quite surprised to see that the Hotel opposite and the streets were alive with all types of people. I admit I thought London had gone crazy and felt annoyed with the world in general. I returned to my bed, determined to sleep. It was impossible, the rush of cars and noise of heavy traffic was deafening. I tried counting sheep but to my horror found I was counting human footsteps. I think I must have dozed off when I was suddenly awakened by a man's voice shouting through the keyhole, 'Nurse, it's a quarter to five.' It was the cook. That seemed to me the last straw. For a moment I wondered if he had taken leave of his senses, but the steady tramp of feet on the pavement outside brought home to me in a flash that the Great Day had dawned. 'At least', I said to myself 'I hope their Majesties are also getting up at this unearthly hour.' I dressed and after the inevitable cup of tea I went to the nursery.

*F: 28: single: children's nurse: C. of E.: Conservative.

Journeys to the Route from three points:
2.30–6.15 a.m.

19. (CL.83.)* On this memorable day of May 12th my friends and I got up at 2.30 a.m. all bright and ready for the coming day's work. One of my friends, a young fellow named D——, was on duty selling Official Souvenir Programmes. As for my other friend and myself we were special depot 'runners' with some important messages to take from the Home Office as quick as possible to the Admiralty. Quickly we got dressed in our smart, spotless uniforms and had some breakfast which was kindly prepared for us by 'Mrs. Chief'. Then off we went in Mr. M——'s car after having picked up Jack and Eric. When we arrived at Liverpool Street Station Jack suggested that we should walk to our depot. The idea soon caught up with us, and with the accompaniment of whistling we set out. Starting to whistle *Tipperary* we were surprised to hear that all the passers-by and the road sweepers had joined in.

When we arrived at the depot we found a large amount of money tins and about 1,000 programmes in neat piles of twenty, each with its own paper carrier. The next thing to do was to issue the programmes to the boys. Having done this we were told that we could go and see the procession which was just about to come. We had been given badges which could be used to enable us to go to front of the police.

20. (CM.1.)† My wife set the alarm for 3 o'clock, the first train to Town being at 3.49. I woke up without hearing it; lay awake for some while and then heard the church clock strike 4. I got up bad tempered. The alarm had not gone off. My wife got me some hot coffee, and packed my sandwiches. At

*Schoolboy: 13: Ilford.   †Blackheath.

4.15 I left the house. There was a thick ground fog or river mist, but clear deep blue sky above. No buses. I walked a mile across the heath to the station. At first there was no sign of life. Then a car came driving carefully in the mist. An owl hooted in the trees by the railway. Three well-to-do houses have their front door lights burning, the front door left open, the gates ajar. Then the sound of a train. Then women's voices and quick steps. Four more houses have lights on in top windows. In a poorer street near the station, women are leaving in the dark with shopping baskets packed. Sounds of a car starting. More lights in top windows.

21. 4.20. The station is lit up—about 50 people on the platform—a dozen Boy Scouts. There is a train immediately, nearly empty. At Lewisham there are some ambulance men. At London Bridge a big crowd, including sailors. A woman carrying a folding chair. The train is about as full as it is normally at 10 o'clock—less than rush hours. At Waterloo there is less mist—the platforms and rails wet and shiny—the buildings black—the lights white—the sky and distance deep blue in all directions.

An oldish couple in the train, dressed up for the occasion, say to each other 'We've never done this. Never been up so early. We've been in town at midnight. There's the old river—misty. Now we're across the bridge: here we are.' They have red, white and blue button-holes of real flowers and an official programme.

22. At Charing Cross there is a burst of cheering. It is 4.52. Endless Scouts being marshalled on the platform. There is a rush from the station to Trafalgar Square. It is stopped by the police barrier at the bottom of the Strand: shut except a little door. This side of it there are people and police about thirty deep: 'Ticket holders only.' There is a general move back and round into the top side of Trafalgar Square. Here the street is fairly clear. Outside the National Gallery

there are roughly a hundred and fifty police and twenty-five ambulance men. In front of St. Martin's a police loudspeaker car is in position at an open barrier. The bottom side of the Square and the Nelson Monument are solid with people. The leader of a Chinese party of about fifteen holds high a red flag covered with white Chinese lettering as a rallying point. There is a general move towards Piccadilly. Scouts are trying to get into the basement—what they call 'the Engineers' Entrance'—of Canada House. A police loudspeaker says politely 'Those people standing on the King Charles Island will not be allowed to stand there. Move off please. Thank you.' Good tone—pretty intelligible—slight echo.

23. The bottom of Haymarket is impassable. There is a big sale of periscopes. Balconies and stands are still empty. People with tickets are waiting for admission. A group warm their hands around a brazier in Suffolk Street. Police carefully tie their capes to rails. Waiters in evening dress in the empty lighted rooms of a club are arranging things on tables. Coming up Haymarket a newswoman cries 'Morning paper'. A passer-by: 'What morning is it?' 'Wednesday morning.' Seat holders—silk hat and opera glasses, grey topper and grey waistcoat and button-hole—move slowly along Charles Street. The smell of a Turkish cigarette.

Lower Regent Street. A man is ringing the bell of the National City Bank of New York. A pigeon alights on a window-ledge. The torches in Waterloo Place are burning. The crowd is not large here. Big cars and taxis are moving easily from St. James's Square. Police talking contentedly. Comment of arrivals: 'This is nice, isn't it?' Smart women discussing how to carry furs. 'Look at the torches, Mum,' from middle-class man. The National City Bank door opens. The man has gone. The caretaker says 'They come too early. I told them 6 o'clock. It's not 6 o'clock, is it?' A man cries 'Periscope! Don't forget your periscope!' Shop-girls giggle at schoolboys in top hats. There is a queue of fifteen for the Men's lavatory in St. James's Square. There is a queue of eighty for the Ladies'. This is 5.15! Cars with green labels are being directed. People leave a car with a brown label: police direct chauffeur how to get it away. There is a group of mounted police in Pall Mall. The St. John's ambulance men seem lost—trying to find something or some place. Rovers are walking up and down. Nurses with attaché cases.

There are one or two people in the Pall Mall stands. The back of Stratstone's is open. The caretaker is sitting on a box. Men inside are setting tables with cloths, glass, etc. A guitar plays *Pack up your Troubles in your Old Kit Bag.* A motor coach crosses the Square. Duke Street is full of parked cars. Seat holders are arriving now.

24. (CL.2.)* 4.30 a.m. Woken by conscientious male cook stumping about in kitchen overhead. Troubled by vague necessity for waking husband with suitable greeting. Sleepily wondered whether a 'God Save the King!' would be appropriate (husband likes Happy-New-Years and Many-Happy-Returns). Finally awoke enough to realize that a shaking was sufficient.

4.45. Call children. Find Ann (9) has had her first nightmare.

5 a.m. Breakfast. Commit lunch basket to husband's care. Collect dog, William, (scottie), put child in pram and start off with two children, pram, dog, and my own aunt (husband forgets latch-key and goes back for it). Surprised to meet very blasé friend (the bearded kind). He is rather ashamed of being caught so early going to his seat. Walk comfortably to Hyde Park Corner where crowd gets thick. Realize that husband has left lunch behind. Recriminations. He goes back for it. We have a few minutes' tussle in crowd. By now

*F: 34: married: atheist: Left-wing.

I have bought rosettes for 2 children and dog but not for my-self or my husband (my aunt arrived from the country well decorated). Notice many people wearing national colours with green and yellow introduced into them.

25. 6 a.m. Reach destination in Arlington St. Dispose of pram and find husband's room. None of the senior staff has come to see the show (a few have seats elsewhere). Our company consists of 3 typists with their aunts and brothers and one senior office boy. Husband arrives 6.15, having secured lunch and a taxi.

Wonder how I will get through the day—get out Link-later's *Life of Mary Queen of Scots* and bottle of beer for husband; also portable wireless set.

Find myself perfectly happy watching the crowd (*Mary Queen of Scots* is never opened once). Children equally happy (we have some sandwiches) especially as they find a back window overlooking first aid station, and can watch crowd casualties. Notice queer swaying movement—like a parrot on perch—that seizes different sections of crowd from time to time. They rock faster and faster, and after a fainting form (usually female) is dragged out.

Condition of Regent's Park—Piccadilly—Regent St.—Oxford St.—Hyde Park: 6.20–9.20 a.m.

26. (CM.9.) 6.25. Leave Bernard St. in H. T.'s car—old Morris 8 with Red Label (Oxford St.) on windscreen. Weather cold and grey.

Seen from car:

'Parking Street' notices ubiquitous—weary-looking crowds in Euston Road—men hallooing by Euston Square to keep spirits up and bodies warm—solitary office girl looking 'Hell and what's a coronation anyway'—marked absence of decorations on cars—flags absent from taxi cabs—very different from Tuesday night. 6.35. Warren Street Station. Hawker: 'Don't forget your coronation colours, sir, tuppence each!' Traffic moving slowly but in orderly fashion. Despondent labels in brown and dark blue (Pall Mall and Regent St.). Notices 'No Left Turn'—'No Right Turn'. Advert. S. side of Euston Road reading 'Morris Commercial Vehicles—a Body for every Trade' heavily draped with decorations. Diversion round Euston Square. Extraordinary diversion at Albany Street: 'Straight on all colours' says notice on road going due North.

We turn left with determination into small street with notice NO ROAD. Police let us pass.

27. We reach outer circle of Regent's Park—turn right—travel at 25 m.p.h. (Speed limit 20 m.p.h. in park.) Circle great camp at north of park—only sign of life, 3 soldiers moodily kicking a muddy football—a row of smoky camp kitchens without attendants. Notice MILITARY TRAFFIC STOP. Outer circle almost deserted till Clarence Gate where join Park Road and Baker St.—crowds moving south past Baker St. Station. Abbey Road Building Society offices well bedecked. Man out of crowd to cab driver, 'Where's your decoration?' No answer from cab. Unemployed singers very miserable outside Baker St. Station—crowd very quiet. Notice ONE WAY STREET, USE OF BOTH SIDES. Notice BUSES ON LEFT, TAXICABS ON RIGHT. Cars converge on barriers at bottom of Baker St. Slow down. Stop.

28. (CM.2.). 6.20. Green Park Station. Most of the St. John's Ambulance men and passengers dismount. Coming out of the station one sees Green Park gate marked 'Ticket Holders Only'. Top hatted men are passing through the gate with their wives.

6.25. Corner of Piccadilly and St. James's Street. A crowd 7 deep is gathered. In the Bell Punch Co.'s building, and other buildings, balcony seats and window seats already occupied.

Girl sitting on soiled newspaper is reading *Daily Mirror*. The caption reads 'Three women wait 25 hours; lead line up for the big parade.' A man's folding stool collapses; girls giggle, rather hysterically.

6.30. Same place. Three horse police pass down route. A middle-aged woman, a tripper, says 'We shall have to get one of these 'ere glasses'—she holds up her fingers to indicate periscope—'It's the only way now.'

A police wireless van takes up position, guarded by 7 policemen—a curious crowd swarms round and submerges it —youths climb on back to get better view of route—police do not prevent them—hawker cries 'Genuine periscopes, the only periscope you can see through—see over the top of the car—see your next door neighbour whenever you like.' A girl in the crowd who has purchased one says 'The periscopes are quite good, but (with grim humour) there's a long time to wait yet.'

29. (CM.1.) 6.50. The barriers at the bottom of the Hay-market are now shut. There are two motor ambulances in Piccadilly Circus, and at least three hundred police of whom a hundred are specials in a long line up Shaftesbury Avenue. A paperman repeats endlessly: 'Coronation Number—Keep from going mad, doing nothing: Read while you wait.'*

7. At the corner of Glasshouse Street there is a single wooden latrine like a sentry box with a sacking curtain for a door, marked 'Troops only'. Suddenly there is a burst of music as a brass band with a cockaded officer on horseback, and a drum-major with a whirling stick, come down Regent Street leading a column of troops in blue uniforms. There is

---

*Cf. Q. D. Leavis on the English novel, who quotes a report of troops in the war sharing a newspaper in fragments, even the advertisements, merely to pass the eye over print as a kind of sedative. This popular joke that you might go mad if you waited without reading gives a striking view of our universal education and neurosis.

immediate interest. Then the band stops and the crowd laughs. As the troops go by a family point to the other side of the road: 'That's our window—the blue.' Kingly Street and other small streets off Regent Street are full of upper-class ticket holders, getting to their seats, and looking out of place. They try to buy papers. A small paper shop has sold out of *The Times*: 'Only the *Telegraph*.' They are coming down from Oxford Circus Station. These streets are littered with dirty paper, orange-peel, broken bottles, cigarette packs, and squashed fruit. Hawkers cry 'Wear your colours! Wear your colours!' Periscope sellers: '*There's* your favourites' —'Look how many's in front of ye.'

30. 7.20. At Oxford Circus nearly everyone has periscopes. The police loudspeaker says 'There is a fair amount of room in Lower Regent Street—at Piccadilly Circus.' Troops are marching down through Cavendish Square. One tough shouts to another: 'George, what's the matter: haven't you seen any of *them* before?'

7.45. Opposite the H.M.V. building in Oxford Street there is music from a loudspeaker. The crowd is only 6 or 7 deep here. In the intervals between music it sings *Alone*. A blind man taps his way along Wigmore Street. Outside W.D.O. there are half-a-dozen Post Office vans marked 'Supply Services'. A driver explains: 'It gives us privilege to go on the streets without being held up by the police.' There is a queue of about thirty employees at the back of Selfridge's. In small hotel in Granville Street people are having breakfast. A maid pulls back a muslin curtain to look at the people in the street. They are mostly moving quickly to the staff entrances of Oxford Street shops. They are reaching their seats far more easily than the people in the Mall. The *Mirror* is having an enormous sale.

31. Hyde Park. Big Ben strikes eight from a loudspeaker, from another loudspeaker come snatches of popular songs: *Auld Lang Syne, It's a Long Long Way to Tipperary, Land of Hope*

and Glory. Children hum it as they play round the trees. Against a tree on a box sit two working-class men, smoking— one with a red, white and blue paper top hat. They are backs to the crowd. Beyond them is a path slippery with rain and orange peel. Pieces of paper blow along it. The crowd is about twenty deep on this side of the route. The police have just given up trying to get people down from trees. The stands opposite are full. Boys lie asleep against the trees. Outside a wood and canvas milk bar the grass has been trodden black. Against the uprights there are heaps of used white cardboard milk cups. They are reflected as they lie in puddles. A tenor from a loudspeaker sings *The Yeomen, the Bowmen of England*.

All down the side of East Carriage Drive there are as many people lying on newspaper (the grass is soaking) or wandering along, as there are lining the route. Ambulance men and women huddle under trees. Old women sit on stools under thorn trees. Hot-dog and Choc-bloc sellers in white coats stand in groups and shout 'Here you are!' The loudspeakers play snatches of music. A man dances to *A Life on the Ocean Wave* and a little grey ambulance woman smiles and lifts her feet in time to it.

32. (CM.2.) 7.55 a.m. Conduit Street. Can see huge tier of seats sloping upwards 30–40 ft. above Barclays', Regent St. Photographer perched on pediment. Woman coming up street points to crowd in Regent St. and says 'They're only going to see it down here, you know.' A band audible. People coming up Conduit St. almost run when they hear it. St. John's Ambulance women have bought periscopes—look more like hopeful spectators than nurses.

8 a.m. Corner Conduit St. and Regent St. woman says 'There's no crowd, is there? It's foggy and cold' (this is not true). One woman asks another 'Have you been here all night?' 'No.'

Proceeding north up Regent St. crowd catcalling and whistling—reason not visible, except that troops are stationary and police inspectors in centre of route. Cheers when military band finishes tune, troops passing constantly. Again shrieks of laughter. Apparently horses dropping dung. Sweepers putting dung in cart.* Girls waving and calling to troops, some of whom smile back.

8.5. Two smart women at large in crowd 'I've never seen anything like it before (looking at decorations) though I was in the boat coming back from South Africa at Marina's wedding.' Mounted policeman near band patting horse to soothe it. Sudden crash of drum sends it, with its neighbour, bucking 10 yards across the street. Crowd again cheers band's tune—woman says 'It's late now.' Another, middle-aged, looking at spectators who have periscopes, says 'There is a happy land far, far away.' She hums to herself.

8.10. Corner of Hanover St. Woman tells husband 'You know, this is nothing like the Jubilee. We couldn't get anywhere then.' 8.15, same place. Two ladies talk to their children, aged (?) 5, about their bowels. 'Will you try again while we are waiting.' Boy not interested, points suddenly to a scout: 'Oh, look there!' One woman keeps reassuring another: 'We'll be all right my dear, it's nearly quarter past.'

Opposite National Provincial Bank P.C. eyes passing girl appreciatively.

Swallow Place. On wall is chalked notice 'Mind Britain's business'.

33. 8.20. Oxford Street, opposite John Lewis & Co. Woman leans against wall, inhaling smelling salts. She wears a red white and blue bandeau. A lady drops something from

---

*The *Daily Express* had an instrument called the cheermeter for measuring the noise made by the crowd; the three loudest sets of cheering in order were for Queen Mary, the King and Queen, then the scavengers who cleaned up after the horses. Even though this is 'laughter in church' it is hard to believe people would have done it before the spread of motor cars had made them less accustomed to horses.

a reserved balcony. The crowd shrieks with laughter. Spectators remonstrate with new arrival, then 'Place belongs to a lady who has gone to have a drink.'

Policeman reading over my shoulder while I made the last note. I ignored him, completed it, and walked on.

There are numerous spectators asleep on folding stools.

8.30. Corner Oxford St. and Hanover Place. Widespread community singing of *Land of Hope and Glory*.

8.40. Oxford Street opposite John Lewis & Co. One policeman, grinning, remarks to another 'Which way do we send them now?' The other, resigned and grim: 'It's getting a bit scraggy now.' Bystanders laugh.

8.55. Police wireless van speaking, but words inaudible at back of crowd, at least.

Woman to woman friend: 'He said, Hurry up and get dressed. Didn't you have any sleep too? Neither did I.'

Woman pointing to balcony seats down Princes St.: 'How on earth do people there think they are going to see anything? It's just to say they've been there.'

34. 9. Oxford Circus barricaded off. Little woman, about 34, asks white-haired little lady, who is jammed in centre of crowd, 'Can you see anything, Mum?' She obviously cannot, but nods head cheerfully. There is a crash of glass, and an exclamation 'oh' and 'glass gone'. A woman behind the narrow gangway says: 'Someone ought to complain to the policeman. No one can pass without treading on my toes.'

9.5. With good-natured chivalry, man about 40 puts little woman into his place: 'There, you'll be all right now'—but she isn't really any better off.

9.15. Conversation subdued whilst troops line up in front of spectators. Man jokes with woman: 'And no washing up done.'

9.20. One cockney girl to another: 'How long 'ave we been 'ere—since six?' Her young man behind says: 'We have just two-thirds as much again to wait.' 'Then', slowly and determinedly, 'We'll TRY to make a bold rush somewhere.' Girl, laughing, echoes 'Somewhere'. Same girl, comparing one periscope with cheaper model, says 'It's a better class.' A man, on same subject: 'We could have got the mirror from the bathroom.' Woman, to man, possibly her husband: 'we left him to himself for a week, and he did well. He's a good painter'—another painter was dearer, charged £13, and 'in 6 months you couldn't tell there had been any paint there—he admitted it himself.'

9.25. Cheering and laughing where crowd thickest. Girl looks through periscope and reports 'Oh, someone else has fainted.'

9.30. Woman to boy: 'Have you been there all night?' 'Yes.'

Weather still grey, but possibilities of brightness. Crowd singing out-of-date dance tunes.

9.40. Opposite Helen Kaye's. Linking arms and leaning on to crowd to hold them back are policemen, some of them seem boys, hardly more than 16. Proof, besides features, bagginess of trousers, much too long. A mounted policeman hands them a message, which they pass along the line, reading. One leans ardently on a girl he is holding back.

The sun is appearing. Woman says 'Oh look, the sun's coming out.'

35. (CM.9.) (Outside Selfridge's.) 9.20. Long conversation with two skilled labourers from Llanelly (Carmarthen) who ask what this building is (Selfridge's). 'It's as long as our main street. Is it always like this? We're going back to-night at midnight . . . the fleet's in London . . . yes, how far's Southend . . . thought London would be much fuller . . . yes, we saw King Edward . . . wanted public sympathy . . . lot of good it did him . . . too long to wait . . . what small policemen you have in London, not like ours.' It at last dawns on them

that most of Selfridge's got-up face is only temporary—one lends me field glasses to look at scaffolding behind street decorations.

Contrasted reports of Procession to the Abbey

36. (CL.25.)* The time was then about 8 a.m. We took the tube from Gloucester Road to Victoria. I was relieved to see that there were very few people on the train. We decided to get to the Mall. We had some difficulty in getting through the roads that were blocked. Once I found myself wandering past three stalwart policemen on my way to the Abbey. They soon put me on the right track and we arrived at the Mall about 8.30. We were standing between the Palace and Marlborough House. I was amazed to see the people who had brought out mirrors of all types and sizes, to enable them to see what was going on. By the scraps of conversation I picked up I gathered that the majority of the vast crowd had taken up their positions about 10 o'clock the night before, others had been there since 5 and 6 a.m. I looked at them in amazement and admiration. The women looked tired, the men very unshaved. But they seemed quite jolly, and cheered quite lustily. Towards 9.30 I think most of the crowd began to get faint from want of sleep. I was beginning to wonder how I could manage to see really well, when a very large lady with a very large parcel announced if she didn't get out and get some air she would faint. I gladly made way for her and not being very large myself I quite easily got into her place and had a good view. There was a sudden stir of excitement and the Procession began. Shaving mirrors, hand mirrors small and large were held high and Periscopes appeared miraculously. I held on to mine and with its aid I saw everything quite plainly. Princess Margaret Rose

*v. para. 18.

looked very much a little princess from a story book, I thought, and the Queen looked really charming. There was real genuine excitement and feeling when our beloved Queen Mary passed through, also for Princess Marina and the Duke of Kent. Up until then I could not help feeling that the people were like a lot of sheep and came early because others had come, as I heard one or two of the crowd remark that they had come much against their will.

37. But when the beautiful Fairy Coach came into view with the King and Queen the crowd sent up a cheer worthy of a British subject and as I gasped in admiration at the look of calm dignity on the face of the new King I recalled the words of the Duke of Windsor when he abdicated, and realized that with his charming Queen and happy children he was well chosen to be our King. All good things come to an end and with the passing of the last of the procession we wended our way with the crowd. While waiting for some hundreds to disperse we got sometime into conversation with one of the Guards who gave me a knob of sugar from his pocket which I am keeping among my souvenirs. On our way through St. James's Park I could not help smiling at the hundreds of people lying asleep on the grass and seats. To think that I had appeared at almost the last moment and seen all and these thousands had been there all night and some saw nothing as quite a number fainted just when the procession began. A policeman directed us to St. James's Park Underground. But the queue must have consisted of thousands. We decided to go to Victoria, but in passing the back way of St. James's Underground we were amazed to see not a soul about. We went in, got our tickets and were home enjoying our lunch by 12.30. For the second time that day I was struck by the thought of how like sheep we humans really are. We just follow the flock. To think of the thousands of people in that waiting crowd not one had thought of going to the other entrance.

38. (CM.1.) 9.40. Belgravia is practically deserted, but in certain roads the police are stopping people. A street seller is turned back. A sergeant gives orders, and says 'Bar the King—don't stop him.' 9.45. The Chelsea pensioners come along Wilton Street. 'Old soldiers never die' says a policeman. 'Are we near the saluting point?' says one. 'We're going in the back way,' says another, as they go into the back of Buckingham Palace. A street piano and fiddle are playing *God Save the King*. A beach-photographer says, 'Some of these people look as though they were going to a funeral not a Coronation.'

9.50. Victoria. A glimpse of sun. Smart upper-class man in grey lounge suit and brown soft hat buys the *Daily Worker* outside the Victoria Palace—looks for a moment at front page, folds it under his arm, takes a key out of his pocket, and opens a door between two small shops in Victoria Street. All down Victoria Street are lines of expensive cars parked. The chauffeurs—about a hundred of them—are standing smoking pipes, or listening to a short little red man in a paper cap playing *Who's your lady friend* on a cornet. A parade of school-girls, 10-14, all with tickets tied to their button-holes, march towards St. James's Park.

39. In the Park people are sitting on seats as usual; one woman is taking a photo of the Lake. One can hear bands playing in the Mall, and some cheering and clapping. Electricians are testing the floodlights among the bushes. The processions are now well started. From a gap between two stands a boy is carried out fainting, and about a dozen people are let in to what is a pretty good view of the troops who are passing. One or two women simply won't believe that they are allowed in: they say 'Ticket holders only?'— 'No,' says the policeman, 'Free. Free seats. Last house till 1957.' The drums beat and the cheering begins in earnest. Facing the lake two fat women sit on a park bench, smoking and looking at the pigeons: 'That's not what you'd call a white pigeon, really.' Some people are having trouble with their periscopes: 'I keep seeing myself and looking quickly away!'—'It makes me giddy looking at this thing.' One man has brought an antique periscope from a gun or a ship, which has to be focussed.

40. 10.30. Some men on stands call to a woman that they will take her two children up, which they do. She is worried. 'Will you please send them back as soon as the King and Queen have passed?'—'Yes' say the men 'and the guns.' 'No. I don't want them to see the guns—only the King and Queen.'

10.40. There is real excitement for the Empire troops: Indians and Australians—especially for the turbans.* There is a higher-pitched cheer and waving of hats. The roof of the gold coach comes into view past the end of a stand:

> Women: 'I can see it wonderfully *without*!' (without a peri-
> scope).
> 'How *wonderful*!'
> 'What a marvellous coach!'

A man: 'You got a good view of it there!'

A girl: 'You can see it *still*—down there!'

A woman: 'I don't think we'll see any more.'

41. There is an immediate movement of the people who had been standing away from their positions—boys jumping over fences—the Guards who had been lining the route laughing and losing step as they come off duty. The lawns which had been empty five minutes before are now covered with Guards, who have got their arms piled and their bear-skins off, and with people sitting on the grass eating. The loudspeakers in the Mall have already begun talking to them. But here (opposite St. James's Palace) there is so much noise and tramping of feet on the paths that it is impossible to hear what they say. There are dense crowds in the Mall consisting

---

*This enthusiasm for Indians and Australians (mentioned together) comes into many London reports.

of the people who had been standing on the other side of the route.

42. (CO.32.)* 6.30 a.m. Was woken by phone. Felt particularly sleepy, and disagreeably aware that I had to attend on duty, in charge of boys from my school. As I got up I thought how nervous the King and Queen must be. My wife and I supposed that the young princesses must be nearly off their heads with excitement. I decided to wear my old socks with a hole in the heel, rather than change them.

7.30 a.m. I went out. The day was going to be fine. How empty Bayswater was, emptier than on a Sunday morning! I had not expected this. How strange the flags looked in the empty streets! The underground was not crowded. I noticed how solemn everyone was, and thought it would be more appropriate if someone would sing. Near me, there were two children of ten or eleven. They were quiet, and stared fiercely with excitement. Few people in the carriage spoke at all. A young American woman opposite yawned all the way.

Using my pass, I went through a police cordon, and down an empty street. A company of Guards went by, whistling some tune. I felt moved, because they were so tall, wore such bright uniforms, and marched with such a swing.

43. 9 a.m. Went with my party to our place. A policeman, making way for a car, repeats the same phrase 'Now come along please', twenty times. Boys of seventeen complain in superior voices of being hustled. The drapery, the tiers of people, and the crush, made me think of *Ben Hur* and of nineteenth-century paintings of Roman chariot races. 'Bread and circuses.' . . .

9.30. Parliament Square. In front of me the perspective of Whitehall. Blue uniforms on each side. White helmets of marines, white caps of sailors. I can see as far as the Cenotaph

*M: 27: married: schoolmaster: 'inactive Left'.

ahead of me, and to the right as far as Westminster Bridge. A hollow wireless voice is talking from somewhere in the air, but the wireless loudspeaker nearest us has been disconnected, it is said, by a pigeon. The crowd is quiet, apparently not very excited, inclined to joke. A dispatch rider gets a faint cheer.

9.35. Dominion Prime Ministers passing. Mr. Baldwin in his carriage, with a face like a whitened canvas mask. I felt tearful at the sight of the mounted escorts from distant parts of the world, the Indians, the Australians. It affected me to think that England's influence reached so far. I separately asked two boys of about fifteen whether they looked forward more to seeing the King and Queen, or to seeing the troops. They both said to me, 'The troops.' A clergyman said the same.

9.45 a.m. Some scavengers removed dung. People tittered. A group of seventeen-year-old boys gossiped about Princess Juliana: 'When I was in Paris she was there. Everyone liked her.' They criticized the ugly decorations of Selfridge's and other buildings, and discussed their careers. The crowd seemed apathetic, and I felt so too.

10.10. Carriages passed, containing the various Duchesses. There were very small cheers. A boy of sixteen said, 'Can't say cheers were excessive!' I thought the Duchess of Gloucester was attractive, which I had not thought before. 10.15. Scavengers removed dung; there was some laughter.

44. 10.45–11. The main procession. I noticed that the crowd cheered loudest troops from the most distant parts of the Empire, the Indians, the Australians. But these were picturesque too. The cheers were also loud for bands if they were playing—not otherwise—and for troops in red, as far as I could judge, rather than those in other colours. Scotchmen and pipe-bands were loudly cheered. For my part I liked the Indians best, because they were strangest and brightly coloured. I also liked pipe-bands, guardsmen on foot, and guardsmen with breastplates on horses. There was a piebald drum-horse which the crowd cheered affectionately. I admired it, but did not feel so affectionate. The King and Queen got the loudest cheers of all. They looked young and very small in their heavy gilt setting. The Queen was friendly, and smiled a little. Her hair looked informal and astray like a woman's who is getting up in the morning. It was a darker colour than I expected. The King, in his flat cap, was bony, frozen-nervous, staring. He looked like a thin head on an ancient seal.

45. (CL.63.)* (Parliament Sq.) After an hour's wait the first portion of the procession arrived, the others following at intervals until the King and Queen arrived, the former looking extremely uneasy. It was during one of these intervals that I heard one of my neighbours remark that she thought it was like dog-racing—something to see for a short time and then nothing for considerably longer.

Diffusion of the Abbey service to spectators of the processions: 10.35–1.50 p.m.

46. (CM.2.) 10.55. Regent Street. Cheers break out for no visible reason. One man suggests 'He's arrived at the Abbey, I think'; his wife says 'They're cheering the sun, I think.' The cheering actually comes from a powerful wireless set relaying in the Piccadilly Hotel. The voice of the commentator can be heard, but not his words. 'They must be giving an audience,' says someone. Khaki-uniformed officer, walking in mid-street, glances up at windows from which sound comes, then lapses into thought.

At door of Piccadilly Hotel words audible: 'Red white

*M: 24: single: schoolmaster: C of E: Conservative.

blue yellow . . . lovely blue dresses . . . most glorious day of his life . . . ringing out now . . . of male voices . . . state coach . . . beautiful.'

47. (CO.9.)* I leave home at 10.35 and walk through the almost deserted streets to the nearest Underground Station. The journey is uneventful, except for the B.B.C. announcer's voice on the numerous radios in the neighbouring houses.

I arrive at the station at 11 a.m., meet my friend, a middle-class lady who is extremely patriotic and is wearing a button-hole in the national colours. We go in the tube to Leicester Square, from where we walk to St. James's Square. My friend is very anxious as to whether we shall get there all right as the streets are rather crowded. However, we arrive there and enter a shop in Pall Mall by a back entrance. I lose my friend and am shown into a seat on the first floor. I find myself between a well-to-do business man from the Midlands, who is reading a 'crime' novel, and two good-looking twins who are speaking a language like Danish and are learning English words from a Pitman's book. I can see the road quite well—the route is lined with soldiers who are standing in front of a mass of people who look like refugees from Guernica. Some are asleep on the pavement, all are yawning, looking white, very tired and slightly peevish, but are keeping their tempers as it's Coronation Day. The sides of the road are covered in newspapers.

48. (CM.2.) 11. Regent St. The loudspeaker of the Piccadilly Hotel announces: 'He's moving up to the doors now. . . . He's very shy.'†

11.3. Piccadilly Circus. Girl sits suddenly on folding stool.

*M: clerk.

†This is a thing more likely to be imagined over the radio than heard.

It collapses. She falls heavily. She is not badly hurt but red with humiliation. The troops are provided each with a paper bag of refreshments. One picks up his bag, takes out apple, and begins to eat it. Removes core with a penknife.

11.7. In Swan and Edgar's middle window a father and son stand, talking at intervals. The father smokes a cigar, the son yawns.

11.10. A young good-looking policeman is joking with girls at front of crowd in Piccadilly Circus. A girl is balanced sitting on a railing used as a barrier. A youth is leaning against it and supporting her with his arm, embracing her closely in so doing. She laughs and replies to him in loud harsh voice: 'It ain't gonna rain no more.'

11.15. Piccadilly. The huge tiers on the roof of Simpson's are packed. The crowd cheers two army vans which are passing. A woman returns to the place from which she has been absent. In a Lancashire accent 'Eh, I can't get in now, can I?'—'Yes, you can get in' say two young men, getting her in. A lady says 'Have you had some cake?'—'No, but I've had some tea. You can get a nice cup of tea over there.' Another lady says 'They're all Lancashire or Yorkshiremen over here.'

11.20. R.A.F. man passing through crowd, tells his companion, 'Yes, he's just left a good £3 a week job.' Loudspeaker at this (Piccadilly) entrance of Piccadilly Hotel is describing the members of the Royal Procession. Then: 'The procession is moving up to the door. . . . A very pleasant sight!' (The crowd as a whole pays no attention to the relay.)

49. 11.25. The black tipster distinguished by the title 'I've got a horse' is passing along Piccadilly in front of the Piccadilly Hotel, wearing bright native costume inscribed with his motto and a tricolour headdress. 'All I want is a smile' he is telling some ladies in reserved Hotel front seats. He attracts considerable attention everywhere. While he is talking to the ladies a man taps him on the shoulder: 'A friend of mine would like to snap you.' He turns round. In cultured voice: 'With pleasure.' He is snapped by the friend from the next window seats of the Hotel. Laughter and admiration for him while his photo is being taken. Then he moves off again saying 'Good-bye' again in his showman voice. A minute or two later he can be heard in the distance—'I've got a horse.'

There is community singing of *Abide with me* echoing in Piccadilly from Regent Street. Against it in counterpoint can be heard the raucous voice of the relay: 'The Queen is moving towards the door . . . the Coronation service is due to begin.'

The organ introit peals from the loudspeaker, followed by flourish of trumpets. Then enters the choir. The wireless is too loud so that some of the soprano notes crack.

50. (CM.1.) (11.25, St. James's Park.) In the Park behind the stands there is an area of black mud strewn with pieces of torn newspaper. A woman sits alone in the mud surrounded by the paper, her head in her hands.

Three girls in trousers are joking with the soldiers.

A policeman coming off duty eats two thirst quenchers.

A girl lying on the grass pulls back her hand from under the Guardsmen's feet just in time. At this moment from the loudspeakers in the Mall the Abbey organ begins. Fanfare. Prelude. The choir. Reproduction of music excellent. Drowning the sound of rustling paper under people's feet. Drowned in turn by the crunch of the Guards' feet as they return. Waterloo steps are covered with torn newspapers and broken bottles. There are groups of people sitting on the steps eating. At the top is a policeman. He shakes his head. No exit this way. 'But' says a girl 'I want to go home and go to bed.' Policeman: 'And I'd like to come with you.' In the stands sit the ticket-holders, their programmes open on their knees, listening and eating.

51. The only way out is across the Park towards Victoria. The responses from the loudspeakers roar across the lake.

The crowd are watching the pelicans(?): 'Aren't they wonderful!' Queen Anne's Gate is the only way through. The crowd is solid from inside the Park to St. James's Square Station. There are only two or three policemen. Then it appears that it isn't the only way—one can walk down to Buckingham Palace Road.

12. On the right the Abbey service pours out across the Park. On the left the Marines' bugles blow in the barracks. Down the centre stream thousands of people. North country father to little girl: 'Ah! You'll have to forgo it for a bit—can you manage?'

52. (CL.1.) (Pall Mall.) Unfortunately during the broadcast of the service a great many people in our stand talked, walked up and down stairs, and drank sherry. They did not seem to realize that this was not only irreverent, but inconsiderate to other people who wanted to listen.

53. (CL.2.) (Arlington St.) 11.45. The other people in the office (they have been at other windows) come in to listen. The Abbey service is going on. They first make jokes with the children and William (dog) and talk, but gradually get quiet and thoughtful and I find I have to hush children and dog as they are listening intently. Feel I must not smoke. My aunt has already left us for a basement room also with a loudspeaker, where she can listen undisturbed and as if in Church to the service. She has a book of the words.

12.20. Decide that I cannot decently feed my children in this now reverent assembly and so take food and dog and children to back office and we all eat lunch (I think this and the early start are the high spots of the children's day). Husband takes dog into street. Aunt refuses to leave service. Children make frequent visits to room overlooking first-aid station. Few casualties to report. They do not want chess, cards or books. We are all quite happy, staring vaguely at the people in the street.

54. (CM.1.) At 12.40 at Hyde Park Corner the sound reproduction was definitely not good. The large numbers of wandering people distracted attention from the Crowning. On the words 'His Majesty King George VI is acclaimed' there is a moment of indecision among the seat-holders—whether to stand up or not—and by all whether to take off hats or not. The seat-holders cheer first, then as the Abbey cheering comes through they stand up. About half the men in the general crowd raise or take off their hats. Two ice-cream boys push each other about in fun because one hasn't taken his cap off. Then the crowd in Hyde Park cheers and the first gun goes off. All this inside half a minute. Then someone in Piccadilly gives a long single cheer and odd people near me laugh. As the organ swells up a periscope-seller lurches forward with an almost drunk mock intonation.* Coming away from Hyde Park Corner the guns continue and a little boy with his mouth full of ice-cream asks his father 'What they firing the guns for? What they firing the guns for?'

55. (CM.2.) 12.50. Lansdowne Theatre. Sixpence to hear relay of the Abbey ceremony. Small cinema about one-third full. The relay says: 'The Queen, attended by her two bishops, approaches the seat of the Almighty.' The voice of the commentator is unctuous. 'The Queen kneels with her two bishops.' In the seat in front of me a coloured man with smallpox-bitten nose is apparently sleeping. Behind me three

*Imitating voices on the radio by way of irony has been very little recorded, though it seems easy and tempting; in a way you are present at the service without responsibility. The man who ordered tobacco in the Archbishop's voice may be parallel (v. p. 282), but he may have done it automatically. Street salesmen on the Coronation route were feeling the strain (cf. the man who said 'Buy a paper! Keep from going mad doing nothing! Read while you wait!" Chap. 2, para. 29).

Americans (or at any rate wealthy visitors) are listening attentively. Elsewhere one young man has his arm round another. Odd people leave at intervals, especially when some pause gives them the opportunity, *e.g.* the silence while organ plays offertory. In this silence the Americans say 'What do they do in the next hour till 3 o'clock?' Then the relay: 'The Archbishop receives the King at the altar and lays a blessing upon him.' . . . 'May they live in righteousness all the days of their life.' . . . 'With them may we be partakers of thy heavenly kingdom.' . . . The choir is singing. American girl to her father and mother: 'I think there is nothing quite so lovely as a boy's voice. I'd like to go to Westminster Abbey sometime.' Then the relay voice: 'The most solemn part of the service has come. It is the communion of the King alone.' Atmospherics disturb the solemn tone. 'The King and Queen are returning to their thrones.'

56. (CM.1.) In Hyde Park at 1 p.m. it is much warmer than in the morning. There are many more people—more standing and many more walking and lying down on the grass. Many of those at the back of the crowd are standing about listening quietly to the loudspeakers outside the Dorchester. Every climbable tree has boys on it. Some moments of sunshine.

1.30. Twelve cases inside and outside the St. John's Ambulance Tent near Achilles are being watched by a crowd of about fifty. A television camera on Apsley Gate is being fixed looking up East Carriage Drive. On the rising ground by Achilles the crowd is forty yards deep in places. Through it soldiers move backwards and forwards, relieving each other.

At 1.50 by Apsley Gate clock *God Save the King* from the loudspeakers exercises a slow but finally compelling effect on the crowd. By the last line almost everyone is silent and standing still, the men with their hats off. They do not sing, but immediately after they give three cheers.

Eight accounts of the Return Procession from early parts of the route: 1 p.m.–3 p.m.

57. (CL.63.)* (Parliament Sq.) Until the broadcast was relayed to the stand I walked about in Palace Yard trying to keep warm and had something to eat in Westminster Hall, where I met my mother who, quite unknown to me, had got a seat in the next stand. The voice of the announcer on the wireless seemed quite in keeping with the ecclesiastical atmosphere of the ceremony, but the time seemed to pass very slowly lightened only by the feeding of the troops stationed in front of us.

The most stirring incident was the unreasonably (so it seemed) fervent cheering I felt compelled to give with others to the King and Queen on their return. The wait of many hours was forgotten in the overwhelming desire to show my appreciation of what I felt the King was doing to preserve the stability of the Crown, the Empire and therefore the greater part of the world in these days of general lack of sound, guiding principles.

58. (CO.32.)† (Parliament Sq.) 12.0–2.20. I sat on the ground till I was sore. Ate Patum Peperium and liver-sausage sandwiches, and felt less tired afterwards. I much admired the endurance and healthy look of the soldiers, with this exception, that some of the cadets had boils on the backs of their necks. I didn't drink the coffee in my flask, because I didn't want to have to search through the crowd for a lavatory. Without drink, I felt I wouldn't need one. I was sorry for the soldiers opposite. I had not seen them eat since nine o'clock, and their only rest was to be marched to the lavatory.

*v. para. 45.   †v. para. 42.

In contrast with the toughness of the soldiers was the spirituality, the ghostliness, of the Abbey ritual which was coming over the wireless. Our loudspeaker had been mended. Submissive look of those who were gathered listening to the long music. 'The meek shall inherit the earth.' . . . Around people were laughing, talking, eating.

The King over the wireless was making a succession of tremendous promises, which he is quite unable to fulfil. Thought: Who is really undertaking to fulfil them?

59. 2.20. Troops have meanwhile marched to Westminster Bridge to wait there for the procession returning from the Abbey. Their drumming and marching has clashed with the organ music and intoning over the wireless. Affectionate remark: 'The sailors never could march.' Noticed a lascar(?) in the crowd, fat and jolly, wearing a red, white and blue tie. I thought, 'Why should he bother?' During this time I had been bored and tired, and felt I had not seen so much as I had hoped.

When the King was crowned, and the guns were shot off, I thought of the ancient court of Denmark, so far out of date, and of Hamlet and Horatio listening to the guns and trumpets. *God Save the King* was sung weakly, mostly by women's voices.

The celebrities return from the Abbey, with their escorts, Australians, Indians, Lifeguards. A dark, hanging sky. The cheers are all louder this time. When the King passes, I wave my hat, to avoid criticism. All I want to do is to stand and stare. He and the Queen are looking straight ahead of them, and are very upright. The King's eyes bulge, and he draws big breaths through his mouth. Is he moved, or exhausted merely?

I study the faces of the Lifeguards and Artillerymen too, see the harsh ones and the gentle ones. More faces are harsh than I had thought.

They have gone past. I am glad it is all over. It is raining.

60. (CL.73.)* (Victoria Embankment.) 1 p.m. The procession commenced to march and ride past. This took forty minutes and contained the Colonial contingents and detachments of our Army, Navy and Air Force. Australians and Indians received most cheering. Then there was another wait and people thought something had gone wrong, until the announcer on the wireless gave us time for more lunch.

2.15. Procession of Prime Ministers and Colonial Rulers and Foreign representatives passed in coaches. Our own Prime Minister received a particularly hearty cheer, although there was cheering and waving all the time. The procession of the Royal Family received more cheering, especially Queen Mary and the two princesses. The children became excited, and most adults said, 'Oh, aren't they lovely!'

When the State Coach with their Majesties went by the cheering from the children became intense and rang through the air. Most adults clapped their hands and cheered, waved their hands and stood up. One or two women looked as if they were going to cry.

61. (CL.1.)† (Pall Mall.) Just before the end of the service, it must have been about two o'clock, the beginning of the troops arrived. The people, who had been waiting all night, or for many hours, naturally started to cheer. It was a pity the wireless was not turned off. The cheering continued at each fresh arrival. Not only the troops, but all the Prime Ministers were cheered. Mr. Baldwin got a special ovation. When he passed us, he was looking out of the window, waving his hand. There was a burst of cheering for Queen Mary and the little Princesses. People were cheering to their fullest capacity for them. The noise died down after they passed, to be renewed with equal vigour for the King and Queen.

*F: 34: married: housewife: C. of E.: Conservative.
†F: 26: single: L.C.C. sec.: Anglo-Catholic: Left-wing non-party.

My seat was too far back for me to be able to see them very well, and at moments of emotional stress such as that, it is always hard to take scenes in quickly. I have rather a blurred picture in my mind of what I saw.

62. (CL.2.)* (Arlington St.) 2.15. Procession begins to pass. Surprised to find lump in my throat and tears in my eyes. Have no impression of cheers in crowd.

2.30. Hold up in procession. Feel normal again. Crowd looks tired and dull—more people faint.

2.45. They start off again. Crowd now cheers hopefully (they had given occasional impatient cheers during halt). Now for me, and my husband says for him, the spell was broken. The state coaches passed, but we could not see the faces of the occupants. Only once more did tears bother me. (I am not given to tears at ordinary times.) This time the stimulus was the mounted band in golden Herald's dress, riding black horses—the most beautiful sight of the day. Two army chaplains provided comic relief as they passed us 2 abreast (4 in all and widely spaced). They got badly out of step with the band and with each other and, glaring fiercely at each other, proceeded to do a fantastic little dance until the rhythm caught them up and they disappeared from sight. When the Royal Coach passed it was cheered like the others— the only sincere cheers seemed to be for Queen Mary and her Grand-daughters.

When the show was over I found Lydia (5) still croaking dreary and monotonous cheers until I stopped her.

63. (CM.2.) (Regent St., Vigo St.) 2.30. The troops have now been stationary 35 minutes. Girls on the balcony of the Goldsmiths' Company are waving to the 5th Lancers. A girl who hears the military band start says 'Oh, they're

*Cf. para. 24.

starting again.' But they do not move. Woman led away by Ambulance man. 'Looking tired' says girl. 'It is a shame.'

2.35. Woman led away by Ambulance man. Husband accompanies them, trying to look as though he did not belong to them.

The band plays again. Tremendous cheers. Along the top balcony of Lloyds Bank Buildings, a whole line of spectators is waving each a Union Jack, beating time to the band. They are just above it. People in the crowd begin to whistle the tune.

2.40. Crash of drums from Piccadilly Circus, then bagpipes: *The Camels are Coming*. Biggest cheers of all.

Man: 'What time is he due here?' Woman: 'Five minutes to three.' She speaks in an anxious voice.

The Camels stops. Huge cheers. Woman says, 'False alarm.'

2.45. Horse-guard consults his watch and makes a wry face at mounted P.C.

The troops move. A girl jumps up and down. 'They're going, they're going.' The cheers are deafening.

On the right comes a crash of glass. We all look round for just a moment and a P.C. moves towards it, but no one comments and interest switches back at once to the troops. Woman: 'They all carry bayonets.'

64. 2.50. Large spots of rain. Woman: 'I hope the rain keeps off.' One girl shrieks with shock of sudden heavy drops. 'The rain'—pulls mackintosh round herself. Another: 'Good thing we didn't get wet this morning. I can get home once it's over, now can't I?' It becomes very heavy.

Woman says: 'The busbies look lovely.'

2.54. Woman: 'There won't be any more [i.e. regiments] now.'

Woman: 'They look more like the Salvation Army.'

Woman: 'Lovely piebald.' Man: 'I didn't see it.'

Girls, commenting on soldiers: 'Isn't he young?' 'Yeh, young kid, isn't he?'

Young man, moving along parallel with troops: 'Can't get through here.' Another: 'There you are.'

2.57. Expectant cessation of cheering. Sound of bridles.

Woman: 'Now the carriages.'

2.59. Whole crowd joins in the marching tune of the band.

Woman, commenting on Horse Guards: 'Aren't they lovely?'

3.0. Woman: 'One thing, it's not a heavy rain. If it only comes in bits and bits, it's alright.'

Men again astride barricade opposite Vigo St. Not moved this time.

Woman, pointing to street: 'Look at those nurses.' None are visible.

Hundreds of periscopes are in use.

65. 3.3. Crescendo of cheering. Man: 'Here they are.'

Two ambulance men push through, 'Excuse me.' They duck under the barriers, and make for the street.

3.4. The sailors' detachment marches past. Man says: 'John Bull.' Woman says: 'The sailors.'

Woman points to man astride the barricade: 'Look at those there. And then people pay £4. 4. 0. for a window seat!'

Woman: 'Stanley Baldwin is in the last carriage.' The rumour is tossed about.

'Here they come. Here come the Life Guards.'

3.7. The first set of carriages are black and closed.

Woman: 'You only see them after they're gone.' Another: 'That's all we'll see of the King and Queen' (i.e. a white-gloved arm at the window.)

Woman shouts 'Hurrah.' Man joins in loudly.

Woman: 'See, his head against the window.'

The two Ambulance men are attending to someone stretched out at roadside.

66. 3.10. The troops lining the route unfurl the Royal Standard and present bayonets.

Woman: 'No, not yet. I think the Duchess first.'

Another: 'That's the Queen.' Then, disappointed: 'No.'

'That's Queen Mary.'

'That's Princess Marina.'

'Princess Royal, that is.'

'The Queen of Norway.'

'I saw Marina.'

'I'm sure Queen Mary's next.'

Man shouts: 'Hullo, George, boy. Well, Marina.'

Woman: 'This is Queen Mary's coach next.'

(It is evident that no one in the crowd actually knows who is who.)

3.13. Hats off. Men yell 'Hurrah.' People are pointing and jumping. 'Queen Mary, that is.'

People hysterical.

'There are the Princesses. Aren't they sweet?'

Woman: 'They're well trained.'

'After the King comes the Duke of Gloucester.'

'That one's a piebald.'

A policeman's eyes are shining.

Woman: 'I saw Queen Mary.' 'Did you?' 'Yes.'

'See, here's the coach.'

Again a man's particularly raucous 'hurrah'.

Woman laughs at uniform of Horse Guards.

67. 3.18. Woman: 'Yes, I see the coach. It's coming very slowly, ever so slowly.'

Hysteria again. (Hysteria renews in waves. When crowd finds itself mistaken in thinking one lot of coaches royal, it greets the next lot.)

'Oh, look at that. Look at that!!'

'Hurraaaaaaaahhhhhhhhhhhhh!!!!!!'

'What a coach!!' (ridiculing because of gilt decorations as well as praising).

As the coach passes crowd breaks up, rushing in pursuit.

Woman: 'I didn't get a look at them.'

'The two Dukes at the back of course, being on horseback.'

'Yes, I saw them.'

'That's the end.'

'That's that.'

'That's the tail-end of it now.'

'Two more coming.'

'Black Maria coming now.'

The crowd moves off in pursuit.

'It's best to follow the crowd.'

Father, to young daughter: 'We've seen something we shall never see again.' Mother: 'She may, we shan't.'

Father (justifying his remark): 'Well, I mean, she may not get the opportunity. We may not be this way again.'

68. The Vigo St. corral is not yet unlocked. The pressure on it from the crowd wanting to escape is terrific.

Woman, terrified of pressure: 'That's what makes me nervous, when a crowd gets wild.'

Barricades opened, people pour out.

3.25. Dispersing crowd.

'We'll see where this takes us to, I think.'

Then another regiment is heard passing. People stop in their departure. Some run back, but not many. One: 'Look what we're missing.'

A youth: 'Well, I saw the King. I didn't see the Queen though.'

Another: 'I did.'

The crowd is in a state of merriment.* A man and a girl are caressing one another as they walk away. There are shouts of 'Oh' and 'Whoopee'. Bells near Burlington Gardens are playing *Loch Lomond*. The rain is ceasing a little.

69. (CM.6.) (About 2.30.) Walk down to Great Marl-

*Note the relief after a state of emotional tension: *cf*. para. 41.

borough St. Stand behind barricades. Work my way up to about 3 deep. Speak to red-haired woman enthusiast (working class) with a son on right side of barricades, 'So that's all I'm worrying about. Me son's there, and I can wait 'ere till he comes through.' Constant spirited backchat between red-haired enthusiast, two girls, Violet and Doris, self, and two very handsome policemen. The police had been on since 3 a.m. without a break and were going on till 12. Looked dead tired, hands trembled.

About 3.5 cheering at procession we can't see begins. Constant rumours as to who passes. Violet says she can lip-read people's mouths on balconies as to who passes, but seems to get same people twice. Much cheering on balconies for King. Not much cheering from behind barricades—more as a joke at procession no one can see.

Horrible accident when woman hanging on to join in barricade doors gets fingers badly jammed. She and several other shrieked for several seconds before door could be moved.

70. (CL.65.) (Oxford St.) All the crowd were good humoured though I heard two rows between people who pushed forward and those who were left behind. People fainted at regular intervals, mostly ones who had stood since six o'clock. About two o'clock pressures developed and a voice from a police van asked us to 'play the game'. He was answered by cheers and laughs from the crowd. A rather stout policeman on a horse who thought that we might be better for a left turning movement was the butt of many shafts of wit.

At three o'clock the first of the procession came along and the people cheered loudly. The first cheer seemed to be a relief of the feelings of all who were waiting. As the troops marched along the cheering tended to die slightly till the coaches came. However, fresh bursts occurred whenever any part was arrayed in striking or spectacular costumes.

The more spectacular the costumes the greater the cheering.

Stanley Baldwin got a very good cheer, and Queen Mary an excellent one. The crescendo was reached when the Royal Coach came past. Several people seemed as much or more amazed by the coach itself than the couple inside it. The King looked slightly nervous but sat up well and proudly. I did not see the Queen very well.

Simultaneous accounts of relayed cheering—later sections of return route—rain: 2.40–4.30 p.m.

71. (CM.3.) (Marble Arch: about 2.40). Bells ringing through loudspeakers: majority of the crowd quiet: comparatively still. Red Cross nurses were climbing up Hyde Park railings.

A tipsy party came towards Hyde Park: 'He's got a bottle of beer and I've got a bottle of beer. Hold the glass!' (there was only one). Roars of laughter. They started singing and then joined in the children's cheering coming over the loudspeaker. Started singing *It ain't gonna rain no more* as the sky overcast, and followed it with *Loch Lomond*.

The loudspeaker asked people not to throw paper streamers from the windows (repeated twice). There was a faint ironic cheer from the crowd.

2.55. 'Here's the band coming, in't it?'—'There's something coming through now—see the white hats.' Mild cheering from the crowd and much more general conversation—excited. Clapping from houses. Cheering and flag-waving taken up by back of crowd in ironic spirit. Two people climb a tree; a bobby climbs after them to bring them down—crowd laughs at that.

Cheering from the Regal as different things in the procession appear.

72. (CM.9.)(Marble Arch.) 2.50. The Procession is already fairly late. (It was timed to reach Marble Arch at 2.31 p.m.)

Man of 30 commenting on scarcity of crowd says to me, 'Half-past three would have been good enough.'

Loudspeaker: 'Please don't throw streamers out of the window. Thank you.' The crowd listened quietly to this announcement then broke into laughter and cries of 'We're not' —'We haven't got any'—'Thank you for nothing.'

73. (CM.1.) (Apsley Gate: about 2.40.)* Now cheers and bells from earlier parts of the route are being broadcast from near Hyde Park Hotel. This is behind most of the crowd and makes them look round.

*At this point we have three Observers who, independently of each other, have arrived in the same crowd at the same time. It is therefore interesting to see how far their accounts correspond. Not only do they agree with each other, but they show the same stimuli affecting different parts of the crowd, and the same impulses travelling through it. Such simultaneous but independent accounts fix the events described with added force—and this force is a direct result of the Mass-Observation method.

Two accounts mention the ringing of bells at 2.40.

Two mention the broadcasting of cheers from a different part of the route being heard by people who had not yet seen the procession. In one case they are not clear where the cheers are coming from, and in the other it makes them start cheering themselves. Then real cheering at Marble Arch is heard at Apsley Gate, which has not yet seen the procession; this does not make them respond by taking up the cheering.

When it starts to rain, at both Marble Arch and Apsley Gate, people immediately begin to sing—it is the same rain and has the same effect. Singing is regarded as an aid to keeping up the spirits, or a kind of moral support.

Both Observers at Marble Arch report at the same moment that the (presumably *police*) loudspeaker asked people not to throw streamers from the windows. Both Observers being on the park side of the road (opposite to the windows) record irony from the crowd. About 8 minutes later, rain having started, the Observer at Apsley Gate notes that people on the Achilles mound are throwing balls of wet paper. An impulse to throw had, it seems, developed along this part of the route. It should be noted that the people in Hyde Park were among the earliest to arrive and the last to see the procession.

2.50. Mounted police are clearing a way between Apsley Gate and the Television Mobile Unit sixty yards back. The news cameramen up on the gate sit huddled together. It is getting colder. The crowd is still gathering—standing in long lines dictated by gaps between obstacles.

2.55. It begins to rain. Up goes an umbrella over the G.B. News camera. Ex-servicemen on the roofs of motor coaches begin to sing.

3.0. There is cheering at Marble Arch. It gets wetter and colder.

3.5. On the Achilles mound people are throwing balls of wet newspaper at one another.

74. (CM.3.) (Marble Arch: about 3.0. p.m.) Bobbies turning more people off the pillars. Woman in crowd: 'Mouldy old codgers, just standing up themselves and seeing it.'

Father and mother to children dressed in red white and blue on their shoulders: 'Shout to them. Wave to them. Shout "Hurrah!"'

'There goes the Salvation Army'—band came by.

'Just occasionally I see a head go past, presumably on horseback.'

An old lady on the shoulders of a respectable citizen: 'I can see the top of them. Dark blue uniforms—rifles—now I can see a band—jolly officer with beret, not cap. A magnificent line of bayonets all down Oxford Street. I can see without a periscope. Am I not a strain on you? It's a band. Awfully pleased, that's all. That's why they're making a noise. Now they're Scotties—marching—they always adore Scotties. Now I can only see tops'—two women speaking German passed me in the crowd—'Now John let me down for five minutes and then they'll be coming. I saw all their tops down to their shoulders—busbies in yellow. Scots band playing.'

Someone else on shoulders: 'Just going through the Arch. Ooh, there's crowds before the Arch. All Life-guards. No

sign of a coach yet, Fred. Let me get down, you'll be tired.'
More soldiers in dark blue.

'Here's the coach coming now . . . something with wheels
on . . . no, it's a gun carriage.'

'They're still going by with red hats on—you want to get
those red signs there; you'll see them easy then . . . same lot of
sodgers . . . on horseback . . . mounted band . . . different lot
now though.'

'I can see right up Oxford Street—whoops! I'm coming
down!' 'Do you mean to say you couldn't help it?'

Stretcher came by—one girl to friend: 'One darned thing
after another.'

A young bobby was explaining to an old lady how to use a
periscope. 'Sorry to disappoint you; you won't be able to see
much; I can't' (in good humour). Three silly girls were
giggling at him and he was distinctly interested.

'See the old policeman?' 'Ah, I see them every night; I
don't want to see them.'

A girl on two others' shoulders as the royal coach came
past: 'Look, look there's the two Princesses.' '*Look*, she
ays!' 'Lord Lascelles!' 'Whose coach is this?' 'I saw Lord Lascelles.'

'Eeh, we'll never get through this crowd.'

(Scots accent): 'Don't squash my knee.' 'Royalty white and
red.' Long dissertation on uniforms, who was coming in the
procession, etc., followed.

Rain coming on—about a third of the crowd departing. A
man at the street corner selling noisy balloons, 'Coronation
Raspberries'.

Great Cumberland Place. People were climbing up the
barricade. Four men with a step-ladder in the street—a fifth
on top of it. People were leaving the stands.

Voice in crowd: 'Isn't it fine. And the old Queen and the
Princess, I think she's sweet.'

75. (CM.9.) 3.0 p.m. 'Here we are.' First sight of procession passing Marble Arch.

Periscopes looking for head of procession (after waiting for 7 hours or more). Claps for Rifle Brigade (the first band) then cheers sporadic. As African soldiers (from Nigeria?) pass a woman (35, working class) says 'Ooh, look at the Japanese.' Cheers for Australians—'Up Aussies!' Mounties! Big thrill in crowd. R.A.F.—A Londoner (skilled worker, *c*. 30) says 'We've been cheering this lot for 6 weeks, they've been out route-marching every day.' Sikhs. 'Look at those funny little blokes'—'They all look alike.'

Women looking through mirrors.

Troops with bayonets drawn.

Policeman: 'Well, there's not much cheering going on here.'

Lancashire girl standing on box behind, to policeman: 'Well, what do you want me to do?'

Second ditto: 'It's a pity not to give them all a shout.'

Third ditto: 'Look at the medals.'

Second ditto: 'And still they come.'

Big cheer for busbies.

Of uniforms, a woman's voice: 'It's marvellous, you know.'

3.30. Woman (45): 'Where 'ave they 'oused all these soldiers?'* A well-dressed man (of about 35) goes up to policeman and says with obvious joy in his tone and facial expression, 'It's going to rain *at last*.' Woman: 'These are sailors; give them a cheer.'

RAIN starts.

Dominion Prime Ministers pass.

Baldwin who has his head dogwise over the ledge of the carriage window and his tongue out, gets the biggest cheer. Cheers for Viscount Craigavon mistaken by our part of the crowd for Princess Juliana.

*In spoken English you would more often talk of 'housing' an emu or an elephant; the idea that soldiers are pet animals seems to crop up here. *Cf.* the similar use of this word by *The Times*, Chap. 1, para. 9.

Princess Marina. Women behind: 'Isn't she lovely.' 'Isn't she wonderful.'

Cheers for Princess Royal, Princesses and Queen Mary.

Cheers for mounted officers.

Gold coach: 'Isn't it lovely.' 'Isn't it gorgeous.'

76. (CM.1.) (Apsley Gate.) 3.14. A huge burst of cheers. G.B. camera man focusses—turns over the lens-turret—gets his eye to the viewfinder, and his left hand on the panning handle. Shoots. He turns the turret over again, looks through, turns back. Shoots. Next unscrews telephoto lens. A band in the procession comes playing down the drive. He turns over again, has a look, pans to a new position. There is a rush of people forward and cheering. 3.20. He turns back, comes back to viewfinder and shoots. 3.21. He opens the camera door to see the film is not jamming, shuts it, shoots again. Loud hand-clapping. He turns over, tilts right down, has a look, turns back. Shoots. He swings the camera right round to have a look at the front of the lenses, and back again, the umbrella revolving with the camera. He turns over, looks, back—shoots.

3.25. Drummers. People stand astride between two motor coaches parked next to each other. A baby howls. 'Why don't you get up on one of *them*?' 'Because it don't belong to me.'

3.35. Raining hard.

3.44. 'This is an amazingly warm little coat and skirt though it doesn't look it.'

3.45. Rain still worse. Man asks a policeman, 'Where is Grosvenor House?' He wants to get to it.

3.50. 'Here comes somebody.' Mounted police officer says the Royal coach will be here in four minutes.

3.55. 'Here is the coach with the King and Queen. It's gold. Now stay quiet and you may see the top of it.'

'Oh! Isn't that glorious!'

77. (CM.8.) (St. Martin's Lane.) 3.30. It begins to rain. Man selling the three card trick—he asks you to select the queen, turns the cards over and when you draw out the queen it is an eight. He sells one to a young boy who shows how easy it is. He talks, telling people the reason why they walk up and down is because they won't be educated. At the next pitch man is chaining up partner prior to release act— 'I put another half hitch round his waist (thighs, chest, ankles, etc.) so——.' He first takes the collection and complains at the way they are mocking his partner by not contributing enough. Says he is a white man (this with much feeling) and points to Union Jack above. He says it covers four corners of the universe and it does not matter if you are yellow or white or black, if you are British, you are a sportsman and expect a fair wage for your work. He is not getting that; if any gentleman will change places with his partner he will get the wage and he himself will give him a £1 besides. Now of course if no one will be a sport and contribute something he will have to unchain his partner, etc. At last a young man comes forward and offers to take the place of the partner. I nod to a man by me 'He's in the swim?' 'You're about right.' Rain pelts down. General rush to shelter in doorway of pub. I find the card-trick seller already there. He has brown eyes, brown uneven hair, blue coat and bowler worn at an angle—looking at him I think of the Mad Hatter and Charlie Chaplin in *The Gold Rush*. Behind him is the boy who bought the trick—he gives the boy a cigarette. He catches my eye and grimaces at the weather.

78. (CM.9.) (Marble Arch.) 3.45 p.m. The procession has now passed. We all move towards the small gate out of Park Lane. Slight drizzle. The jam becomes very bad. People stationary at front. Cries of 'Don't push.' 'Damn the police, why don't they open the other gate?' 'Why don't they stop the people coming out of the stands?' 'Hell.' 'Are we moving?' 'Mind the child.' 'Why aren't we moving?' Educated

voice in crowd: 'I didn't think the Royal Family seemed very pleased with themselves.' 'Terrible.' We escape at last and the rain pours down.

We crowd at Marble Arch—the station is closed. Police voice from loudspeaker: 'Please don't push through the barriers. Portman Street is open.' Further instructions drowned in buzz of crowd. At Portman Street we are swept by police on to pavement. Soldiers march down the route. I turn up Orchard Street right at Somerset Street. RAINING VERY HARD.

79. (CM.1.) (4.0 p.m.) There is immediately a rapid walk in the rain towards Knightsbridge. Knightsbridge station becomes completely jammed with people. Sheets of rain. Half-way back up to Hyde Park Corner there is a tangle of cars, horses, and people: they peer into the window of a smart car. People inside have evening dress on. The crowd taps on the window: 'Oo! Carnival Queen!' Coming down from Hyde Park Corner is a man with no hat, and his head right through the middle of an *Evening Standard* poster. A well dressed woman with an official programme open on top of her hat.

4.30. At Hyde Park Corner Rovers are hurriedly putting up a metal barrier in the centre of the street where a lot of cardboard boxes (left by periscope and chocolate sellers) are lying on the ground in the rain. They are now as slippery as banana peels. A girl is lying on the ground in the arms of a policeman.* He says: 'Open your eyes—let me see you open your eyes.' People have to be helped one at a time down the steps into Hyde Park Corner station. Men are dismantling the television apparatus.

Along the East Carriage Drive the side of the road is

*This is the climax of a series of stories (paras. 48, 50, 69, 74) involving policemen and young women. Unlike the soldiers to whom all thoughts are turning, the policemen are in physical contact with the crowd and so they make the best substitute.

actually an inch deep in sodden newspapers, cigarette packs, rubber mats, and filth. Seat holders in covered stands are waiting for the rain to stop. The open stands are empty. The statue of Byron shines in the rain. The police are reforming their units.*

London: 5 p.m. till past midnight

80. (CM.1.) 5.0 p.m. In Piccadilly, crossing-sweepers have already got the refuse into heaps—carpenters inside Simpson's are taking down seats—there is a pile of dismantled barriers in a side street. Two ex-servicemen with a barrel organ covered in a Union Jack are giving a superb performance with spoons and plates in the middle of the road. The queue for the Piccadilly tube is four deep as far as the Popular Café.

81. (CO.38.) After tea, at 5.25 p.m., I walk to Charing Cross Road, meeting the thickest press of spectators in the

*Out of many possible studies of the Coronation crowds, it seems worth while attempting to list the uses to which they put paper. Paper was used in newspapers, notices, tickets, maps, programmes, radio-lists, plates, drinking-cups, for wrapping cigarettes, knives, forks and food, as bunting, flags, house decorations, hats and suits of red, white and blue, for rosettes and streamers, in fireworks, in cardboard periscopes, for sitting on, for sleeping on, to shelter people from the rain, and when thoroughly wet the stuff was thrown about as a kind of bomb. The stands and pavements were positively drowned in paper. It seems possible that this had a psychological effect on the sale of newspapers. People came to feel that there was so much paper about that you did not want any more. At any rate the triumph of organization which brought out early editions of the evening papers was not well rewarded in London itself. The papers did very well till ten in the morning, when the radio started along the course; after that the sale of papers practically stopped, even where the radio was inaudible. The organization, however, deserves to be remembered. By arrangement with the G.P.O. special runners took photographic plates to motor launches in the Thames, and a special edition of all evening papers was on sale (for example) in Buckingham Palace Road by 12.20, containing full report and photographs of the procession which had reached the Abbey by 11 o'clock. For a statistical survey of May 12 see *Shelf Appeal*, May 1937.

Soho streets, who are rushing to find teashops, cafés, any place to shelter and get some refreshment. All the adults look weary and depressed—very few have raincoats or umbrellas and the children by now are all being carried, some of them fast asleep in parents' arms. Piccadilly Circus is in the hands of a street gang who seem to be coping with several tons of paper, broken boxes, wrecked umbrellas, torn flags, hats—and mysteriously—one good silk stocking which becomes the basis for an unprintable remark, which I overhear, from one of the sweepers.* Overwhelming numbers of young women—far more than men—who all seem to have enjoyed the show and are going to keep on enjoying it, despite the rain.

82. (CM.I.) 5.30–5.45. In a pub off Piccadilly, shop-girls are drinking port and champagne cocktails—

'Wasn't it beautiful! She was crying and I had tears in my eyes—we were dead drunk!'

'The way they wheeled on their hind legs!'

'At *God Save the King* all the customers got up in a rush!'

Story of the American who had come all the way from America and heard them in the Abbey intoning, and wanted to hear the *women*.

'These glasses' (champagne glasses with hollow stems) 'are deceptive: you've got more than you think you have. I've got some at home. V. uses them for milk. You don't drain them. And if you don't wash them up till the morning all *that*'s gone curly.'

5.55. 'I'm not going home till 8. I'm going pub-crawling. Good-night, Else. Good-night, Queen. Good-night, Daise.'

6.0. 'When I went back to the girls I went through the men's place. Oo! One man was washing his face. I thanked God for that.'

*Observers seldom refuse information on this ground when more fully experienced.

'When I got there they said: "Got a ticket?" I said "Ticket! I'm going up to work." '

'But *Piccadilly*—I looked out—it was pouring with rain— the *newspapers*—it did look awful. Before and after!'

'That lovely coach—they say it's solid gold.'

'What have you got?' 'Manhattan.' 'I like the man not the hat.' 'The man without the hat on.'

'Did you see us throwing sweets out of the window? We were feeding the troops—just feeding the troops.'*

'I loved it when they put their bayonets through the balloons.'

'He ate his orange though.'

'I wouldn't throw them at the horses though—it's hard—it comes down with a force.'

'They're marvellously trained, those horses.'—'Oh, they're lovely, those horses.'

6.10. 'We've had a marvellous day, Joe. Everything went as smooth as that.'

'That service' (buffet service in store) 'was marvellous! It'll take them twenty-five years to get up that energy again.'

Waiter: 'It was a fine spectacle. I wouldn't have missed it.'

Other girls come in, and they all get rather drunk. '. . . who's afraid of Big Old Ginger?'

She: 'I'll kiss you if you're not careful.'

He: 'I feel scruffy.'

She: 'So do we all.'

'I was sitting on one lavatory, and she . . .'

'Amami Night to-night!'

*Compare the Observer in para. 57, who found that the time passed very slowly, lightened only by the feeding of the troops. There was an article in the Coronation Number of *Pearson's Weekly* by Lieut.-Col. T. A. Lowe, who has never forgotten the egg sandwich given him by a girl while he was on duty as a subaltern at the Coronation of George V. It seems clear that soldiers at such times are regarded as pets, and you feed them as you give sugar to horses (who, however, must be treated more carefully, see text).

83. (CO.38.) It is turned 6 p.m. and the underground entrances are choked with people, most of them becoming just now very bad-tempered. At 6.15 p.m. I am making a way back sheltering occasionally from the now heavy rain. I reach house of friends in North Bloomsbury about 6.45 p.m.—forty minutes late for informal cocktail party. Meet five strangers, two male, three female, and three friends. Two of the friends very excited by fact of having seen procession accidentally and yet completely in comfort. Says girl (aged about 24, secretary-typist), 'We lunched quietly near Leicester Square and were actually trying to avoid the route and the crowds when a policeman saw us in a crowd at the end of an alley and pushed all of us into the back of a crowd in Regent Street. We saw everything without any trouble or waiting.' She seems tremendously excited, having been carried away by the appeal of colour, mass and glamour. The friend who had accompanied her declared, 'It was a good show, in the way a good Disney is a good show.'

84. (CO.41.)* Early tea, then some friends called and a party of us went to Victoria and made our way to the Palace. (About 6.30–7 p.m.) Crowds not nearly so dense as we had expected. Made our way easily to the railings outside Palace and joined lustily in the shouting. Were told the King would not appear again before 9.30 as he was resting. Crowds dispersed in a most orderly fashion. Everything well organized, everyone in good humour; no apparent drunkenness in pubs or restaurants. We went all over the West End, able to move wherever we wished. Crowds in underground nothing like an ordinary working morning in the rush hour.

Spoke to various policemen. All in good mood, not unduly tired. The decorations which pleased me, personally, most were those of D. H. Evans in Oxford Street, which I thought very restrained and artistic.

*F: 39: single: typist.

The greatest crowds we encountered were outside Selfridges, where there was dancing. A lot of R.A.F. men dancing. Some people with banners 'Washed in the Blood of the Lamb', etc., and revellers fastened rosettes, balloons, etc., on them, but everything passed all right, no bad temper. We obtained a comfortable meal in Lyons' Marble Arch place, no undue delay. Band worked very hard, playing medleys of old-time favourite songs, and people sang and waved an occasional flag, but they really seemed more concerned with munching. By no means a hilarious scene, like a New Year's celebration in a similar restaurant.

Excitement caused at our table by a balloon which we had fixed on a long wire into the salt-cellar subsiding gradually into a rather rude shape. People kept potting at it. A man from another table placed a paper hat on it and then everyone around threw things, even a dour elderly lady who looked as tho' she were on her way home from church.

85. (CM.11.) (Oxford Street.) About 6.15 p.m.
Three women knitting on the Coronation seats in a shop.
A girl about Selfridge's decorations: 'They've got a thing! What about it?' Her father growled.
A woman: 'It's been worth coming to see this.'
Another woman: 'It's lovely.'
Another woman: 'It was "Britannia" last year.'
Another woman: 'Statue of Peace?' 'Yes.'
A lower middle-class woman: 'It's wonderful that—the figure.'
A woman: 'You've got to stick together.'
An upper-class woman: 'It goes right on to the Armistice.'
A woman to another: 'It'll cost 'em something to take it down.'
An old lower-class woman: 'Mr. Selfridge—I wonder 'oo 'e is.'
The street was filled with a loose crowd of people walking

in couples or threes or fours, with seeming purposes, mainly going west. Some music was playing. Men were selling programmes of Selfridge's display and shouting loudly. A string of boys in Coronation caps came by, blowing whistles and making the usual strident Xmas noises.

86. (CM.10.) (Oxford St.) About 7.15: Drage's windows attract interest. A banjo player—oriental—on left of porch. Left shows in background a representation (2-dimensional) of Balmoral Castle. 'Isn't it nice.'—'Look at that steeple of that there chapel—that's the sort of place he has once in a twelvemonth' (a discontented tone of voice). 'Is that the Duke of Windsor's place?' 'No, that's Bálmorál.' In centre of floor of window is shown a pseudo-Jacobean table. A bill is displayed: 'You and your home by Jane and John.' In centre window are wax models of King and Queen in Coronation robes. King on Edward the Confessor's chair. Crowd here thickest. Other window right similar to one on left, only this one has instead Windsor Castle as a background. An invitation to 'look round with no obligation to buy' displayed in foreground of window.

Vendor of Coronation medals wearing an imitation crown.

Roussel's shop displays card 'Civilization brings overtaxed heart respiration—risk of rupture, etc. Wear a Lina Belt.' Portly man—well dressed—gazes intently: eventually, without a word, continues his strolling along pavement and his wife takes him sympathetically by the arm.

87. (CM.12.) 7 p.m. *Victoria Station*. Gravesend-Rotterdam platform. Middle-aged American lady to a group of foreigners: 'Especially *maintenant*, especially *maintenant*, especially now when everyone wants cars.'

Waiting room. Some asleep, some half asleep. Some look at their shoe heels and exclaim how they are worn. Three Norwegians come in; and an Air-Force man looking for someone. Overheard: 'Didn't some of them look terrible?'

Notice on Buffet:
The Commissioner of Police for the Metropolis has granted these premises a Special Order of Exemption permitting the service of Alcoholic Liquors from 11 p.m. till midnight on May 12, 13, 14, 15 and 17 and from 3 p.m. until 5.30 p.m. on May 12.

Outside. R.A.C. motor-bike man in red oilskins. Boot cleaners in red coats. Crowd along pavement at lower end of Victoria Street cheering most passing cars. Man with a trumpet playing *It's a sin to tell a lie.* Man with small concertina playing the same tune, accompanied by a dog and a dwarf wearing huge boots back to front, who held the hat. They said they hadn't been playing long and, considering the rain, weren't doing badly.

A party of foreign boy scouts. Some men all in black velvet, cocked hats with a baton and sheaf of papers in their hands. One in white gaiters, waterproof and monocle. I overheard the words 'he darted into a cinema'.

88. *At the Abbey.* 7.30 p.m. Boy scouts enjoying themselves helping distressed aristocrats, getting their cars for them, etc., and always saluting. Some admirals (?) were leaning against the scaffolding supports with the invariable baton and documents. A party of boys came down from the bridge singing to the accompaniment of a trumpet and bashing of basins. Very few people in Westminster tube station. A negro parson studying a map.

7.58. Rain heavier; crowds shelter in subways and lavatories. The announcer introduces Rt. Hon. Stanley Baldwin, etc. Voices in the crowd 'Up Stanley!' 'Come on, Stanley!' etc.

King's broadcast. Crowd apparently not very interested. They looked listlessly around. Cars more and more frequent. A block between Victoria Street and Whitehall. Rain very heavy. Cars going to the Abbey were lettered N/R, etc. Some had names on them, Sir Edward Poulton, Major Hollis. Some had boy scouts on the step. *God Save the King* went on much longer than the crowd expected. They twice began to put their hats on at the wrong place. Singing very half-hearted. The last note (which was delayed) took them by surprise.

Two small middle-aged women remark first 'It's a quarter past now, isn't it?' Then 'That was lovely, wasn't it!' etc. Men: 'He's gained in confidence a bit.' Others mostly silent or discussing weather. 'Let's make a push for it.'

Crowds inspecting wreaths on Cenotaph.

Seller of *Evening Standard*: 'All the pictures! Here they are kissing each other at Buckingham Palace!'

Public bar full. Soldiers and men of all the services. But except one tommy they were not singing as lustily as the rest of the crowds of all ages and conditions. Mostly jingoist songs. *Tipperary, Daisy, Pack up your troubles, Silver Lining, Lady of my Love*, etc.

89. (CM.10.) 8.0 p.m. Trocadero bar. Fairly full. Middle class, well dressed for the most part.

'Got up 5 a.m.' 'Pretty good that.' Barmaid remarks she has not seen new pennies, but adds, 'Have you seen the half-pennies? They are nice.' Two men in evening dress engaged in conversation: dogs one of the topics. I overhear another group. 'They were done by W—— beautiful—Pyorrhea just after was terrible—if ever you want to go to see a man, go to him. I'll tell you who he was treating same time as myself, Old P——' Bar grows more crowded. 'I'm only warning you, joking apart. Hullo'—to someone who transfers his attention to this group from one to which he had been talking—'S—— was in plus fours by my table. He dropped away. Oh, it was damn good: had two Americans with me'—speaker quotes the latter—' "By gad, this is marvellous: stuff of a 1000 years" —carried away with themselves, and it was genuine: they were carried away.' A box of bottles is dragged along the floor through the crowd. A reference to the Great War. Empire.

'Oh, it was marvellous, mind you, magnificent—all those bloody people—only diamonds: everyone puts their best on. Uniforms were gorgeous. Somebody was responsible—very English—more than English—Imperial! It had to be—half the people running things to-day are not English—Strabogli' —a reference to the Dominions—'English-speaking nation, that's what it is'—quotes again—' "Wonderful" they thought it was. There's a lot in what I say. Give Hector my love. Cheerio!'

90. (CL.1.) I had supper with a friend. After which we listened to the King's speech. Its simplicity and obvious sincerity, and the slight difficulty he had in delivering it, made this a very moving experience, after all the pomp and ceremony of the day.

We then went along to Buckingham Palace and saw the floodlights come on, shortly after which the King and Queen came out, and we joined in the cheering. As the Mall was entirely blocked we went into one of the stands, in the hope that they would come out again. A police car announced that they would not reappear, so we walked down Birdcage Walk, across the beautifully illuminated Horse Guards Parade, to Trafalgar Square. Two policemen on Nelson's monument were laughingly preventing a very good-tempered crowd from climbing up. They sang *For he's a jolly good fellow* and other songs, finishing up with *Knees up, Mother Brown*, which is sung and danced in a circle.

91. (CO.38.) Piccadilly Circus and every inch of street surface everywhere around is coated with a sort of papier-maché paste of old newspapers, bags, flags, pieces of cloth, etc., well mixed with a mud basis. Most people seem to be drunk; all are singing in groups, small parties of three or four, or in crowds of about a hundred. We link arms (nine of us) and struggle through to a pub in Sackville Street. The bars

are jammed, beer splashed all over the floor, and the more easily destructible furniture is stacked away in corners. The beer is awful and we are detained by an inability to negotiate a passage down the crowded stairway. No soldiers or sailors about here, and most other people—youngish, and of artisan or factory hand type, with a few students and 'commercial traveller' types—obviously just enjoying an occasion which gives excuse for indiscriminate drinking, singing and fraternizing. It is 9.10 p.m. as we leave the public house. We find our way through bands of singers, instrumentalists, and a few hurrying earnest persons with some purpose, into Regent Street. The crowd jams the road opposite some club or restaurant on whose balcony the band plays patriotic and popular songs for the crowd's delight. I find this infectious and our group, tied up in the crowd despite our efforts, joins in. The radio of a police car pleads with the crowd to 'keep moving' but no one pays any attention. There are enormous numbers of semi-drunk and quite drunken people all round, but no one minds; when a small fight breaks out people in the crowd stop it and pacify the parties concerned, before two policemen can wedge their way through the crowd. We finally get clear and find our way to a pub in the wilds of Mayfair somewhere. Comparatively quiet, and good beer, so we settle into chairs and drink and play 'shove ha'penny'—the women easily beating the men's team. The middle-class girls I find are medical students and one of them decides that we are not celebrating the Coronation correctly, so we all move off into Piccadilly and somehow find we have picked up a very objectionable youth who bitterly resents our caustic remarks anent his hat (we all being hatless perpetually). He is trying to make up his mind whether he is big enough to hit me, when a very charming soldier and his companion intervene. Their technique for stopping fights is to make everyone join arms in a ring and sing the popular ballads of many years ago. I feel very hungry and ask about food—we find a smelly café in Jermyn Street but it is full; so the soldier obliges by giving me first an excellent cigar then a large slab of chocolate which he produces from a pocket somewhere in our crowd. We find a fairly quiet street and the soldier gathers us round him and begins to tell a long-winded story but laughs so much that he never gets to the point and most of us are laughing too before he has gone far.

92. (CM.11.) I went out at 9 p.m. to Piccadilly Circus.

There was a terrific crowd packing the Circus—a bell was ringing furiously somewhere, and people were cheering.

A woman said, 'Doesn't it give you a terrific thrill walking across streets?'

In the middle, near the barricaded statue of Eros, some men were dancing in a bare patch in the mud with legs bared, for the amusement of the people around.

A young girl said, 'They're just ringing the bell up and down the street.'

A young man: 'Oh! Wanting something to do? Go on.'

A party was marching round singing, in file.

A man was selling 'Ladies' tormentors.'

One middle-aged middle-class man to another, 'Only 2 hours! What'll it be like at midnight?'

Parties were driving across the square from Piccadilly to the E. sitting on the backs of cars and taxis, or on top. Balloons were being thrown about everywhere, and the noise of Xmas whistles and cheering was unceasing. The crowd was closely packed, but it was easy to jostle one's way through it as one wished. People were smiling, laughing, looking, shouting, and conversation was mainly exclamatory.

A party of boys passed with a pin, with which they pricked people (?). 'Give us one,' someone said.

A young man: 'Only about three of them started that row, didn't they?'

A man—half drunk—had climbed up a lamp post in the middle and was shouting 'Oiee' repeatedly.

A young man was sitting on the back of a taxi with a glass of beer in his hand.

Someone said: 'There's one coming here.' (A taxi.)

There was shouting, and confetti was being thrown.

The crowd was blowing horns—and then the old gang passed again with the insistent bell and horn. 'Manners, boys, wait a minute.' Cheers.

Someone shouted '1—2—3—4.' The crowd pushed and jostled on. Men in uniforms were in the crowd. There was de-sultory singing and humming as well as the perpetual noise.

'Oiee' still went on from his perch. He and his companion were eventually pulled down by a bobby, though only about 6 ft. up. He retaliated when the bobby had gone with 'Oi'll teach 'em.'

Someone shouted to 2 men on a taxi-roof: 'Come down off there.'

A big balloon was thrown up above the crowd, and for some time amidst cheering they tried to keep it as high as possible, then it was broken, and cries re-echoed.

At the end of Piccadilly a man with two women and an-other man said: 'Yes, come on—what about a drink.'

Someone passed beating an oven-tray. Some public school cads were singing. It was now 9.40.

93. Near Lyons' Corner House at the E. end of the Circus a respectable, but half-drunk woman was admiring a window full of chocolates 'That's nice, isn't it?' Her daughter repeated the remark inanely.

One man to another: 'Only 5s. There's another thing called Siton(?)'

One young man to another: 'It's Coronation, so we've got to celebrate it, so whoopee,' and crowned his syllogism by transferring his pork pie to his friend's head.

I returned to Piccadilly Circus, where some lightning lit up the scene for a moment, or perhaps merely a flashlight photographer, from the photo-van. At the entrance to the Circus the crowds were pushing vigorously both ways thro' the narrow entrance, between the wooden walls. Some taxis were being rocked inside.

Three men: 'Three cheers for the Empire.'

A sober man: 'Look what's happening here—the police.'

One sang 'Do Re Mi Fa So La Te Do.'

The police were shouting 'Keep on the move, please', and pushing.

It was raining again.

An upper-class man: 'They'll call for somebody to come out.'

Some squibs seemed to be exploding.

94. His friend said to 'Oiee': ' 'Ave you found 'im?' (presumably meaning the bobby). 'Where is 'e?' And then he collapsed on his friend's shoulder worn out.

One young man said to another: 'Think!' (scornfully) 'I know.'

A man, ironically: 'Oi'm surprised at yer.'

The crowd were now 'rocking' cars as they came thro' from the west, pushing the body first on one side and then on the other so that it rocked on the springs. Some of the occupants accepted it calmly—others were furious.

A woman: 'There's that bell again.'

A Highways Dept. car passed.

A man, out of curiosity: 'Got a swastika round 'is arm.' He repeated it.

Men selling whistles pushed them to my mouth to induce me to buy them. I refused scornfully.

Bags of confetti were being sold, '2d. only'. The sellers were cheating with the change, but gave way to the 'Come ons' of some soldiers who saw the trick as they bought it.

'Oiee' was up another lamp-post, completely drunk, 'I want my captain, I must have my captain. Oiee' (very hoarsely). 'You're drunk.' 'D'you mean it?' He came down, and embraced his veracious friend with mock emotion.

Some marchers, an even larger band than before, pranced by—their class seemed much higher than one might have expected. They were rushing along, much faster than others.

There was more singing, and the crowd was now more rowdy. They were occupied seriously in 'rocking' cars and trying to push them over. One driver got out furiously, and his anger quelled the timid pushers, but as soon as he got in again the pushing was repeated. At last his car got off.

'The police have got 'em thro'. What a shame.'

Three more cars were rocked—the crowds were dense. A torn and tattered umbrella was thrown about to general laughter.

'Sink it, brother,' as another car approached.

Two Australian soldiers passed. 'Up the Aussies.' 'The Australian contingent.'

95. A weary, good-humoured bobby to three girls on an island: 'Where are you going to? Who are you with?' (Then to one) 'Who are *you* with?' 'No one.' 'Like me.' 'Where are you going?' (Then more talk to the girls.) 'Everyone's moved but you three. Well' (with a chuckle) 'd'you know I'm lost?' (An exchange of toffees. Comment from nearby: 'They're still 'ere.' ''E's funny, you know.') 'Well who 'it me? Was it you?' (of small cut on nose). Then ferocious to crowd in Circus, in spite of size and years, 'Keep on the move.' (Some mounted men were in the Circus amid cheers.) Returning after a good effort, a dubious smile to the three and left them standing, as more talk engaged.

96. (CM.10.) 9.45. Shaftesbury Avenue. Disorderly procession led by youth banging dustbin lids. Sing *Glory, glory Hallelujah!*

Women gaze in hat shops. A group: 'Where's best pub?' and to some sailors, in passing: 'God bless the navy.' I follow the group.

Pub off Shaftesbury Avenue. Packed with lower classes. Sailors get back-flaps pulled by a young girl in doorway, and later also by an older woman who had to get up to do so—doubtless remembering her youth.

Song—*Long, long way to Tipperary.*

Man, about 35: 'My next neighbour's 150 miles away.'

Youths and maids now throng in jubilation. Buy Union Jack and fly it. Start fight with cars in a jam: they are joined by a few more of same age. 'Here's to the good old beer, mop it down.' Crowds from pavement amused. The lorry they have mounted sways and bulges. Women in crowd: 'The fun is just starting.' Two youths stop for a moment on pavement —'We'll surely find some maids.' The other 'Can't find bloody rubies.' 'We've pee'd there once.' Lorry now stacked with people. Shrieks of laughter from crowds on pavement. 'Right on—right on.' From pavement: 'They'll be falling off in a minute.' A Trocadero hall porter: '4 ton on a hundred-weight lorry.'

2 red flags fly from the lorry amid many Union Jacks. Remark from pavement: 'Shot 'em all off, look!'

A youth from the lorry, after it had just turned left into side street: 'Come on, everyone.—Anything else but Italians.'

Lorry has given a jolt. 3 are chucked off and hurt. A crowd gather. 7 policemen in attendance. One: 'I thought that was coming.'

An elderly man, attended by two women, is ambling about putting panpipes to his lips intermittently.

A car, checked in traffic jam; its driver rings a fire bell lustily.

Remark from pavement: 'Wish it were dry and a really hot night.'

Group of seven youths, wearing Union Jack, singing *Tipperary.*

Some men are standing on top of a full taxi. Woman passes

carrying a child. R.A.F. men and others in uniform. Long procession wearing union jacks.

Piccadilly. Crowd dense in many parts. 'Can't get out of 'ere.' 'You will.' 'Someone's conked out.' Two or three mounted police disperse the crowd here. 'That 'orse bit 'is ear.'

A man is clasping a girl very voluptuously high up on a lamp standard, high above thick crowd at his feet. Several humorous remarks. The girl is evidently enjoying herself and the man proud of himself—display.—A medical student (?): 'Give me a ring when you're through.'

97. (CM.11.) (About 10 p.m.) *Regent Street.*

It was raining quite hard now, and some wind was blowing. Some boys passed with flags, some musicians were playing as before.

Some boys in a circle shouted 'W-A-L-L-Y. WALLY.' (Simpson.)

A band in Hope's was playing on 1st floor to a crowd collected in the street, *Daisy, Daisy*. The crowd was swaying, and the mass effect was good. *Best of friends must part*. Another tune. In the windows of Hope's were some men in evening dress. *Auld Lang Syne* after an indistinguishable tune. Cheers. 'The King.' Some took their hats off, some kept their hands in their pockets. Cheers.

A linked group of men and women passed singing *Pack up your troubles.*

A horn led another huge procession, in step or trying to be, followed by a rabble.

A party went squawking after a dog, and looked quite ridiculous.

A row of people came dancing along.

A long entangled chain of people came along.

A man to two women: 'You ought to have worn a mask.'

Some were kicking a box about.

Some more people were singing with flags.

The street was being cleaned by men with a dirt-cart.

A pleasant P.C.: 'You'll get plenty of notes to make to-night anyway.'

John Brown's Soul was sung by someone.

At a traffic jam—A man: 'Get out my way.' A woman. 'You are a bully, it was only a Baby Austin.' The man. 'Hurrah, we can go at last.'

Three or four marched along in time, singing.

98. (CM.12.) *East End.*

Raining fairly hard. Few people in streets.

Dirty Dick's. Upstairs 2 stories in one with Old English beams etc. Barrels all along one side—on the other hams hanging. Stair down to Vault bars.

Overheard: Girl: 'Pleased to meet you.'

Man: 'No love lost.'

Downstairs packed with miscellaneous crowd mostly soldiers, some with girls. Several Indians.

In an alley called Artillery Passage—thickly decorated: grocer's shop packed with children in red white and blue aprons, etc. and faces blackened with soot. As I passed I heard 'We want Joe!' loudly repeated. Then 'Sh——' prolonged. Then one of the children started to sing a ragtime: *I love you and you love me* etc. He was encouraged and helped by the shopkeeper, who leaned benevolently in the background with a young Jewess and another kindly old woman. There were also several women gathered under an umbrella at the door listening. Loud applause at the end, though sometimes his singing made them laugh.

Every pub you went past roared with singing. I went into one. As soon as I put my head in one, they asked 'Have you got a lady?' Crowds of Jews. The pianist was a Jew with an absolutely emotionless face. Everyone danced with tremendous gusto—jigsteps or in rings even to foxtrots. The lavatory-man was complaining some woman had sat on the basin and it had given way. 'She must have shit herself, but it'll cost me a fiver.'

Fish and chip shop. Obstreperous drunk. 'May I ask you a civil question? Will you give me my right change? . . . Who do you think'll win the Derby? Without meaning any offence, allow me to say —— will win the Derby.' Then the waitress came in. 'Do you know the first thing I'd do if I were king? I'd have her killed.' Voice: 'Then she wouldn't marry you.' He sat down again at a further table and drank a cup of tea by pouring it (spilling most) into the saucer and tipping it up.

99. (CO.33.)* 11 p.m. Many people alight at Leicester Square and as we go up the escalator we are amused to see a young man, hugging a soda-water syphon, come sliding down the belt of the bannister; as he comes in contact with a lamp stand on the slide the bottle is broken, and he sails on his way merrily, too drunk to mind anything.

When we left the station, we walked down towards Trafalgar Square. On our way we notice many young men and girls, wearing red, white and blue paper hats—the colours are beginning to run as it is raining hard. Many of the young men carry 'ticklers' (a sort of brush on a piece of wire, which are being sold at 2d. apiece by hawkers in the street) and wave these in our face.

We stop to look at some Coronation photographs displayed outside a news cinema, where the commissionaire is shouting that they are open all night. Two working class men are also looking and they are making remarks about the people in the picture—'Look at the old girl, she looks as if she's got toothache' and at another picture of the actual crowning: 'Look they're just putting it on his nut.' I said to one of them: 'You're not very loyal are you?' 'Oh I'm patriotic all right.

*F: 34: typist: non-religious: Left.

I've been up all night waiting to see the procession.' I said 'Why did you do it?' 'Oh, something inside me made me, and after all it's nice to be able to tell your pals that you've seen it.'

We pass on and walk down past Trafalgar Square. I notice a group of 2 soldiers and 2 girls all huddled together and singing some quick jazz tune and dancing together. The fountains are playing in the square and it all looks very wet and cold with the rain also pouring down. In another corner of the Square there is a crowd watching some people dancing up and down, arm in arm and singing *Knees up, Mother Brown* —they appear to be working people.

100. (CM.11.) 11 o'clock. In Oxford Street men were cleaning stands high up above the streets. A man was wearing a black 'pork-pie' upside down. Ice creams were still being sold. A girl was wearing a trilby. Men were selling shellfish. The crowds were mainly marching West. Two drunks reeled along. Huge bands of people in 'regiments' passed.

Regent Street. Some women were talking about brollies. Two 'lines' of people were charging each other. A trumpet sounded. Two Australian soldiers with a Union Jack and two men were marching down the centre. I saw some more Australians. A man knocked on one of the wooden barriers at the side of the pavement, and shouted, 'Who's there?' Someone replied, 'Knock, knock', from the street.

Someone pulled a woman's umbrella, which infuriated her.

Near Hope's a crowd was again collected, singing *Daisy, Daisy The King*; most hats came off—cheers. *Jolly Good Fellow.*

Piccadilly Circus. It did not seem so crowded now. A man was walking about with a placard 'Business as usual' on his chest.

A man: 'Don't forget to see; my hat's bloody wet.'

A party of cheerers passed.

'Trains'll be running all the night.'

Near Lyons' there was a band of 'marchers'. Men were selling 'To-morrow's *Sketch*, Sir.' 11.50.

Near Piccadilly Circus there was an ambulance case, what I could not see. Quite a lot of people had collected in a 'Black and White Milk Bar', all very quiet; at Lyons' there were huge queues waiting to go in. The police were now occupying the centre of Piccadilly, the steps around Eros, and keeping off the crowd which had been there before.

A number of people were now drunk. I heard *Daisy, Daisy*, and *The music goes round and round* (the only modern tune I heard). A woman was carried by two men across a very muddy patch of street. I thought I saw a flash of lightning. A doleful voice shouted 'London's burning.'

101. *Regent Street*. It was now much clearer. Three young boys charged down shouting: 'The Campbells are Coming.' Near Oxford Street a man was standing on a soapbox, completely insane; someone pulled his shirt out; he remained as he was, making gestures of extreme modesty for the edification of the public.

A middle-aged lady, leaning against a lamp-post, with her left hand on one of the workmen's red lights, shouted as I passed, for want of something better to do.

Oxford Street. There was some 'ballroom' dancing in the middle of the street to a public wireless. A Royal Mail van drove through them and scattered them, as they thumped on it.

A piper was playing, and collecting money.

A man: 'Seems singularly deserted—where's everybody gone?'

The street was not much more crowded than normal now, tho' some people were walking in the street itself.

A man waving shouted, 'Wave to me.'

A slow hymn dirge issued from somewhere.

There was a thick crowd round Selfridges'; some were singing; others seeing the sights. *Smile, smile, smile.*

In Orchard Street they were still selling ices, at 12.30. Some girls sang, *I'm tired and I want to go to bed.*

A drunkard was singing himself a very wandering path home. It was raining.

102. (CM.10.) *About midnight.* I had just started down Regent Street in direction of Oxford Street when I came across a crowd looking expectantly up at a 1st-floor window. Soon there appeared from the window a man in evening dress waving a Union Jack. Shouts from the crowd 'We want the flag.' He is unresponsive, but begins to conduct their singing and soon gets a trombone player from the dance band from the interior of the room. Others from the dance—including girls—come to look down upon the crowd. The 'conductor' is rather conceited and evidently enjoying this opportunity of displaying to his 'nice' friends and girls on the dance floor what a clever chap he really is in getting the crowd to be so responsive to him—and they really were. They sang the same old songs to the trombone. At a loss how to end this procedure, for he did not want to stay out in the cold and damp night directing community singing interminably, he had *God Save the King* struck up and so could end appropriately after having roused three hearty cheers for the King. A girl in a deep red evening dress and dark hair waved a sweet kiss to the crowd as they went inside.*

103. *Oxford St.* A girl to a soldier: 'Where do you live?' . . . A soldier, drunk, of a Scottish regiment, is serenading a policeman, to the amusement of the crowd. A woman: 'Jock, you go off, you'll be getting into trouble.' Policeman goes off. Crowd disperse.

*These people on the balcony seem to have gone on conducting a private balcony appearance for some time. Two Observers record it on three occasions. *Cf.* para. 97 (10 p.m.), para. 100 (11.50 p.m.).

'Damn good, you know. Marvellous show.'

'Ain't it wonderful?'

Band.

A man is walking home with an Australian's hat;* remark: ''E's got an Aussie's 'at, anyway.'

Gloucester Place looks very empty. I am passed by a little middle-aged man very sozzled and straddled across the pavement staggering from one side to the other: sings at the top of his voice waving bowler hat in hand, *God Save the King*—words drawn out as long as they will bear.

*The hats seem to be what made the Australians so popular with the crowd. This man has got a kind of trophy. 'In the Warramunga the headdress which is invariably worn for Kingilli ceremonies is roughly knocked off by an Uluuru man.' *Australian Totemism*, Prof. Roheim, p. 256. The emu feather in the Australian hat is itself, of course, borrowed from aboriginal totemism. *Cf.* the man just above (para. 91) who bitterly resented laughter at his hat; jokes on Manhattan (para. 82), putting the hat on the balloon (para. 84), problems about taking your hat off, swapping hats, wearing pork-pie hats upside down (para. 100), the man who crowned a syllogism in this way (para. 93), and the man selling Coronation medals in Oxford Street at 7.15 p.m. in an imitation crown.

Chapter 3

MAY 12: NATIONAL ACTIVITIES

Délire officiel d'une grande ville pour troubler le cerveau
du solitaire le plus fort.

BAUDELAIRE, Le Splendide Paris.

1. The effects of the Coronation were nation-wide. In fact, the point was continually stressed that by means of broadcasting and modern communications the whole British Empire—and thence by a short step the whole world—was sharing in the celebrations. Every town, every borough, nearly every village and hamlet, had its own ceremony; one might almost say in every street and in every house there was a separate celebration of the Coronation—though when we reach this far, it appears that amidst the general rejoicing there are *some*, perhaps an isolated few, who are holding aloof or are at any rate apathetic. The local reactions vary according to the local conditions. The celebrations take numerous forms according to local need or fancy. All have in common a reference to the central celebration at Westminster Abbey, but it would seem that in quite a number of cases this reference was not as marked as might have been expected, and the celebration tended to reflect the local loyalties more than the central ones. For instance, an Observer in a Scottish town records that there was no mention of the Coronation or of London throughout the day, while the 'success' of the town itself was the general theme. The street celebrations also were nearly always extremely exclusive; strangers were not allowed to take part and barriers were put up to prevent them from 'gate-crashing'.

2. In this chapter a picture is built up, from CO. and CL. reports, of the national activities of the day with a few records from other countries as a 'control'.

We have reports from the following towns besides London:

Glasgow, Birmingham, Dublin, Belfast, Swansea, Liverpool, Manchester, Leeds, Nottingham, Newcastle, Halifax, Hull, Oxford, Southend, Southport, Middleton, Cambridge, Ipswich, Douglas (Isle of Man), Sandwich, Donaghmore (N. Ireland), Macclesfield North Shields, Blackpool, Croydon, Worcester, Evesham, St. Bees, Ruislip, Hertford, Ashford, Aberdeen, Ilkley, Watford, Prestwick, Stranraer, Beer, Brighton.

There are also reports from Lausanne and Montreux, and from Vienna. There are reports from small villages in the following counties:

Gloucestershire, Somerset, Co. Durham, Buckinghamshire, Hertfordshire, Norfolk, Suffolk, Sussex, Co. Dublin, Kent.

In many cases several reports, sometimes as many as seven or eight, have come in from the same place, often from quite independent sources.

The Break of Day

Newcastle—Belfast

3. (CO.34.) At 12 o'clock on Tuesday night I was at Newcastle-upon-Tyne Central station. A long queue was still waiting for the London train. There was a general feeling of excitement. I was wearing my nailed climbing boots and carrying a rucksack. As I passed the waiting crowd somebody called out and asked whether I was walking to London—there was a general tittering. Everybody seemed very friendly and congenial, the man at the ticket office was not, for once, disgruntled.

My train left at 12.50, ten minutes late. I dosed intermittently, the train seemed to shunt backwards and forwards at

Carlisle dozens of times. At dawn we were running through wild rock-strewn country behind which the mountains were misty blue; but we glided past a placid lake around which a few sheep were peacefully grazing.

I looked across at the young man opposite me. He smiled and asked me the time. We passed a few remarks about the time we were supposed to arrive at Stranraer. He went along to the lavatory and returning took an apple from his case, cutting it carefully and meditatively he gave me half. The rest of the occupants of the compartment were still sleeping.

After some ten miles there were cottages, some of them had union jacks flying from the bedroom windows. Sunrise was very beautiful, fiery clouds preceded the sun, even the drab stone walls which separated the fields were touched with pink. I seemed suddenly to have come upon the spring, for the beech trees were out, the larches pale green against the seemingly black firs. The gorse was aflame far more than in Northumberland. As we ran into Stranraer at 6.45 we passed the park laid out in readiness for some sports and with flags flying in the cool morning breeze from the little grandstand.

We went directly on board the steamer, a clean, tidy little vessel. As we sailed out of the harbour everything was flooded with warm sunlight, in the town behind us there was scarcely a flag visible.

Birmingham

4. (CO.29.) At midnight on Tuesday, May 11, I was at a friend's house; there were two men there (D. and N.) and one woman (B.). N. pricked his ears and said 'The bulls are going.' B. said 'God Save the King.' I said 'God bless him.' B. went on with her sewing (on a machine). The rest of us sat round the fire, singing to ourselves songs: popular, obscene, and hymns. N., happening to sing the hymn in which the line 'Light of knowledge in our eyes' occurs, explained at

some length that the line had been originally 'Light of science in our eyes', but that J. A. Symons had had it changed because at the time Darwin was worrying the Church.

5. The fire was going out and we were getting cold. About 3 a.m. we went to bed. N. and I were to sleep in the room, on a couple of chairs. We first walked about a quarter of a mile to buy some cigarettes. N. bought them as I had about 4d. left. We went without coats and it was cold; a policeman on the corner looked suspiciously at us but did not trouble to speak to us. Coming back, we found a sleeping-bag, one blanket, and various coats ready for us. N. had sleeping-bag and coats, I the blanket. We each took a chair; D. went. N. said he wasn't going to sleep, because it was too uncomfortable; would read a book. He read *Low Company*, while I read the first chapter of Silone's *Bread and Wine*. The chapter was some 22 pages long, but I was tired before finishing it, and when it was finished, put the book down and tried to sleep. I fell into a light sleep and when I woke up N. was no longer on his chair but stretched full length along the hearth rug in his sleeping-bag; asleep. I thought it was half-past eight by the clock; but it was half-past seven. I did not move from my chair but reached for a book. Picked up a Shakespeare and read the closing scene, *Othello*. Between ten to eight and eight o'clock N. woke and stretched himself. He said he had slept for an hour. (The light was still on.) At 8.15 we moved and went upstairs to get two dressing-gowns. We came down and made tea. We could find only one small piece of brown bread which we cut into three and toasted. The milk had come very early, so we took it and the butter into the living room and had breakfast. Afterwards N. took up *Low Company* again and read. I was cold and cramped and we did not talk. I read Freud's *Introductory Lectures*.

6. I read the *Introductory Lectures* until about 11 o'clock, in utter silence. At 11 N. suggested that the pubs were open. We

let ourselves out of the house and walked to the 'Ivy Bush', about a quarter of a mile away. Went into the Men's Smoke-room. There were about three men in there; one woman; and a small boy (about three years old?). The boy was drinking something which N. said looked like a double whisky. N. ordered two halves of bitter. Told me about an old house at Quinton, now very dilapidated, which had once belonged to a certain family, long since fallen in the world. The local people knew of their downfall and now systematically de-stroyed the house; youths came on Sunday afternoons ('re-spectable, clerks and such like') and threw stones at the win-dows and roof. There was another house, also theirs, and also deserted, somewhere in the Black Country, which received the same treatment; only it was ornamented with iron stan-chions since the ground of its site was sinking on account of pit shafts; the locals stole the iron and made money by selling it as scrap 'in the iron boom of 1933'. Outside a man was playing a whistle. There was not much decoration in the pub; most noticeable was an illuminated address to the publican and his wife. The barmaid called N. 'duck'. He raised his eyebrows. The room began to fill up gradually. We had an-other half each. N. started talking about women. Said he was 'really seriously considering . . . had never been like this be-fore. Wanted to get married.' But, he said, most women were not worth much. Also told me he had been commissioned to write a history of Dudley a few days back. Had declined. We went back and read until 12 o'clock.

Vienna (translated from the German)

7. (CL.75.) Slept badly and restlessly. Dreamt a lot but could not remember the dreams on waking up. Woken at 4 by the song of the birds. I thought that hundreds of people viewing and taking part in the great show in London had not slept, and thought that I could not raise any interest or ex-citement for anything after a sleepless night. About 7.30 got

up, talked to my daughter, S. We discussed the book *Bread and Wine* of Silone, which we were both reading. It is wonderful how Silone describes the life of the poor Italian peasants, the misery, the ignorance and the superstition in the mountain villages.

N. London.

8. (CL.64. Female: 23.) Got up at 4.30. Sold *Daily Workers* and pamphlets outside Belsize Park tube from 5.15 till 8.15, with five or six others. The mass was not so great as one would have expected, and it was not the sort of crowd which usually buys the literature we had to sell. Many of those who bought pamphlets did so with a mistaken idea of the contents. A very peppery old officer with rows of medals asked for an official programme; I said: 'This is a guide', but he snorted and threw it back at me after a moment. A rather drunk young man in top hat and frock coat (at 5.30 a.m.) asked 'Is this the official whatnot?' But he also did not take one.

Five platoons of soldiers arrived, and were quite the weediest collection of young men I'd ever seen; and they were supposed to be training for the defence of the Great Empire!

A comrade arrived from Aberdeen at about 8.0, looking very dirty and unshaven and bleary, disgusted because the Clyde district had broken out into decorations and he felt ashamed of his countrymen.

A very swell car rolled up containing 4 people. The chauffeur got out and bought a *Times*. The owner said: 'And a *Daily Worker*.' 'We haven't time, sir,' said the chauffeur. 'And a *Daily Worker*,' repeated the owner. So I sold him one of my pamphlets also. He said at first: 'No, we only buy programmes from Boy Scouts.'

An ambulance man said: 'Coronation? I'm working 14 hours a day!' But for some reason he wouldn't buy our publications.

9. (CO.21. Quaker.) The Y. Hostel at St. Bees is much cleaner and better arranged than many, but my wife and I were the only visitors for last night. She slept on the women's storey, and I in the men's—the top floor, with fine views.

After a good night's sleep I arose at 5.5 a.m. and was out by 5.35—creeping silently. As at most hostels, the warden had no fear of my emerging without locking door behind me. My 'holidays' are really leafleteering campaigns—I have brought over 1000 leaflets (for the 6 days' trip) and went systematically to the houses and shops, in the early morning quiet. For a long time no sound, but later at two houses dogs barked at my stealthy approach.

Back to hostel about 7.20. Brewed tea for wife, and helped with breakfast operations, etc.

Ilkley, Yorks.

10. (CO.3.) Now the rising bell has rung, and I am seeing mile on mile of misty moor from windows high up over the valley, with 'Ilkley, the gem set in heather' of the posters lying among its trees in the valley below. Trees swaying and straining: cold and nearly raining. But this isn't the south, and the moors can loom bigger for a bit of mist, and it is a grand hearty wind (bang goes a door). The trees sound like the sea. Looked up curve after curve of 'our moor', but our beacon is in the mist at 1300 feet, and so is Beamsley Beacon opposite. I remember George V's Coronation night, yelling round our beacon, after stumbling up the track past White Wells; and then tramping back with my bigger brother to Dick Hudson's to count bonfires down the dales. We put 'the flag' on 'the flagpost' and lit 'the beacon' in those days. All traditional stuff. No Woolworth's bunting.

'Well, isn't that just what our Government would do, put Coronation on a wet day?'

The postman, radiating cheerfulness 'Well, it's just about as bad as it could be.' Black oilskins dripping.

South London

11. (CO.44.) I was uncertain as to the exact time I opened my eyes on May 12th, I know I was dreadfully tired, the cheap clock on the mantelshelf had stopped, my watch had been in tick for some weeks, anyway the day being a holiday and I being financially short so that I would be unable to enjoy the revels I decided that I would enjoy the luxury of lying in bed until midday.

I tried unsuccessfully to reach my cigarette case and matches, which were on the dressing table, without getting out of bed, the distance being too far. I had to make the effort of getting out, I lit up and blew a cloud of smoke into the air, drew away the curtains and took a look out of the window, it was a depressing view, my room faced the back garden, such as it is, at the end of the garden runs a high warehouse, at least that is what it looks like and as I am a lodger here I have never asked what it is.

It had been raining and by the look of the clouds it looked as if it would rain some more before the day was far advanced, the grass on the lawn wanted cutting, and on the border it was hard to tell which were plants or weeds, the garden next door was much tidier. I saw several flags stuck in a rustic arch which spanned the garden path.

On the dressing table were three books, my own, *Sanders of the River*, Snowden's *Wages and Prices*, a relic of my student days, and *The Book of Mormon* which had been given me by a Mormon missionary. I picked up *Sanders* and got back into bed. I didn't read much of it. I could not concentrate, so continued to smoke and gaze around the room.

12. There is not much to look at in my room, a dressing table, wardrobe, a chair and bed compose all of the furniture, most interesting of all is the solitary picture which hangs on the wall, I sat up in bed and had a good look at it. I had never noticed it before as I only had moved in a week pre-

viously. I was surprised to see that it was a picture of a young lady in the nude reclining on a divan, she appeared to be admiring herself in a mirror, I should imagine the previous lodger had placed it there as I was perfectly sure my landlady would not tolerate such goings on in a single young man's room. A couple of cigarettes later I heard my landlady climbing the stairs, she rapped the door and entered carrying my breakfast on a tray.

'Good morning, Mrs. ——,' I said, 'lousy weather for the Coronation.'—'Serve them right all the fools who have gorn up the West End,' she replied. 'I wonder what the old Duke of Windsor is thinking of this morning,' she continued. I observed she always refers to the Duke of Windsor as the old Duke of Windsor, though she herself is 74.

She placed the tray containing the breakfast on the chair, commented on the number of cigarette ends lying about and the untidiness of the room in general, as she was about to leave I said to her it was an excellent cup of tea, 'go on' she said with a smile 'you ain't tasted it yet'—when one is in the precarious work as a vacuum cleaner salesman on commission only you have to get on the better side of your landlady as you never know when you will have to ask her for a week's credit.

Swansea

13. (CO.28. Female.) 7.20 a.m. Get up. Feel rather liverish, with a headache.

Put on dressing gown and bedroom slippers—go down to kitchen—put small copper kettle (find myself thinking 'Fancy this still going'—it has leaked slightly for years) on methylated spirit lamp (i.e. open container on a stand). This is not in the kitchen proper but in a sort of china pantry—I go into the kitchen and note some dead black beetles (? or cockroaches—not sure) on the floor—on their backs, my mother having used 'Flit' the night before. I feel slightly revolted and hesitate to clear them out of the way partly because there is nothing handy with which to do it—I go across to a pantry to get tea caddy—put cups and saucers, sugar, milk on tray— also cut 2 small pieces of bread and butter and put on plate on tray—and finally go into the wash-house and find a pan and broom to sweep up the beetles (note that there seems slight movement in the legs of two of the six), tip them into a piece of newspaper and leave on top of the range for them to be burned when the fire is lit.

14. About 9 o'clock. I go downstairs. My mother is now clearing out the 'drawing-room' grate—the coffee is perco- lating and the milk in its saucepan on kitchen range. I lay breakfast and help to cook the breakfast—Welsh gammon ham and laverbread (a kind of sea-weed—found locally and very popular, locally, fried with bacon or ham). My mother prepares apples ready to cook prior to putting between pastry later in the day—during this period my mother opens the front door and from there calls out to me that the general servant of the house opposite is hanging out a flag.

Lancashire

15. (CO.36.) 9. a.m.
Mother: It's 9 o'clock. I'd no idea it was so late.
Sister (Spinster aged 36 yrs.): What does it matter.
Mother (calling me, who am still in bed): Why didn't you put this coat to dry last night on the rack like I told you to?
You wouldn't, because I told you to, or you wouldn't take the trouble.
Wouldn't take the trouble I suppose.
Self (spinster, aged 37 yrs.): Will you cook my bacon with yours pop?
Father: D'you want your egg poached or fried.
Self: Whichever yours is.
Father: Make that toast.
What, haven't you finished yet.

Fill up the teapot.

It is mashed.

And the kettle.

Mind the steam doesn't scald your hand.

Just think what you're doing, and don't go about in a dream. When I do anything it comes natural to me to think in order.

You've filled the kettle too full now.

This tea suits me but it won't you. It's too strong.

Self (to mother, listening to Coronation broadcast): What have you turned the wireless off for?

Mother: I'm going to get my work done, and I thought you didn't want to hear anything about it.

16. 11 a.m.

Self: What are you doing to-day Father?

Father: Collecting rents.

Self: I'll come with you part way, in spite of the flag (on the car).

Mother: You'll be lucky if you find anyone in.

(While travelling in the car.)

Father: I bet those men are butchers.

Self: Why? d'you know about them?

Father: No, they look like it.

These trees are pruned to keep them small and compact. I like them that way. That's what I wanted to do with the apple trees along the side of the garden, only ma gets vexed if I attempt to prune them.

Self: How quiet it is.

Father: Just like Sunday.

(I alight and walk to a friend's house.)

Hertfordshire

17. (CO.44.) I wake at about 9 a.m. first conscious of the chattering of starlings on the roof and the bustle usually as-

sociated with the place in which I live (a Roadhouse). This seemed more intense and purposeful to-day somehow—maybe they are hoping for a busy day. The sun was shining when I woke—now the skies are grey—I wonder if it will keep fine —indifferent personally.

The church bells start ringing—they depress me often—but don't seem to this morning.

The Royal and devout will be on their way to church to thank God for the British Empire and their new King. Bladder full—must go to Bathroom. Get up also conscious of indigestion which I have had intermittently for last few weeks, it worries me a bit; not used to ailments; must see a Doctor I suppose.

Landlord comes in to tell me the girls refuse to cook my breakfast unless I put in an appearance soon—not sure that I want any.

Radiogram switched on downstairs—jazz as usual—how I hate it.

Breakfast—Bacon and eggs with landlord and another resident—the conversation divided pretty equally between busstrike and Coronation—we are all agreed that it is good that the Busmen did not allow any consideration of the Coronation to force them back to work before their claims had been considered.

A young husband and wife with two children drive into car park—enter dining-room and ask if they can get a breakfast without much delay—they look nice—the children are charming—they talk little and eat rapidly—I cannot catch their snatches of conversation.

Norfolk

18. (CO.6.) Woken at 6.0 (approx) by the nurse bringing in baby. Went to sleep again. The maid came in at 7.15 to call us. I heard her apologizing to my wife for being late as she had overslept.

7.55, got up. Had my bath and dressed. Came down to breakfast 8.35. At breakfast my wife and I talked of the weather (it was not raining, but it looked very dull). A friend had sent my baby daughter an Ed. VIII coronation mug. We talked about and admired this. I said 'What exactly are we going to do this morning?' My wife replied 'There is a service in the church at 10 o'clock. I cannot go but I think you should go to represent us.' I said 'I will go.'

Cumberland

19. (CO.18.) 7.10: Got up. Shaved carefully all except position of possible side-burns for carnival make-up. Although feeling tired, I was determined to throw myself into making a day of it. Did not have the usual cold bath, but washed my feet, which were tired after a hard day yesterday, Tuesday. Put on my best grey summer suit, clean white collar, and bright (royal, *not* Communist) red tie.

7.45: Went downstairs. Made tea, and while drinking it, had a good practice on the mouth-organ, of the French song-tunes to play in the procession with my Modern Languages group in the School's section.

8.20: Postman came at the usual time, bringing one $\frac{1}{2}$d. letter, with the first of the new King's stamps that I had seen. I liked it. The letter inside was from the U.D.C.—a good stroke of propaganda. I shall send it to my wife in London.

8.40: Started decorating my bike with red and blue (not 'blue and red', I mentally note!) tissue paper. The mud-guards and other parts that I had enamelled white were already quite dry. The decorating took longer than I had expected. At 9.0 I was still in the middle of decorating my bike, and only finished doing so at 9.40, when the church bells of the local parish church warned me to hurry—for the 9.45 service. I got a buttonhole of forget-me-nots, red primulas and white wild cherry, took a bite of bread-and-butter and set off at 9.42 for church.

Short 'Days'

20. (CL.26.) I was a Gold Staff Officer in Westminster Abbey (or Usher). I walked from a near-by flat to Westminster Abbey in time to be on duty there by 5 a.m.

The most stirring, the most peculiar, and the funniest thing I saw were all one. After the last guest had been shown to his seat it was still only 8.30 but we had already been on duty for three and a half hours and had hardly had time to draw breath during this time. As we stood about resting several G.S.O.'s said what they would give for a drink, whereupon one G.S.O. in a particularly magnificent cavalry uniform said: 'Didn't any of you bring anything? I brought a little champagne, but I had to smuggle it in.' We followed him to the foot of one of the temporary staircases inside the Abbey, where he produced three cases each containing two dozen bottles of Bollinger. The sight of the bottles being produced was, to me, the most stirring incident of the day. The loud popping of all the champagne corks within the Abbey during the Coronation service was the most peculiar. And the faces of those sitting immediately above and around us, who could hear the popping of the corks, but who could not leave their seats to join us, was the funniest. (We had finished the six dozen bottles by eleven o'clock.)

I remained there on duty till 7.30 that night, with only one snatched break of twenty minutes during the middle of the service, when, wishing to rest my feet, I walked out into Dean's Yard. The only place to sit was in the State Coach, and I sat there and smoked one cigarette before returning to my post. At 7.30 I was dismissed, and walked back to the flat where I had a light supper. I received an invitation to go and dine in Park Lane and look at the crowds afterwards, but refused.

Cambridge

21. (CL.39. Domestic servant. 17.)

6 a.m. Up, did necessary work.

7 a.m. Breakfast.

9 a.m. Made beds, etc.

10 a.m. Went to the market hill and heard the service relayed from Gt. St. Mary's.

11 a.m. Went to see the decorated procession.

12 a.m. Visited the Colleges.

1 p.m. Lunch.

2 p.m. Listened to the procession on the wireless.

3 p.m. Washed up, etc.

4 p.m. Went to Jesus Green to see sports, etc.

5 p.m. Rained, so went home to tea.

6 p.m. Listened to the wireless.

7 p.m. Played games indoors.

8 p.m. Listened to King's wonderful speech to the Empire.

9 p.m. Went to a dance at Corn Exchange.

10 p.m. Dancing.

11 p.m. Home to bed.

11.30 p.m. In bed.

22. (CL.96. Boy. 14.) I rose at 3 o'clock, with my father, mother and little baby brother. We walked to Ilford Station, catching the 3.35 a.m. train, which I might say was crowded, but full of good spirits and Coronation goers. After walking for 'miles' and taking a taxi, we reached Constitution Hill and were directed to our seats. After waiting for some hours, a cry was heard.

'Here comes the KING'!!! Soon the Procession came into sight. My father held up my little brother, who cheered excitedly. After some soldiers and open carriages had passed, the glass Coronation Coach hove into sight.

I shall never forget that sight as long as I live. The King smiling and the Queen bowing her head, at the people. More soldiers passed, dominion soldiers included. After we had lunch, and went and looked at all the decorations, returning home at 12.45.

23. (CL.51. Wife of retired Major. Over 70 years.) Listened to wireless in morning. We live in a small hamlet on the Cotswold Hills. 8 miles from a town. 1¾ miles from larger village (one shop). We combined with them to celebrate the Coronation and about 80 out of 100 people in our village went over there.

2 o'c. till 8 o'c. Watched races, sports, tugs of war. Teas. (Evening party followed but we left.) About 400 people—all gay and happy and friendly—an assembly of various households.

(Most stirring incident.) God Save the King in the Abbey and the cheering later. (Funniest incident.) The old villager who said that since last Coronation his under storey could not support his upper.

24. (CL.60. Postmistress. 50.) *Gloucestershire.*

Yes. I was very keen on going to London to see the Coronation and I was lucky enough to get a ticket through the Women's Institute. What impressed me most in the crowd was that they were all jolly and good tempered, and out for a good time, and I think a general holiday is very good especially for the working class. I got to my place at Constitutional Hill at 8 a.m. and did not have a dull moment, there was something interesting passing all the time, and I saw all the Coronation procession, the only thing I did not like was the rain, and it was too funny to see people with Brown Paper and Newspapers over their heads.

Yes, my neighbours were quite keen on the Coronation, and those who did not go to London had quite a good time at home, and the children were all very eager to put their flags up.

Halifax

25. (CL.54. Middle-aged female.)

9.30–10.30 a.m. sewing. 10.45–11.20 a.m. Church. 11.20–11.50 a.m. walk.

11.50 a.m.–12. tried to find a window from which to see the firing squad and soldiers who were assembling outside, and failed. 12. heard and counted the salute of 31 fired as a royal salute. 12.15–1.15 p.m. dinner.

1.50 p.m. Set out to walk to town, to catch a bus at 2.20, returned for another coat as I was cold and missed the 2.20. Walked a longer route to town, passed ex-servicemen arriving in small numbers for parade; passed a continuous stream of people making for the 'moor'. Caught a bus at 3 p.m. for Bingley, was one of three passengers at first, and one of six at most all the way. Passed through four small hamlets gay with flags and saw small groups of people in each. Arrive Bingley about 4 p.m. Passed a park full of people. Walked along main road to Bradford about a mile, turned right between a river and a golf course; counted 20-25 cars at golf course. Continued half a mile between fields and returned to Halifax bus by same route. Caught a bus at 5 p.m. at Bingley, arrived Halifax about 6 p.m.

6.30–8 p.m. read. 8 p.m. supper. 9 p.m. bath and bed.

I saw nothing stirring or peculiar. The only funny thing was the name of a row of houses, Amble Tonia.

Swansea

26. (CL.48. Charwoman. 62.)* Got up at 8 a.m. (usual time in working day). Breakfast—after about 9–11 a.m. engaged in decorating own house as part of street decoration—streamers across street and festoons (of *Xmas* decorns) round doorway.

*Written up by CO.28, 'with Mrs. H.'s permission and knowledge of object—information obtained mostly by questions.'

11 a.m.–1 o'clock. Housework with sister (single) 1 o'clock dinner—bacon and eggs.

After dinner 2 p.m. Watched from corner of street 'Street Procession', i.e. pony and cart bearing 'King and Queen—Mayor and Mayoress'. These were young adults—followed by children on way to street tea.

3.30. Children's tea. Helped to cut up and wait on children. Children had 'Blanc Mange Jelly, Cream Slices, Pastry like'—volunteered to do it.

4.0. Adults' (women) tea—waited on by 'Committee' for the tea.

'Ham and Tongue and Pickles and Pastries and Cake' and tea.

This was followed by tea for men of street.

Then 'Committee'—Mrs. H. went home to listen in.

6.30–8 p.m. Walked round neighbouring streets to see what they were doing.

8 p.m.–12 midnight. Watched dancing in nearby streets—walking about—windows open—and radios on.

12 midnight. Chiming as they had supper. Just cup of tea—'I never take anything else.'

27. (CL.31. Hospital nurse.)

Coronation Day. I went up to see what I could see. Went to St. James's Park—walked through the park and stood right at the back of the crowd, near a policeman at the end of a gangway where the fainting and dying were coming through. I could see beautifully right down the opening. I was in time to see the small princesses, Queen Mary and the King and Queen.

After the King and Queen passed, I slipped away, and walked towards the Abbey, heard the beautiful bells, and saw the King and Queen into the Abbey without any trouble whatever. How remarkable! after people staying about all night.

I saw the lady get into the police car, the mother of the child who was killed.

It was a wonderful sight to see the soldiers outside the Abbey. I have never seen anything like it before. The Caval-cade was beautiful. One would feel they were in the Historic days. Their clothes alone. Had there been more sun it would have been more beautiful.

I was going to sit on the kerb and wait until they came out at 2.15 p.m. BUT!!!! when I saw the people on stretchers going into Westminster Hospital, and I had been up all night, I thought I might be one of the victims. I came back to Putney.

28. (CL.79. Boy. 13.)
Coronation day, although a very historic day, it was, at Ilford at least, raining nearly all the day. During the morning I listened to the running commentary on the procession and the Abbey ceremony. Although the ceremony in the abbey became rather boring at the end, I stuck it out, and heard the crowning of the King and Queen. This took practically all the morning. We had dinner and prepared for a pretty dull afternoon.

But my mother had a good idea and my father went to the organizer of the street tea party, which was to take place in the afternoon. He told her that as it was raining he was pre-pared to allow them to use our shop. Soon the shop was full of screaming, yelling, crying, laughing children. The food was placed on their tables and it took a lot of time to stop them starting to eat before saying Grace. Soon the place was pretty quiet, the children were munching away at the cakes and tarts. My father persuaded me to get my piano-accordion and play them a few tunes. Soon instead of eating they were shouting (or as they called it, singing).

At six o'clock the shop was clean and quiet, the children had gone into the street. My mother then took us to the pictures. At the pictures we heard the king's speech. When this was finished we saw the other film and went home it was practically time for bed so we had our supper and went to bed. In bed I lay awake for a while thinking of the tea-party, but soon I fell asleep.

29. (CL.27. Female. 21.) On May 12 I was in a small village in Essex. I went to a Church service in the morning, a service planned by the Archbishop of Canterbury for general use for the Coronation. (I might add I went out of politeness, I was visiting a Rector.)

After that we listened with a crowd of villagers to the broadcast of the service—I enjoyed the music and the trumpets but the rest didn't interest me as I didn't like the style of commentating—it was well done, no doubt, but I felt as if they were trying to impress me and I wasn't interested so I went for a walk.

After lunch I helped to serve free supper to the villagers and helped to make the dance after a success. After this I went to a more sophisticated dance at a nearby town where they had a pageant representing the different colonies in the Empire—then home to bed at 4 a.m.—slightly whistled!

30. (CL.47. Character actress in a repertory company in the provinces.)

On May 12th we rehearsed as usual. I left my rooms shortly before 10 a.m. The town was deserted and had the air of any rather wet Sunday morning. Except for a mild amount of red, white and blue decorations there was no feeling that it was different from any other Bank holiday. We finished work at 1.30. There were more people about the streets than there had been at 10 o'clock—most of them wearing a bit of ribbon or a disc stuck in their coats. I came straight back to my room —had lunch, slept for an hour. At 4 o'clock I started to learn my lines; this I did for two hours, then had tea. At 7 p.m. I went out thinking to go to a cinema (I ought to mention that I was not working in the evening, as the play we were rehearsing was the first of a season which began on Monday, May 17th) but the queues were so long I saw that there was no hope of a seat. So at 7.30 I went to the Theatre Royal and stood at the back of the circle. The theatre was full and there was some sort of 'Round the Empire' broadcast going on, to which no one was paying the slightest attention. There was more or less quiet for Mr. Baldwin's speech, and absolute quiet for the King's. The house stood for *God Save the King*—relayed, with a soloist. There was proper attention for two verses and a few brave spirits joined in for a phrase or so but it wasn't taken up, and the timing was a little unfamiliar so they got a bit restive for the remaining verses, and sat down at the end with sighs of relief, and a return to conversation and chocolates; almost immediately, the lights were lowered and the play began. I left after about 20 minutes. It was now pouring with rain. Outside the theatre I met a member of the company and we went to a pub and had a couple of drinks. The room was very full; there were many remarks about the weather, and hopes that it wasn't like that in London. One or two were comparing notes on the broadcast of the Coronation service, but the conversation did not become general. I left about 9.15 p.m.—came back to my room and was in bed by 10.30 p.m.

Lausanne

31. (CL.69. English girl at school. 17.)
Participation in organized celebrations were almost compulsory for us.
(*a*) Service in the English Church.
(*b*) Relay of Westminster Abbey service on the radio, to which we all listened for the full three hours.
(*c*) Lunch.

(*d*) Fête organized for the English colony at a large Lausanne hotel. Incredibly dull, uncomfortable, and badly organized.

(*e*) Special dinner at the Pensionnat. Champagne for toasts, tables decorated with gentians and red tulips, and relay of King's speech.

(*f*) Dancing.

(*g*) 12 p.m. Secret party in bedroom. Toasts drunk again in white wine, from tooth glasses. Twelve girls sitting round on 'duvets' laid on the floor, propped against the walls of a darkened bedroom. Clad in pyjamas and dressing-gowns we celebrated at midnight our National fête, by smoking strictly forbidden cigarettes under cover of night.

Ilford

32. (CL.80. Boy. 13.) In the morning I got up at seven and had my breakfast. Then I helped my father repair some shoes. Then I listened to the Coronation on the wireless until tea time. After tea my father had to go on picket duty at his garage as the strike was on, and my mother and I went to my uncle's where my father was going to join us later. At my uncle's house we listened to His Majesty's speech and the Coronation variety on the wireless. After leaving my uncle I went to see the bonfire and fireworks in the park. I went to bed at 11 o'clock.

Leeds

33. (CO.28.)

(*a*) Statement from an old-age pensioner (female). (Write-up ½ hour later). 'Me and Jane never stirred out all day. It wasn't fit. We didn't even go to t' pictures. And my poor feet was awful, awful!'

(*b*) Statement from a middle-aged weaver who lives with her sister. (Write-up 1 hour later.)

'I never went out. You see we have the hens. My sister

wanted to hear the King's speech, but she went to bed too early. She didn't seem very well.'

34. (Written up by CO.33.)

London

(*a*) Report of 'Annie'—the lift girl, which I collected the day after the Coronation.

'Annie, will you tell me how you spent your day yesterday?'

'Oh, yes, certainly, what do you want it for, a newspaper report?'

'Well, not exactly, but I do want to know how people spent their day.'

'Well, I went to take up my place in Northumberland Avenue the night before.'

'Didn't you find it cold and tiring?'

'No, not a bit—we spent the night singing and cracking jokes and drinking hot tea.'

'How did you manage about the lavatory?'

'Oh, we had to tell the policeman where we were going, and that was alright if you didn't mind that. We were escorted by a policewoman to the lavatories—I said to my friend—"Blimey, I've never been escorted on a job like this before".'

'Did you see the procession.'

'Yes, I saw every bit of it—it was marvellous, except much to my sorrow, Queen Mary, but I think she got most cheers of all, everyone likes her much more than the others—yes, it was all marvellous and worth every minute of it.'

'Did you have trouble in getting home?'

'Well, yes, there was a bit of a crush, but not so bad. I got home about a quarter to five and had tea, then I went to bed for an hour, then went over to my boy's place and listened to the relay of the service as we didn't hear it in the morning. Then we went up to the pub and stayed there until midnight, getting blind drunk and singing and dancing and mucking about in general.'

'How did the workers have enough money to buy drink in the middle of the week?'

'Well, we knew it was a holiday, so we saved, and I expect the poorer people borrowed from their neighbours.'

(b) 'Well, Maggie, did you have a good day yesterday?'

'Yes, I enjoyed myself fine.'

'What did you do?'

'Well, I got up fairly early—did the housework at home and mucked about, then I went on the spree.'

'What did you do?'

'I went up to the pub first and had some drinks, then all my relatives and myself went to a neighbour's house and we spent the rest of the day singing and drinking until midnight.'

'What did you drink?'

'Guinnesses, of course,' said she and slapped me on the back.

(c) *Letter from unemployed man. Liverpool.*

The day dawns in Lpool grey but bright periods and a bit cold in the streets there is that feeling of festivity. all through some people look serius, I suppose they are like me, if a person has an empty pocket well his hearts empty however this is all a side issue.

Enclosed* I have sent you all that happened in L-pool. I watched it and in the evening I went to Sefton Park where there is a fair everybody was having a good time. and I hope you were.

Bulawayo, S. Rhodesia

35. (CL.115.) Reporter. On May 12 I slept till ten. From ten to eleven I read the paper with interest until I came to a half column of news giving the time schedule of the Queen's dressing arrangements on that morning. It may be true as the London *Times* said in a leader that the Royal Family's private

*i.e. Newspaper cuttings.

affairs are now the common possession of the nation, but I cannot agree that it should be so. The amount of powder and lipstick the Queen puts on her face for a public event is her own affair entirely and among intelligent people it can only be a matter of regret that the details are broadcast in the English press of the world. It seems to me like dragging the Queen down to the level of a film star.

So I put down the paper, bathed, dressed and went to breakfast. Before lunch I forgot about the Coronation celebrations and reviewed a book. After lunch I reported for duty and went with a colleague to report the local celebrations. The afternoon was hot, dusty, annoying and rather pointless, especially when it came to transcribing the shorthand notes of a speech to the children by the Minister of Justice and Defence. Going very slowly over the words of a man who is attempting to foster a rigid idea of Empire upon a crowd of children is very monotonous indeed. That night I reported the fireworks display which was beyond anything else the most interesting event of the day.

Lagos, Nigeria

36. (CL.114.) (Female. Married.) I should not have gone up to town to see the Coronation procession if at home. Out here, the festivities were more interesting, and I went to the canoe races, the Trooping of the Colours, Fireworks, etc.

In the early morning went to the Trooping of the Colours. Spent the rest of the morning on the race-course with husband, measuring out plots for the school to stand. In the afternoon watched the children's parade. In the evening watched the fireworks.

The Coronation benefits the country to the extent that it brings a certain amount of work and with the Africans a considerable amount of pleasure. They love illuminations, dancing and the general party feeling.

The most stirring incident was the march past of 8,000

school-children, wondering what would become of them all. The most peculiar a high official at a dance dressed up to represent a libertine king, and his wife, a famous courtesan. The funniest—His Excellency bounding on to the field on his white charger, feathers flying, and A.D.C.'s galloping behind; and his hasty retreat three minutes later, when a smart shower came on.

Local Celebrations (i)

Prestwick

37. (CO.2.) 9.45. Church-bells begin to toll. I go out. Slight breeze now. The air is vibrant. Splendid day. Cool, yet fairly warm. I notice that I am more 'extroverted' than usual.

At the Cross about 400 people waiting for procession. Chiefly shop-assistants on holiday—many pretty girls—and visitors. Shop-assistants seem better dressed than visitors.

Large crown on G.P.O. Many flags on Town Hall. Three-quarters of the shops (i.e. 3 out of 4) decorated. Chiefly bunting—tricolour.

9.50. Newsagent's wife asks me to buy a tricolour badge, 6d.; I do so. She tells me that they are selling the small tricolour badges to the men. 'It wouldn't look nice if you hadn't one.'

38. At 10.20 comes the procession.* Band playing *Are we downhearted—No!* The Marshal's white horse is restive. The

---

*The procession will be in the following order:
1. Marshal and assistants (mounted).
2. Town Council and Public Bodies.
3. Prestwick Pipe Band.
4. Decorated lorries, staging tableaux depicting incidents in the history of the burgh.
5. Decorated private motor cars.
6. Decorated commercial vehicles.
7. Decorated horse-drawn vehicles.

Marshal is ex-provost and Boer War veteran. About six mounted assistants in riding habits. One of them is a young butcher's assistant. The Govan (Glasgow) Burgh Band (Brass) follows. Scarlet uniforms. Members of town council, and ministers, in limousines. Councillors in top hats. Ex-servicemen and freemasons. Decorated lorries representing Prestwick's trade and history. Two or three humorous tableaux. Young man on velocipede attracts much attention. Boys' Brigade Band. Model lighthouse on lorry. All the schools represented. There are only a few 'Royal' suggestions on lorries. Everything has a strong *local* flavour. An original presentation by Prestwick Laundry.

Procession takes about 15 minutes to pass. I take walk along main street from 10.40 to 11.30.

Postman says to me that he is very pleased with procession, and that earlier in morning he had directed lady to the place of starting. He is wearing new Coronation uniform. Most of the stationers and tobacconists are open (owners on duty). A cinema-operator expresses satisfaction at splendid decorations on Broadway Cinema. He explains how ladders were used to put them up. Tobacconist says he is pleased with the procession. Woman newsagent says it is better than she expected. Stationer says the 'spirit' of the day is right. Camaraderie. No sectional interests allowed to intrude. I say that I wish it could always be like this. He agrees. *Note*. I did not hear any reference to London in the conversations.

Kent

39. (CO.42.) 10 a.m. approx. I walked briskly from W——station to the village green where I found that all the children

8. Decorated motor cycles.
9. Fancy dress cycle parade.
10. Passenger coaches.
Two prizes will be given in each of the above classes, which will be presented at the Dance in the Town Hall during the evening.'
(*Burgh of Prestwick. Coronation Souvenir Programme.* 12th May, 1937.)

of the village had just been given yellow Coronation mugs stamped with portraits of Their Majesties. The children and important persons of the village had gathered round a hole in the green where the following ceremony took place. The crowd moved to the village green to witness the setting up of a permanent memorial to the Coronation of His Majesty and also to Mr. J. H. Beans, whose name is imperishably associated with the preservation of the beauties of W——.

Mr. H., W——'s oldest parish councillor and former chairman of the Parish Council, performed the ceremony. After firmly planting the tree Mr. H. said:

'We all know that in this Empire wherever our countrymen are found this day will be celebrated in one way or another the Coronation of a new King. In our village we are choosing the occasion to recognize the memory of one who assisted in preserving the amenities of the village in its beautiful setting, the late Mr. J. H. Beans. It was to Mr. Beans to whom they had to turn grateful eyes when they looked round in the spring and saw the beauty of Nature in the fields which he planned'* . . . and much more in the same strain. The Coronation was very briefly mentioned once more before the crowd dispersed.

Hertford

40. (CO.18.) 11.45–12.15. I was in the grounds of Hertford Castle, where there were perhaps 2,000–3,000 people (? I m no judge of the numbers of a crowd) on one side of a river which flows through the grounds. On the other side of the river was an Artillery Battery, a Company of Territorials and a Military Band. The crowd was composed mainly of lower middle class, with many of the poorer people. The upper middle class seemed to be entirely absent. There were many youths and girls who might have been factory hands. Small children

---

*Cf. the view of *The Times* (1, para. 174) that the necessary centre of life is the crown.

were playing on the tennis lawns. There was a general buzz
of conversation—nothing much overheard. One middle-aged
man was distinctly surly when I pushed him in the crowd.
The first round of the Artillery Salute caught the crowd un-
awares. Most people 'jumped', and after a short pause of surprise, the crowd broke into general wave of laughter. Some
frightened children cried, and some girls put their fingers to
their ears. One said, 'Oh, it does hurt my ears.' The repeated
playing of *The King* seemed to cause some irritation, but most
people stood still while it was played. One youth kept his hat
on, and a man, aged about 60, held his hat just above his head.
When the salute was completed a girl said 'Is it finished
now?' The crowd quickly began to move off.

*Birmingham**

41. (CO.29.) We went through decorated streets among
crowds who without exception seemed to be smiling. The
women were dressed in coloured dresses and the men fav-
oured red, white and blue fezes. There was a queue in front
of the 'Home-Brewed'; also an accordion player. We found
that the shop we wanted to go to was shut, but walked on
until I noticed a dairy open. We bought a tin of Heinz baked
beans and asked if bread was sold there. The woman said no.
We looked at each other in concern and said 'We shall have
to walk until we find bread.' She said she would sell us half
a loaf and did. Shortly after we came back J. arrived in khaki;
he had taken part as an O.T.C. corps officer in the parade in
Birmingham earlier that morning.

We walked down the main streets—New Street and Corporation Street. They were congested. On a bus some chil-

---

*'The story of Birmingham's demonstration of loyalty to the King and
Queen at their crowning is one that will be told and retold with pride in
years to come. This was a day, it will be said, when England's second city
showed, to the last man, woman and child, its devotion to the Throne
and its pride in the Empire.' (*Birmingham Post*, 13.5.37.)

dren were singing. They sang in rapid succession *God Save the King*, *Pennies from Heaven*, *Daisy*. Half way down New Street we met T. and his wife and little girl.* He was 'observing'. We walked on, and in Corporation Street D. said he wondered if a girl just behind was observing too, for she was walking slowly along the street looking quietly from left to right of her; her expression was expectant and attentive—so much so that it was noticeable.

42. We went up to the office. M. arrived (a Scottish reporter) and asked if any of our reporters had been up. I said I didn't know. Asked M. if he'd any news. He had seen a lot of drunks in one side street. I asked him to lend me some money. He took out a handful of change including 1s. and two half-crowns. I thought I'd ask for 1s., then said 'Could you do half-a-crown?' 'I might' he said. Then he took out his pocket book and showed that he had three or four pound notes. I borrowed one of them, much to my surprise.

We went to a little pub in Snow Hill, with a little bar, few decorations, and about half a dozen men inside. We stayed there an hour or longer. I drank about two pints, B. P. three perhaps, the printer one, and D. four pints, at least. (D. had already borrowed 5s. from B. P.) I did not buy any drinks—or perhaps one round—because I was getting more and more morose about being bored and thwarted. B. P. talked about dogs with the proprietor behind the bar—a small man with waxed moustache, and the thumb missing from his left hand. The printer said Alsatians had 'something of the wolf' in

*'In New Street we met R. (a University student) with a young man we didn't know. We were not introduced.

R. told us that he had not got up till twelve and that he was now going to his friend's office to finish off his thesis and that his friend had some stuff to write up for his paper and was then going to start typing his (R.'s) thesis. R. said to me: "Are you taking notes or writing up your impressions at the end of the day?"

"Taking notes," I answered. "I'm getting quite brazen—writing it down in front of them."' (CO.35.)

them; the bartender and B. P. said they hadn't; the bartender said that the 'Alteration dogs lived in Alsatia, and if you went to Alsatia you wouldn't find a wolf, because the Alterations had never seen a wolf in their lives.'

Birmingham

43. (CO.35.) 10.0. A., L. and I waited for a bus to town.* A small crowd was waiting. In Shakespeare Street two men were smoothing out flags which had been curled up by the wet. Three buses went past with the chain across. We caught the fourth by grabbing the handrail and holding on. Only one other person was allowed on.

We got off at the Bull Ring. A burly man in a muffler was selling rosettes. He spotted a young man without an emblem walking towards the city centre, and called out, 'You'll cop it, you know, going up there without one of these on.' The young man bought a rosette.

10.30. Walking along New Street we could hear the sound of a radio at Webb's radio store. We could tell it was the voice of an announcer but were not near enough to hear what he was saying. A few people were hanging round the door.

There was a barrier at the corner of New Street and Corporation Street. We didn't know whether the constable would let us across the road or not. He saw us wavering and said, 'Come along, if you want to go across.' We crossed over. There was only a single line of people on that side and there were gaps in it. We took up our stand on the kerb. I wondered if I would have time to post an answer to an ad. in the *Birmingham Mail* letter box. But the pavement was filling up rapidly and I stayed. But people stopped coming sometime before the procession came round and were never more than four deep on our side of the road. And I could see that on the other side people could walk about behind the crowd.

Some young men climbed on to the roofs of the telephone

*A. : daughter, 5½. L. : wife.

kiosks in Stephenson's Place. They could have found plenty of places on the pavement if they had wanted to.

A boy standing in the front row on the opposite corner watched these young men for some time, then pushed back through the crowd and climbed a traffic light standard. A policeman called to him and he came down and squeezed his way to the front again.

44. 10.45. An aeroplane went over, flying low.

A cigarette card fluttered into the street from a high window behind us. It fell face up. It was out of Player's Coronation series.

Two girls rang the bell at Greaves, the hand bag shop. They didn't get a reply so one of them stepped out and called 'Coo-ee' to an upper window. A little later the door opened and they went in.

An old man said to his wife: 'The buses were slow for an occasion like this.' She answered 'Very slow'.

A news-seller came along the street with a bag of *Daily Mails*. 'Pages of London pictures,' he shouted. He didn't sell many.

When a burst of cheering came from the radio at Webb's a man about 60 years old who wasn't wearing any r. w. & b. said to a young man wearing an enormous rosette: 'Did you see 'em at Trafalgar Square last Sunday?'

'Christ,' answered the young man, 'half of 'em never seen a thing.'

'What about the old girl who got there yesterday afternoon?' said a plump young man with a red face.

'Let them sit up as wants to,' said the old man. 'I wouldn't. Ought to have a gold medal. She'll wonder why she's got the flu next week. After all, he's only a human being.'

'You've said it,' said the young man with the big rosette.

'I had to stand eight hours to see the old king lying in state,' said the plump one.

'It'd have to be more than one king for me,' said the old man. 'When you got to him you only saw a union jack over him.'

'That's it. That's just about it,' agreed the plump one.

Three young women (one of them holding a baby) and two young men took up a position behind us, leaning against the shutter of Perry's the jewellers. The three girls were wearing picture hats and very pretty r. w. & b. dresses with tight bodices and full skirts. The young men were in blue serge suits and white mufflers.

A dejected-looking little man in steel-rimmed glasses went by holding open a periodical to show two coloured photographs of the King's daughters. He didn't say anything until well past us then I heard him call out: '*Tit Bits* Coronation Number, three pence.'

45. Some girls farther up the street began to sing. Their voices were good and carried well. No one could discover quite where they were. They sang songs from *Follow the Fleet*. They sang *All the nice girls love a sailor, Land of Hope and Glory, Tipperary, Bicycle made for two, Pack all your troubles in your old kit bag,* and *Gentlemen, the King*—in this order.

I heard the young man with the big rosette say: 'The other day I said to an Ansell's chap, "How's the beer trade?" He said, "Rotten! Got no beer." That's how it is all the way round.'

He spoke to the old man about London: 'It did look an old barn of a place the first time I saw it,' he said. 'And I was disappointed in Buckingham Palace.'

'And the cenotaph!' exclaimed the old man, disgustedly. 'Look at ours compared with it. It's only because it's London. They can get away with anything.'

A soldier came down Corporation Street on a green motor cycle and turned into New Street. He was received with sporadic cheering and laughter and a little man with a Hitler moustache who had two schoolgirls with him said, 'That will be all for to-day, children.'

A man in a r. w. & b. suit came along on the opposite side, selling r. w. & b. hats. He had some of the aplomb of Maurice Chevalier. A girl about 16 ran over to him from our side. He put one of the hats on her head, stood back to look at it and adjusted it slightly. He got a big laugh. The girl took the hat off her head, gave him some money and ran back with the hat in her hand.

46. We welcomed the first band with enthusiastic cheering,* but people could not keep it up for contingent after contingent of ex-servicemen in mufti and troops in equally drab khaki. So there were only big waves of cheering for the three other bands, the Legion of Frontiersmen, the contingent of the British Legion in which every member carried a banner, the airforce men in blue-grey and the nurses.

There was a big cheer for an old man in one of the ex-servicemen's sections who was wearing navvies' corduroys and a r. w. & b. cap. He carried a whip, had a pair of dumbbells slung over one shoulder, and at every few paces did a little jig. I couldn't cheer him because I had burst into tears. I remembered Eisenstein's dodge in *Potemkin* of allowing one sailor to turn his head when the dead mutineers were carried past.

*'Massed bands played in the Square before and during the parade. When at last the procession arrived, cheers echoed and re-echoed along the route. The Deputy-Mayor (Alderman S. J. Grey) accompanied by a number of Service officers, took the salute from a dais in front of the Council House.

The detachments of ex-Servicemen went by....

Then the light-blue uniforms of the R.A.F. detachment came into sight.

V.A.D. nurses marching along in their blue uniform dresses with white aprons and caps ... were given a chivalrously warm welcome.

Two pigeons, the only brave pair that remained of all those that usually haunt Victoria Square and Chamberlain Square, wheeled and flew above the khaki-clad ranks marching with fixed bayonets, whose burnished blades added yet another tone of grey to the sombre picture.' (*Birmingham Gazette*, 13.5.37.)

Another man in an ex-service section was in a r. w. & b. fancy dress and walked in imitation of Charlie Chaplin.

At 12 o'clock the procession was still passing. Mostly khaki-clad sections now, and the remarks were becoming more caustic.

The girls in r. w. & b. dresses behind us kept calling to the soldiers to smile.

A woman in the crowd near us called out to a soldier: 'Oo-oo Bert.' And other people in the crowd took it up, shouting and waving to imaginary Berts. Occasionally a soldier whose name perhaps was Bert turned his head and looked hard at the crowd. The shouting was redoubled then and caused a lot of amusement. The soldiers seemed a bit hazy as to what was going on and some of them looked a bit resentful.

The girls at the back who hitherto had been calling to the privates started on the officers.

One of them called out to an officer: 'Ay you in the front, give us a smile.' And to another: 'Ay little 'un, give us a smile. Show 'em what you can do.' And the man with the Hitler moustache turned round and said: 'You don't want him to lose his false teeth, do you?'

To an officer at the rear of a contingent one of the girls called out: 'Give us a smile, sargeant.'

And the old man who wasn't wearing any r. w. & b. turned round and said: 'You'll cop it, calling him a sargeant.'

When some cadets went by without bayonets on their rifles one of the girls called out: 'Oo, look! They've got no ends.' The laughter which greeted this sally had a quality in it which made people who hadn't heard it ask what had been said. And I heard the remark being repeated up and down the lines.

A fat officer passed by at the head of some little boys in khaki and someone said: 'God, he's eaten all the breakfast.'

'Oh the little mites!' exclaimed L. And the girls at the back said: 'Oo, ain't they little 'uns' and 'Go it, little 'uns'.

I heard L. say to the woman standing next to her: 'The army look an underfed lot.'

The woman said: 'I wonder what they'd do if anyone came?' And L. answered: 'Same as us, I expect—run.'

When four soldiers passed on motor cycles one of the girls called out: 'Oo-oo, take us on the pillion!'

When an officer glanced round at the soldiers he was leading one of the girls said: 'You shouldn't look round, general.' Another one said: 'They're all there.' And the first one said: 'We'll tell you if they do anything.'

The contingents of nurses representing various nursing associations were the ugliest collection of women I have ever seen.

47. Walking towards the bus stop in Albert Street we saw the Deritend Jazz Band getting into marching order, in Union Passage. There were four men and about thirty girls all dressed in yellow blouses, black trousers and white canvas shoes. The men carried drums and the girls megaphones— through which they hum tunes. They marched away to the beating of a drum.

12.40. On the bus we all packed the windows when we went past two women wheeling an elaborately decorated pram.

Behind us I heard a poorly dressed man say, to one who looked like a commercial traveller: 'They've all got their answer to-day.'

'We've called their bluff,' answered the other, with an air of finality.

1.15. While we were at lunch I saw a man and woman pass by in elaborate r. w. & b. costumes in the Spanish mode.

A procession returned to St. John's Rd. from a tour of other streets. It was headed by three men—one with a big drum, one with cymbals, and one with a dustbin lid which he was beating with a stick. They were followed by children in r. w. & b. dresses, some of whom were banging on toy drums and clashing saucepan lids. Two women with perambulators brought up the rear. They were all singing *Rolling Home*.

1.30. A drunken man in a pin-striped suit was getting along by pressing his hands against the hoarding round Burtons the tailors' new site.

1.47. Two young soldiers in khaki who no doubt had been in the parade waved to two girls who had just gone up Durham Road. They did not stop.

A middle-aged man walked slowly to the pillar box, fetched a letter out of his pocket, stared hard at the collection plate, scratched his leg through his overcoat pocket, spat twice, then reluctantly posted the letter, bringing it half-way out again before finally dropping it into the box. After staring hard at the collection plate again and wiping his nose on his hand he walked waveringly across the road.

2.0. Two men in Shakespeare St. were dancing sedately together to a piano. They were the same two who were smoothing out flags at 10 o'clock. A little later they were playing ring-a-ring-a-roses with some children.

A. went out with her skipping rope to look at the children in Shakespeare St. She went close up to them. All the children knew her well. But to-day they did not speak to her.

Swansea*

48. (CO.28.) 1.30. We leave the house and walk through the town through some of the poor streets and past some of the

*'Yesterday's programme of Coronation Day plans throughout West Wales brings out clearly the outstanding part played by local initiative as distinct from official action. This is something new; and a very difficult problem it is for some 'advanced' people to explain. The institution in which a new epoch commences to-morrow is seizing the public's mind as never before.

If decoration and celebration were confined to purely official pro-

much decorated ones—We could see in the distance a crowd of about 40 people at the end of one street (Maddock Street referred to elsewhere), of which we had heard from our char-woman the day before—they were obviously excited and amused—In passing along another street—we saw a horse .dray—untidily trimmed—with two chairs on it (from dining-room suite—dark wooden frames and brown 'Rexine' seats)—a girl (of 15 or 16) in some sort of costume of r. w. and blue ran out to talk to the young man on the box—who wore an old top hat with red, white and blue band on it—About 25-30 people from the houses round were on doorsteps to watch and one very poorly dressed man was standing on a window-sill taking a snap—There was a fair amount of chatter, laughter and excitement—A tramcar came along at that moment (single decker still in use on one or two routes here because of the bridges) and the man had to turn the cart round to get out of the way. My mother spoke to a woman standing on her doorstep (she knew her as having done much public work in the district)—small, rather grey-haired, gentle, very respectable type—She asked what it was all about and the woman said it was for 'the King and Queen of Maddock Street', and that they were going to 'parade'. 'For a bit of fun, you know'—Mother then asked her how she was and her manner became much subdued as she said 'Not very well' and in reply to my mother's 'What's the matter?' said 'Something here' and tapped her chest.

We walked on in still a poorer neighbourhood and saw still fewer people—partly because there are not so many houses there—more offices etc.

As we passed a small public house I heard about 4 or 5 men

grammes, party capital would be made of it at once. But the mass of people has been aflame with enthusiasm, and the results in the small streets and tiny hamlets have been half comic, but touching in their exuberance. "Eat, drink and be merry" is the national watchword to-morrow.' (*South Wales Evening Post,* 11.5.37.)

inside singing *God Save the King* very emotionally and raucously —they sounded half-intoxicated.

We passed a 'Workmen's Lodging House', and I noted about 12 miserable little carnival flags outside—I found myself thinking what a 'mockery' that was.

49. 1.55. We arrived at our destination—a small low building used as an unemployed men's club-room—My mother had been asked by the voluntary organizer if she would attend the Coronation Day luncheon and bus ride to Gower.

As we approached the centre we saw 5 or 6 men—older, middle-aged—working class in appearance—talking and caught the words 'If ever —— that bloody horse——.' My mother laughed and made some remark now forgotten—The speaker was short, slightly tubby, wearing light grey suit and cap to match. We passed the group and entered the building —a man just inside the door asked if we belonged to the concert party. My mother did not quite hear what he said and replied that she had her tickets—He repeated his question and she explained who she was—He was very apologetic and very anxious to make amends saying that he had heard of her very often but had never seen her before—He was wearing a rather large r. w. and b. rosette—Very soon the organizer came along, he shook hands with my mother, using his left hand, his right appearing to be in his pocket but I later decided that it was an empty sleeve—He was about 5 ft. 7 ins.— with a slight Manchester accent—He was introduced to me and held my hand very firmly and rather hard and long when he shook hands—He quickly explained that a certain table was for 'The Visitors' and even suggested which places we should sit in, putting my mother and I next to each other at one end near him—next to each other so that 'You won't feel so nervous'—I understood the 'you' to mean me so I replied that it would 'Take more than this to make me nervous'.

50. The walls were very dingy painted dull green half way up and then darkish yellow to ceiling—There were streamers of r. w. and blue paper across the room which made it feel that the ceiling was low—Actually it was rather high—There was

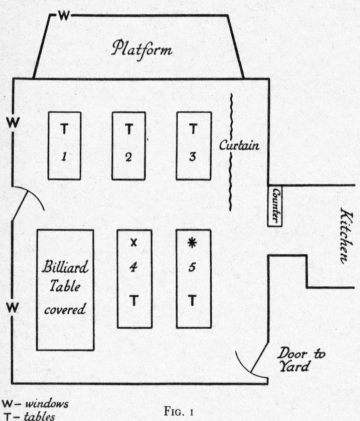

W – *windows*
T – *tables*

Fig. 1

r. w. and blue bunting over windows and on tables over white cloths, r. w. and blue crinkle paper fixed in strips.

There were 2 or 3 vases containing a few flowers on each table—there were set out on 4 tables plates on which were pieces of beef, ham and tongue—knife and fork at the side and a bread and butter plate—in front of each place a spoon, and on the right of each place on 2, 3 and 5 a ½-pint mug—cream with a picture of King and Queen and a royal crest or such on one side—In the middle of the table were jars of mixed pickle (very mustard yellow in colour) and pickled cabbage-dishes of salad (lettuce, tomato, egg, cucumber). Plates of bread and butter cut medium thickness and in triangular pieces—I noticed that on the 'Visitors' ' table, No. 4; there were cups and saucers of grey with Chinese or Japanese figures on them—These were grouped at X and had milk jug and sugar basin near them—There were also plates of slices of fruit cake.

On the platform were a few girls of ages 10–14—perhaps 3 —wearing royal blue satin skirts (knee length and pleated), white blouses with short sleeves, r. w. and b. bows, white socks and black bar-slippers—There were also a few youths of about 14–16 one in blue trousers and white blouse and red sash, others in ordinary clothes—There were a few adults in ordinary clothes—All were talking or unpacking instruments such as mandolins, a drum, triangles, etc. Over table 5 was a fair sized model of a sailing ship and hanging underneath it a brass bell—obviously supposed to be from a ship.

51. The men were 'let in' by producing their ticket at the door—Two and a half tables were filled and more places had to be set on the third table. The men varied in age from 20 or so to 65—and in type—All were quite neat and tidy—some especially the younger ones being quite fashionably dressed —There were one or two who made one feel that they must have been sailors and one or two old ones who looked as if they would never look well-kept or in good circumstances—I remember one with two very long front teeth and a long 'walrus' moustache—There was one negro—They sat down in quite an orderly way and we sat at our table—finally my mother was placed at the foot of the table and I on her left (again so that I shouldn't 'feel nervous'). She was called upon

to say the benediction—after silence had been called by beating the bell with a spoon, the result being a very thin tin-y sound.

As soon as we sat down pots of tea were brought and a jug of hot water and my mother started to pour out. Some milk was already in the pot with the tea.

Mr. D. announced that when everyone was served with tea he would call on Mr. E. to propose the toast to the King and that we would drink it in tea.

52. When ready for the toast, Mr. D. asked someone to tap the bell and then he referred to Mr. E.'s kindness in helping to audit the accounts and explained that each man could keep his mug—emphasizing the fact that they had bought them themselves and were entitled to them—(perhaps I should explain that the centre had made a profit of £20 and this had been used to provide the 'party'). He also said that those who didn't want to carry them home to-day could leave them in charge of Mrs. —— and take them when they felt like it— Then Mr. E. got up to propose the toast. He said he was pleased and honoured to be asked to do it—said that he was pleased to help the centre and would be willing to help any other such centre and then went straight on to 'Their Majesties, the King and Queen'—I was surprised that he made no effort to make any sort of a topical or patriotic speech.

53. After everyone had finished the tables were cleared by anyone who felt like giving a hand—I had noted at one point that there was no smell of hot human bodies as so often happens in such circumstances and also that although everyone appeared to be enjoying the meal none were eating at all greedily.

Just before 3 o'clock—when we had all turned our chairs round to face the platform and after some of the men had gone out to the yard—presumably to the W.C.—Mr. D. came to us visitors and remarked: 'We are going to start with the King and I want to have it as full as possible—so help me, will you?'

54. 3 p.m. The concert began with *God Save the King*—Everyone seemed to be singing but the effect was very thin.

After that the party got going—they were mostly juveniles—and not very skilled—they opened with a sort of massed band and the opening tune was *I want to be Happy, but I can't be Happy till I make you Happy too*. This was followed by several others quite familiar to me. Then the programme proceeded with 'mandolin solos'—tap dancing by the 3 children on a sort of tap dancing mat the size of a large hearth-rug placed on the stage—Then an imitation radio cabinet was placed on the stage and a child 'elocutionist' gave out of it, heard but not seen, a ballad on local history—very bad verse and very bad speech—with several insecure ' hs'—There was also a 'tenor' who sang *In the chapel in the moonlight* and afterwards apologized because he had 'not yet found the key of the piano'. He sang a second sentimental ballad and then returned to *In the chapel in the moonlight* so that we could join in—From then on there was a very great deal of this community singing—done mostly to mandolin or accordion playing—I remember that some of the songs were—*Just a song at twilight, I can't be happy* (second time), *Daisy, Daisy, Oh, Oh, Antonio*—Several more modern ones whose tunes were familiar, although I hardly knew any of the words—*Isle of Capri, Tipperary* (near the end of the programme). The majority were popular songs of 20 years ago at least—We all joined in where we could and hummed, la-la-ed the rest.

55. There was a comedian who came on in frayed trousers, an old top hat, etc., white cotton gloves and carried a monocle which he incessantly put into and took out of his eye, breathed on, cleaned, etc. He gave a little very feeble patter and then proceeded with *Burlington Bertie* taking it *much* too slowly and finding it very difficult to fit in with the accompanist—a slightly fat young woman in a white linen frock with red flower design all over it and navy blue collar, cuffs and belt—It was quite popular, however, and he came back in a very battered bowler and no monocle but with an incessant cough and sniff to sing *I was standing at the corner of the street.*

The small boy elocutionist came on—not inside the cabinet this time—to give a comedy recitation (forgotten what) dressed in long trousers, navy blue, and blue jacket, yellow pullover, bowler hat, carrying a silver-knobbed cane—with which he incessantly pointed and fidgeted. As an encore he gave *Albert and the Lion*—in a very poor imitation of Stanley Holloway. He could not manage the accent—there was a great deal of S. Wales accent which did not fit the style of the piece. After this he gave the lines:

> 'I went to the pictures to-morrow.
> 'I took a front seat at the back.
> 'I fell from the pit to the gallery, etc.'

much to the disgust of the boy behind me who remarked 'That's stale'

56. At about 5.15 mother and I decided that we must try to find a W.C. She asked a woman and we were escorted into the yard, with apologies, to the men's W.C. It smelt abominably and it was a very small place—the floor was rather wet with urine and there were 2 sinks or whatever you call them. There were also 2 closets and with firm injunctions not to sit on the seat the woman left us—My mother—even more insistent—echoed her warning and went into one—I could not face it and returned to the room. I knew that we had a bus ride to face so that I had to find somewhere to go—We discussed quietly going home but there wasn't much time for that. Finally my mother thought of a restaurant which might be open—It was just across the street—I went out to it—At first, although the door was open, it seemed quite deserted—

I found a room with tables round the sides and a dance floor in the middle—The ceiling and walls were decorated for a carnival with balloons and paper festoons of all kinds—The tables were set for dinner and had silk r. w. and blue ribbons pinned diagonally across the white cloths—It was only dimly lit. As I got to the door a brisk young woman on the far side saw me and came towards me. I explained that I was stranded in the district and was there a cloakroom I could use—She willingly showed me to it—explaining that they were very busy getting ready for a dinner dance that night—she offered to get me a clean towel and brought me a clean roller towel—red and white striped turkish towelling. I took off my hat and combed my hair—and powdered my nose.

57. I gave the waitress 2d. and went back—to enter the hall together with the black man—or so I thought but when I got inside I found that it was a second one—not present before—There was a boy of about 12 singing, unaccompanied, hymns—local favourites. As I returned my mother got up and asked if he could sing the one just done *in Welsh*, the boy could not but he could sing *Calon Lan*, a very well known one —He did—but my mother was shaking her head and muttering 'He can't say the words properly'—After that Mr. D. suggested *Aberystwyth* but finally it was *Cwm Rhondda* that was sung—in English—After that we all sang *Hen Wlad fr Addau*—in Welsh—standing—I have learnt the first verse once but could only manage half the words correctly.

Then someone started *For he's a jolly good fellow*.

The concert finished just about 6 p.m.

Towards the end a lot of the men had wandered out— some had returned, some had not.

Just before the end while *Daisy* was being sung a man got up and waltzed round with a chair in his hands—People laughed and clapped and he was hauled on to the platform to do it again. He appeared to me to be dumb as he smiled a lot

and looked at the rest of us but did not speak—He started off
on the platform and then the man in charge of the concert
party pushed forward a woman attached to them (but not a
performer)and she waltzed with the first man—to the strains
of *After the Ball was Over*. They were quite good waltzers. The
men appeared to have enjoyed the entertainment.

58. 6 p.m. The assembly broke up and it was understood
that between 6.15 and 6.30 the party would start in buses for
Gower—Everyone appeared a little tired and disinterested by
then—Mr. D. had slipped across to the restaurant to see if we
could have some tea there. He reported that it wasn't really
open but that they would make us some tea. I was not very
anxious for it but it was suggested that I had better go with
the others as it was not very suitable for me to stay behind on
my own—So I went—The party that went consisted of Mr.
and Mrs. D., Mr. and Mrs. E., the girl of 15 and the boy of 12,
my mother and myself—There was one corner table not set
for the dinner dance and we sat round this—A waitress was
sent to us and we said we'd just have tea and biscuits.

Mr. D. told us that there had been a lot of food left over—
as the secretary had insisted that 10 oz. of meat would be
necessary, arguing that most of them were old sailors and
that he knew what old sailors could eat—He told us that the
women had cut sandwiches to take on the ride with us—
Someone remarked how clean the men were and another
person—I think Mrs. D.—said that she had been surprised
that there was no smell of hot bodies in the room at all—We
all agreed and I recalled having thought of it during the concert—She then explained that, frequently at a certain
mission in the town, she had to go out as she became naus-
eated by it. Mr. D. proceeded to relate that the men had
scrubbed out the place themselves and had used a certain
amount of disinfectant on it (I forget the quantity quoted).
He also related the story of his asking for volunteers to do the

scrubbing and how someone had said 'Well are you prepared to do it?' and he had said 'Certainly if you want me to'—After this five had offered and he had then said that they would be paid 10s. between them, upon which there had been some grumbling from the others who said 'Why didn't you tell us that before?' Apropos of all this he remarked that of course there would always be a few 'of that sort' but that they had more or less weeded them out and that now there wasn't 'one bolshie' amongst them—He also told us how the men themselves had insisted on having *real* flowers on the tables.

59. 6.30 p.m. The bus started. We were taken past some of the streets in which teas had been held—in passing one I saw an old man in grey trousers and waistcoat, white shirt, white canvas shoes, paper hat—with a whitish short beard—holding a small child in his arms doing a sort of dance to an audience of a few neighbours.

The bus I was in led the way—When we were about 4 miles out of the town and on a piece of common, someone said that the other bus was no longer following and there was slight consternation because we had branched off the main road. Someone suggested that the others had stopped at 'The Black Boy'—public house 1 mile further back—This caused a little amusement—It was decided after 3 or 4 minutes to go on as they knew the route—By now the sun was shining and it was a beautiful slightly hazy evening—There were ponies with foals to be seen on the common and the man in front of me pointed out a crested lapwing—Both he and the old man sitting next to him (who, I noticed, had had some sort of rash and was now skinning so that the collar and shoulders of his navy blue suit were covered with pin-head flecks of dry skin) were interested in the scenery etc.—and at one point he told me that he wanted to find some violets, having promised his little girl to take her some. 'She's all for violets' he remarked.

Almost as soon as the journey started Mr. D. started to sing and several people joined in—sometimes all the bus-load except my mother and Mrs. D., who were absorbed in their conversation. The songs were some that had been sung during the afternoon. I remember *Daisy, Daisy, Just a song at twilight, Oh, Oh, Antonio, Chapel in the moonlight, Molly O'Grady, Loch Lomond*—Quite fresh were *Pollywolly doodle, Early one morning, One man went to mow.*

Olton, near Birmingham*

60. (CO.14.) 3.30. Set out to walk ¾ mile to next bus route. From a house half way along the main road comes the sound of the wireless broadcast. A young couple stand by the gate listening. As I pass I hear 'Now the Royal Marines are passing . . .' On reaching the main crossroads I wait a few moments to see if the 3.36 is coming then resume my walk. About ¼ mile from the second bus route the 3.36 overtakes me. I stop it and get on. I sit down in front of two young working-class girls of about 17 or 18 and take my notebook out of my handbag to take down any conversation I may overhear. The conductor takes my fare. Conversation of two girls: 'Ron was telling me about a girl he knew down —— Road, she was only 15.' 2nd girl: 'Those at the hall on Monday night were not much older,' further inaudible remarks— 'There is nothing doing all along here, is there?'

As we go on I notice—a large poster, now very old, on the hoarding of the local parish church advertising a meeting in the Birmingham Town Hall, where various recently returned

**'The red, white and blue symbols of Imperial unity hung from almost every house and vehicle, and were proudly displayed in the costumes of the people who crowded the streets. The centre of the city rang for hours with the voices of children singing the National Anthem and with the cheers that greeted each fresh outburst. Everywhere there were celebrations—organized, impromptu, dignified, clamorous celebrations by single families, by whole neighbourhoods and by the representatives of the population of the city.' (*Birmingham Post*, 13.5.37.)*

people from Abyssinia were to speak; a crowd outside a
public house, nearly all wearing red white and blue paper
hats, particularly two working-class girls in long trailing
dresses with coats over the top, arms round one another's
waists talking to a youth who suddenly starts to dance with
the two of them. The bus stops. A working-class woman of
about 35 runs after it, as she approaches the bus she drops
something which tinkles on the pavement, she stops to pick it
up, it is a knife. She gets on the bus. She is hatless, but wearing a coat and clutches to herself a badly wrapped parcel out
of which sticks the top of a large bottle. She puts the knife,
blade uppermost, in her pocket. We pass several working-
class people in fancy dress—a fat man dressed in blue sateen
trousers, a much fatter woman wearing a checked gingham
skirt, and paper coal-scuttle bonnet, and carrying a very
small umbrella or sunshade—the general effect being Betsy
Prig. Here the bus stops, and the woman, with the knife
sticking up dangerously out of her pocket, gets off.

61. The bus passes through meaner streets, past a council
school playground full of middle-aged men and women
dressed in all types of costumes, hats, and false noses, apparently playing some kind of game (Nuts and May?), a poor
looking girl of about 18 is watching them unsmilingly
through the gate. A fantastically dressed couple of about 45
walk past wearing false noses and looking round to catch the
approval of passers by. Further along a woman walks a little
unsteadily along the pavement. She is wearing a long transparent mauve dress with some kind of diamante embroidery
upon it, it reaches her ankles, under this she wears a short
white petticoat reaching only to her knees, on her head is a
red white and blue Napoleon hat. Her face is old and hag-
gard and she leers dreadfully at passers-by. On the next corner we wait for traffic lights and I see two youths supporting
between them a third youth who has evidently drunk more

than is good for him, a policeman is crossing over from the other side of the road to speak to them. I stop the bus and get off outside a public house. A man in clown's costume is crossing the road, he is very completely made up, even his face and head being covered with whitening. Against the wall of the pub leans a girl of about 20 dressed in a flimsy red white and blue costume, a discontented expression upon her face. I turn the corner into a side street. An old woman is leaning against the wall, but starts to shuffle along a few steps as I pass her. A youth of about 19 looking sorry for himself, lurches past me into a latrine. A very fat girl dressed in tight blue sateen trousers crosses the road accompanied by a young man. I overtake a well dressed working class man accompanied by two older ladies, as I pass one old lady says 'And do we catch the bus at the top?' the man replies 'Yes, about as far as you can go, isn't it?' At the top of the road on one side of the pavement is a long line of kitchen tables with children sitting down or running round eating their tea. Further on a very tinny piano has been brought into the street and is surrounded by children and young people singing *It's a sin to tell a lie*. I now reach the top of the street and enter another main road. I pass another crowded pub where a not-so-young woman dressed in sateen trousers is executing a dance on the pavement.

Birmingham

62. (CO.35.) The bus we wanted seemed to be a long time coming so we crossed the road and boarded a bus to the city-centre.

At Camp Hill we saw a little tea-party in progress, outside a fried-fish shop. There were about twenty small children huddled together round two kitchen tables.

At the corner of Bradford Street we saw an old woman come out of an entry. She was wearing a dress made of union jacks and a r. w. & b. Phrygian cap. She looked like one of the furies of the Revolution except that when she saw us looking at her she beamed in a most friendly fashion and proudly smoothed her dress over her belly.

Halfway down Bradford Street an old man was swaying and waving his hand, by a request stop. He slipped off the kerb but managed to keep on his feet. 'Watch him!' shouted the conductor to himself. And as he helped the old man aboard he said: 'One more step and you're safe.'

The old man fell on to the back seat by the conductor. He had a yellow withered face which emerged from a tall old-fashioned collar.

'Going to ask old Brown to tea?' said the conductor.

The old man replied with a song; at least, he replied in a singing voice, but I couldn't make out any tune and the words were so mumbled as to be inaudible.

While he was singing the conductor said to him: 'Ah, we're a bit too far away from London. But I'm singing *Knees up, Mrs. Brown* as soon as I'm finished here. At five o'clock I'm running.'

The old man was still singing and a little later the conductor sang: *We'll ask old Brown to tea.*

Four smartly-dressed people got on the bus outside the Empire Vaults—A young couple and a middle-aged couple. I took the latter to be the parents of one of the young ones.

The young woman said: 'I've lost my hat, my beautiful hat—look at it.' And she held up a r. w. & b. hat.

'How do you mean—lost it?' asked the other woman. And they all burst into laughter.

The bus was waiting for a big heavy man to cross the road in front of it. Every time he raised a foot it looked as if he would topple over backwards but he got across all right.

'Now then,' said the older woman, and she waved her arms as if conducting, then began to sing, in a powerful voice, *Lily of Laguna*. We all took it up. The conductor smiled indulgently but didn't join in.

We then sang *Nellie Dean* and *Boo Hoo*—and we were at a standstill in New Street by then, in the biggest traffic jam I have ever seen in the city. It was mostly private cars doing the circle to see the decorations, and motor coaches filled with children and adults shouting and waving flags. There was a persistent honking from the motor coaches. The honking was an imitation of hunting horns.

Inside the bus we turned round and laughed at one another as we sang. A. was delighted and said: 'Shall we sing in a bus to-morrow?'

63. 4.10. The police band began to play the Overture from *The Bohemian Girl*. It sounded very finicking and thin in the open air and we went across to Paradise St. to catch a bus to Harborne.

We waited a long time. A 3A came along at last but it was full. More and more people gathered at this stop.

Two fairly well dressed women were standing by me. One of them said: 'Did you see the mess they'd made of her hair? She'll never want a drink again.'

They were joined by another woman who told them that she didn't have to be on until 7. 'I'm in the bar,' she said, 'the cheap side. But I expect I'll be doing anything to-night.'

A little later I heard the tail-end of an incident this woman had been relating. 'Yes,' she said, 'he got a knife out. Everything had been ever so jolly before that. It put a damper on everything.'

Three drunks were waiting at this stop. Two men about thirty and a woman about forty. They were all lower-class. The woman had a big set of false teeth and was very poorly and drably clad, but the men were flashy, with exaggerated waists and a lot of padding in the shoulders of their overcoats. The woman looked drawn and ill. She lolled against the two men with her eyes closed and screamed out *Tipperary.*

One of the men who was very tall repeatedly shouted at her: 'Enjoy yourself!' The other man did not speak once within my hearing, but had a sinister snarling grin on his face all the time.

Every so often the man with the grin would break away with the woman and hurtle down the line of waiting people grabbing on to anyone to keep his balance. He had his arm tightly round the woman's waist and she was simply dragged along like a sack. The tall one would follow them and start mauling the woman—turning her round with his hands on her thighs, then on her breasts, and crooking his arm under her chin and bending her back, and shouting at her: 'Enjoy yourself!'

The crowd was exchanging wary smiles.

The two men looked as if they might be quarrelsome and seemed antagonistic to the other people waiting there. I had to keep shifting my ground for fear they might fall against A. The tall man seemed to sense my uneasiness. He came lurching against me from behind and shouted: 'We're as good as Broad St. We're as good as Hagley Road.' (These streets belong to the 'west-end' of Birmingham and all the buses stopping here were going in that direction.)

Suddenly he grabbed me by the shoulder and said: 'We can enjoy ourselves, can't we?'

I agreed, and he closed his eyes and screamed at the sky: 'Enjoy yourself!'

The woman begged a cigarette off the bus inspector and then got him to give her a light. She inhaled deeply then screeched: 'Are we downhearted? No! Am I downhearted? Yes!' And all three of them went corkscrewing down the line and back again. The tall one shouted: 'If I was Al Capone I'd bump some of these off!'

We had moved away from the kerb towards the shops and when they came back again they stopped and stared at us. Then the tall one said to me: 'I fought in 1914.' He tore open his overcoat and continued: 'I ain't got any decorations up, but I fought for England.' He put his hand on A.'s head and A. grinned up at him. 'This little girl', he said, 'is as good as the woman who was crowned Queen to-day. Ain't she?' He gave me a threatening look as if he would give me a punch on the jaw if I didn't agree. Then he continued: 'She's as good as royalty, the little duck. I fought for England, for the *people* of England. Not royalty.'

The woman leaned over between the tall man and me and chucked A. under the chin. 'Oh, the little dear,' she said. 'She's the one who counts. She'll remember this when we're dead and gone.' Then the man with the snarling grin pulled at her and they reeled away.

The tall man shook hands with L. and said: 'Enjoy yourself duck.' And then with me, saying: 'And you, enjoy yourself, we're the people.' His finger nails were short and broken.

Two dwarfs, one with a humped back, passed by on the opposite side, dressed in r. w. & b. costumes. The hunchback was playing a small accordion.

64. 5.0. We decided not to wait at this stop any longer for a bus. Another 3A had come along full-up. So we crossed the road, as we went I heard the tall man shout: 'You wasn't there, that's why you don't raise your hat you son of a bitch.' He was staring at someone in the crowd and he was holding open his overcoat again.

5.35. We rang the bell at my mother's house in Harborne. My brother-in-law answered the door. He looked depressed. 'The show here has been pitiful,' he said, 'Just like stuck-up Harborne. Didn't even stop the buses for the children's procession. The terraces struck up a cheer but no one took it up. They just gaped at the poor kids.'

They had just had their tea but my mother began to lay the table for us. She said: 'So glad you've come. It's a bit gloomy here.'

She had been to the sanatorium to see W. 'They gave them a tuppenny packet of woodbines and a glass of lemonade for the Coronation,' she said. 'He didn't like to see me coming away. He said: "I expect everyone's going crazy outside." '

My mother also told us that on the bus coming back to Harborne there was a girl about 17 years old who had been backwards and forwards to town three times because she was too drunk to get off. It seemed that this time two well-dressed men took charge of her and said they would take her to their house in H——Rd. give her some tea and then take her home. She lived at Small Heath.

My brother-in-law said: 'The boss is paying the work-people for to-day provided they get in by nine in the morning.'

My mother gave us a boiled egg each for tea. One of them had cracked and some of the white had seeped out and she gave that one to L.

Sussex

65. (CO.16.)

3.0 p.m. Dash in and change at top speed.

3.15. Up to sports and tea—over a mile, mostly uphill. One neighbour looks out of window and says how well broadcast coming over. Neighbouring family offers me a lift half way.

3.35. Arrive. School entrance very finely decorated. Sports field is just opposite. 2 placards with texts have been stuck up outside (unofficially of course!). See younger women's walking race in progress—many shorts, red or white blouses, very muddy legs. Go straight to tent, feeling guilty about late arrival, being on tea committee.

3.45. Children's tea ready, announced by megaphone. 3 long trestle tables in marquee of poles and slack sheets. Children only use $1\frac{1}{2}$ tables. White paper on tables and red-white-and-blue paper down centre of one. One had had to be re-done because rain leaked in. Children very quiet. Didn't start till bread and butter offered to them. We go out and collect strays. I find one 5-year-old stranded by gate very unhappy. Children continue quiet and don't eat big teas, tho' encouraged to do so.

Clear tables after children go, hard at it but stop occasionally to watch race as it passes near front of marquee.

4.30. Tables look nice for first sitting of grown-ups' tea—meat and ham rolls, mince pies, cakes, tea. People mix up well and sit down anywhere, not cliquy according to social differences at all. Quiet. Loudspeaker put on for a few minutes—crowd calling for King to come on to balcony. Don't think our people listened.

Men's one mile caused some cheers and clapping but it is heavy work on muddy field. Rain a little lighter.

66. 5.15. 'Second tea' starts coming in too soon—due to committee not keeping them out with rope or something. We and caterers get anxious about counting the numbers as we pay by number exactly fed. Tent much fuller now. More people coming along as rain is stopping. Real hard unsatisfactory job getting tables cleared, tidied up and set, with people already sitting there, the ground of the marquee becoming steadily more worked up and sticky but all cheerful and no one grumbles. Gradually all served the atmosphere of muddle not dispelled. Proprietress offers me a cup of tea 'in among'—new pot just brewed, and some cakes. Committee about to have tea but, tho' sorry, I have to leave.

5.55. Watch very small children's egg and spoon race, very funny and watchers much amused. Sports are well run by Scoutmaster and retired London teacher (with megaphones) and the headmistress and one or both assistants of village school. All very nice with the children and encourage them to go in for things but nevertheless I hear then and next day some 'too shy'—older ones as well as younger, and competing only with children they have known all school lives.

Beer, S. Devon

67. (CO.1.) When the Children's Tea was announced for 4.30 at the school at the opposite end of the village there was a joyful stampede of children in that direction. The joy of feeding together is a great thing in the lives of these bairns. When we got to the school, there were some of the younger ones in tears due to weariness and hysteria, but they recovered at tea. Coronation mugs were given to all children, even the baby born on the previous day. The oldest man, an old sailor, and the oldest woman (from the almshouses next door) presented the mugs.

A lady of the district (not present) gave each girl a silk handkerchief and each boy a sixpenny piece in the new coinage.

Lancashire

68. (CO.36.) 3 p.m. (Crowds of folk are hanging about street ends. Singing in a pub near by. We pass 2 people playing piano accordions. People seem to be saying little, but mostly drifting slowly down streets or standing at the ends of numerous cul-de-sacs. Children are playing about in desultory fashion. In a few streets and cul-de-sacs women are setting tables. At the end of one elaborately decorated cul-de-sac is an enormous crowd, because a rock garden has been built, and this street has a reputation for 'doing things in style'. An old man and myself suddenly confront each other, and we both smile.)

Old Man. A——

Self. D'you remember me?

O.M. Ah! a should think a do. Y' come on Sunday. Y' were with ——

Self. Yes, that was me father. We were taking photos.

O.M. Ah! I remember.

Self. Well, I've come to take some more, and if you'll let me, I'll come to your tea party. That is if people agree. Pay of course.

O.M. Ah. You'll have to see Mrs. W.

Self. We don't know her.

O.M. I'll take you.

69. (We go to a house half way down street, and over which is a sign 'Moneylender'. We notice nobody else attempts to come. He knocks at an open door. A sad looking woman appears. They talk. She shakes her head.)

No it can't be allowed.

Self. Very well.

(To old man) We are sorry. We wanted to stay.

O.M. Come to our house. I'll tell my daughter.

(In the centre of the street a table say 12 yards long, gaily decorated. All the women in party frocks, men in suits. Old man goes across. He speaks to wife and daughter at doorway. We are beckoned in. On table and sideboard are jellies, blancmanges, iced cakes.)

J. and self. Oh, how nice. These look lovely. This is a real party. How beautifully made!!!

Daughter (aged 28-ish, working class, in long green silk dress). It's all been paid for by Mrs. W. and Dr. ——'s maid has made all these. That's the maid in the blue dress. Dr. —— is a lovely lady.

J. Is that Dr. —— in the blue dress?

Daughter. Yes.

J. She looks a fine woman; aristocratic.

Daughter. Mrs. W.'s paid for all these. Five pounds. It was her husband's dying wish. He's only been dead two months. When he was alive he was that generous. It didn't matter what it was. Jubilee the same, bonfires; he was always ready to give something. He went before his time.

O.M. If he'd been alive it wouldn't have been like this. Twice as good. You wouldn't have known this street.

J. Why, it's beautifully decorated now.

O.M. Not what it would a bin. That generous.

Daughter. Yes. This morning we all went to the cemetery and sang a hymn round his grave. Mrs. W. paid for everyone to go in a chara.

J. Is that why all the children are wearing mauve frocks?

Daughter. Yes she bought one for every girl, and ribbons to match. They'd only shoes to buy.

(They go out into street.)

Self. We are interlopers.

J. Absolutely.

Self. We've been offered tea, so we'll stay for that, and then go. For this we'll have to be hard-faced.

(We wait in house alone.)

70. (I go out. Children take places at table.)

Man. Now all stand for *God Save the King*.

(They sing.)

Now sing grace.

(They sing.)

Now you can all dig in.

(Children eat: women hand food.)

Mother. Will you have a cup of tea now? Sandwiches?

(She goes to another house and brings in sandwiches.)

J. I think we ought to go after this. While you were taking photographs some people came in and went through into a back room. I overheard the mother say 'I don't know how long they're staying'.

Self. I wonder what else they said.

Mother (reappearing). Don't be frightened to eat.

J. It's all very beautifully arranged.

Mother. Yes. Shall we be seeing the photos sometime?

Self. Certainly. I'll come down with them.

Mother. When?

Self. After Whit. The week after Whit.

71. (People come in from back room.)

Mother. This is a cousin of mine and his son.

Cousin (a man aged 40-ish, working class). We don't often come. But to-day . . . I expect you young ladies'll make a bit out of this.

Self. No, we aren't being paid.

Cousin. Don't tell me. Nobody does owt for nowt.

Self. No, really!

Cousin. Well, if you're not being paid for coming, you'll send it to a paper and be paid for what you write.

Self. We're here because we want to be.

Cousin. No. . . .

Self. Yes, for love.

Cousin. Nobody does anything for love. Nobody does anything if there isn't money in it.

Self. Anyway we're going now.

Cousin. What about the photos?

Mother. They're coming with them after Whit week.

(We took our leave. Thank you's and Good afternoons.)

(At the end of the cul-de-sac is an altercation between a man slightly drunk and the residents. He wishes to come in the street, but they refuse him.)

J. and self. Glad to be out of this. So'm I. What time is it? 4.15.

Self. I feel blazing about that man.

J. As though you can't do anything without money.

Hertford

72. (CO.18.) Balls Park celebrations, Hertford. From second hand information.

4–4.30. *Children's tea*. After the tea the children began throwing plates, cups and saucers, and practically everything was smashed. Finally they tore up the table cloths.

Damage to property.

7 p.m. onwards. The caterer lost 8 dozen glasses, the Cricket Club 4 dozen glasses. Six cricket club deck chairs were missing the next day, and were most probably thrown on to

the bonfire (200–300 yards away). Other chairs were damaged, and scattered all over Balls Park under the trees.

Hertford

73. (CO.26.) During the afternoon a free tea was given for the school children in two marquees. I got the following information the day after—The tea was uneatable and undrinkable—the kids started hurling their cardboard flasks all over the place—cups and chairs were smashed and finally the table cloths were torn to shreds. The committee in charge of this apparently were not there—they had gone to see the Coronation. Also mothers of children were behind the marquees pinching cakes etc., as hard as they could.

Birmingham

74. (CO.37.) Between 6.50 and 6.55 in a well-to-do side street. Saw a group of about 8 people laughing and chatting, three highly dressed up, and found it was the guessing-weight-of-cake party. They proceeded towards a man at his gate about 30 yards away, who wore no decorations and was dressed in cap and working coat. He grinned broadly as though rather nervous about the whole thing, and began conversation by shouting at that distance.

A short way along the street, a boy of about six was walking with his mother. He held a decoration in his hand, and called, 'Mummy, I'm looking by the trees, because I found this one by a tree.'

Later I passed a sedate elderly couple discussing loose pieces of coloured paper blown about the road.

Note. In these better-class streets decorations appeared to suit the houses, 70 per cent. to 80 per cent. of people were wearing paper hats, and street games were organized: three-legged race, blowing up balloons, dancing to pianos on pavement. Adults appeared to welcome the opportunity to play like children.

7.5. Entered Digby Park, to see two groups of 50 or 60 each in possession. A man about 25 played with dog on grass over a piece of paper decoration. According to regulation, dog should have been on a lead.

7.27. Approaching poorer quarter. Observed man emerge from a public house unable to walk straight. A woman coming the other way, with push-chair and two children, appeared disgusted, and shepherded the children past him.

7.30 approx. commenced to rain, and was still raining at 10.30 when I returned home. This put an end to street games.

In this district the houses have no front gardens, are dirty, of dark-red brick against which decorations appear incongruous. I passed two women on a deserted street who were gossiping about a third person, of male sex. They stopped talking when about 12 yards away, although I did not look directly at them, and began again immediately they had passed.

75. 8.10. I observed a drunk going round corner of Miles St., a corner which is railed. He staggered continually across the seven or eight-foot space between the rail and garden fences. A boy about five blowing a trumpet in a doorway stopped to watch him with troubled eyes, then ran inside. Two girls, the elder about 11, came out unconcernedly from a house right into the man's path without noticing him. He pulled up and succeeded in passing behind them, while they went on without showing any sign of seeing him.

8.15 in Miles Street a number of people had gathered in an archway, and several were jigging up and down to what sounded like piano and drum. A man on the outskirts, wearing a paper-blue hat in the style of the French Revolution, was banging a tambourine on his knee.

8.35. Proceeding up Ravenhurst St., where a rope was stretched across the road. (Have heard that some streets applied for permission to close the road, but were told permission could not be granted, police would not see anything that did happen.) Police car approached containing two capped officers, presumably superintendents. They smiled as if enjoying a joke, and turned down another street. Almost at once another car containing two constables approached from within the roped-off portion. I lifted rope for them to proceed.

Leeds

76. (CL.65. Italian.) I walked on. Newspaper vendors were shouting their papers. A young mother dragged her six-year-old son along the crowded pavement. He was mumbling something.

'Now keep quiet, Coronation doesn't come every day.' Again she shook him by the arm. 'Coronation doesn't come every day, you know.'

On one of the side streets, a young couple parked their perambulator in the middle of the sidewalk and stopped to read the results of the Coronation procession in London.

Toward 7.30 I made my way to Woodhouse Moor. The rain had come again. The few people who were gathered around the bandstand were preparing to go home as the band played its last number for the first half of the programme. I walked through the park for a few minutes and not finding anything of interest to see or hear, I turned into a lane nearby that led to the cemetery. Here I read the inscriptions on several tombs and thought how different Italian burial places were. Night was approaching, I was chilly, I turned and walked home.

Lancashire

77. (CO.36.) 7.15 p.m.
Self (to bus conductor). To where the pageant is.
Conductor. Don't know.
Elderly woman. (Lower middle class or upper working class.) It's on the field by the side of the church. We're going.

Self. Oh thanks. Looking forward to it?

E.W. Yes, we are, yes. . . .

(On arrival at pageant field.)

Self. Is it going to keep fine?

Amateur Ticket Seller (at entrance to pageant field). I don't know. I'll pray for you, but I sometimes get the wrong wavelength.

J. Isn't it disgusting, 6d. to stand on this damp field. I think someone ought to complain. When all these seats are vacant you'd think they'd let us sit down. I feel thoroughly annoyed. Just look at these children. That man has an impertinence to suggest they should sit on this damp grass. They're awfully good too. Look how still they're sitting. Even the little ones.

Pageant Master (through loudspeaker). Very fitting on this red letter day that the history of this village should be told in pageant. Preparations have been going forward since October last. P——, like a young man who looks forward to promotion, so we too, look forward to furthering our civic dignity, and becoming a non-county borough.

Tender grateful thanks to all who help to make it a success. All profit will be given to local charities.

All who are here to-night will be asked to give it the advertisement it deserves. Ask your friends to come on Friday and Saturday evenings.

(Introductory music in progress.)

J. Isn't it astonishing what people will stand. 2/- for those seats, and all those people standing around looking at empty places.

Nobody seems to be doing anything about it.

You can't get anybody to say anything.

Why don't people complain I wonder.

(The announcement of the King's intention to give a broadcast speech calls forth the following comment, given by man, apparently 35-ish, black coated worker, suburban dweller.)

And they can't even give him a clap in. (He commences to clap.)

78. (Overheard conversation among a group of about nine youths and girls approx. 17–22 years.)

Youth (seeing Father Time approach). Someone's wearing the sheet. Go on. All clap.

Another. Deserted world this.

Another. Very good, what we've seen so far.

Another. If we look like a lettuce, will they lettuce in those seats.

Others. It's an invasion.

Have a toffee.

Ooh. . . .

Have one on me.

Don't take any more than one.

(As local 'St. George' canters about the field.)·

Youth. That's 'Lady Maureen Stanley' if you want to know.

Youth. They're playing the Dead March.

Others. Gooseberry.

Knock, knock.

Here's a policeman, so you'll stop where you are now.

Eh up! It's a policeman. What you playing at?

Wish I hadn't on an open shirt this weather.

Draw somebody.

Here's a pencil.

What?

Anybody in sight.

Draw the band.

(I move elsewhere.)

(As 'cave' man and 'cave' woman squabble over large bone.)

Working class mother. What are they? I don't know.

(As 'prehistoric beasts' appear.)

Didn't know there was ever anything in —— like that.

What are these?

Arabs?

I don't understand it.

Daughter (aged about 11 years). They're Druids. We have it at school.

W.C.M. They ought to have some one telling us what it's all about.

Self. Yes, it would be helpful.

W.C.M. I think 1d. for children and 3d. for us would have been enough. Fancy 2/- for those seats. And they're damp too. How do they expect people with families to come and pay all that. It'll keep folk away. They'd get a lot more people if they only charged 3d. and 1d.

How do they expect people to support the cause.

It's slow.

It's time we'd something to eat.*

Glasgow

79. (CO.40.) We lounge about in the sun by Loch Lomond, and have milk since we can't make tea, and return to Glasgow at 9 p.m.

The town is in a ferment. Buildings floodlit, and special trees planted in George Square, centre of the city.

The Municipal Buildings are festooned with cheap-looking red velvet. LONG LIVE THE KING! says the Socialist administration.

Up High Street, oldest and poorest section of the city,

---

*'In spite of a cold evening and the Coronation celebrations all over the district, a goodly number of people were present to see the first performance of the P—— Historical Pageant on Coronation Day. The pageant itself was somewhat late in starting, and was further delayed by the King's broadcast speech. As the programme advanced, the players and all taking part behind the scenes became more accustomed to the vastness of their stage, and the pageant was brought in its final stages, to a very successful close and was warmly appreciated by the large audience.' (*P—— and W—— Guide*, 14.5.37.)

crowds are running about with no apparent aim or purpose. There are a great many drunks. Women in shawls and girls are rubbing their faces with 'make-up' that is used for branding cattle in the markets. Streaked with blue and red they look like Maoris, or painted savages in a war-dance. They seem capable of anything.

Small gangs in side streets are lighting fires that may become definitely dangerous in congested areas like these.

The atmosphere is electric. The people seem to feel that tonight the police are powerless. They can do what they like.

'Workers in our factory' a man tells me, 'have ordered sixteen barrels of beer. How they expect to get them back to work on Thursday I don't know.'

'The whole thing's been badly planned' another thinks, meaning the Coronation and Whitsun holidays should have been combined.

So to bed, at 11 p.m. when scuffles were developing in various parts of the city—for no reason at all, except excess of spirits, or reaction to oppressive surroundings and an imprisoning environment.*

*'Hundreds of people who live outside Glasgow found themselves stranded in the early hours of this morning. The good nature of the sightseers, which had been a feature of the congestion in the centre of the city, disappeared later when it was realized by them that they would be unable to catch buses for home. There followed a wild scramble for the night tramcars, but they were unable to cope with the hundreds of people who loudly voiced their opinion of the transport arrangements.

One of the passengers told an *Evening Citizen* reporter that the scenes were worse than anything he had witnessed on the occasion of a big football match. Women screamed as they struggled to get near the tramcars, and many received kicks and bruises in the scramble.

The firemen had their busiest night for many years. Between 6.30 p.m. and 12.30 this morning they answered no fewer than 40 calls to bonfires. Many of the fires had been set up on dangerous sites, and they had to be extinguished by the firemen. Others were lit on tarmac roads, to which considerable damage was done. Much of the material for the fires was obtained by raids on buildings marked for demolition, and also wooden fences.' (*Glasgow Evening Citizen*, 13.5.37.)

Aberdeen

80. (CO.22.) 10 p.m. Had a snack before going out. Discussed events of the day.

10.30 p.m. Left for firework display. Passed Town Hall and Marischal College both brilliantly floodlit, the college looking like a fairy castle. We proceeded through old Aberdeen working class districts at which wife exclaimed 'It is awful that people have to live in these hovels'. People here were out in the streets looking at the fireworks which could be seen down towards the sea beach. Then passed old King's College—an old pile—also floodlit to great advantage. The stone crown on the top was particularly beautiful. We stopped here a little while to admire it. Next proceeded to esplanade to see what remained of the fireworks. The display was good but not very outstanding. We had probably missed the best of them. The esplanade was lined with cars parked on each side, and three lines of moving traffic. The display ceased at 11.30 p.m. so we wended our way homewards, but, owing to the density of the traffic this was difficult. We arrived about 12 midnight.

Prestwick

81. (CO.2.) 9.30. I go out. About 2,000 people at Prestwick Cross waiting for torchlight procession. Four or five bagpipe players intoxicated. Scores of buses bound for Glasgow, many of them carrying intoxicated men and women. People in buses singing and shouting. One or two narrow escapes from collisions between private cars. Shopgirls and typists with 'boy' friends. Many of the young men bare headed, though evening is now decidedly cold. Five sets of illuminations go on at 9.45. Admiring comments from crowd. These illuminations are amid trees. Men and women motor cyclists with 'crash' helmets come up from the motor-cycle races on the shore. Several women in crowd make derisive comments about women motor cyclists. 'Look at her.' 'Is it twopence to look at her!' Motor cyclists go into hotel for a drink. Young man and two girls (brightly but cheaply dressed to resemble film stars: working class) on way to dance. Everyone cheerful.

82. At 9.50 torchlight procession arrives. Headed by local pipers. There are about 200 children, young men and girls—working class—carrying torches, singing a marching song, and shouting. At least six torches are dropped. Shouts from crowd. 'Someone'll get burned.' Boys and girls walk on, almost over burning torches on ground. They blaze for about a minute. People block a road and have to get out of the way of motor. There are now about 4,000 people making for the shore. Many start to run. Cars and people close together. Crowd breaks on to golf course and streams towards bonfire. (*Note*. Up till now I have not heard a single remark about the Coronation). Police have to move back crowd. Young working class youths make 'wisecracks' at a policeman. 'You take up space yersel'.' (I cannot remember these 'wisecracks'. Four or five were being shouted at the same time.) Enthusiasm when the torchlight procession climbs the slope singing *Blaze Away* (two-step) and arrives beneath the bonfire at 10.20. With shouts and cheers the torches are thrown on the pile. Several torches are badly aimed and land in or near crowd but no one is burned. Great flames shoot up from bonfire. The embankment catches fire but nothing can be done owing to the heat. Grass burned; no real harm done. Young boys of 8 or 9 run about near the flames. Several intoxicated youths begin to dance and sing Scotch songs. Torchlight processionists sing *God Save the King*. There is a pandemonium of noise, shouts, laughs and songs. Weather dry and cold.

83. Some good remarks:
'Whaur's Mrs. Simpson noo!' (very few people laugh at this).
'The wee barrel's sticking it well' (reference to barrel near top of bonfire).

'Gie us *The Bonnie Wells o' Wearie*' (laughs from crowd).

'Good evening!' (intoxicated youths to young girls).

One girl says 'Don't get funny'.

'Biggest blaze I've seen' (it is certainly a monster blaze).

Small bottles thrown at bonfire by working class youths. A squib is thrown into crowd. Three working class girls are frightened. 'I've had enough of this!' No remarks about Coronation. At 10.50 I leave bonfire. Many people are returning home. Roads choked with cars and pedestrians. A lady says, 'I've never seen Prestwick like this!' People speak as if they had enjoyed the day.

The Day in Central Europe

84. In contrast to the day in England, the day recorded by this Observer in Vienna is almost free from the influence, both direct and indirect, of the Coronation. In the evening, just before 8 o'clock, she is reminded by reading the papers of the events taking place in England, but it is fairly clear that normal life was not seriously disturbed by them so far as the Viennese were concerned. It is just as well to remember that large as is the area over which the Coronation is of paramount importance, yet once over the national boundary and the spell is broken.

85. (CL.76. Medical student, female, 23, Swiss-evangelical, single.) (Translated from the German.)

7 a.m. Woke up or rather was woken by my friend, who said: 'You must get up, if you want to get away early.' I lay a few more minutes and blinked and was annoyed that the sky was grey and not blue and that it was so hard to keep one's eyes open. Then we had a short discussion which of us should get up first and suddenly I jumped out of bed. My temper

suddenly got much better. My friend didn't want to shave, although he was no longer clean-shaven, so we had a brief wrangle about washing. Then he read to me out of the newspaper, still in his pyjamas, while I told him to get dressed. In the end, naturally, he was dressed before me. While we dressed we drank our cocoa and ate a radish together, my friend also ate his roll and butter, but I took mine with me. Then we went off together to town. In the street we bought another paper, then in town we separated, and I telephoned a friend who had fallen ill the previous evening. I found he was still in bed, and promised him I would come and see him before lunch. Then I went to the dentistry. Then as quickly as possible through the general hospital to the surgery lecture. On the way I met a student whom I knew by sight. He seized on me eagerly by the arm and said, 'Do you know that I have passed my exam. in children's diseases, with distinctions.' I congratulated him and asked him what questions he had. He had had to examine an infant with tabes and cutaneous eruptions, etc., and that it had been very difficult. Then he said all at once: 'You look so nice and pretty, and you have got much fitter.' I laughed and we parted. I thought how in all men the small boy keeps popping up.

86. The lecture was very crowded and oppressively hot. At the end I had to squeeze my way out, so as to reach call-over in time. Then I went to see a business friend I know, whose business is near the hospital. She had taken it over a short time before, and had made it all beautifully neat and clean, and she herself is always so clean and tidy that I specially enjoy visiting her. Also everything is green in her shop and she always dresses in green clothes. She gave me a pamphlet which her sister had sent me, on social conditions.

Then I bought biscuits and rusks at a cake shop for my friend who is suffering from indigestion, and went to visit him by tram. He told me about a book on Napoleon III which he

has just read. I examined him, took his temperature, told him
not to smoke and went off. Then I went home for lunch. All
the time I was travelling or on the tram I read a frightfully
interesting book, that I simply couldn't put down: Willi
Bredel, *The Test*. It is about concentration camps in Germany. At home I found a letter from England and a weekly
paper. I turned the radio on, then noticed that the earth was
disconnected. It worked all the same. It was the usual midday concert. I sat at the window in the sun and read and
thought how nice and warm it was for once in a way, quite
like summer. Then mother came in and my two brothers and
we fed: mushroom soup, ham and green peas and salad and
stewed rhubarb. We talked about the food because we
thought a meal without meat and with only stewed fruit to
follow was too little.

Then I buried myself in my book again and read for two
hours without interruption, in spite of pangs of conscience.

87. Then I had to leave home quickly, to meet a friend in
town, who was just going for five weeks to a Czechoslo-
vakian spa, and wanted to say good-bye. She works for the
telephone and telegraph department and is very capable. We
met in front of the Urania and I talked to her about her work
and said that she must look after herself well so that the cure
would really do her good. She gave me a lot of interesting
news about her job, etc. Then off I ran to the University Sur-
gical Hospital where I had a practical. We were at the
casualty ward and examined the cases that came in. In the
one hour there were a butcher's assistant who had run a
shaving deep under his nail, a little girl who had had her
head hurt by a stone that someone had thrown, a soldier with
a broken arm, a tourist who had been brought by ambulance
to Vienna from a trip to the mountains with a broken leg, and
an old lady who had fallen down in the street and broken her
arm.

88. Then I went slowly back through the town, looked at the marvellous lilac and chestnuts which were now in full bloom, went through the city and met by accident a German Catholic friend with whom I had a short conversation. Then I had a rendezvous with a man from the Institute of Statistics in a café. As he was late, I read the papers and remembered for the first time that to-day is Coronation Day. I read the detailed reports in the papers and felt sorry for those taking part and for all who had to be in London that day and felt glad that the bus strike was still on, as in this way the ghost of tradition had to face the modern world a little.

At 8 o'clock I went to another meeting, held by the League of Nations Union. The subject: Are armaments economic? The lecturer made a sharp attack on the illusion that armaments are good for trade. Armaments are in every respect a waste of money.

At the lecture I met my friend and others, with whom we discussed the probable arrival of Maurice Freres in Vienna and about Mr. Butler of the I.L.O., who was due to speak at the L.N.U. on May 24. Then my friend and I went home together and ate a cold supper consisting of sandwiches and various kinds of cheese. Then he wrote out his French exercises, I read the papers and at midnight we went to bed.

Local Celebrations (ii)

Belfast

89. (CO.34.) 9 a.m. to Midday. As I walked from the station into the sunny street the first thing that drew my attention were the revolvers worn by the police; next the placards outside the newsagents—the *Irish Times* said 'Exciting scenes in Belfast', the *Irish Independent*, 'Rioting in Dublin.' I expected to see some disturbance before the day was over but at the moment everything looked very peaceful, there were only a few people about, an occasional tramcar clattered along the cobbled street, the policemen stood indolently with their hands behind them.

I walked down a main street looking for a café for breakfast. I passed two or three very disreputable and dirty-looking places but they seemed to be the only ones open. I came finally to the City Hall in Donegal Square. All around the square the high façades were draped with bunting, bedecked with flags and crude pictures of their majesties. The trees were a fresh green, the lawns around the City Hall strangely unspoilt; there were colourful beds of tulips, wall-flowers, forget-me-nots, and before each window of the building there was a mass of flowers.

There were holiday makers seated waiting in charabancs and as I came noisily along with my nailed boots there was a nudging and peering. Still in search of a café I began to return by another route. I asked a policeman if he was able to show me a place, but upon my suggestion he agreed that the railway restaurant was probably the only one open. As I walked back, however, I passed a café which had just opened, the girls were still sweeping the floor and cleaning the tables. I ordered tea, sausages, fried egg, bread, butter and jam, and while the waitress was laying the table I asked her what was happening in Belfast that day.

'Oh, the Coronation, you know,' she answered.

'Yes, I know, but is there a procession or anything else?'

'No. There will be some bands and music.'

'When?'

'I don't know, they will just come out and play when they feel like it. There is no special procession.'

90. After breakfast I walked back to Donegal Square, there were more people about now, they seemed to be just strolling about aimlessly, waiting for trams, and enjoying the warm sun.

The attendant at a public convenience told me that there was to be a procession at 2.15 but he did not know of what it would consist.

I sat in a seat in the square, my neighbours were mainly old men wrapped in dowdy overcoats and growling spasmodically to each other. I continued to read *War and Peace* which I had started at breakfast time. The sun made me sleepy. I was only half-conscious of the things going on around me. I heard the quarter hours strike on a clock close by, there was the continual racket of tramcars, the ceaseless roar of motor traffic. I was repeatedly roused by children selling Coronation badges and pieces of ribbon, there were scores of them about the streets and periodically one of them came into the City Hall gardens and pestered all the people on the seats.

Until 12.45 I basked in the sun. I was not hungry for I had breakfasted late, and having decided to wait and see the procession I had still some time to pass. I went to a small café near the docks and had an ice cream and some cakes. When I entered the wireless was wheezing incomprehensibly something about the Coronation celebrations, but after a few minutes somebody switched it over to dance music. About 1.45 I returned to Donegal Square to my seat. Soon a bagpipe band came marching past dragging with it a horde of followers. They went round to the back of City Hall. Then there was another bagpipe band with its accompanying mob. There followed four other bands at short intervals, two accordion bands, a fife and drum band, and a silver band. In the meantime at one side of the square members wore in addition orange cuffs, some had the privilege of carrying unsheathed swords on their shoulders, others little spears and banners.

91. When it struck 2.30 I was becoming impatient at wasting so perfect an afternoon in the crowded centre of a city. I

thought regretfully of the Mourne mountains and decided to leave unless something happened very shortly.

Playing about on the grass were little groups of dirty children. One small child, clothed only in a straight coloured dress, was trying to stand on its head and displaying its naked body to a seemingly inattentive crowd. Another little boy had saliva running continuously from his mouth, the front of his blue jersey was soaking wet, his eyes were curiously screwed up, but the other children romped about with him apparently not noticing his peculiarities, and he unprotestingly submitted to their buffetings and pushing. Some of the accordion bandsmen lay on the grass, one of them softly playing dance tunes. Almost everybody making any attempt to look respectable was cheaply and flashily dressed.

Just before three, when in my impatience I had gone to ask a policeman where I could catch a bus for Ballynahinch, the procession started. It consisted entirely of the bands and the Orangemen. I asked a man who stood next to me what L.O.L. meant on the orange collars. He said he didn't know, he was a stranger.

'So am I. Where are you from then?'

'London. So I don't know what all this is about. It's damn silly at any rate.'

'Why didn't you stay in London?'

'It's been bad enough there all the last week, what with the bus strike and everything else. I'm jolly glad to get out of it.'

92. (CO.30. *A sanitary inspector.*)

At 9.50 I went into the general office in order to await any cases of infectious diseases or nuisances which may arise during the day (inspector on duty) and chatted with the clerk on duty. He had a Coronation souvenir paper and read aloud the heading 'Smiles that charm all subjects' and added in a disappointed tone 'they have failed to charm me'. This amused me and I chuckled for some time. The food inspector on duty came in and said that he had hung the red flag out of his window. At 10.30 the chief came in and the clerk was very self-conscious in his presence. He blushed deeply and was obviously ill at ease. When the chief left the clerk expressed his opinion, in an insulting manner, that the chief was a nuisance and better out of the way. The clerk then started talking about babies and how they urinated on one's knee. From this we started talking about babies' urine and thence to dietetics. A workman remarked that the King and Queen would be a long time without a meal to-day and the clerk said, amid laughter, that they would take a snack in their pockets. From this evolved facetious and imaginative remarks on the crowning ceremony.

At 12.30 the meteorologist came in together with a girl friend, whom I know. Whilst he was writing up his report the girl friend engaged in conversation with me. She talked about her holidays and travel generally. There was no mention of the Coronation.

At 1.30 the clerk came back and I went to lunch. On my way home I saw some soldiers on parade and felt ill at ease when I remembered that as a child I was very excited to see them. Indeed the sight to-day seemed a nauseating affair. When I reached home the wireless was thundering *God Save the King* which left me unmoved.

Cambridge

93. (CO.20.) 10.30 a.m. Went along to Trinity to join up with other sellers of the *Daily Worker*. Passed the market place where a small crowd was listening to a sermon which was being relayed by loudspeaker from an adjoining church. The voice coming over the loudspeaker was very indistinct, and I could not make out what was being said. The *Worker* and pamphlet sellers were organized in small groups of about half-a-dozen and the leader of each squad kept in touch with the organizer by telephone. I was sent along to Jesus Green to

join H.'s group with reinforcements of pamphlets (the three pamphlets in the 'Plain Man's Guide to the Coronation' series issued by the Communist Party). I sold a dozen of these pamphlets in a very short while (not more than 20 minutes). Some of those who bought them probably thought they were programmes of the local festivities. One girl bought one and said (a little archly): 'You're all a lot of nuisances.' One little man wearing glasses and a stiff collar took a look at one and said unpleasantly: 'What's it all about? Anti-British stuff, is it?' Then I got some *Daily Workers* and started selling them. Some of the other sellers had said they didn't want the pamphlets because it was the *Workers* that they were selling like hot cakes. I found that the *Workers* sold all right at first, but after a bit I couldn't get rid of any more—the crowd seemed to have reached saturation point. One foreigner (he looked like a Turk, I thought) to whom I had sold a pamphlet earlier on, stopped me and asked for the two others in the series. Then as the crowds began to disperse (this was about 11.45) we were given a large number of leaflets to distribute headed 'May 12th, 1937. The National Government presents . . .' All the passers-by took the leaflets very readily and I must have distributed several hundreds in about three quarters of an hour. One elderly woman cried out 'Up the Reds!' and one undergraduate shouted from an over-crowded sports car: 'When's the next war going to start?'

About 12.45 I went back to Trinity and handed over the money I had taken. There were already over 400 pennies on the table though many of the sellers had not come in. One of those there said that at the Jubilee the pamphlets had sold very much better in the afternoon than in the morning. Walking back to lunch I met an old lady wheeling another old lady in a bath-chair, and heard the one in the bath-chair reading aloud slowly from the leaflet I had been distributing: 'Speed-up in Industry: 5 men now do the work that it took 6 men to do in 1932.'

Yorkshire

94. (CO.3.) 10 a.m. Roads empty. The only sign of Coronation in the wide swept dale were one or two grim looking old flags on towers, who'd seen wind and rain before to-day. Went by Ilkley's favourite moorside walk—the Tarn of 'Bout 'at' fame. They ducks were there, and swans nesting on the path, with hurdles to keep folk off. One old lady with a bun, a dog, and sensible shoes was in sight. Then came a boy of 13 with two spaniels, whom he tugged back from the swans while asking me to see if the eggs were hatched out yet. He said 'It's frightfully awkward for me because I seem to have left their collars at home'. Discussed cameras and live stock.

Went on towards bandstand, where 19 small boys watched one territorial, four guns, and a lot of tarpaulins. Asked a child 'What's this?'—'Guns!'

'Whose?'—'Territorials.'

'Camping here?'—'No, ours.'

A more accommodating youngster chipped in 'They are firing them at dinner time.' Others volunteered 'Firing twenty-one guns' 'Them as use the drill hall.'

Knots of working-class men began appearing. Two boy scouts with souvenir programmes greeted with 'Left, right, 'shun!' from the onlookers. 30 territorials stodged up the hill toward the guns.

Shop window labelled 'Empire of India' full of toy lions 6/11 to 2/11. Broadcasting from a shop, no one listening. One Holiday Girl in trousers caused much mirth.

Bought programme from very polite little scout.

11. Went through grim rows of Ilkley's back cottages to see a dear old woman who used to be our cook. She lay dying with the London broadcast on, and her husband (going blind) nursing her. I sat with them, and they talked.

She: 'I didn't think I'd live for the Coronation. I'm so tired, I don't want to wait.'

He: 'I'm 80 years old. I remember the last Coronation. Those were good days.'

Noon. Twenty-one guns: someone else pretty near had some guns too—Ben Rhydding from the sound. Wet Weather hooter—so the sports and bathing beauties and processions are off.

Montreux

95. (CO.11. American.) The streets seem very quiet, like Sunday. We meet one or two groups of self-conscious schoolmistress types of people, with heavy, thick, tri-colour ribbon favours. A few schoolgirls. The flag on the Dutch club is the French flag. A few English flags, but not to notice, as the town is often decorated for foreign visitors and various diplomatic delegations. The 'Zermatt' herb advt. has been replaced in the principal pharmacy by an 'Eno' fruit salt herald. I noticed that, a day or two ago, and all here were amused. The round plaques of gilt-covered chocolate G. and E. medallions are all sold out in the chief confectioner.

96. (CL.56.) My mother and I went to see the decorations planned by the Town Corporation in the main streets of North Shields. These consisted of garlands strung from painted poles on either side of the streets, and being simple and dignified were pleasing to see. As there was a constant drizzle of rain, few people were standing in the square, and the open air service was as brief as possible. An expected procession of the corporation officials back to the town hall did not take place, so the small number of people who had lined the route in anticipation quickly moved off. There was a little disappointment at this, but not much.

Near Croydon

97. (CO.15.) Noon–3 p.m. We came back through the park; there were not so many people listening to the service

as I had thought. Only about 50. In the park were 4 marquees, 2 large roundabouts and 1 small, 2 coconut shies, a fortune teller's booth—granddaughter of 'Gypsy Lee'. In a sunken part was a platform for a band in an enclosure railed off by wooden palings for dancing. There was a kind of square stage affair, carrying decorations round the top of 4 poles, one at each corner. I didn't realize then what it was for. I discovered afterwards that it was a bandstand. There was a railed off enclosure for a fire brigade display, and another for a bonfire: a tall pile of brushwood was ready. Outside the park there were very few people about. I went into a tobacconist to buy some cigarettes. The man said: 'Better than we'd expected.' I said: 'Yes, it was terribly wet yesterday.' No further comment. There were sea scouts selling programmes of Carshalton festivities at one of the entrances to the park. I bought one. 6d. Nobody seemed to be buying them.

Suffolk

98. (CO.45.) Just before noon I go up to the Castle (a cement-bound ruin with a caretaker's room, which can be climbed for a small fee) where perhaps twenty people have collected in drizzling rain to drink a glass of free beer to the health of the King and Queen. The local M.P. is haranguing the small crowd from a platform, leaning earnestly over the iron balustrade at the entrance to the castle. We are too far off to hear what he is saying until he is about to give three cheers for the King. Two men are hurrying round among the people, filling the Coronation mugs (which they have prudently brought with them) with beer from large enamel jugs. Miss B. and I have brought nothing to drink out of, so a local farmer provides us with blue glasses, which are on a table where the prizes for the morning's ploughing match are laid out; three copper kettles of different sizes, and a lemonade jug with six glasses—the woman's prize.

People stand about dismally in raincoats, fumbling with

their mugs; several have rosettes of red, white and blue. The one rollicking figure is Mrs. S., a village woman of 65 or so, who has a Coronation scarf round her neck, another round her hat, an over-dress of crinkled paper in red, white and blue panels. All round her large umbrella are hung Coronation pompoms.

Guns are heard somewhere in the distance, and we drink the health of the King, then the Queen, then the young Princesses and the rest of the Royal Family. The wife of the local member comes up to Miss B. with a look of personal enthusiasm and relief, and says ringingly, 'Well, he's crowned and that's all that matters.'

Cotswolds

99. (CO.7.) We eventually started about 12.20. The country was misty, still and very bright green. Lanes very quiet, a few girls walking in groups and boys cycling desultorily in circles. Worcester unusually empty. Girls walking in pairs with tricolour ribbons in their hair or comic hats, and most of them had had their hair newly set.

I was still upset with calomel and my period, and we had to stop at a pub at Pershore. In the bar parlour the letters 'G' and 'E' had had 'ordon' and 'velyn' added in blue chalk. R. noticed that here half pint glasses are called sticks. Streets quite deserted, being lunch time, though someone was decorating a lorry.

Some miles on we saw a small crowd in a meadow watching what appeared to be a large corpse burning, tied by head and feet, presumably a cow being roasted whole. Later we stopped to buy asparagus at a roadside stall—125 heads for 3/6. The old man said he had several acres of it. The yield had not been very good this year, but he was not sorry as the traffic had been much less than usual during the last few weeks. Apparently he never sent it to town. We ate sandwiches as we went along.

Evesham was very quiet; Broadway was full of parked cars, as usual on holidays, and here we were stopped by a procession of serious children in fancy dress, escorted by a nervous, untidy teacher. After them came private cars and decorated tradesmen's vans, advertising their goods. The crowd had fixed smiles and occasionally cheered, sometimes for reasons not apparent, but particularly when a lorry full of people in fancy dress, with labels in ink on white calico 'Stars of the Great Broadway', 'Come up and see me sometime.'

I noticed how very countrified country people still look. Even lads in smart overcoats and girls with neat hair have fresh coloured, vacuous faces, and the old women shaped like Mrs. Noah have beehive black straw hats.

Outside Bourton-on-the-Hill we stopped to steal stone from a quarry, and collected a sackful. People walking along the road, some carrying milk cans, shouted and guffawed to each other, but took no notice of us. Bourton was quiet as usual.

At Moreton-in-the-Marsh they were forming up for a procession and we saw groups of girls in fancy dress and people standing about watching them, and others arriving in cars. We met a young man coming into town dressed like an old lady in bonnet and beaded cloak.

At Chipping Norton they were having something that looked like school sports with pegs in a field. We met three old men coming from the workhouse with knives and forks in newspaper.

100. (CO.12. English.) 3 p.m. Went to Montreux again, drove slowly past English church. Girl Guides and Boy Scouts were ranged along the road, waiting to march in to the service. Many English were crowding into church. There were a number of cars outside, including some belonging to Swiss people, as far as I could gather, owners of large villas or those whose work brings them in contact with the English. Walked

down main road and noted that some of the obviously tourist shops had flags out over postcard stands and in one watch shop, they had an arrangement of flags, a globe, photographs of King and Queen, souvenir boxes with the King and Queen, etc., underneath. Went round other streets but all was absolutely calm. Chauffeur to whom I spoke (Swiss) asked me if I had news of the bus strike.

101. (CO.25.) 2 p.m. Washed and left the house with my friend. We walked down a hill and remarked that the air was good and that the rain had ceased. We travelled to Leeds by tramway past many once gaily-decorated but now bedraggled streets. In one street we saw the housewives endeavouring to make good the damage of the storm. A deaf and dumb couple were gesticulating in front of us. Many people bent on pleasure, I thought, and well-dressed, boarded the tram. Leeds was crowded with people.

We observed the decorations. Many of the adorned buildings attracted my attention. Some were decorated in restrained and pleasing schemes whilst others were riotous with colour. We were surprised to find the Town Hall open to the public. At about 3.5 p.m. we joined the throng and passed through the corridors and lobbies. I was attracted to the City Court. Some middle-aged women had seated themselves in the comfortable chairs in the Barristers' Room. Scenery had been erected in the front of the organ in the concert hall in readiness for a performance of Edward German's *Merry England*. People were quiet. Then along to the Civic Hall in front of which rhododendron bushes had been placed. There were lights in the large windows, gentlemen in evening dress were to be seen, and persons whom I thought must be important emerged from the large doors and entered cars.

102. (CO.21.) The day has been dull, with slight rain about 11 and after 4. A wonderful quiet day, to St. Bees Head

lighthouse, mostly by road going, but returning mostly by fields. Passing through small villages of Rottington and Sandwith, hardly any people were to be seen, and beyond the sound of an occasional wireless set, all was quiet.

Shepherds seemed friendly, even when we were trespassing (footpaths seemed erratic): supposed to have holiday, but sheep seemed rather restless and inclined to follow some foolish leader who jumped into wrong fields. In one field, the sheep (and lambs) seemed so interested in us that we lay down and allowed them to come very near.

Wonderful views at times of distant hills of Lake District. Lots of seagulls; also heard larks, and cuckoo for first time this year.

Chatting briefly with shepherds, Coronation was only mentioned as to whether London was rainy.

At 3 o'clock a wife in one of 6 shepherds' cottages kindly allowed us to climb stone back-wall and down ladder into her garden (we had again lost our footpath!). She showed us her kitchen, and then the newspaper with map of Coronation route with times. 'What a time to wait about! And what an expense it all is: all the unemployed might have been given a stone of flour instead.' Her son age 23 has been in Peel House police college for 3 years and 500 of these have been called up for special duties. She was going later to the big tea.

At 3.30 we came across a suburban resident viewing from binoculars: says he enjoys the scenery that way. Mind not on Coronation.

West London

103. (CO.17.) When the game of chess finished, my brother went home, and my wife and I had dinner. After this meal, I went out for a walk. I chose to stroll round a poor neighbourhood not far from my house. To my surprise, the display of decorations in one of the poorest streets was on a really large scale. Every house had a string of flags fluttering from its roof guttering across the roadway to that of the house

opposite. Many large flags and small ones were sported here and there, and loyal emblems in gilt letters enlivened the drab grey brick walls. Even the kerb-stone had been coloured red, white and blue the whole length of the road on both sides! And the middle of the roadway itself was given up to the children seated at long tables and freely indulging themselves in tea and cakes, and flaunting paper hats of all sizes, shapes and colours.

Cricklewood

104. (CL.12.) In afternoon went to see children's tea given on Westcroft Estate—poorer houses decorated more than middle class—everyone happy; mothers and fathers dressed up to entertain, cats and dogs decorated with red, white and blue bows.

Midlands

105. (CO.24.) 5.15. Hostess insists on going out for a walk. She has tried four times to ring up friends *re* the evening outing, but cannot get connected. Family atmosphere heavy and dull. Host is evidently reluctant to take the car out later. All go out in the rain to 'get a breath of fresh air'. They walk aimlessly to the city square.

Decorations are chiefly heavy rain-proofed red, white and blue blobs of chains. The guild hall has four illuminated bells. No other decorations and there is little planning or co-operation.

Host and Observer, having pictured a beautiful picnic day and the country, are bitterly disappointed.

Not many people about. Queues for picture houses.

Party goes to look at when the Coronation film will be shown at 'News House'. The notice says 'to-night'.

Hostess says disconsolately, 'This is a rotten walk you've taken us. We all come here every day.'

Family's temper gets more strained.

Observer says: 'If I had twopence I'd buy some evening newspapers.'

Host immediately buys two different local papers.

Observer says: 'Let's go to the Museum.' (There is a special antique furniture exhibition on.) Son, after a hurried conversation with his mother, disappears home with the newspapers under his coat. They pass a V.C. hero's statue in the park grounds. Observer thinks it a pity he is dead.

Hostess says: 'He was a wild fellow,' but Observer is not comforted.

The deserted bandstand has 'Extra' still on.

Few people about, mostly young couples, everyone very restrained.

Near Leeds

106. (CO.25.) At about 4.10 p.m. we took tea in a charming café. Everything appeared very usual and I overheard no remarks about the day or its proceedings.

At tea my friend and I discussed ceremonies, a Cingalese dancer, our fascination by dancing—native dancing—the art of dancing, mentioning Havelock Ellis's essay 'The Art of Dancing,' the Greeks, religious and secular festivities, the Eleusian mysteries, the Dionysian mysteries, Euripides' *The Bacchae*.

5 p.m. A mention of the fatigue of protracted listening-in, of the fatigue of the people taking part in to-day's ceremony, of the feeling of Royalty after such an eventful day and especially of the feelings of the Queen-Mother, of Princesses Elizabeth and Margaret Rose and of the Duke of Windsor. We overheard no remarks about the Coronation although the room was full of people. We heard a waitress say that the children's costumes had been judged. My friend and I washed ourselves. On paying my bill I bought a packet of sweets. Outside, things were very quiet. Numbers of hikers and cyclists were to be seen and people leaving places of ceremony, but I witnessed no actual proceedings.

107. At about 6.30 p.m. we leaned over a wall and saw a bed of kingcups. I climbed over the wall, poised myself on a tuft of dry grass in the marshy bed and gathered two clusters which we pinned in our coats. Along the road we passed through Beamsley where several of the houses had simple decorations. We endeavoured to sight Beamsley Beacon but we were unable to decide which of the numerous hills it was. All the way we chatted about the things we saw. Our tongues were rarely still for an instant. Through a small triumphal arch we passed to the main Harrogate-Skipton road.

108. The train approached, reversed and set off for Leeds at 7.33 p.m. We had an empty compartment. The train stopped at every station. There were no signs of gaiety along the line but I thought that one porter at Burley-in-Wharfe-dale, wearing, not uniform, but a rusty-brown suit, was probably dressed in his best for the occasion. In the train we discussed the pictures in the compartment, and in particular one of the Roman baths at Bath. My friend remarked that she thought the Romans would be cold taking open-air baths in Britain. We talked about a colour scheme that pleased us and criticized the pattern of the carriage upholstery. We alighted at Calverly station. As we walked along the platform a man higher up the train glowered at us through the window. In the booking hall we admired posters advertising holiday resorts. And so to my friend's home where her father was laying out the patience cards on the red table cover. We told the folks of our day's excursion and they gave us a report of the broadcast we had missed.

Isle of Man

109. (CL.42.) In the evening I went to the cinema in Douglas, the Island's chief town. The show was interrupted at 8 p.m. so that we could listen to the King's speech over the wireless. We saw the first films of the procession, and there

was also a picture called *Crown and Glory* depicting the chief incidents of the new King's life. We strolled about on the Promenade after the show, looking at the decorations and the various floodlit buildings. A larger crowd was assembled than I have ever seen there before, the whole island coming out at night, each because everybody else was doing so. As our bus left for home at 11 p.m., we did not see the best of the fireworks. The bus was crowded, but nobody was intoxicated, and, although all were cheerful, they were rather sleepy. We arrived home about 11.45 p.m. and went straight to bed.

The only incident within my knowledge which could possibly be called stirring was when, after waiting for a few minutes in the cinema, *God Save the King* was heard over the radio as a prelude to the King's speech, spontaneously, but without excitement, everybody rose to their feet.

Just before the bus left Douglas on the homeward journey, a woman with a large family asked a friend whether she had seen yet another of her children, who had got lost in the crowd. What was peculiar about this was that the mother seemed rather amused than upset at the loss. But I think the father was looking for the child.

The crowd behaved in a most orderly way on the whole. Thus it was rather funny when a man cheerfully called out 'Good-night Cathleen!' to a girl (with another man) who by her surprise evidently was unacquainted with her well-wisher, because it was the only incident of its kind. Any of the phlegmatic Manx crowd who noticed it looked deeply shocked.

Belfast

110. (CO.34.) 9.30. At half past nine I went and stood at the cross-roads by the hostel. The nearest village was two miles away, but the country was plentifully scattered with farmhouses. A peasant came along very soon and putting down his buckets, which he was taking to the well, he sat on the grassy bank and started to talk. Farming was the first

subject, he asked what type of farming was prevalent in my home county and pointed out how it differed from that of Ireland.

Five minutes later three other peasants came along, two dressed in their working clothes, and one with a bicycle and dressed in a navy blue suit. Having mumbled a good evening the two flopped down on the bank, the third stood leaning on his bike in the middle of the road for there was no traffic about.

'You bin crowning the king to-day ——,' said the first peasant to the man with the bike. He gave no answer but looked only sullen. The first peasant turned to me and said 'Now he's off to the dance at the Orange Hall.'

There was nothing else said about the Coronation so the first peasant, who was well-spoken and intelligent, lapsed back to agriculture. The other two sat silent, one of them occasionally emitted a guffaw. After about ten minutes the man with the bike rode away without a word. 'He's bin having some whiskey to-day,' said the first peasant.

The flies became troublesome and all four of us were continually scratching the backs of our necks.

'What's that?' exclaimed one of the other peasants pointing to where, just above the horizon, a shower of stars were falling from an exploded rocket.

'That's where they're letting off the fireworks at Hillsborough,' said the first peasant. We watched a few more rockets disinterestedly and silently.

West London

III. (CO.17.) We came out of the cinema at 9.45 and on our way home, stopped at a public house called the 'White Hart'. We went in at 10 p.m. There were not very many people inside, but the public bar was noisy. After about half an hour it became noisier, chiefly due to the efforts of some strong-voiced but unmusical singers. Outstanding among them were a man and a woman. The woman had a good voice, though unrefined. Rather amusing was the struggle they were evidently having to keep things going, their repertoire being limited to a very few old well-remembered tunes. Patriotism would occasionally well up, and in honour of the day, instigate *Rule Britannia* and *Three Cheers for the Red, White and Blue.*

The bar itself was decorated, but not elaborately. Emblems in buttonholes were in vogue, I noticed, and near me was a man in argumentative mood. 'How easy it is to lead the mob by the nose!' he was saying. 'The non-working class puts on an act now and then to show the working class who is boss. And the damned fools of workers jostle each other and wait up all night to be properly impressed by the show. They have to pay for it, too.'

'But it has made work for some poor devils,' said a woman in the party.

'Work!' scornfully retorted the man. 'For how many and how long? And isn't there anything more useful waiting to be done? A young man is set up by his class and the limelight is turned on him in order to attract our gaze his way and so away from the intrigues and jobbery of the real rulers of this country—financiers and big business!'

I found myself in agreement with him. Soon afterwards we left the place and walked home in the rain, arriving there at 11.30. Supper took twenty minutes, and I retired at midnight. I spent some minutes thinking of a word competition I was going to enter, and then fell asleep.

The End of the Day

Birmingham

112. (CO.35.) Yates' Wine Lodge in Corporation Street was packed. There are only a few seats provided along the walls so most of the people were standing up. There was a

great deal of noise and if you didn't move to let people pass they simply fell against you. There were little groups of people singing and a ring of young men with arms round one another's shoulders just staggering about. And amidst the groups there were many people standing in ones and twos, drinking and smiling, watching and silent—like ourselves.

About half-way up the room two young women of the lower-classes were dancing to their own singing, facing each other and holding out their long coats at the side. They danced coolly without excessive animation.

A young man in a r. w. & b. clown's costume came up and began to dance with them. He was very excited and used a great deal of energy. One of the girls dropped out and he danced facing the other one. Once he had to stop because he was laughing so much and the girl continued to dance, smiling. Her friend joined in again and he leapt between them and took each of them by an arm and they all danced together. Sweat was pouring off him and he had to stop again, exhausted. He was holding his chest. The first girl went on dancing and smiling and he wouldn't be beaten and gritting his teeth began again, more violently than ever.

Kensington

113. (CL.25.) I really had intended to go out again in the evening to see the floodlighting and hear the King's speech. But the weather decided that for me. I was sorry it turned out wet. It did I'm sure spoil things a bit. I decided a hot bath and an early night would be a good ending to a perfect day. As I crept into my comfortable bed at 9.30 I decided that Coronation Day had been my lucky day and fell asleep to the sound of music of a nearby wireless playing *God Save the King*.

Birmingham

114. (CO.29.) By nine everyone, including the Sergeant, was merry and N., D. and B. P. were drunk. I wanted to get

drunk myself, but though I drank steadily I stayed sober (I had eaten a fair amount during the day) and merely felt very comfortable. At ten o'clock I began to talk about arranging to take some bottles back to B.'s. B. P. went collecting and I helped to scrape up about 6s. I ordered 20 small bottles from the sergeant, which came to 5s. 10d. Then I went back and had another pint of bitter with M. The licence allowed drinking till 11.

After the party had been in progress for a quarter of an hour another bunch (mainly unknown) came in. Among them was a young girl in glasses who walked across the room to where I was. I gave her my chair and her escort, who was a bit tight, sat on the arm, but she started talking to me. She had been drinking beer and knew that she was near to being tight. She didn't like the people there, nor her escort, and she said I seemed to be different from the rest. I was sitting on a typewriter and drinking beer very rapidly. She smoked the cigarettes I gave her one after another in quick succession. I told her to take strong tea without milk and put in a lump of washing soda if she still felt a little drunk; that, I told her, was a sea-cook's tip which was a very effective one. She had never been drunk before and told me she was an elementary school teacher from Walsall, and that she was 23, a Roman Catholic, and very much afraid of facing her land-lady that night. She said she had been around with the fellow with her for some time, but that he was very jealous and not very trustworthy. I suggested that she'd better go and talk to him or he'd be more jealous, but she didn't, and after a while he went with another man who had a car, to buy some food. They were absent for half an hour. All the time she talked to me. She had never been to this sort of party before and at one time when B. and the only other woman there happened to be out of the room she got very frightened and I had to ex-plain to her that the people who looked such wicked brutes were really quite nice people.

115. One fellow started talking to me about reality and illusion, 'the table in the room,' the Berkleian theory and when I got stuck I said: 'Imagine a fairy godmother transporting this table, these chairs, and all these drunken bastards outside this room.' The other asked me to prove the existence of the fairy godmother. N. was looking a little gloomy, though he was still tight, so I said at once: 'The truth is that in reality Joe himself is the fairy godmother.' N. was surprised and hadn't an answer. 'I postulated a fairy godmother . . .' I said, but N. said, 'Postulate my arse.' Beer had run out by this time, and I was drinking tea without milk. I offered the student of Berkeley three aspirins, which I said I always presented to people with whom I perceived a common bond; and I said he could have the rest of the bottle of fifty if he cared to take them. Just before the Walsall girl went I went across to her and asked her if she was feeling better now. She said she was 'but what a man she'd got'. She went (at about 2.15). The rest stayed till about three.

Leeds

116. (CO.25.) 11 p.m. Soon after this hour I set out for home, accompanied by my sweetheart who bid me good-night in the lane. I could see the glares of five beacons. The streets were deserted and most of the houses in darkness. I reached home at about 11.25 p.m. to find the living-room full of my family and visitors. Clothes were strewn about the chairs and sideboard. Dance music was coming softly from the radio. My aunt told me how she had visited a friend in Yeadon. She said: 'I held my umbrella over my face and so they couldn't recognize me at first. Then D—— said: "Well, if it isn't K——!"' I turned off the wireless, said good-night and went up to my room.

Olton

117. (CO.14.) I prepare supper and we eat it. Listen to news. I continue to read. Several times we think we hear M.

out of bed, but upon investigation he is fast asleep. We then discover that it is the sound of fireworks coming down the chimney. I suggest that it may be better if I sleep in M.'s bedroom and H. by himself in the guest room, so that H. will not be disturbed every time I have to go to M. in the night. H. agrees. I go upstairs and prepare M.'s bed for myself (change sheets, etc.). Come down and read a little more. Go up to bed. Usual preparations, bath, etc. 12.30 just dropping off to sleep when M. calls, go in and make him comfortable. Return to bed.

Hertford

118. (CO.18.) 10–11.30 p.m. Went to the pub next door to find a friend I hadn't seen for 3 months. Exchange of reminiscences. One man insisted that the profit on decorations all went to the Jews. Another man produced cigars, which he said he had had since Christmas. (The atmosphere felt vaguely Christmas night-ish.)

Went back to the Pot; talked to a waitress, and made love to her a bit. She said she was tired with the Coronation—probably in a literal sense, anyway, as there was a big rush from tea-time onwards. 1 a.m. Was taken home to Hertford by a man I had never met before, who knew one of the other waitresses.

Near Croydon

119. (CO.15.) I got into bed at 11.15 p.m. Lying in bed I could hear shouting, dance-music, syrens (perhaps the kind you blow down, but fairly loud), distant trains, rain-water falling from overflow pipes and a noise of escaping steam, probably from the large roundabout. I got out of bed just after 11.30 p.m., and saw that the bonfire was now going. Before I went to sleep I heard the church clock at Carshalton strike midnight. All was quiet then.

Chapter 4

INDIVIDUAL REACTIONS ON MAY 12

'Social psychology is in general little concerned with the manner in which the required continuity in the psychic life of succeeding generations is established. A part of the task seems to be performed by the inheritance of psychic dispositions which, however, need certain incentives in the individual life in order to become effective. This may be the meaning of the poet's words: Strive to possess yourself of what you have inherited from your ancestors. The problem would appear more difficult if we could admit that there are psychic impulses which can be so completely suppressed that they leave no traces whatsoever behind them. But that does not exist. The greatest suppression must leave room for distorted substitutions and their resulting reactions. But in that case we may assume that no generation is capable of concealing its more important psychic processes from the next. For psychoanalysis has taught us that in his unconscious psychic activity every person possesses an apparatus which enables him to interpret the reactions of others, that is to say, to straighten out the distortions which the other person has affected in the expression of his feelings. By this method of unconscious understanding of all customs, ceremonies, and laws which the original relations to the primal father had left behind, later generations may also have succeeded in taking over this legacy of feelings.'

FREUD, *Totem and Tabu*.

Reactions to Radio

1. There were various possible reactions to the Coronation. Either one could enter wholeheartedly into the celebrations, religious and secular, or one could attempt to resist the general tendency of the day, by shutting oneself indoors, by closing one's mind to the suggestions forced upon it, or by escaping into solitary places: all these types of resistance are illustrated in the reports, but it is interesting that even those persons who shut themselves up most completely could not escape the day entirely. We have seen the elaborate preparation made by the social mechanism to provide in advance for the conduct of the day. This chapter will show how far the individual will was capable of imposing itself on the prearranged pattern of behaviour.

On the whole the chapter moves from considering the individual in a small group (a family listening to the radio) towards the individual in complete solitude (dreams).

2. The most potent means of unifying behaviour was the broadcasting of the ceremony and processions, and of the King's speech. It meant that a very high proportion of the population spent the day listening in and thus partaking in the central events.

Of the 77 replies to the leaflet questionnaire 43 say what was 'the most stirring incident' of the day. The actual question asked was 'What was the most stirring incident . . . that you saw or that you heard of during the day?' 10 replies to this question were from people who actually saw the processions—they record 'the most stirring incident' as follows:

1. Announcement of crowning on radio and state coach (the only incident from those who saw the procession which refers to the broadcast).
2. Start-off of procession. Mounted band in gold on black horses.
3. Cheering of crowd.
4. State coach.
5. Child crying because foot was caught.
6. Cheering of crowd.
7. Cheering.
8. 'Fit brown men' marching in procession.
9. State coach and cheering and shouting crowds.
10. Feeling of emotion when the King was crowned.

Twenty-eight replies to this question were from people who did not see the procession, but who listened to the broadcasts. Of these 22 found their 'most stirring incident' in the broadcasts, as follows:

1. Hymn from St. Margaret's.
2. King's speech.
3. Cheering.
4. King's speech.
5. King 'riding by'.
6. King's speech.
7. Spoken word of King.
8. Cheering outside palace.
9. King's responses in ceremony.
10. The broadcasts.
11. King's speech.
12. Crowd cheering outside palace.
13. '*Vivat Rex Georgius*.'
14. Cheering. *God Save the King* in Abbey.
15. 'Heart of the Abbey service.'

16. Sound of trumpets.
17. Shouting and trumpets.
18. *'Vivat Regina'* in broadcast.
19. Administering of oath to King.
20. State coach emerging from Buckingham Palace.
21. Singing of *Te Deum*.
22. Singing of choir in Abbey.

Two further replies are directly connected with broadcasting:

1. People quiet in pub to hear King's speech.
2. Spontaneous rising of audience in cinema for relay of *God Save the King* after the King's speech.

The 4 other replies about stirring incidents by people who listened to the broadcasts are as follows:

1. A figure representing Canada in a pageant.
2. Boy Scouts' fire.
3. Old woman singing *God Save the King* in R.C. Church.
4. Seeing a car decorated with Communist flag.

Five 'most stirring incidents' come from people who neither saw the processions nor heard the broadcasts:

1. Military band playing in rain at Richmond.
2. Spring flowers and green leaves.
3. Colleague chased by swan.
4. Pun: Communists ought to cut their dialectical cackle.
5. Glastonbury floodlit.

3. The first part of this chapter will show in more detail how people reacted to the broadcast in the course of the day. Certain problems of behaviour, which are inherent in all occasions when people sit in a room listening in (especially now that loud speakers have

replaced earphones), were more than usually apparent. For example:

Is it permissible to eat during a 'sacred' broadcast?

Is it better to give one's whole attention to the broadcast, or to occupy a part of it with knitting, sewing, reading, bridge, housework, etc?

With what completeness is the listener participating in the ceremonies, and how far should he behave as if he was actually present at them; should he, for example, stand up during the playing of the National Anthem?*

The question reappears at a yet further remove when records of the Abbey service and procession commentary were broadcast.

4. Many apparently turned the wireless on for the benefit of the rest of the family, or of the servants; others put their loudspeakers by the window, so that passers by should be able to hear. As the broadcast went on, a certain number seem to have been bored and to have switched off, but others became increasingly moved, even to the point of tears (and this in the case of some of the more sceptical and hard-boiled). Music seems to have contributed a great deal to this access of interest, though one listener (Conservative and Church of England) considered the music barbarous, and compared it to 'African dervishes'. The hesitation in the King's speech seems to have aroused general sympathy, even among anti-monarchists, and to have operated as a factor in his favour; though this sympathy was closely connected with a feeling of embarassment. Rumours had been current, and had been voiced in the press, that the King would not actually speak and that his speech would be given from a gramophone record. There may have been some con-

*Cf. Chap. 2, para. 49.

nection between this rumour and the fact that it was immediately after the speech that someone managed to impersonate a B.B.C. announcer and gave a commentary on the scene outside Buckingham Palace. The nervous strain of handing out the commentary to the 'unseen millions' seems to have told heavily on B.B.C. officials, as there was a series of similar breakdowns and hoaxes before and after the Coronation.

The importance of radio on the day is made abundantly clear in the reports. They enable us to follow the events of the day in terms of the broadcast.

Watford

5. (CO.12.) 12 approx. After Kensal Rise we passed a building with the sound of singing. The man with the little girl pointed it out to her 'Lovely singing' and said it was the service from London.

'But Daddy, how can we hear?'

'Why, dear, it's the wireless.'

'Will they see him be crowned?'

'Not all the people will see him.'

'Why won't all the people see him crowned?'

Scotland

6. (CO.22.) 10.30 a.m. Arrive at S——— Theatre to connect up radio set to talkie equipment in order to relay the King's speech at 8 p.m. This is being done in 15 shows in town. Many adjustments required to get satisfactory performance. Operators intrigued and very anxious to follow correct instructions. Very little conversation except above owing to operators being busy elsewhere.

S.E. 23

7. (CO. 41.) Was definitely keen to hear the broadcast, so hurried over bath, breakfast, etc. As soon as I heard the announcement of the Royal Family entering their coaches, and heard the cheering, etc., I felt tears coming into my eyes, especially when Queen Mary appeared on the scene.

We listened intermittently from 11 till about 12.30. Compared notes with my married sister, who said she always swallowed lumps when listening to crowds cheering. She said 'It makes my face go wry. But it is hysteria. Anything that is done in unison, even children drilling, has that effect on me.' My sister has never studied psychology or heard of Mass Observation. I thought her comments very much to the point. After a time we became bored with the broadcast. It sounded like gargling in parts. We had a drink or two, then early lunch and a nap.

Listened in when the Royal Family appeared on the balcony, and were again thrilled.

8. (CO.46.) 6.0 a.m. I'm in a seventh floor flat at the corner of Marble Arch and Park Lane. Those present are mostly middle-aged women and a few young women.

7 a.m. All collected. Below in the street a vast lining of people is already fixed, their feet among torn newspapers. In the flat a desultory conversation. Two women, one deaf: 'I've lost my paper. I wanted to know about the Beefeaters.' Many Americans. A man is reading *Angels in Undress*. The weather is cold. One woman says: 'Not like the old King George's days! Every day he came out it was a lovely day!'

8 a.m. A dreary, bored group knowing that hours are before them, not daring to be expectant. An American voice: 'Meet Mr. Miller of Detroit.' Carpets are turned upside down in the flat.

9.45 a.m. Three girls still asleep in chairs. A young man with red socks, red tie and red handkerchief in breast pocket, walks about. Two American women are tracing out designs for a dress with much argument. A row of women is knitting solemnly.

They listen to the broadcast from the Abbey. An American voice: 'Do you know they haven't heat in their churches here?' The street outside sounds like a vast radio shop. Small child in a pink coat: 'What are they shouting away for, sillies?' The loudspeakers are muttering most of the day.

The procession passes. There is a whistling tone in the cheers. Too many chairs have been crowded on to this balcony. There is evidently no protection against the seat ramp. We sit in exceeding discomfort at the rate of 12 guineas each.

Switzerland

9. (CO.23. English Girl.) 9.30. Washed, dressed and tidied my room, not thinking of the Coronation or anything else in particular. Put on a pair of slacks and sports shirt, and went downstairs to practise tap dancing and limbering (my daily ritual). More or less forgot goings on in London, and chiefly concentrated on my own potentialities as Ginger Rogers' future successor, thinking it would be grand if some film director would discover me and write a film scenario which included plenty of crooning and tap.

10.30. Completely hot and exhausted, I joined the rest of my family in the library, which has become our combined living and dining room. The radio is there: we turned it on, just in time to hear the departure from Buckingham Palace. The commentator was a highly poetic Belgian who was in great form; he began by describing how the blanket of grey fog was being dispersed by a minute ray of golden sun which lighted the roof-tops, the millions of chimneys, and the railings of the park. He then went on to telling us all about the 'trepidating emotion of the vast crowds, which echoed across the green prairies of St. James's Park.' All this in French of course. I giggled to myself; it seemed such a very roundabout position to be in: an English person, in Switzerland, listening to an English ceremony being described in French. . . . The commentator was particularly impressed by the costumes:

couldn't stop enlarging about the magnificent velvet, 'cramoisie' silk and embroideries passing before his eyes, and the grandiose apparel of the 'Yeoman Guards' (pronounced all in a gulp, as in French, which also sounded a bit odd) and the 'white boots' of the Highlanders.

London

10. (CL.21.) Suffered tortures of the damned listening to the wireless from 10 a.m. till 11.30 p.m. as my old housekeeper who was unable to go out to join in the fun was revelling in all the fuss. I was also trying to read and knit and answer futile questions as though I enjoyed it.

11. (CL.6.) 10.30. I return to the wireless. The King has left Buckingham Palace, having presumably had a bath earlier and is now jolting along Whitehall. I go back to bed, leaving the wireless on. I hear my two maids rustling on the stairs so I get dressed and go into my sitting room and make them come in too to be comfortable. I go on with my friend's book, interrupted occasionally by the Archbishop of Canterbury, the King and the Garter King of Arms. This surprises me for I am interested in the book and I am doing my best about it but I feel myself quite unusually moved by the music of the ceremonial. I find myself listening to it quite a lot of the time and once or twice especially during the hymn from St. Margaret's, find tears in my eyes.

12. (CL.9.) 10 a.m. Switched on radio and tuned into National station for Service. Continued household duties and then sat down to sketch (my hobby). It was peaceful in the room. Parents were gardening.

11 a.m. My sister C. (aged 14) sat beside me with a Bible, opened at the Psalms, and a copy of the *Radio Times*. She was too busy listening to talk.

12.0. C. and I still alone. We have carefully followed the

service. C. curious and serious. I also serious, but critical; my feelings were very mixed. I love my country but the patriotic jingo of flag-wagging, etc., has never appealed to me. Rather I am impatient at the childishness of the outward show. Love of my country goes deeper than that. I was nearly moved to tears once or twice (I couldn't say why but I always react in that way). Lunch time. We ate in almost complete silence because we were still listening to the radio. My mother kept remarking on the lengthy service and how weary the King and Queen must be. Also she wondered what the late King Edward was thinking about the Coronation.

North Shields

13. (CL.56.) 11 a.m. When we got home we found that Father was listening to the wireless, so we joined him with the *Daily Telegraph* supplement to enable us to follow the service intelligently. I did embroidery and mother mended while we listened.

I found that my interest was decidedly quickened as the service proceeded; mother was much more prepared than I was to be thrilled. I liked the music, especially the fanfares of trumpets, and as the ceremony proceeded I found myself surprisingly moved, until I felt that I wanted to cry. That certainly surprised me as I am not easily emotionally moved by plays or novels. It might have been the music or the profound solemnity and significance of the service.

S.E. 12

14. (CL.71.) *Stirring:* when *Vivat Regina* was broadcast. And other parts of the Abbey ceremony.

Funniest: when we couldn't quite hear the words of the ceremony and some of the phrases sounded like 'Gawd blimey' and 'swelp me bob'. We all joined in mock interpretations and there was much laughter.

Swansea

15. (CO.28.) 10 a.m. Start to clear away breakfast things
—my mother turns on the Radio without making any comment whatsoever. She places it in a position where it can be
heard by us as we do our housework in and near the kitchen
—in the doorway of a small sitting room.

10.55. I made my bed and returned to the sitting room
with some stockings to darn while listening to the broadcast.
My mother sat there too and from time to time went out for a
few minutes. She followed the service in a book she had
bought several days previously. We did not talk much.

At one point she remarked that a certain local Labour
leader had been staying at a seaside hotel nearby and had
spoken against all this and she continued '—but when he was
mayor he was very anxious to have a 2nd term of Office.'

After the first fanfare she remarked: 'I always think the
fanfare is wonderful.' I agreed, having been thinking it myself. It gave me the first emotional quickening of the day.

During some of the time my mother was cutting her nails—
much to my annoyance—I hate to see and hear other people
cut their nails especially anywhere but in a bedroom or bathroom.

About 11.40. My mother said: 'It's the Communion now—
I think I'll go and wash' and goes and I proceeded to make
some notes on the day up to then.

Somewhere about now the service reaches the actual
coronation—the crowning, and I leave my writing to listen
and to find the place in the book—After the crowning I called
out to my mother:

'Well, they've got him crowned king now so that's all right'
—and I experienced a sense of relief as if a sense of uncer-
tainty and apprehension (intellectual rather than emotional)
had been lifted.

I had found that the two fanfares—the *Vivat Regina* and

276

the *Vivat Rex* of the Westminster School boys by far the most thrilling moments of the 'show'—Several times during the ceremony I found myself thinking that the ceremony and its symbolism was very fine and very beautiful 'if only they *meant* it'.

Nr. Dublin

16. (CO.10.) Spent the night in the house of my wife's parents, in ——, a small country town in the Free State, 20 miles from Dublin. They have the only Protestant national school in the town; the house and school are in the same building.

I am on holiday (Wed. to Sun.), for the Coronation.

11.35. Immediately on finishing breakfast, wife and I went into the sitting-room, with the intention of hearing part of the service. About 20 children, boys and girls, aged probably 5 to 12, were seated on forms quietly, and looked at me with interest. My wife's parents were there too. Her mother, who is deeply fond of music, gave little commentaries from time to time, naming the composer, and piece. She commented on *Zadok the King*—'You'll never forget that, children.' I wondered whether she really believed that, and wondered too whether the children's quiet and fixed expressions hid a real interest in the music or day-dreaming.

Sussex

17. (CO.16.) 11.30. Go upstairs and make the beds, can hear a fair amount. Listen in again. Very impressive, but this gorgeous glitter of birth and wealth is set against background of distressed areas, war in Abyssinia and Spain. Wonder anxiously about Spain to-day.

12.0. Go out and see to chick food hoppers and fill up lamp for youngest chix. Heavy rain comes on.

12.30. Return and write up (in rough) report so far while listening. Stop at archbishop's words preceding actual crowning; seems irreverent to go on writing. Offer a prayer with

277

him for the reign tho' vision I see of England's future is probably different from his.

Lancashire

18. (CO.36.) 12 noon. (At friend's house.)

(The Coronation broadcast has been in progress in another room all this while.)

J. (Girl, 30-ish, upper working class, suburban dweller, factory charge hand.) This music is most stimulating. It upsets and stirs me but I like it. If only we could direct the flow of people's emotions into proper (?better) channels. I love trumpets and brass bands.

Self. It's those English horns. They are marvellous.

J. They're doing their best to make it seem all from God.

Self. Last night —— and I had a walk round, when we came to a house with a picture of Albert Edward and Elizabeth tacked up, and underneath to bathe it in an aura of light was an electric lamp. —— said, 'Oh look at this holy image,' then out it popped. She said, 'Now look what our derision's done.'

Ruislip

19. (CL.100.) 12 noon. The inn was full, very full, very noisy and above the din a loudspeaker was blaring forth the ceremony being enacted at Westminster Abbey.

At 12.30 came the words 'The King is acclaimed'. A rather noisy hail-fellow-well-met man in plus-fours shouted 'The King God bless him'. People stood for a minute, then resumed their seats, continued drinking, and apparently forgot there was a Coronation.

Cricklewood

20. (CL.8.) On the actual crowning of the King, my little girl (6) remarked, 'Can't the King crown himself? isn't he big enough—is that why someone must do it for him?'

278

On the starting out of the King's coach she burst out . . .
'What a fuss they are making—it seems they are having a
nice game playing at Kings and Queens!'

Most people I overheard speaking of the Coronation were
interested in the *spectacle* of the procession.

Southport

21. (CL.24.) I was 'on duty', *i.e.* in charge of a handful of
youngsters (all boys) for the day.

From 11.0 to 12.30 we listened to the service at Westminster in a cinema which was opening its doors free. The
boys sat in silence, but were apparently less bored than I was.
I heard no comment from people near except when the King
spoke. A woman said 'He's got a nice voice', and somebody
imitated the long pause between 'promise' and 'to do'.

Being sympathetically conscious of the King's nervousness
was the only sensation the business produced in me.

When we left the cinema one boy said 'Well, they've got
him crowned,' and they all went on to discuss the bad behaviour of three other small boys who had been sitting in
front of them, drinking 'pop', and fighting almost incessantly.
I was surprised that no adult took offence at the noise.

Midlands

22. (CO.24.) 12.30. Observer arrives at friends'. They
have two Union Jacks out. No one is playing on the Club hard
tennis courts opposite, tho' two young men have just arrived.
Observer is met at drawing room door by host, who says:
'Talk of angels. We thought you were never coming.' Observer explains she was waiting till a good moment came to leave
the broadcast. (These people are Civil Service—Church.)
Hostess is embroidering a fire-screen. Son, age 19, is reading.
The wireless is on, and from time to time they consult the
Daily Telegraph Supplement; host offers Observer a sweet but
by mistake holds out bird's peanut tin. Shows Observer a

newspaper photo of a crowd waiting on the edge of a wet pavement all night.

Says: 'Can you understand how anyone can do this? How they have the physical strength I can't think!'

Hostess shows her embroidery, and they discuss going, later, into the country to see a beacon lighted.

Says: 'What did you think of the King's voice? Very good I thought it.' Alludes to 'All this paraphernalia'. Says lunch will be cold as maid has been let go away till to-morrow morning. 'They enjoy it more than we do.'

Nottingham

23. (CL.47.) My hairdresser on Saturday, after asking if I'd been to London on the 12th said that she'd listened in to the Service. They'd had their wireless on from half-past ten to half-past four—'And you should have seen my mother—she sat in front of it all day—and all through the service while he was being crowned and that, the tears were pouring down her face and she kept moaning "*Oh*, it ought to be Edward—it—it—it ought to be Edward"—My mother's a scream!'

Sussex

24. (CO.16.) 1 p.m. Lunch—which we take into sitting room so that we can go on listening. Involuntarily stop for hymn from St. Margaret's and closing music. The *Te Deum* is glorious, quite beyond words. Glad to think that people on route, Dominions, U.S.A. and others would hear that.

Southport

25. (CL.14.) 1.30 p.m. Had lunch in Southport in an extremely modest café—Coronation 'serviettes' red, white and blue favours on the table. Asked the waitress if they'd crowned him yet and she said 'Oh yes' very reverently.

South London

26. (CO.45.) When I got downstairs the time was nearly 1 o'clock, the radio in the dining room was on at full blast, three people sat round it, my landlady and Mr. and Mrs. F. who is a chauffeur and his wife were deeply interested in the ceremony from the Abbey. At intervals Mr. F. would say, 'I wish I were there,' my landlady appeared to be rather scornful and said she wouldn't give a thank you to be there not after the dirty trick they had played on the old Duke of Windsor, Mrs. F., stout and forty, sat listening with damp eyes every time the commentator commented on Princess Elizabeth and Margaret Rose, she said, 'how sweet,' Mrs. F. has no children of her own and cried and smiled all through the service.

At 1.30 p.m. I left the house to get some cigarettes. . . . When I arrived back the F.'s had departed when the broadcast of the service from the Abbey had ended, the radio was still going strong with the roar of the crowds as the procession was on its return journey, what impressed me most was when one commentator told us how a group of disabled soldiers had been singing *Old Soldiers never die*, when the crowds began to shout 'We want the King' outside of the palace my landlady came into the room and switched it off, she said that a friend of hers had told her that the old Duke of Windsor had come over to London disguised and in secret to see the procession, she further remarked that she would have went up and cheered if he had been king.

Beer, S. Devon

27. (CO.1.) After lunch, got into conversation with proprietress of café. She turned on the 'wireless' for us and we listened in from 1.20 to 2.20. This was mostly from within the Abbey. While the prayer 'Wherefore with Angels and Archangels and all the Company of Heaven' was proceeding, there was much clamping about in the kitchen, and at the 'Sursum Corda' there was more bustling and banging. While the Archbishop was reciting passages in the Holy Communion—'Hear what St. John saith' a customer came into the outer shop and gave his order in the same ecclesiastical tones, for tobacco.

2.45. A Mr. B——, builder and decorator, and organist in the congregational chapel, had been listening in to the Abbey Service. It had moved him tremendously. His emotions were stirred by the ancient traditions, the setting, the music (which he was proud to think was all English, except the Handel) and the religious connections of it all—this from a Congregationalist, the most direct representatives of militant Puritanism at present in England. I encouraged him in his respect for antiquity and we parted good friends. I met him later with his wife at the 'Social' where again he voiced his enthusiasm for the historical, the aesthetic and the religious aspect of it all. The Holy Communion in particular he mentioned as giving the ceremony meaning. The ecclesiastical commentator had said that the taking of the bread and wine marked the culminating point. It was here, said the commentator, that the power and strength of Christ was partaken of, and heaven blended with earth. (Here was a clatter and disturbance in the café kitchen.) The commentator had collected as much emotional connotation as he could—*e.g.* the splendour of the King's crown was likened unto the glory on the face of Moses and the Black Prince was mentioned in connection with certain gems (a ruby I think) in the crown.

Hertford

28. (CO.18.) 1.30. Went back to the cricket ground for lunch. When *The King* was played (the radio, which was on all the time in the pavilion) the men lunching on the balcony at once stood up, but those at the large table in the pavilion remained seated. Those outside noticed this, and rapped on the windows, and one put his head inside the door and said 'Stand up you chaps, *The King*.' Those inside then got up.

Cambridge

29. (CL.16.) Morning. Listened in to part of commentary on ceremony in common room with 9 people (4 conservatives, 3 liberals, 1 fascist, 1 fabian). General reaction: embarrassed grins, and outright laughter when the commentator was outstandingly loyal. Fascist stood for National Anthem. Conservative remarked 'bloody fool!' It was generally agreed that the Coronation was a good thing because it improved trade, gave ruling class prestige and broke down class barriers.

Scotland

30. (CO.22.) 1.30 p.m. Mother-in-law wants to listen to Coronation broadcast again. Sister-in-law arrives, delayed by the crowds assembled for procession. She hasn't been listening to the broadcast, but has spent the morning in bathing pool.

During lunch all listened to broadcast to the end of the Abbey ceremony. Mother-in-law interjects that the business is marvellous. She is evidently very Royal in spirit and looks at me reprovingly when I suggest that some of it is bunkum. Wife remarks that one of the announcers sounded like Oliver Wakefield.

2 p.m. After lunch over a cup of tea, we further listened to the broadcast of procession leaving the Abbey. Wife and sister-in-law wish to hear bands instead of the descriptive talk but are disappointed.

2.30 p.m. Still listening to B.B.C. more or less in silence. Mother-in-law forgets for a moment and remarks that sister-in-law's fingers are turned back, this, she says, betokens 'greedy' fingers, listening resumed. Mother-in-law remarks what an ordeal for the Royal family to go through with all

this ceremony—and now we have a new King and Queen—
just listen to the crowds—what do they do for food, they must
be starving.

2.40. B.B.C. broadcasting crowd noises. Table cleared and
preparations made to receive O., friend of wife. Wife says
there is awful lack of bands, they should be playing all the
time.

3.40. Still listening to the B.B.C. Mother-in-law intrigued
to know how troops lining the route all day relieve themselves. This problem is to be referred to a soldier we know
who is one of the said troops.

Hertfordshire

31. (CO.44.) The Radio is going full blast in 'The Plough'.
The procession is on its way back to Buckingham Palace—the
commentary is disjointed and indistinct—we hear mention of
the eight Windsor Greys. Sir Gerald Woolaston—louder
cheering than any we have heard hitherto; the announcer is
talking about the 'last glorious moments'.

Cambridge

32. (CL.16.) Afternoon. Saw televised procession* in
home of local tradesman. His wife and parents-in-law con-

*'Analysis of the reports received by the B.B.C. on the reception of the
Coronation procession television is showing that the audience was larger
and more widespread than imagined. The number of viewers may now
be estimated at 60,000, and the pictures were received as far away as
Brighton, Ipswich and Cambridge. Ipswich, the farthest point, is 63
miles from the transmitter, and reception there provides further proof
that the original estimate of a 25-mile range is too modest.

The B.B.C. has under consideration a proposal that a census should be
taken of those who saw the Coronation procession on the television
screen. It is thought that the figure may help to convince the Government
of the rapidly growing interest in television, the Government may be prepared to allocate to the B.B.C. for television development a proportion of
the £1,000,000 a year still retained by the Exchequer from radio receiving licence fees.' (*Daily Telegraph*, 18.5.37.)

stantly remarked: 'Isn't it all wonderful,' 'After all, it just
shows all this socialist nonsense up, doesn't it?' 'This is the
only country where you could have a ceremony like this,
without fear of someone throwing a bomb.' They also ex-
changed anecdotes about the Royal Family, all of which had
the same point—that the Windsors are really quite human.
They were very concerned lest the King and Queen be over-
tired by the ceremonies.

London

33. (CL.11.) Woken up about 3.30 p.m. by return of
cousin, having walked off from Westminster as soon as procession had passed. Get up. Ask, as at weddings, the inane
question: 'Did it go off all right?' 2 other young naval officers
and 3 girl friends arrive. They can't stay very long but they
knock back a bottle of gin. The wireless of crowd outside
Buckingham Palace leaves no doubt that England has scored
when the Royal Family come on to balcony. I'd been rather
proud of those uniforms, swords and things—even when one
broke one of my best glasses sweeping the head off like a
tulip.

Birmingham

34. (CO.14.) 4.10. I arrive at my mother's house. I find
my father and sister listening to the wireless, which has
reached the stage where the crowds were awaiting the King
and Queen outside Buckingham Palace. I go upstairs where
my mother is packing ready for a journey on Thursday. She
comes downstairs with me and says on entering the drawing
room 'Have you still got the wireless on? the noise makes me
feel queer in the head.' Father 'They're coming out on the
balcony in a minute.' He then switches off the speaker in the
drawing-room and goes through to the dining-room to listen
in there. General conversation ensues about measles, holidays, relatives, etc.

35. (CO.10.) 4.30. Wife and I left by car for Dublin. The only flag to be seen was the college flag over Trinity College. Clery's (a municipal store), which usually has half-a-dozen flags, had none. In a small tobacconists' the conversation was obviously about the Coronation (5.45 p.m.), for I heard the remark, 'I'm sure he's tired out.' I said, 'Did you listen in?' (without specifying what to). The tobacconist said he had. 'Did it go off well?'—'It did, indeed. And he spoke very nicely too.' We agreed that we were sure the King was glad it was over. It is almost certain that the tobacconist is a Roman Catholic.

Sussex

36. (CO.16.) 6 p.m. Leave field at top speed. At the gate two people want to know how it goes—retired teachers—fear of asthma and the wonderful broadcast have kept them at home. *Very* thrilled with the way people called for the King and cheered him. Further on we meet deafish lady and her friend. 'How has it gone?—too wet to come up and how was the broadcast? No they had not their wireless.' The friend obviously feels mad to have missed it. 'Was weather in London fine? Were there any incidents?' Very pleased, especially, that no incidents occurred. Two more people ask how sports have gone.

6.30. Arriving home ask mother (for whom sports and tea too far in the rain) what 6 o'clock news was. Only sports so hope really nothing to tell about Spain.

Dash round feeding chickens. Milk goat. Mother takes dog a short run.

Scotland

37. (CO.22.*) 7.40 p.m. Went over to R—— Cinema, arriving at 7.48. Found operator in a slight panic so took over. B.B.C. a bit late, Mr. Baldwin speaking after 8 p.m. At the end of Mr. Baldwin's speech fanfare announced National

*Sound Engineer.

Anthem. Machines stopped and radio switched over and volume faded in. Audience—a full house—stood to attention during the Anthem, then followed the speech. Voice clear but somewhat hesitant as though King had been told to go slow if in doubt over a word or if having difficulty in pronunciation. After the speech another fanfare at the end of which we switched over to the film show.

Chief operator said that the Coronation to him seemed to be for the Archbishop of Canterbury, not for the King. He expressed the opinion that the King was in the hands of the clergy. Edward wouldn't stand for this so was kicked out. He further said that he had heard that Edward was going to make an announcement after the Coronation and blow the gaff so much that the country would be split into opposing camps.

8.4 p.m. After disconnecting the radio from talkie equipment and leaving instructions to return radio sets to dealers, went over to S—— Theatre. Assistant manager reported excellent results. He considered that the King's articulation was greatly improved and accent and style superior to that of his Father and Brother Edward. Boy then arrived with flash copy of Movietone News (8.17), which had already been shown at another cinema at 7.35 p.m. Plane arrived at airport at 6.40 p.m.

9.15 p.m. Went to T—— Cinema, they reported fine broadcast results; no flash copy of Paramount News Flash.

Advised by phone that Gaumont News had arrived at 10.20 p.m. by plane and was shown (one cinema). All cinemas had advertised their respective news-reels as to be shown after 7.30 p.m. but only Movietone and Gaumont arrived at all. All cinemas had men waiting at airport and spent much money on phone calls.

Leeds

38. (CL.65.) The tea-shop I usually frequent was filled to the last table, mostly young couples of the working class dressed in their Sunday best and enjoying the day off. There was a poster in front of the door about the programme from London that you could hear from their wireless, but during the hour I spent there I heard nothing but orchestral music which no doubt came from one of their gramophone records.

Towards 7 o'clock I was back to Briggate Street again. More crowds than ever. The Rialto Cinema had a sign out to the effect that no Coronation news-reel would be shown to-day as the plane was held up in a fog.* There was a long queue waiting to get in nevertheless.

Buckinghamshire

39. (CO.4.) At 7.15 we had supper, a cold meal, and listened to the Empire broadcast. I thought the choice of U.K. speakers particularly good, and was surprised at the French-Canadian girl who used no English. We heard the King start his speech, and I then had to get out my bicycle and go to work.

It was not my normal working time, but an extra night shift was put on to deal with news-reel prints for the Paramount Co., and my assistant who was starting up was the youngest of the shift workers, a boy of 18, so I went to help. I arrived first, as the time of starting had been postponed during the previous night.

9.0 p.m. When my assistant came I was already getting the various liquids for the film developing machines ready, and he was surprised. I asked him how long he had been up, and he said 'Since four'. (He worked the previous night.) We got two machines ready for work, slightly delayed by the fact that he went and was sick. I asked him if he felt all right, and he replied 'Yes, I've been wanting to do that for a

*'Owing to fog only one of the special aeroplanes that were expected to reach Birmingham last night with films of the Coronation ceremony was able to arrive. Hurried alternative arrangements were made, and most of the theatres showed films of the scenes in London, although they arrived later than was anticipated.' (*Birmingham Gazette*, 13.5.37.)

long time.' I gave him a dose of magnesia in a little water and left him to work alone, another man would come and help him at midnight. (I heard later that the film to be copied arrived at about 2 a.m., about 80 copies of a special edition of the day's news-reel were made for European use, these were put on an aeroplane at dawn on a private aerodrome half a mile away, and rushed to Amsterdam to be distributed by the usual mail planes.)

West London

40. (CO.17.) 6–9 p.m. After tea we all left for the Regal Cinema, Hammersmith. It was not so crowded as I feared. At 7.40, the films ceased, the lights went up, the curtains swung to across the stage. From behind them a loudspeaker relayed to us the voices of representative persons in various parts of the Empire broadcasting their country's tribute to the new King. Then several dignitaries in London followed, and at last the climax—the King's speech. The lights lowered discriminatingly, and created an atmosphere of intimacy. Everyone listened intently. At the end, we stood as the National Anthem came through, being played and sung, a little too lengthily. Then the film programme was resumed. A rush 'news-flash' of some of the Coronation scenes was shown.*

*'Observer goes to see Coronation film. Attentive, but not hypnotized audience. They stood quite spontaneously and naturally when *God Save the King* was sung during the Abbey service.

They laughed at:

(1) The Archbishop twiddling the crown round over the King's head, and the King sitting lost and overwhelmed in the Throne immediately after with it on his head.

(2) Princess Margaret Rose twisting about to see as much as she could of the proceedings.

(3) Gloucester, Kent and others making obeisance and trying to get down the steps in their robes, backwards.

They cheered at:

(1) Mr. Baldwin in his carriage.

(2) Queen Mary.

(3) The Royal Pair on Buckingham Palace balcony.'

(Reported from Nottingham, week following May 12.)

Ruislip

41. (CL.100.) 8 p.m. Broadcast of King's speech preluded by the National Anthem. Audience restless while speech lasted; more than restless when it was followed by endless renderings of the anthem, including singing by a soprano who was flat.

Birmingham

42. (CO.35.) Evening. 7.58. We could hear a man's voice on the radio now. No one was listening. My friend asked the barman if it was the King. The barman looked at the clock and said 'Ah! Must be.' (Afterwards we discovered that it was Baldwin.)

Some young men and girls in the opposite corner were singing. Two of the girls were blowing on combs and paper. They sang: *When the poppies bloom again* and *It's a sin to tell a lie*.

The legionary was over at the bar now. A fair-haired young man was there too. He looked a smarmy, ferrety sort of fellow. Suddenly he turned round, raised his hand and said: 'Gentlemen, the King.' We fell silent but we didn't stand up.

While the King was speaking this young man stood with bowed head, the picture of reverence and humility.

A well-dressed, well-built man came in and walked deliberately towards the bar. He glared when people said 'shsh'. Then he stood still and took off his hat.

Four people came in to an accompaniment of 'shshs' tiptoed to the empty middle table.

A red faced woman in a r w & b cap looked in and went out again.

A little man came in through another door. He didn't make a noise, but he made fussy impatient movements, craning his neck to look at the bar. He didn't take off his hat, and after a minute or two went out with a look of annoyance on his face. A man near us said something about him in a disgusted tone.

A lanky man with a long pale face came to the doors and held them open, grinning feebly; when I looked again he was standing inside the room, but still grinning feebly.

The man who had asked for silence must have been a bit tipsy, for his bowed head went lower and lower until it bumped against the chest of the barman standing facing him. The barman pushed the man's head away. He looked up and winked. The barman spat.

As soon as the King had finished this man jumped on to the table and started *God Save the King*. He was so keen that he was ahead of the radio and had to wait until it caught up. People laughed at him, but he sang with great fervour and we stood up and joined in. I noticed that several people moved their mouths without singing.

Hertford

43. (CO.18.) 8 p.m. During the speech those at the tables went on eating, pouring out tea, etc., except for one elderly man sitting alone, who sat with his head on his hand. The waitress brought some food to one table; the people there at once began eating. She made some clatter clearing another table, but no one showed any particular annoyance. (She told me later that she didn't dare to come in again to clear tables until the speech was over.) In the middle of the speech the wireless faded completely for ten seconds or so. The women and the elderly man showed great irritation and disgust; the others looked at each other with puzzled expressions. At the end, when *The King* was played everyone stood up without a hint of hesitation. One man continued to stir his tea. At the beginning of the second verse everyone sat down except the airmen. One woman made some remark and laughed when the second verse started. When the third verse started the airmen were 'standing easy'; two at once

came to the attention again, and lasted out till the end. The other two looked at each other, and walked off, rather guiltily and clearly in two minds.

North Shields

44. (CL.56.) I should also state that while listening to the Abbey service we passed few remarks, but wished that the King had had to make some reference to toleration for other sects besides the Anglican church. We had lunch during the service in order to allow the maid to go early, but this was done as quietly as possible.

We made a special point of listening to the King's speech, which we liked, especially his references to the unemployed and to children. We noticed the long pause before he began and sympathized with him in his difficulty. My mother would have been much more interested had it been Edward VIII who was crowned; she feels that he was more independent in outlook than George VI who, she thinks, will be likely to do just as he is told. We liked Edward VIII for the interest he took in social problems; at the same time we feel that George VI is both conscientious and hard-working, and that he was sincere in his dedication of himself at the Abbey.

When we heard the crowds round Buckingham Palace shouting 'We want the King' for so long before the King appeared, we all grew rather anxious about it, and my Father grew quite annoyed. He kept repeating that Edward VIII would have come out long before, and that if George VI did not soon appear, the whole day would be spoilt for many people. It was a relief to hear eventually that he and the other members of the royal family had appeared on the balcony.

9.30. After supper my mother and I walked along the coast to see bonfires and Whitley Bay and Cullercoats. By this time the rain had cleared off, and as the King's speech was over, people felt free to leave their wirelesses.

Cricklewood

45. (CL.12.) In evening went with friend to have a beer at the local; found everyone laughing and singing *For he's a jolly good fellow*, including people who on Tuesday said that the King is epileptic and stutters—that we're crowning the wrong man, etc. Heard the King's speech relayed here and all applauded the sentiments expressed but deplored his diction. 'Never mind,' said a man, 'he's like his father and his heart's in the right place.' And another, 'You're right, them as say most, do least.' I left as they all joined in song again.

Sussex

46. (CO.16.) 8.10. B.B.C. announcer—'all over Empire people are having parties.' We say we wish we were. Knock at door—surprise visit—my cousin with 5 fellow-students from London physical training college and man friend about same age. 5 of them pretty hefty and all came in 2-seater car with dicky. Shorts, enormous bare legs, one or two with large scarves round necks, mackintoshes.

'Just thought they would blow in', camping from previous evening till Whit. near Sevenoaks. Full of spirits. 'We've just listened in to the King's speech on a portable and there was an old boy with a row of medals coming along the road. So we asked him if he'd like to listen. He stood stiffly at the salute during *God Save the King*.' We asked if they had seen the procession—'Oh! no, got to camp late last night.' 'Spent morning in camp; listened in to all Abbey service of course.' 'Can't see village near for bunting' (amused evidently).

Swansea

47. (CO.28.) May 13. Mrs. H. (charlady): 'Did you hear the King's speech last night?'

Observer: 'No' followed by explanation of why and then 'Was it good?'

Mrs. H.: 'Yes, it was very nice—just like his brother's (meaning Edward VIII) thanking everyone for their kindness to him and the Queen and saying that he'd do his best for everyone.' This was followed by a reference to the fact that he did not stutter but that he stopped periodically. 'You know, you'd think he'd finished and then he'd go on again' but that he couldn't pronounce his 'rs'—She reported that several people had commented on it to her as very noticeable.

She remarked, however, that in view of the strain of the day, etc. 'He did very well.'

For and Against the Coronation

48. One would expect to discover from the answers to the CL. questionnaire not only whether individuals were for or against the Coronation, but some more general indication of popular feeling. Analysis shows, however, that people's estimates of popular feeling must be treated with caution.

In the first place the proportion of varying religious and political views was as follows:

Politics
> Right wing, 14.
> Left wing, 33.
> Non-political, 31.

Religion
> Church of England, 17.
> Other denominations, 19.
> Non-religious, 42.

In the second place, in answer to Question 6 (Were your neighbours mostly keen on the Coronation? What did they say to you about it?), *67 replies attributed to friends and neighbours' views which coincided with the Observer's own views.*

Among 77 replies, only one failed to answer this question.

One reply (from a student at Newnham) stated that neighbours held views other than her own.

Two replies state that neighbours hold more extreme views than the Observer's.

In the other six replies which depart from the general rule, neighbours are stated to hold different views from the Observer, but another group is mentioned as agreeing with him. For example, CL.52 (a teacher) was against the Coronation and stated that neighbours were mostly keen; but that certain teachers and educated people were *not* keen.

CL.102, CL.104, CL.105 are all members of one family, and against the Coronation, though all state that neighbours are keen.

49. The following are examples of the way in which the great majority describe their neighbours as thinking like themselves:

OWN VIEW	NEIGHBOURS' VIEW
CL.12. Wife and mother. 'Most stirring incident when men and women stopped their revelling and stood silent to hear King's speech.' Pro-Coronation.	'They like the King because he is a family man.'
CL.24. Approves of a mid-week holiday, but deplores political harm.	'The boys welcomed the holiday, but were clearly not excited.'
CL.25. No genuine desire to see or hear anything, but went with friends. Pro-Edward.	Overheard members of crowd saying that they had come against their wills. Pro-Edward.

OWN VIEW

NEIGHBOURS' VIEW

CL.33. Against 'except as symbolical affirmation of unity of British Commonwealth.'

'Few people to be seen outdoors, and these were mainly ex-service men wearing their medals, on way to local procession.'

CL.35. No wish to see Procession. Most stirring incident: King's responses in Coronation Ceremony.

Indifferent; most listened in; had sympathy for the King and Queen, thought King got through his speech remarkably well.

CL.36. Keen. Wholeheartedly in favour of a King and Queen.

'Everybody was keen; where there was little or no display, it was because of expense.'

CL.39. 'There is no other country that has such a wonderful King as ours.'

'Yes; my neighbours said it was marvellous.'

CL.42. 'Little desire to see Coronation. One King is much the same as another.'

'Our neighbours all hung out flags, but they could not be called more than mildly interested.'

CL.50. No desire to see.

Neighbours indifferent or considered too much fuss was made.

CL.60. Very keen: saw Procession with Womens' Institute ticket.

Neighbours keen. 'Children all eager to put their flags up.'

OWN VIEW | NEIGHBOURS' VIEW

CL.63. C. of E. Conservative. 'From a Conservative point of view, most gratifying.' Anti-Edward.

'The people around me seemed v. keen. One lady made much of the fact that the Church was responsible for the crowning of the King.'

'Obvious respect and veneration for the Crown.'

'Reception to S. Baldwin only surpassed by reception of K. & Q.'

CL.66. 'As a spectacle, yes; as an enthusiastic, cheering participant, no.'

'Some were quite keen, but many were apathetic.'

CL.99. 'Most stirring incident administering of the Oath by the Archbishop to the King.'

'Several people expressed the desire to dedicate lives to serve others, following the King's example.'

CL.109. In favour. 'I drank fairly steadily during all opening hours.'

In favour, but some 'were more concerned at the time with the binge they were going to have on Coronation Day.'

50. From these results we can only say that not only were people divided in their opinions about the Coronation, but they had totally different pictures of the popular feelings about it, in almost every case based on their own. In this they were doubtless quite normal: if they had recorded that their opinions were at variance with those of their neighbours, they might have been suspected of having an abnormal sense of being differ-

ent, or persecuted. But it is also clear that in arriving at any generalization about public feeling, it is necessary to call a great number of witnesses in order to prevent individual bias from interfering with its accuracy. This must be regarded as one of the main justifications of the Mass-Observation method.

51. An analysis of the answers to Question 2: (Did you yourself see, or did you want to see, the Coronation procession?), gives the following result:

(a) Wanted to see Coronation and saw it - 6
Did not want to see it and saw it - 7
Did not see but would have liked to - 25
Did not see and did not want to see - 40
(b) Specific statements of dislike of crowds 13
Not worth trouble and discomfort - 14
Afterwards wished they had seen it - 3
Did not want to see it, but were afterwards glad - - - - - 2

52. An analysis of the answers to Question 4 (Do you think it benefits the country to have a Coronation?) gives the following result:

For Coronation - - - - - 42
Against - - - - - 20
Undecided - - - - - 25
———
Total - - - - - 87

REASONS:	Political	Psychological	Social	Commercial
FOR -	15	9	25	17
AGAINST	13	3	8	5
	28	12	33	22

In some cases an Observer was pro-Coronation for one reason, and anti-Coronation for another. The above figures do not therefore represent single persons but single votes.

Individual reactions, and individual accounts of other people's reactions, can now be examined in detail. They are both for and against the Coronation, but the majority of those quoted are heterodox, since they tend to be the most illuminating. Of particular interest are those which illustrate an attempt to resist or escape from the Coronation, and the resulting problems and troubles.

Lausanne

53. (CL.69.) *English schoolgirl.* All were enthusiastic about the Coronation, many unreservedly so. At the beginning of the day there was a good deal of regret for the Duke of Windsor, but by the evening all opinion had veered round to King George.

London

54. (CL.55.) *Chef. 31.* I think it benefits the country to have a Coronation in that it puts money into circulation pretty quickly: example: the men who were selling periscopes did a roaring trade, then there is the sale of the national colours, then again on the social side in the higher circles, and the catering, and travelling agents.

All my friends are pleased about the Coronation, and hope the King will live long to enjoy the goodly heritage which is now his. These very weak remarks may, I hope, be of some use to you, but may I end by saying how happy I am we have a King and Queen. We must have a head over the country, and our King is placed in his position by birth, and I do not think it is right to ridicule him because of his high estate.

Beer, S. Devon

55. (CO.1.) (About 8.30 p.m.) The most noteworthy element in the speeches was that voiced with great sincerity by the local baker—that we had gone through a unique experience that day and it reminded us that there was no country on earth where there was so much happiness, prosperity and freedom as in England, and that we should show 'the foreigner' in no unmistakable terms that we valued our happiness and freedom (no prosperity this time). There was no mention of the King and it seemed as if all mention of him was kept in the background as far as possible, and when mention was made, it was in the direction of implied apology —*e.g.* his deeper voice and his sincerity.

56. (CL.26.) (*Conservative and Imperial. Gold Staff Officer.*)
I think the Coronation probably benefits the country as a whole, but at the expense of great and prolonged discomfort to Mayfair and the West End generally.

A large percentage of people who went crazy about the Coronation, if asked to answer this questionnaire, will do so, whereas most of those who were bored to death will not. There is probably therefore a much larger percentage of people who took no particular interest than your statistics will show.

Swansea

57. (CO.28.) The charlady also proceeded to tell me that she had attended the Street tea although on Tuesday she had implied that she was not going to it but explained now that she did not want my mother to know as the latter had been very antagonistic towards it all and that she (my mother) would give her no peace over it. But she 'didn't want to be different' and had paid her 1d. a week. It was all 'very nice' and 'they' had had dancing in the street 'but no rowdyism—all very quiet—friendly' (implying I think no drunkenness, etc.).

South Norwood

58. (CL.22.) Most of them displayed flags, somewhat tardily. Decorations developed a note of social competition,

each trying to be a little more conspicuous or original than those next door.

Typical remarks (after Canterbury's broadcast): 'Now can you imagine Mrs. Simpson listening to that?' 'How impressed foreigners must be!' 'And so good for trade, my dear'; 'Better than having a Dictator, anyway'; 'The man I feel most sorry for is the King.'

Census of decorations on private cars (100 exactly counted in each case):

May 2 (Surrey)	-	-	-	-	- 39%
					45%
8 (Central London)		-	-	- 48%
12 (Croydon)		-	-	- 70%

Consoling thought: One man who demonstrates is more conspicuous than six who don't!

Beer, S. Devon

59. (CO.1.) It appeared from scraps of conversation that there was much veiled competition between streets and even individual houses, *e.g.*

(i) Friends passing and loudly commenting—'I've seen your house, this morning, it's lovely.' 'Have you? Doesn't the west end (*i.e.* of the village) look fine?' 'Your flags are a credit to you!'

(ii) One man told me (the ex-soldier, aged 45) that he had been up at 6 a.m., putting up bunting and paper festoons on his house. He had some pieces left over so he nailed them in a whip-like bunch on his door, and still having some small pieces of red, white and blue paper, he made a frame of them for a portrait of the King cut from the *News Chronicle* and nailed it on his door. His comment on the whole street (named Common Row) was interesting. He said, 'There wasn't a scrap of decoration to be seen yesterday. And people said "Common Row has nothing showing" but we put it all up late last night and this morning.'

Somerset

60. (CL.62.) I had only been in the district a week and only knew two people. One, a married woman of about 30, a villager, told us that most of the people in the village thought Edward ought to be King, and weren't very keen about the Coronation except to have some fun. This village, C—— D——, refused to have anything put on the rates to pay for their fun. Glastonbury and Somerton have a special rate and are in debt. The other person I knew, a youth of about 22 who helps me in the garden, looked forward to May 12th because he would have a whole day free to work for other people. His ordinary work is on the roads but he likes any kind of work. He spent the morning helping a man to hoe his wheat. He spent part of the afternoon cutting and trimming a pole for my wireless. He just liked the extra time. He saw no bonfires nor went to Glastonbury Tor. He didn't want any money to spend either. I owed him some but he didn't want it. I gathered from these two fairly representative country people, different in age, sex and standing, that the village working class just regarded it like an extra feast or treat, but were not at all excited about it.

Gloucestershire village

61. (CL.51.) They all seem to feel George VI is like his father—a safe King. Villagers do not approve of any irregularity in their Royal Family.

North Shields

62. (CL.56.) My young sister's reactions are interesting. She has lately proclaimed herself a socialist (I do not know why) and she strongly objected to the decorations in the nearby houses. She said that if mother put out any flags or ornamentation outside, she would pull them down, so mother had to be content with red, white and blue flowers and two little flags in the window, about which my young sister made disparaging remarks. She snorted about the Coronation cake mother had made, though she did not refuse to eat it! and she listened to none of the wireless broadcast. She found the day very dull. If she had been able, I think she would have enjoyed most a dance or some other binge with boy friends.

London

63. (CO.41.) *Female Typist. Single. 39.*

I became very bored with the word 'Coronation'. Could not buy cigarettes, sweets, biscuits—not even a suspender belt—without finding crowns and what-not on them. Many people I spoke to felt the same, that it was being overdone and artificially bumped-up. Some people expressed the view that it would have been different if it had been Edward to be crowned, as people really *liked* him, whatever his shortcomings.

I caused a commotion in the typing room where I work by pinning up a rather attractive portrait of Edward (looking very sad, but minus wrinkles and bags under eyes!). Room divided into two camps, violent arguments, red faces, blazing eyes, etc. I left them at it, not caring two hoots either way.

Next day one of the girls had pinned up large highly-coloured pictures of King and Queen facing me, but I made no comment whatsoever, not deliberately but merely through indifference, so it fell rather flat.

I became very irritated with the eternal red white and blue decorations. They seemed to act as a physical irritant. I said they gave me acidosis, and much more of it would result in a gastric ulcer, no less. Nevertheless I thought the city streets very pleasing, particularly Cheapside and Gresham Street, which being narrow and fairly old, caught the medieval atmosphere. One could imagine knights passing through on horseback, spear and lance set, etc.

It also gave me quite a pang each day as I came through the back streets of Bermondsey in the train to London Bridge. These streets were a blaze of colour in their inexpensive way, the meaner the street, the more colour. There was something spontaneous about it, which touched me.

What I saw in the West End decorations did not please me so much. I did not like the mixtures of orange and red in some places, and many things definitely offended my eye. Walking along the Mall one evening while a court was being held, I thought—'So this is the peak of our civilization—martial music, and crowds slouching aimlessly along, admiring the phallic symbols and what-not.'

I must add a word about my personal feelings. I found it most enlightening to analyse my feelings, and those of other people who talked to me. I was surprised how much I responded to the atmosphere of the crowd, the cheering, etc. I felt a definite pride and thrill in belonging to the Empire, which in ordinary life, with my political bias, is just the opposite of my true feeling.

Yet I felt a definite sense of relief that I could experience this emotion and be in and of the crowd. One becomes very weary of always being in the minority, thinking things silly which other people care about; one must always be arguing, or repressing oneself, and it is psychologically very bad. One is fighting against the herd instinct all the time. Therefore you will understand that the carnival spirit of the actual Coronation Day *really* was a holiday for me, and I say this without cynicism. I wonder how many others felt the same.

Reviewing it all calmly afterwards, one sees how very dangerous all this is—the beliefs and convictions of a lifetime can be set aside so easily. Therefore, although people will probably always like pageantry, colour, little princesses, etc., and it seems a pity to rob them of this colourful make-believe element—nevertheless because it makes it in the end harder for us to think and behave as rational beings when we are exposed to this strain and tension—I would definitely vote agin it. It is too dangerous a weapon to be in the hands of the people at present in power in this country.

Hertfordshire

64. (CO.44.) There were more people in the S—— Hotel—the radio is going well with the Abbey Service—no one takes any notice—it does not interfere with the hum of conversation. Several ex-soldiers have their medals on the lapel of their jackets. I am hailed by someone I know who buys me a beer.

The conversation seems to be about the war, and about how some of the Zeppelins were brought down in the district. The man who hailed me is a builder's son—I have never seen his friend before but he is a rotund little man with a complacent look—conversation changes to the local celebrations. Choir on the Radio singing beautifully.

One of my acquaintances explains about a 'Feu de joie' and how it is performed by firing rifles in quick succession all down the ranks. This brings the conversation to the Abbey ceremony—the little rotund man is enthusiastic about how the various Prime Ministers drove to the service, Mr. Baldwin with an escort of mounted police, etc., and the escort of North West Mounted Police for the P.M. of Canada.

At 11.45 I decide to have a drink at the D—— Hotel, the oldest and most important in the Town.

Not many people in the bar—one old retired Colonel type of man talking to another (Col. obviously very deaf). Other man struggles to carry on a conversation under difficulties—the topic is whisky and whisky drinkers in the old days—how they had seen men swallow tumblers and half-tumblers at a time. They did not mention the Coronation.

Another man standing at bar by himself—may be a builder or something of the sort—friends come in and greet him; one says: 'Tcht Hullo Lilly' in a pansy, nancy-boy way referring to a lily of the valley button-hole he has.

He tells his newly arrived friends of how he is going to stay at Portsmouth with a brother who has a position connected with the Navy. He seems to relish the idea of a stay at Portsmouth and reiterates 'All right Boy' with a broad wink and adds 'Sailors don't care' at which the barmaid smiles.

South London

65. (CO.45.) Very few people appeared to be out, in fact it seemed like Sunday in the High Road, I called in a snack bar, ordered a cup of tea and a packet of cigarettes, I was the only customer at the time, and the waiter seemed reluctant to put down the newspaper he was reading to serve, I remarked it was a bad day, he agreed and said that some people would lose a lot of money as a result of it. I said that may be so but the pubs and cinemas would do well, he still remarked that a lot of people would lose money, the conversation came to an end, he was about to pick up his newspaper again when another customer rolled in, this was an ice cream salesman who cursed the weather, I finished drinking and went out.

Lancashire

66. (CO.30.) 6 p.m. I left the office at 6.0 and walked towards the bus. The streets were crowded with people dressed in their best clothes and the whole atmosphere reminded me of a Sunday evening. The bus conductor seemed very dissatisfied that he was not getting double pay for the day which, he considered, was a day of rest. During tea I conversed with my Grandfather who had taken no notice of the Coronation. I asked him how he had liked the day. 'No different to any other' he replied.

67. (CL.66.) 11.30 a.m. Looked in at *Children's Dancing, etc. Display* at Blackpool Football Ground. Wandered round endeavouring to ascertain how people were feeling. For the most part they were dispassionate—outwardly at any rate—with the exception of the children, parents and officials. Here and there, a middle aged man danced an impromptu jig. The enthusiasm which mingled with the applause seemed to be largely parental. The most enthusiasm was aroused by the formation of a 'living Union Jack' by the school children. In the singing and cheering later I noticed that strange self consciousness of adults which does not appear to hamper children. Each man waits to see if the one next to him will sing, and finally, encouraged by a few enterprising singers, all begin to sing in an undertone.

During the formation of the Union Jack, just before the children finally bent down to show the flag at what one might call the 'crisis', I looked at the faces of two young boys near to me—'thrilled and expectant' and that of a woman—'tense anticipation'. Before I was mildly interested. Then upon observing the faces of these two, a strange thrill—apparently quite disconnected from everything—passed through me. I was annoyed, and a little afterwards wondered why.

68. (CO.24.) Observer met a working class man (father of a family) in the train.

After a few odd remarks, he suddenly said: 'Not much heart in it this time. Not like the Jubilee. Leicester was better. Nottingham very poor. . . . Decorations rotten . . . nothing doing. . . . The Duke of Windsor was very popular. . . . W. took all the shine out of it . . . (wistfully) I practically loved him. . . . He worked jolly hard for his country.

'But it all came such a surprise . . . I felt disappointed.

'Even a working man wants something for himself. But this woman was third-hand as it were—with all due respect to the woman. Of course he was a human being after all. . . . This other fellow fancies it, I think, and the Queen. He didn't really want it. I saw him once in Halifax. He looked dreadfully tired.

'Still we have to have a king.'

(13.5.37; taken down mostly at the time.)

Lancashire

69. (CO.36.) 12.45. *J.* (speaks). D'you know, I was the only one not wearing a favour at the shop (factory). Everybody's decorated their portion of the shop. Just here and there are a few blank spaces, and I say to them as I'm passing along giving the work out 'Hello! what's the matter here?' They just look, but of course I know why.

Some of the girls are most ardently patriotic. They amaze me. When it comes to election time they always vote conservative—you see them wearing bows of blue ribbon (conservative colour)—yet they are most ardent and enthusiastic Trade Unionists. The two don't go together, but they don't see it. That's what I can't understand about them.

All yesterday they were singing (while machining) all the patriotic songs they could think of, *Land of hope and glory* and so on.

Self. I'm surprised it's allowed.

J. Well, I'm in charge. How could I stop it? And it's an occasion. Besides they work on piece rates. So if they slow up, it's their own loss.

Last night 6 of the girls went down to London. They'd crotcheted themselves tammies of red white and blue, and a crowd went to see them off.

I said to them, 'D'you expect to be back at work to-morrow?' they said, 'Oh yes, nine o'clock.' But I've promised to leave the door open till they come.

70. 2.15. (While waiting for J.)

Self. Do you know what time the next bus will go?

Young woman (probably Irish, and a servant girl, having the day off). One's only just gone. I don't know.

(Later.)

Self. D'you know what time the next bus will go?

Elderly working woman. No.

Self. Everywhere's very quiet. I thought a lot would have been going on.

E.W.W. I don't know. My son's in the ambulance at H——.

Self. What's on there?

E.W.W. Soldiers parading—firing guns.

Self. D'you enjoy it all?

E.W.W. It's all right. It makes a change. I don't suppose I'll see another Coronation.

Self. D'you agree we should have kings and queens?

E.W.W. It's not what we want, it's what we get. We've got to have them.

Self. Yes, but if we could please ourselves, would you rather have them or not?

E.W.W. I shouldn't like to do without them. The Queen's a good mother and she's two nice children. I've lived in five reigns.

(Arrival of J.)

2.35 p.m. (Servant girl and ourselves enter bus at terminus).

Self. We're going to a tea-party down in ——, that is if we can get invited.

Irish servant girl. I'm going to one at my mother's in ——, but no strangers will be allowed. I don't think they'll let you join in if you haven't some relations.

Self. No, we don't know anybody but we'll ask them if they'll let us join in if we pay.

I.S.G. That won't make any difference. At least not if it's like it is in my mother's street. They only want their own.

Self. Why are you wearing a bow? We haven't bothered.

I.S.G. Oh . . . everyone else has one. They haven't put out any flags where I am.

Self. Why not?

I.S.G. I don't know. Nobody's said anything.

(We comment on the appearance of the streets. An old man looks interested and smiles. I cannot remember how I started a conversation with him. I know I was determined to engage his interest and he seemed eager to talk. He was often indistinct.)

Old Man. Last Coronation I'll see. I'm 77 years old. I was thirty years under King's colours and I wouldn't change. Best country in the world. Been in China, India. I got 6d. a day: sometimes it was only dry bread. I'd do it again. I'd go again to-morrow if I was 17. There's going to be a war soon.

(We alight: walking through streets we see Congregational Church board on which is printed 'God save the King and us'.)

J. In our factory one man has up 'God save us'.

71. 4.15 p.m. (J. and I make our way to a friend of J.'s in the not too immediate district.)

E. J——! How nice to see you.

J. We're down here this afternoon looking at the decorations and tea parties: so I suggested we called here to see you.

E. (a widow, childless; 40-ish; shopkeeper in poor working class neighbourhood). Yes. Take me as you find me.

J. We expect to ...

J. You don't get out much?

E. How can I? It's a good job I'd my good time before I was married. I've had little enough chance since, being cooped up here. The first time I'm able to go out I'll paint the town red. But I think I've almost forgotten how.

(I forget how the following found its place in the conversation, but it did.)

E. The support of tradition was desired by the majority of people in the neighbourhood. They are not concerned who is king, but they desire a king.

Would you like a cup of tea with me? You're welcome to anything I have. Would you like something out of the shop? Ham? Tongue? It's very nice.

J. We're delighted to have anything. We'll get tea while you serve.

(We do.)

You know E.'s an imperialist. She's true blue. She's intelligent though.

E. I wonder if Mrs. Simpson has been listening in? She must be conscious that she couldn't fulfil the position desired of her.

(E. attends to shop.)

Voice of woman being served in shop. I cried when Queen Mary came in. She's so well loved. A lovely broadcast.

E. Yes, I cried too. I felt all bottled up.

72. 6 p.m. *E.* You know I think the Duke of Windsor was ruined. He became a war-minded youth; spoilt by the influence of the war. Early in the beginning the important people of the country and society were called to France, and as leaders went away, all home-influence was withdrawn.

Mrs. Simpson's an ambitious woman who's tripped herself up. The duke was popular, I know, but weak. Spoilt. What he's lacked are home ties.

Self. What do people here say about them?

E. I haven't much in common with them. They just talk about their neighbours. What this one's doing next door, or the one across. Nobody ever swears in this shop, though. I think that's a tribute. Don't you? They do respect me I think.

When I do go out I'll really enjoy myself. But when I have the facility I shall have forgotten how to.

There aren't many communists in this district. People aren't ready yet for anything better.

73. 10.30 p.m. (On the bus home.)

Self. Good evening Mr. ———. You don't know me, but I know you.

Mr. —— (Unitarian minister). There are a good many who know me, whom I don't know. We're coming back from a day on the moors. There's been a really good crowd of 50 of us. All left-wingers. And we haven't mentioned the Coronation once during the day. Our —— contingent joined a group from ——, and we met a third group at —— where we all had tea in a schoolroom. At the end of the evening I suggested we might sing *God Save the King*; after all I thought we are all of this country. We are all members. But a young woman came up to me and said 'I didn't ask that we should sing the *Internationale*, so I don't think you ought to ask us to sing the National Anthem'. So I compromised. No, shall I say we finished off by singing *Auld Lang Syne*.

Hertfordshire

74. (CO.44.) 3 p.m. First call in —— is the urinal under the decorated clock Tower. Here we meet two members of the local Labour Party—they invite us to come with them to 'The Clarion' Youth Hostel, a centre for young people of Left political views started by the *New Clarion* and now constituted on the basis of a friendly Society—but actually being a centre for left propaganda, education and culture. We are pleased to meet some members and accept their invitation—all crowding into the Austin. We find we know a number of the people present, the warden a local County Councillor—and a Communist who addressed a L. Book-Club meeting once—and several other familiar faces—a red flag with the Hammer and Sickle flies in the garden, where we find two young men in earnest conversation—one tall bespectacled and unshaven—the other short, dapper, very dark haired, smart with a sensitive face, a foreign accent, and eloquent gestures of the hands.

We were shown all over the premises by hospitable members—including a recreation hut where billiards and dancing are the pastimes. I join in the singing—and dance with a striking blonde girl whom they sometimes call 'Jean Harlow' (there is a resemblance I suppose). I play the piano for the others to sing, old songs of the Music Hall variety seem to be in request. *Daisy* (a 'Bicycle made for two') etc. also Irish airs. Just to be provocative I play *Land of Hope and Glory*.

This elicits general laughter and chaffing but one middle aged man looks seriously annoyed so to appease him I play the *Internationale*.

75. (CL.48.) *Woman barrister, 37—Left Wing tendencies— but with a love of luxury and pageantry. She wrote:* And now the Coronation is driving London dotty. The decorations look awful—every available cul-de-sac—every park—every square is just one mass of public lavatories—I trust we shan't have an outbreak of typhoid, but I don't see what they are going to do with the sewage. Troughs for the men and I suppose pans or buckets for the women. It intrigues me to know what they will do with it.

Oxford

76. (CL.3.) 9.15–12.0. Dressed. Wrote a poem. Annoyed by patriotic and religious activities at Church opposite. Read a magazine, *Light and Dark*, to which I had contributed. Began to rewrite a criticism of Edgar Poe.

12.0–12.30. Friend came to discuss my attitude to women. Decided I was a pervert. He is monogamous.

12.30–1.0. Went out to observe Coronation activities. There weren't any. A few new whores in the streets. No expensive cars outside hotels.

Southend-on-Sea

77. (CL.10.) I rose at 9 o'clock this morning, glanced through the paper, being much more interested in the news from Spain and the bus strike than the pages of 'historic supplements'. At 11 I switched on the wireless to hear the broad-

cast, but this was for the sake of others in the house, who, by the way, merely wanted to hear because they thought it an historic occasion. After that I read Voltaire's *Candide*, and at 12 o'clock adjourned for a pint to the local pub. Switched on the wireless again at 2.0 for the same reason as before, and off at 2.30. Reading Pat Sloan's *Soviet Democracy* all the afternoon.*

78. (CO.2.) *Prestwick*. Three young men are painting the house and wall, opposite. They are 'down for the day' and are friends of the young working class widow who lives in the house. They are obviously enjoying the painting. They grin and joke.†

79. (CL.4.) *Engineering apprentice*, 21. On the 12th I cycled all day in company with two University students. We spent a glorious day around the Chilterns. Most villages passed through had loudspeakers going and every green had bonfires ready for igniting.‡

80. (CL.22.) Went into the country—very quiet country, remote from towns and main roads, on the Kent-Sussex border. Even so, did not entirely escape from the Coronation atmosphere. Every habitation decorated, and from every cottage came the sound of the cheering. Very few people about in fields or gardens—evidently all listening to the broadcast commentary. At each village there were celebrations in the open air—dancing, sports, brass bands. Somehow

*Reading books is one way of shutting oneself up and shutting the Coronation out.

†These men are not making any fuss about turning their backs on the Coronation. They are just taking their holiday in the way most natural to them; however, they are 'decorating' a house, but in something more practical than bunting.

‡These lads were three of many who used the holiday to get out into the country, and they do not appear to have had any strong sense of guilt about it. Naturally, they found the rustic celebrations in full swing.

the countryside seemed to purify even Coronation emotionalism of its unhealthy fever. It was spontaneous merry-making that we saw, probably little changed from what it was centuries ago.

81. (CL.84.) *Schoolboy*. On Coronation day I rose early to find the weather not too promising for my friend and I to carry out a pre-arranged outing.

However, I packed my sandwiches and puncture outfit in a case which I fastened to the carrier of my bicycle. I called for my friend and we set out.

Reaching Eastern Avenue we saw many others coming from London.

The weather had brightened up as we passed Seven Kings.

On the wide footpath were road signs giving casualty list on that road for 1936.

As we passed Romford we increased our speed till we reached Gallows Corner, where we had a short rest. Here we turned to the left, and after going up and down several hills, we found ourselves opposite Warley Barracks. These were decorated with varieties of coloured flags. Opposite the barracks were many big guns which my friend and I inspected.

A little further on we saw an ideal wood for a picnic, but on asking if it was private, we received the affirmative answer with dismay.

After cycling on again for about ten minutes we sat and ate part of our lunch.

This done we made towards home as the weather looked threatening.

Just after passing through Shenfield we heard a drone above us and looking up we saw an aeroplane stunting. Carrying on we came to an aerodrome, where we stopped just in time to see an aeroplane land and two ascend. There was a Flying Flea taxi-ing along, but it could not gather enough speed to rise.

As the rain began to fall heavily we rushed back to our respective homes.

At half past two I was dry, and eating the remnants of my lunch. I switched on the wireless and listened to the Coronation ceremony. When this had finished I read a book till seven o'clock when my father came home.

I was having my tea when my mother returned. After tea we went into the drawing room and listened to the Coronation party. When this was over I retired to bed rather tired but happy.

This was not the proper action to take on Coronation Day, but I wanted to get away from the overcrowded streets of London.

82. (CL.95.) *Schoolboy.* On Coronation Day we had a holiday so I thought I would have a rest and so I stayed in bed all the morning reading. I got up and had my dinner and then cleaned out my animals which are a dove, rabbit and two guinea pigs. My dove takes a long time as I have to sift his sand. By then it was nearly teatime so I went to the library and changed my books. Then I had tea and afterwards went to my friend's house where I played darts until about 9 o'clock. Then I went home and to my surprise my auntie had come to see us and we stayed talking to about half past ten when I went to bed.

Cricklewood

83. (CL.12.) *Wife and mother, 33.*

Had extra hour in bed and read morning paper. Spent most of morning in garden making enclosure for tortoise as decide simple things are satisfying, but wireless sets are giving off loud cheers and wish secretly I was seeing procession. Dash into house frequently to hear parts of Abbey service and King's avowals—think the commentating boring. Drink

sherry at midday meal, rest of family gloomy, decide broadcast of big events brings feeling of isolation.*

London

84. (CL.5.) *Platonist*.† Soon after my alarm clock had struck,
I got up (at about 7.0). I noticed with malicious pleasure that
the weather was not fine, for I wanted the weather to be bad
to spite the coronation-mongers. I am disappointed that it is
not raining, but bethought myself that it might rain at the time
of the procession. I washed, dressed and shaved in an even more
leisurely manner than usual; for I dislike hurrying over this
operation, since I often feel worried at the beginning of the
day, and I feel the need of time to brood on my worries.
I prepared and ate my breakfast, over which I read part of
the *Communist Manifesto* from Emile Burns' *Handbook of
Marxism*.

After breakfast I put some hair oil on my head, as a pro-
phylactic against threatening baldness, noting the resemblance between the King and myself in respect of this action.
At this time (10 a.m.), when I was in my bedroom, I was a
little startled to see a bird (a sparrow, I fancy) beating its
wings for a short time (perhaps three seconds) against the
window-pane. For a moment I thought it was perhaps im-
prisoned between the panes of the open window. On going
nearer I concluded that it had seen, and was trying to get out,
a daddy long legs or some such creature, which was motion-
less in an approximately upright position (*i.e.* head near
ceiling) against one of the panes. I thought (i) of 'nature red
in tooth and claw' (ii) that the bird was observing the source

---

*Alternative to books as a means of escape is attachment to animals.
You have to attach yourself to something.

†Two very queer things happened to this man who spent his Coronation Day arranging shelves. Both involved feelings of guilt, and the first
was preceded by an act of self-anointing, which he felt to be parallel to
the anointing in the Abbey. Both incidents raised feelings about being
secret and boxed up.

of its sustenance, even as the Coronation crowds would be doing, (iii) that the bird's observation of the daddy long legs ought to be included in mass-observation. I noticed also the terrifyingly fragile and almost beautifully exact structure of the insect (I wondered whether it was technically an insect, and counted six legs on it). I thought also that it was too transparent for decency. This last thought arose from my squeamishness.

85. At about 10.45 I began to take out of some boxes which had arrived on May 11 a number of books and papers, and arrange them on some bookshelves which I had had put up on the previous day, and also elsewhere in my sitting-room and in my bedroom. I continued this occupation with little intermission (I had no lunch) till about 5.45 p.m.

86. At about 5.45 an unexpected incident happened to me, to which I recall no parallel in my life. I opened a 'printed paper rate' postal communication from the Cambridge Preservation Society. This communication had reached me about three weeks earlier, but, having been extremely busy, and perhaps also not anxious to explore a request for money, I had left it unopened. (The envelope bore the words 'Cambridge Preservation Society'.) Inside, besides the printed communication from the Cambridge Preservation Society, I found a sealed envelope addressed to a person whom I did not know, and bearing undistributed stamps to the value of 1½d. Rather impulsively, I opened it, and found inside a document evidently not belonging to the communication from the Preservation Society, and of a suspicious and perhaps illegal nature. In some alarm at my unintentional but still reckless participation in an affair that might possibly lead to legal proceedings, I resolved to send the document to the Secretary of the Cambridge Preservation Society. This, coming at the end of a boring and long-drawn out stretch of work, took me by surprise.

London, W. 11

87. (CO.7.) 9–12. When the announcer began to describe the ceremony R. and I went out to collect plants and earth from the garden. When we came back we found the fuse had blown just as the King was taking the oath, and J. was trying to fix it. He came in and out, and turned the lights on and off and said: 'Sod the Pope and everything—if there's one thing that maddens me, it's electric fuses.'

6–9. Put on gum-boots and built a rockery with the stolen stone and earth we had brought, and planted most of the plants before it began to rain hard.*

Vienna (translated from the German)

88. (CL.75.) . . . In the garden were 2 other young women with 2 young children—already to-day an unusual sight. The 1-year old child who was quite a stranger to me crept towards me and allowed me to take her on my knee, where it stayed quite happily, until its mother said: 'Please drop her quickly, she is as punctual as the clock in her habits.' The owner of the garden told me that her new neighbour who had moved in yesterday had immediately visited her to point out that on her fence was 'Heil Hitler'. He was very surprised at her calmness when she told him that it had been like that for 2 years, that it had been constantly whitewashed and after a long rain always reappeared. We inspected the fine fruit trees which were in bloom; even almonds bloom and ripen there and many years she gets 50 kg. of almonds. There are also asparagus, strawberries and wonderful tulips and irises and a swimming pool; unfortunately the bathing season has not yet opened.

89. Then I visited my solicitor, who had to go out at that

---

*Trees were being planted, and according to a Lancs Observer, rock-gardens being built for ceremonial reasons at this time; but this one was a purely private affair.

moment, and took me with him in his car. He told me that he wanted to go to Asia Minor in the summer to see the Hittite monuments there. I got out at the Opera and walked over to the big market to see what the food prices were like there, but I found that neither meat nor fruit were in the least bit cheaper than in our district. The American apples, which are now almost the only ones on the market, are exorbitant. At 5.30 I sat in front of the Café Museum and got hold of all the Vienna, Prague and English papers. The strong wind soon forced me to go inside. I read details about the preparations and the beginning of the Coronation day. In the evening there was already a telegraph photo from London. A friend of mine came in with her dog which immediately sat on me. Mrs. S. said that she and her son had had a very heavy day as he supplied the papers with photographs and the telephone and the front door had not kept still the whole day. At 8 I came home and had supper. My son H. said it was a pity I had missed the Coronation report on the wireless. We only had a German gramophone record relay, whilst in Budapest they had the direct relay from London. I then listened to a 'bunter Abend' on the wireless, looked at pictures in the *Geographical Magazine*. There was an article about the Zulus in Africa. One got the impression that the life of these people is absolutely taken up with fear for evil spirits and witches and with protection against these harmful influences. Then I read a few pages out of an English book about the Stuarts, and thought how the fight over the unrestricted power of the Crown ended in favour of the people. To-day apparently both King and people in England thrive in this state of affairs.

Middleton, Lancs.

90. (CL.15.) At 8.50 a.m. I left home to play in a golf match. (The Club had organized matches for Ladies and Gentlemen for morning and afternoon and a whist drive for the evening.) However, after the morning match I went home

—not particularly, however, for the purpose of hearing the broadcast—arriving at 12.30 just in time to hear the broadcast of the actual crowning of the king.

West London

91. (CO.17.) 9 a.m. to noon. I awoke again at nine and, remembering that my brother would be calling for me at ten to go for a game of tennis, I got up at once. Sky was dull, day seemed depressing. However, no rain, so some prospect of a game of tennis. By the time I had washed and shaved, and eaten my cereal and grapefruit, it was 10.5. My brother arrived and stayed a few minutes in conversation with my wife and myself. 'It (the rain) will hold off for two or three hours at least,' he said. She replied that it was fortunate for the crowds who had been waiting in the open so long, although she had scant sympathy with such spectacle-greedy fools.

My brother and I left the house for the public tennis courts where we usually play. The weather brightened considerably. On the way, I noticed that only about one house in four was undecorated. 'How deserted the streets are!' I had to remark; 'not a soul about.' It was as if a very early curfew had restricted people within their doors. The chief sign of life was the sound here and there from a loudspeaker delivering the commentator's account of the early part of the Coronation proceedings.

We reached the ground, and I obtained a ticket for one hour on a singles court. We began to play the balls over to each other prior to a serious game. My brother was running to make a return when he fell. I could see he had gone down very heavily on his chest, and rushed round to his side of the court. He had struck his face on the hard surface, and got up dazed with a badly lacerated chin. With the help of the groundsman I bathed the wound and bound it up and we came home. On arrival I took off the temporary bandaging, bathed the badly torn place afresh, and applied a better dressing. My brother took a little brandy as we sat down in the drawing room and played a quiet game of chess. I turned on the radio and so listened to the descriptive account of the Coronation being broadcast at the moment. We seemed fated to hear the actual crowning ceremony, which we intended to ignore when we set out earlier to play tennis.

Lancashire

92. (CO.30.) I laid in bed till 6.15 a.m. and got up, washed and shaved. I ate my breakfast and read the paper. On leaving the house I encountered a tramp who asked if I could make him some tea. He looked a pitiable creature and held two half-pennies in a grimy hand as if to offer payment for the service. I told him I was in a hurry to catch the bus and that no one else in the house was up as yet. Although I must have seemed aloof to him the sight touched me deeply and were I completing the mass circular I should have named that incident as the most emotional. Owing to this delay I missed my usual bus and had to wait ten minutes in the rain.*

93. 3.0–6.0 p.m. Attending to office work. The clerk on duty foolishly tried to lift me up and in doing so caught the back of my hand upon the point of his pencil and caused a bad scratch which bled profusely. I remonstrated with him and he apologised and felt ill at ease for his idiocy. The effect of the act on me was to put me out of humour for the rest of the day. I went into my own room and studied law for the rest of the afternoon.

Cambridge

94. (CO.19.) Lunch time–3 p.m. Just before starting lunch we heard a bagpipe in the street. Five undergrads were strolling along, with streamers from the player, who walked

*Feelings of guilt and pity seem both to have been heightened.

in front. As they passed our window G. W. M. threw a flaskful
of water on them. (He said he knew them—they were Peter-
house men, often in the 'Little Rose', a pub.) Before we knew
what was happening two of them, fighting drunk (the others
were just merry) came up and started throwing their weight
about. G. W. M. did *not* know them after all, and F. S. W. got
two nasty bruises, P. C. C. was tumbled into the fender,
G. W. M. got a black eye, and they then started to try and
take his red bow. One of them said, 'He's got red socks as well!'

Swansea

95. (CO.28.) 9.30 a.m. Mrs. H. (my mother's charwoman)
informed that she had broken her tooth yesterday—She now
thinks she cracked it a few weeks ago and that when biting on
bread roll yesterday she thinks it broke finally although it was
some time after when extracting a crumb from underneath it
that she discovered it to be in two pieces.

A few minutes later she was recounting the story to my
mother and I overheard her add 'So I shall remember the
Coronation'.

96. (CL.4.) As for peculiar incidents, the only one I can
recall is an accident on the Oxford Rd. A sports car lay in a
deep ditch. Between it and the road was a fairly high fence.
It wasn't damaged . . . ?

97. (CL.14.) *Between Southport and Liverpool.* (3.30 or so.)
Passed two men on the road having an argument about
money. One of them threw about 10/od worth of silver in
the tram track, but later came back and picked it up.

98. (CO.11.) On the night of May 11, Coronation Eve, I
was at the flat of my mistress in the London suburb of Leyton,
walking through fog, owing to hold-up in the tram service.

From 9 a.m. we lay in bed, and I discussed with my companion, G., the relations of her married sister, V., with her

husband, R. Of late, R. had been troubled with dreams in which he committed murder, and other dreams in which V. had left him, and V. had been concerned enough to consult the family doctor.

V. was frank enough to tell R. of her visit to the doctor, and R. then told her of an incident, some weeks before, when she had asked him to go to the cellar for a hammer with which to remove a nail from the child's shoe. Having brought the hammer, he remembers coming towards V. whose back was turned, when the thought of striking her down with it entered his head most powerfully. We agreed, G. and I, that the whole story was very similar to cases where a person of apparent good nature and cheerfulness has suddenly run amok and killed his nearest relatives, and we agreed also that minor displays of temper acted as a safety valve against the accumulation of anger to a dangerous point.

Thinking again of Mass-Observation, it occurred to me to wonder how it would be possible, if at all, to measure the accumulation of unexpressed sadism amongst the people, as economic and social conditions worsen, and to draw conclusions as to the probable directions of outlet, when a climax is reached.

Dreams and Phantoms

99. People were asked in the questionnaire for the funniest and most peculiar incidents of the day, as well as for the most stirring.

Note on *peculiar* and *funny*: these terms taken together are fairly obviously distinct from one another, but taken separately they tend to overlap. 'Funny' can often be stretched to cover the same disparaging connotation as 'peculiar'. It is not surprising that the distinction between the incidents in these two categories is somewhat blurred.

324

On the other hand, *stirring* incidents are in a relation of simple opposition to *funny* ones. If someone is not stirred by something intended to be stirring, he will probably say it is funny.

More incidents were sent in as 'funny' than as 'peculiar', partly perhaps because people were doubtful what would count as peculiar. There were, however, many incidents recorded both in answers to the questionnaire (CL.) and in Observers' reports (CO.) which have a peculiar quality, or a quality which is in some sense an amalgam of funny, peculiar and stirring; perhaps what they have in common is that they illustrate a somehow disturbing attitude towards the day, either in the Observer or in those observed; sometimes expecting or hoping for disaster, sometimes using the celebrations as a basis for free fantasy; and among these it is fair to include the dreams which Observers have recorded. In each case one may well ask why it was that the Observer noticed this particular incident or dreamt this particular dream. All, incidents and dreams, are connected by having happened on the same day, but there seems to be more to it than that. The common element is the Coronation. Sometimes its influence is barely definable; at other times it can obviously be interpreted along psychological or anthropological lines. The same element has been discernible throughout the reports, especially in the London night scenes, in Birmingham and Glasgow, and in descriptions of what befell people who tried to shut the Coronation out. It is macabre and atavistic, and suggests a haunting by ancestors; which after all is what one would expect on such a day.

100. Of the 77 people who answered the leaflet, 39 gave a 'funniest' incident and 29 a 'most peculiar'. The following is a list of 'funniest' incidents:

Policemen climbing Victoria Memorial to dislodge spectators.

Two Army Chaplains out of step.

Two men dancing round policeman singing *Rule Britannia*.

Non-appearance of Corporation officials at local celebration.

A policeman who said he was a stranger in those parts.

Not a holiday, a holy day.

Dustmen sweeping up after horses.

Taxi-rocking.

Broadcast misunderstood as rumour of King's illness.

King, Lion and Unicorn, with 'God bless them' underneath.

Woman who saw Queen Mary's coach empty, and expressed wish to ride in it.

Parodying the words in Abbey ceremony.

Football match in female attire.

Broadcast about corns.

Syllabus of 'air raid precautions' in remote hamlet.

Faces of members of Abbey congregation who couldn't get at the champagne.

People sitting in rain watching pageant in local park.

Woman who slept through procession.

People with newspapers on their heads in the rain.

Archaism of broadcast ceremony.

'Highbrow' music of Abbey ceremony.

'Steaks' for 'steps'.

Communist party ought to be renamed Zionist party.

Old lady, 'Did they have a Coronation in London as well?'

Chelsea pensioners very old. They date from Charles II.

Old villager: since the last Coronation, his under story was no longer able to support his upper.

'Amble Tonia' as name of row of houses.

Singing out of tune at country pub.

Midnight party at Girls' school.

Poem by 'Neptune' at pageant.

Drunk undergraduate.

Untidy woman running out to see street musicians.

Neighbour's face three feet away seen through bow window at 8 a.m.

Broadcast reference to 'the Queen' meaning Queen Mary.

Girl swarming up rope into tree to see procession.

Boy in Isle of Man shouted 'Good-night' to girl he didn't know.

Britannia's statue draped in red, white and blue.

Little girl's comments on broadcast (*ingénue*).

101. The peculiar flatness of most of these jokes must be put down partly to the excitement of the day, which made people willing to be amused, partly to a sense of the holiness of the day which easily produced 'laughter in church'. The 'most peculiar incidents' may be summarized as follows:

Mother allotted near seat independently.

Presented with flag by Mayoress; did not want it.

More decoration in meaner streets.

Chinaman in plaid trousers.

American's offer to buy regalia.

Robing and disrobing during ceremony.

No decorations on police station.

American's offer to buy Coronation robes.

Mother with large family, half-heartedly looking for yet another child in crowd.

Champagne corks popping in Abbey during ceremony.

Curious behaviour of crowd outside palace.

Crowd outside palace demanding King, in spite of his exacting day.

Man throwing money into tram-track in Liverpool.

Reactions of indifferent friends under stress of excitement.

Accident in Oxford Road.

Illegal document unaccountably enclosed in circular from Cambridge Preservation Society.
Irish maid asked what 'G.R.' stood for.

102. Now we can look at some incidents which have this surprising or disturbing quality, quoted in full from both CL. and CO. reports, including a number of recorded dreams. They represent in fact that residuum of the day which at present defeats precise analysis or explanation, but which is important as giving it its dominant tone or character, a character which is made up of the totality of the fantasy and image-making of all the individuals.

Leeds

103. (CL.65.) *Female. Married. Italian. 31.*

Woke at 8 a.m., stopped the alarm clock and then turned over and had another sleep. At 9.15 was awakened by newsboys shouting 'Coronation . . . off! Coronation . . . off!'

Is it called off? I thought. I jumped out of bed, knocked at the window for the paper. The newsboy looked toward my direction but made no attempt to cross the road. I knocked again, opened the window partially but the newsvendor disregarded me altogether and kept on shouting as he went along.

Watford

104. (CO.12.) 3.20. Crowds are streaming into the park all the time, and now I hear the first newsboys: 'Ten pages of Coronation Pictures.' I go on working.

'Coronation Tragedy: Ten pages of pictures!' I finish my work shortly and settle down with my book. I wonder if it is an interesting tragedy, and whether I should go out for a paper, but the *Star* only says that there were rumours that a stand had fallen in Piccadilly, when only a glass case had fallen. When it was denied by St. John's Ambulance, Rumour invented a crash somewhere else, and so travelled round London. We conclude the tragedy is off.

Hertford

105. (CO.26.) I saw nothing that really excited me, but one thing I saw did make me think a lot. An ambulance arrived to take away someone who had had a fit on a neighbouring field where races and Punch & Judy show, etc., had been taking place. Rapidly a large crowd formed—many of them running in order, presumably, that they might see something.

Ilkley, Yorkshire

106. (CO.3.) 1.30. Down the village to see the judging. Town Hall and Winter Gardens are chock-a-block, atmosphere 'like Boots Cash Chemist and all the bottles burst'. Went on to the bus garage and saw the tradesmen's vans and lorries. First prize to greengrocer with every apple and potato spit and polished till you could part your hair in it. Lovely great horses—and the judging was done in earnest. Out they came from the cart—off came harness, and for ten or fifteen minutes each horse was gone over. 'He'll be dangling his ticket round Ilkla on his round tomorra.' Butcher's cart with pastoral group of very dead skinned sheep in red white and blue bows. Lorry of Baptist Sunday School in white nighties and gold crowns, with a cross and 'Crown Him Lord of All'.

Hertford

107. (CO.18.) 6.15 p.m. A very heavy storm broke, and the crowd fled into the marquee. We left about 6.45, but by 7 games, races, etc. were recommenced. There was one particular detail. An effigy of a footballer had been hanged under a black skull and cross bones flag. I was told that in a rag hockey match a player was sent off for rough play, and then hanged in effigy. I am not sure what time this happened, but

roughly about 3 p.m. This dummy was left hanging all the evening.

Essex

108. (CL.27.) The *most stirring* thing in the day for me was at the pageant at the dance when the figure in white fur stepped forward presenting Canada and their playing of the *Maple Leaf*. It wasn't the fact that I'm a Canadian but that it seemed so strange to hear that piece in a strange country and I thought of all the people from the Colonies farther away and different races and wondered what their feelings must have been. It just struck me what a good idea this British Commonwealth of Nations was. The funniest incident was seeing three men dancing around a policeman singing *Rule Britannia*.

Sussex

109. (CO.16.) Funniest incident—On the sports field I saw a young woman who had been running. She had on a long coat, open, and an old leather motor bike crash helmet because of the rain I suppose. For the rest—long bare muddy legs, shorts and shirt, with a cigarette and pushing the pram.

Village in Co. Durham

110. (CL.99.) Question. What was the most stirring incident 'heard'?

Answer. The most stirring incident was when I heard (on the wireless) the Oath administered by the Archbishop to the King. It was very impressive.

What was the funniest incident?

The funniest incident was in connection with our village festivities: a football match by men-players in female attire.

London

111. (CO.17.) I saw a man (6 p.m. May 12) near Madame Tussaud's, dressed in striped pyjamas, wearing a silk hat and

a flaxen wig. He was very drunk, and had to hold on to some railings.

112. (CL.47.) The only bright spot in the Square was a young man dressed as a grotesque parson who got on Nelson's monument when the police were elsewhere and kept the crowd roaring with laughter by faintly obscene Church announcements: things like 'Will the young lady who sat on a knitting needle at the sewing meeting kindly return the needle.'

113. (CL.47.) The most peculiar thing I saw was a Chinaman, who was not near the procession route and didn't appear to be entering into the fun or doing any entertaining or anything—but he was dressed in a black coat, top hat and Scottish plaid trousers, mainly red in colours. This was about 1 p.m. in a side street off Holborn.

Leeds

114. (CL.65.) The most stirring incident: A poor old woman with a black shawl on her head singing the National Anthem with a most profound feeling. Her voice was heard throughout the church, she wasn't singing she was pleading.

The funniest incident: a woman hurrying out of her house to see the musicians on the street, her hair untidy and the skirt only partly buttoned from which was seen a protruding stomach. In her hand she held a few pieces of coal, undoubtedly meant for the fire but in her excitement had forgotten all about it.

Ashford, Kent

115. (CO.43.) About 10 a.m. the milk girl came to the back door and I overheard some conversation between her and the maid.

Maid. Well are you going to treat me to-night if we meet in the High St.?

Milk Girl. Are you going in fancy dress?

Maid. I'm going nude with a Coronation medal. (Both giggle.)

London

116. (CO.44.) Leaving the bathroom later in the morning I bumped into Miss ——, who with her mother share two rooms on the same floor as my own.

I said Good morning to her and asked her if she was going to town, she replied, 'No, but it's a pity the rain came and spoiled everything,' she asked me if I would like an orange, pressed one into my hand and hurried into her room, she always reminds me of a rabbit and is just as inoffensive.

117. (CO.27.) At 5.45 on May 12, I saw a policeman on his hands and knees looking under the door of a lavatory in Baker Street station. He called for a ladder, and then climbed over the top of the partition. He spoke as though someone were inside who had been very drunk, and who had fallen from the seat to the floor.

Attendants came up, and I left before they got the man out.

118. (CL.63.) The funniest incident was perhaps my meeting with the policeman (I asked a policeman the way and to my astonishment he replied that he was a stranger in those parts) or a remark made by one of my neighbours that she would like to be a flag hung on a pole, flying.*

*The two following stories, one from a newspaper, the other from an Observer's report on Coronation preparations, further illustrate the peculiar equation: Woman = Flag.

(i) 'A woman's undergarment was seen "adorning" a flagstaff on the Ministry of Health building in Whitehall to-day.

' "Someone must have climbed along the staff," an official of the Ministry said to *The Evening News*. "It must have been a dangerous prank. The flagstaff had to be brought in before the garment could be removed." The flagstaff is part of the preparations for the Coronation.' (*E.N.* 10.4.37.)

(ii) In the last few days more flags have been hung out; and to-day the

Hampstead

119. (CO.33.) 11–12 a.m. Earlier in the morning we had noticed two men walking up and down outside—my sister came in later and said 'Those two men are still there—I'll go out and ask what they want.' Off she went and returned a little later to say that they had told her 'They were watching the house opposite where a number of Indians lived'.

Soon after I went out to them and asked them why they had to watch the Indians, they replied 'that amongst them was a very bad Indian'.... I said 'What do you mean?' They said, 'Well, one can never trust these people at times like this and they might want to make an attempt on the King's life.'

I asked them how long they would stay, they said, 'We've been here since seven o'clock last night and will stay until about four this afternoon.'

I said to them 'Aren't you tired?' they said 'No'—'We are used to this—it's a fine job, tho' of course we don't spend all our time like this.' I said 'What do you do when you are not watching people like this?' One of them replied 'Oh we type'

---

decoration of the front of our building has begun. Since it is more or less a government building, being largely occupied by government offices, contractors are doing the work.

The men don't interfere greatly with our office-work, but M. has had to leave his desk. 'They're putting Mrs. Simpson in front of my window,' he says smiling, referring to a huge Union Jack. (Reported one minute afterwards.)

The workmen are sawing up wood and hammering. It is becoming distracting. Can't say I observed much excitement, except among the men doing the job.

'I don't see that coming down!' says one of the men, looking at the pole outside the window, and the flag flying from it.

We all look. The women are most excited. One of them declares for some obscure reason that the red is 'of no use to her'. She likes the blue of the flag. 'We are not communists,' she says cheerfully, and walks away.

At 3.35 the typist breaks a teacup. No further casualties. (Reported by CO.40, *Halifax*, 3.5.37.)

—I said 'Type what?' he replied 'Oh, records—you would be surprised to know how efficient our service is—we have thousands of photographs of people—I expect we have one of you.' I said 'Why of me?' and he said 'Well, perhaps not of you, but of any people we think dangerous.'

We went on to talk of the Indians opposite—I said 'I shouldn't think there was any harm in them—they appear to be wealthy princes'—one of the C.I.D. men replied 'That's just like all you girls—you get taken in by them—they're a bad lot.' I said 'I haven't been taken in by anybody—I don't know them, but I thought they might be students.'

He said 'Yes, they tell you they are students—do you know they are most backward—they hardly reach matric stage when they come here.' I said 'I thought that as the British Government ruled India, they had given the people good schools and opportunities for education'—he replied 'Oh, no —they have very little education.'

I asked him if the Indians knew they were being watched— he said, 'Oh, yes—he has seen us and he has gone back to bed'—I said 'How do you know?' and he replied 'Oh, we've just seen him passing the window in his dressing gown.'

My greatest desire was to quarrel with them and tell them to clear off, but I found myself asking them if they would like a cup of tea as they must be cold—they said they would.

I took them the tea and then went indoors to get on with some sewing I was doing.

12 noon. I go and prepare lunch and whilst doing so have a chat with the C.I.D. men who are just outside in the street and the kitchen looks on to this. In the course of our talk they tell me how they like their job, but how difficult it is to get into it as they have to know shorthand-typing, languages. They told me they have to go round to political meetings and take down notes of the speeches.

The two men go off and have their lunch, and the house opposite is left 'unguarded'.

After lunch, my sister and I go on with our job of sewing—neither of us feel much like doing it, but we feel we must do something useful on our day off and not indulge in laziness which we both feel inclined to do. We listen to the Coronation broadcast from time to time, but switch off as we find ourselves becoming bored.

London

120. (CL.47.) In a pub was an Indian, of the type who looked as if he ought to be selling scarves, etc., but wasn't. A British sailor in uniform patted him on the back and the conversation went like this:

Sailor: 'You like England, eh? Having a good time here?'

Indian: 'Very glad.'

Sailor: 'You're the best fellows in the world. I've been in your country a lot, and you're all fine fellows.'

Indian: 'Thank you.' (Rather bewildered.)

Then the sailor turned to me as I was just near and said, 'That's the way to treat 'em, you know. A few kind words mean the world to 'em. They get kicked round all over the place and they never forget it if you say something good to them.'

121. The following story of the illuminated omnibus illustrates very well what is meant by a 'phantom'. The event took place two days after the Coronation, but only because it had to be postponed on account of bad weather. The bus is an imitation Coronation coach—it appears and disappears—but the most important thing about it is that, as with the State Coach, its glamour is imaginary. The whole incident is a piece of make-believe such as children indulge in. The same *might* be said of the Coronation procession, if there were not such a weight of feeling attached to it that the make-believe side of the proceedings is almost wholly concealed.

Birmingham

122. (CO.37.) Friday, May 14.

10.30 p.m. A crowd, or rather scattered groups totalling about 80 persons had collected on Coventry Rd. by the corner of Heybarnes Rd., to see the illuminated omnibus, due to pass at 11.5 approx. Two or three groups of women were engaged in 'third-party' discussion. Three men were gossiping about the vices and virtues of policemen known to them personally. Mixed groups of young people talked about topics not directly concerned with their lives, but the exchange of witty personal remarks was absent. Boys from 10 to 14 played among themselves, occasionally chased one another, and pretended to see the bus in the distance. One woman about 24 approached two women friends, and called loudly, 'Have you seen my mother?'

'No—did she go to . . .' (the name of a suburb).

'Well, I expected to find her here.'

'Oh, did you, well I haven't seen her.'

A man in breeches with dog on lead was conversing in low tones with male companions some yards back from the roadway, for there was an open space on the corner.

About 11.0 o'clock there were close on 300 people round this spot—on either side of them were only people walking on their usual excursions. About this time the conversations became much louder, but there was no increased traffic or other noise to account for this. A cry of 'There is it!' came from a boy in the doorway, with arm pointing. A few moved forward to see, and as the top of the illuminated crown showed over their shoulders, most of the people began to move forward. Some of the younger ones crossed the road, for it was approaching on the other side. As it drew abreast, a woman of 45 or more exclaimed, 'Oh, how lovely' in tones which indicated she had unconsciously prepared the words beforehand. Most people were full of staring, as if they could not see too much of it, and remained dumb. The shape of the vehicle, which was a single-decker, the big crown on top of it, and the portraits of the King and Queen together with the words, 'Long live our King and Queen' were outlined only in electric bulbs of various colours. Half a dozen youths rode behind on bicycles. Scarcely had it gone by, much less disappeared into the distance, than three-quarters of the persons on my side of the road turned, and in the quiet stolid manner of charladies, walked away up Heybarnes Rd. None showed any signs of enthusiasm.

123. The dreams which follow are from the night of May 11 except where otherwise stated. They are all from Observers (CO.) who are asked to put down their dreams, if any, in the course of normal day-surveys. There was no spontaneous recording of dreams under CL. replies. The Observers are trying to act as recording systems, and we can use them as recorders among other things of certain fantastic aspects of the day. At a time of dramatic national consciousness people's propensities for fantasy are strongly stimulated and also get caught up into connection with the central symbolism. There is evidently some relation between the fantasy of these dreams and the fantastic incidents in real life on this day, such as those already recorded.

124. It would be quite possible to apply to these dreams the ideas and discoveries of Freud and of Frazer, but at the moment it is perhaps sufficient to analyse them in terms of the people and things involved rather than in terms of the incidents, in order to bring out their social content as far as possible.*

Persons in area 1: Of the eleven two were absent friends, four dead friends, two were local acquaintances, two were wives (of the dreamer), one his fiancée.

Persons in area 2 *and groups in* 2p: Chorister, butcher,

---

*v. Chap. 1, para. 20, *footnote*, and Part 2, para. 2.

policeman, lady, elderly woman (? Queen Mary), child, the doctor, workman, strange man. Groups of children, Coronation crowd (twice), two crowds of people dancing, cocktail party, group of workmen, some men with a horse and dray.

Persons in area 3: Christ, the Bishop of Norwich, the King (twice), Primo Carnera, Gen. Franco, photograph of film actress.

Animals: Rat, bull, octopus, mouse (moles), tortoise, pigeon.

Vehicles: Taxi, tram-car on a dray, a train that turns into a car.

London

125. (CO.17.) I awoke, or rather half awoke, at 7.30, breaking off a dream in which I figured. I was somewhat anxiously obtaining six pennies for a sixpence (having some vague idea of 'phoning at the back of my mind) from a local shopkeeper, whom I know very well. Then I must have turned over and slept again, for I had another dream, in which I was providing a hungry rat with sustenance in the form of a pink sweetmeat.

Buckinghamshire

126. (CO.4.) Awakened about seven by church bells, I saw that the weather was fair, and went to sleep again. I had been dreaming that I was the guest of a strange man with a house in a village, that on the side of the house was a grape-vine, which now bore the shrivelled and raisin-like remains of last autumn's grapes. I was surprised at finding grapes which had matured in this climate (a vine in our village failed last year) and opened a grape, finding a little sweet juice and many pips in it. Then the man called me to see a strange sight in a flower-bed, a tortoise attacked by a pigeon. But the pigeon could not keep the shell open, and had to leave the tortoise alone.

London

127. (CO.7.) Dreamt that I came out of a station—vaguely Victoria—and to my consternation found myself in the middle of a Coronation crowd. Where thickest they were blocking the road, backs to me, looking at something I could not see. When I got my bearings, however, I found I had turned right instead of left, and that the road in the other direction was clear.

Ilkley, Yorkshire

128. (CO.3.) 'Chorister. Children borrowing soapbox from butcher to stand on to get sandwiches for the train. He had apples, but it didn't suit. I'd just had a salad. I wanted policeman to find a lady to share a taxi on to the station.' That was intended to remind me of a dream, but it has entirely disappeared.

Switzerland

129. (CO.11.) Usual breakfast in bed, woke early with a start, wondering, thinking 'we will be helped' and putting this for unusual reason (for me) into conventional religious symbol, 'Christ will help us,' recalled that it was morning of Coronation, wondered if it were raining. Remembered dream. I was talking to older woman, pleading for a much younger writer, I will not name, well-known in London cinema and literary circles; I said to this older dream woman, 'X. is after all very clever. I may have made fun of him in the past but am truly very loyal.' In dream, I am in old-fashioned room with lace curtains (Victorian England?). I change my chair and lean nearer to this older woman (the old Queen?) to say, 'Yes, X. is *really* very clever and I am sure he should be praised (accepted).' The talk goes on this way, I am half excusing myself, half pleading for said X. Is X. the new King or is X. Edward? In any case, I seem to take an older-sister half-protective interest in this X.

Norfolk

130. (CO.6.) *Dreams.* I was back at school (a mixture of school and Cambridge). My class was to be taken by the Bishop of Norwich. I could not remember in which classroom, or where the classroom was and this worried me very much. I had not got my undergrad's gown or my bicycle, I had left them in college. I had to walk miles to get them as my wife had taken the car. I gate-crashed into a cocktail party. I remember saying to the hostess, 'I am afraid I have come without an invitation but I thought the chief constable was here.'

(*Notes.* I had seen a picture in the *News Chronicle* of the Bishop of N. arriving for the Coronation. I think he was formerly a schoolmaster. A week or so ago I had meant to go to a cocktail party the chief constable had given at the club in Norwich but I changed my mind and did not go. I had an invitation to this.)

Cambridge

131. (CO.19.) I dreamt of the pedication of a child (sex identity unknown) at which I was indignant, with a paternal (or fraternal) interest. (I have no brothers or sisters.)

I dreamt my fiancée had come up to see me, and that we were very happy together.

I dreamt of having breakfast, while I sang the *International* in 'Swing time' (how, I don't know!).

Cambridge

132. (CO.20.) *Dreams:* I was in a train and we passed torrents of flood-water flowing over a small cliff and across a field where normally there was no river at all. Later the train entered a railway cutting and the line itself was under water. Eventually the train was held up on a bend where there were some workmen at work. After some delay the train had become car and I was asked to drive it.

After an interval I was once again in a train. This time it was in a station and I left my compartment to buy a film magazine with a photograph of some film actress on the front. While I was on the platform the train moved slowly out of the station, but I was not disturbed by this, as I knew it would stop just outside the station and I should be able to walk along and get into it again.

Scotland

133. (CO.22.) Dreams vague, of Primo Carnera and I at the doctor's for examination, but before being examined (I was for neck complaint) the dream faded. Other dream of wife and I at theatre, before commencement of performance, dream faded.

Cheshire

134. (CO.21.) *Dream:* Last night I dreamed that as we had not 'decorated' in the slightest degree, our windows were broken! (This probably due to hearing of adverse comments in office made by neighbours. Our Irish chairman had not decorated, and when neighbours commented, he showed his war medals as his 'decorations'!)

London

135. (CO.31.) 6.30. Rose and got my husband's breakfast. (He was going to the Coronation.)

7.30. Went back to bed and dreamed that I saw a dagger under the King's pillow and a note on the pillow. Then I dreamed that I saw a yellow tram-car coming along the Coronation route which overturned in the roadway. Nobody except myself took any notice. I opened some windows and the people began to climb out. Everybody was hysterical, but nobody was badly hurt. Then some came with a horse and a dray and lifted the tram on to the dray. The horse easily dragged its load away. Then I fell off my seat and rolled down a bank into a river in a new yellow dress.

Lancashire

136. (CO.30.) I awoke at 6 a.m. just in time to prevent the alarm clock from ringing. I recollected my dreams and remembered how I sat in a meadow and what I imagined to be a cow came up to me and I seemed unafraid. It turned out to be a bull and tossed me in the air. I somersaulted and fell on my feet and was caught again by the bull. This continued many times until I was finally tossed high over a fence and awoke before I fell. I remember falling asleep again and very vaguely remember talking to a member of our clerical staff who has been deceased eighteen months, he was talking derogatorily of the work of a certain person who happened to be himself.

Hampstead

137. (CO.33.) Awoke at 8 p.m., realized it was a holiday and with great sense of relief at not having to get up, snuggled down into bed again. Fell asleep and dreamt that I met an old girl friend, whom I haven't seen or heard of for about six years, on her way to the Coronation to take up her position and wait all night.

Birmingham

138. (CO.35.) *Dream:* Two crowds of people wearing white dresses bedecked with coloured ribbons were singing and dancing in a wide street. But one crowd represented the Distressed Areas and the other represented the Devastated Areas and under the surface there was a great deal of bitterness and rivalry.

Phrases formed before fully awake:

'The price increased over the vegetables.'

'For her not coming to his room in night attire the charge was as little as six shillings.'

Norfolk

139. (CO.6.) Dreams on the night of May 12. (I include these two dreams I had as they seem much more concerned with the Coronation, or at any rate one of them is, than my dream on the night of May 11.)

(1) I met General Franco by the side of a lake. He said to me 'I have taken Bilbao.' I said 'Oh dear! I have just re-painted the whole place.' He replied menacingly 'Do you know what I am going to do? I am going to scrape off all your new paint.' This so infuriated me that I attacked him with a garden rake which I was carrying and knocked him into the lake. As he fell in he pulled me in with him. As we were struggling in the water together an octopus appeared and seizing him by his white beard with one of its tentacles it dragged him down. I was afraid the octopus would get me too but a workman in a rowing boat helped me out. After-wards I was anxious lest I should get into trouble for mur-dering Franco but I was both relieved and puzzled to find that the papers next day made no mention of his disappear-ance.

(2) I had a seat in Westminster Abbey to watch the Coro-nation. The King was handed first a pair of large spectacles. —To enable him to see better for his people, I thought—then a bull's-eye electric torch (similar to one I possess)—to enable him to see them in the dark, I thought. I was rather em-barrassed when he turned it on to me picking me out from the crowd around me. These things had all come out of a suitcase. The last thing looked to me like a pair of garden trowels but the suitcase was handed up to the King who exclaimed, 'Oh it is a mousetrap and there is a mouse in it!' I saw then it was a trap similar to what is used for moles.

343

Hertfordshire

140. (CO.44.) 9 a.m. I dreamt considerably, the only dream which I could remember was concerned with meeting three people (unrecognizable as acquaintances) whom I had thought were dead. The meeting place was a kind of subterranean vault. There was another dream which was too obscure to remember.

Part 2

THE NORMAL DAY-SURVEY

'It is obvious that the different kinds of habits based on training, education and discipline of any sort are nothing but a long chain of conditioned reflexes. We all know how associations, once established and acquired between definite stimuli and our responses, are persistently and, so to speak, automatically reproduced, sometimes even although we fight against them. . . . We know also how different extra stimuli inhibit and disco-ordinate a well-established routine of activity, and how a change in a pre-established order dislocates and renders difficult our movements, activities and the whole routine of life'. PAVLOV. *Conditioned Reflexes*, Lecture XXIII. 'Applications to Man.'

1. From a scientific point of view, this book so far has no doubt been of interest in showing the kind of behaviour which Mass-Observation can observe. But it has been mainly arranged in a simple documentary way, without much attempt to suggest further possibilities of analysing the material. The unity of the material on May 12 is due to all the social life of that day being hinged on a single ceremony of national importance. On any other day, this unity will tend to disappear, and it is for social science to discover the unity, or lack of it, which is typical of a normal day. We do not claim to have been able to hunt down unifying elements on Feb. 12, March 12 and April 12 with any great success, though the experience of hunting has given us certain criteria for future use. But the purpose of Part 2 of this book is to show another way in which the material of the Day-Survey can be analysed. This method of analysis (which was suggested in a footnote on p. 14) can of course be applied to other reports besides those on a specific day. But the Day-Survey report is a rough and ready means of obtaining data about *all* the everyday activities of a given Observer, and is therefore a good basis for analysis, until it can be decided *which* of these activities need more specific investigation. The following paragraphs will explain the method of analysis by social areas, and a number of surveys made on March 12, a normal working day, will then be analysed by this method.

2. *Social area of an Observer:* The social area of an Observer consists of all the people with whom he is connected socially. For the purposes of the day survey, this area may be sub-divided into three concentric circles.

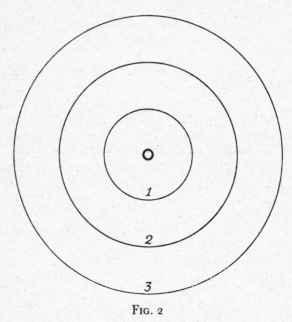

Fig. 2

Innermost is a circle, (1) which includes the Observer's family, household, people in same employment, regular customers, regular tradespeople, roundsmen, postman, etc., friends, regular political or religious acquaintances, next-door neighbours: singly or in groups.

Next comes (2) which includes strangers, newcomers, chance acquaintances, people known to a second person, unusual tradespeople, unusual customers: singly or in groups.

The outermost circle, (3) consists of people and institutions whose pressure and contact is less direct and personal, but no less effective. It forms the social horizon of the Observer, a penumbra which surrounds his day-to-day acquaintances and encounters. In it are groups, institutions, classes, official persons, celebrities, people acting in a public capacity, ancestors, literary and mythological figures, public mouthpieces (newspapers, radio, etc.) and such abstract collections as *The People*.

3. *Social incidents:* The record of the day given by each Observer may be divided into a series of statements; some Observers give a fairly full statement of routine activities which take place every day, but on the whole all tend to record mainly incidents which are in some way deviations, however slight, from the normal routine. A rough definition of a social incident would therefore be an occurrence of sufficient importance to be recorded by the Observer at the end of the day. It may be an encounter, or conversation, or piece of information which enhanced the Observer's social consciousness; a satisfactory performance, or hindrances to performance; social offers, acceptances, problems solved and unsolved; and so on.

4. In analysing the records the incidents may be narrated as happening to the Observer or in some indirect way, *e.g.* told to the Observer by a second person. In the analysis a convenient notation for this difference is to class as incidents to the power of 1 ($\mathbf{x}^1$), those in which the Observer describes himself as:

Meeting people
Seeing people
Talking to people
Hearing people
'Phoning people
Writing to people
Coming into physical contact or collision with people.

Incidents to the power of 2 (x^2), include:

Hearing of people
Talking of people
Reading of people
Listening in, to or about people
Seeing pictures of people
Thinking of people
Getting letters from people

Incidents to the power of 3 (x^3), include:

Hearing of people known to the person one is talking to but not to oneself.
Reading an account by a second person of a third.

The points raised in the preceding paragraphs will be made clearer in the analysis which follows.

5. This was the directive sent out for March 12.

The aim of the day's survey is to discover what happened to each Observer on that particular day. What is required is primarily a factual statement; then an account of any feelings he had which seem sufficiently important or noteworthy for record.

(1) State your name, address, age, sex, married or single, politics or religion, if any, very briefly.

(2) State your job or occupation during the day. (State whether it was a normal day for you, or if abnormal, in what way.)

(3) State your health on the day in question.

(4) Describe the weather; also striking dreams, if any.

(5) Describe any local events—sport, crime, political or other meetings, etc.—what films were showing; and send relevant cuttings from local press, stating what paper they come from, what page they appeared on, and whether they were prominently displayed.

(6) Describe briefly and factually the events of your day, giving times; report any conversations, if any, with

different types of people. However ordinary the events may seem to you, they are of interest in this inquiry.

(7) Keep your feelings out of 3–6. Then describe your feelings during the day, if possible, in a final section.

The following suggestions may be of assistance:

(1) If any speeches are given as direct speech (*i.e.* in inverted commas), it should be stated if shorthand was used. If not, how long after the conversation took place it was reported. (*N.B.* direct speech is very often incorrectly remembered in detail, although the gist may be accurate.)

(2) In conversations, give status of speaker.

(2*a*) If you mention the status of a speaker, *e.g.* 'business man', or 'two young matrons, upper middle class', say how you judged it: *e.g.* by clothes, by accent, by knowledge of the individual or how.

(3) Try to write down notes as frequently as possible. Do not interrupt anything to do so.

(4) When stories are given, state authority of story, *e.g.* gossip, newspaper, from interested parties, etc.

(5) In all cases it should be stated *when* the observations were written down, and when finally written up.

6. We now present three complete day surveys of March 12 representing the average working day of a mill-hand, a bank clerk, and a housewife.

7. *Mill-hand, Bolton*

(1) Age: 28. Male. Single. Atheist. Non-political.

(2) Side-piecer employed in a Cotton mill. This was a normal day for me.

(3) Health: slight cold. Rather dull.

(4) The weather at 7.30 was very cold and wet.

(5) The events of local interest: The main one I would say is the Wanderers, the local football team, the consistent loss of points is causing a lot of talk and anxiety to their host of supporters.

A musical festival has been held during the week, the local paper has given a lot of space to it all through the week.

Reported in to-night's *Evening News* is a meeting at the Conservative headquarters addressed by the senior member for Bolton, Sir Cyril Entwisle, this meeting was for Bolton Women Conservatives.

A Unity Campaign is advertised for Sunday evening organized by the local Communists.

The Little Theatre (Amateur Dramatics) are giving to-night (all week) a performance of Shakespeare's comedy *Much Ado About Nothing*.

No crime to speak of in the *Bolton Evening News*. The biggest headline in the *News* is given to 'Lloyd George's Attack on the Chancellor' but this is closely rivalled by 'Wanderers' Winger suspended', 'Club warned by Football Association'. The estimates for the Navy are the subject of the editorial column.

8. I left home for work at 7.30 a.m. It was raining and very cold. Working hours in Bolton Mills are 8¾ hours per day, 7.45 p.m.–12.15 p.m., an hour for dinner, 1.15–5.30.

1^2 My brother is in the hospital recovering from an operation for appendicitis, he is to be removed to another hospital on
3^2 the outskirts of the town, Blair's Hospital. Mr. Blair was the donor of the house which has been converted into a hospital for convalescents. Asked questions about the whereabouts of
1 Blair's of a piecer, as I walked into the mill and up to the eighth storey in which room I work. The man gave me the information, and said he knew because his father had been in.
2^2 He had been knocked down by a bicycle and had his skull

fractured. 'He was black and blue you couldn't see any white about him.' He went on to say his father had never worked since.

The engine in the spinning mill starts up about 7.39. Piecers and spinners begin to oil. Wheels are running full swing slightly before 7.45.*

9. This morning our little piecer was late, that is he came *1* into the room about 7.42. As a rule people are expected to be in the mill ready to start before the engine starts up. Clothes have to be taken off and overalls to be put on. Dirty oily shirt and overalls and bare feet is the uniform. The piecer had evidently got up too late and rushed to work in a splutter, for he walked into the wrong wheelgate (pair of mules). There is a great scarcity of little piecers, and this piecer is shared between two spinners, one day for one, the next for the other. The piecer walked into the wrong wheelgate, and the spinner rather bad temperedly told him to go on the next *1* pair of mules. Piecer not concerned about coming late, not interested in the job.

Spinner had to do a slight job that the piecer should have done on Thursday night, but had forgotten.† He was annoyed and said 'I told him to do this last night, and he didn't.'

10. 8.30. The spinner on the next pair of wheels seeing me *1* doing the cleaning said he would give me a lift now and then (humour).‡

*From now on these footnotes will indicate the nature of the incident to which they refer along the lines laid down in paragraph 2 above. The present incident is a perfect example of a statement about routine, but in the next sentence an incident occurs in which already routine has broken down. It may therefore be termed a 1a incident, and in future all such will be numbered in the footnotes simply as 1a.

The reference figures in the margin refer to the *persons* mentioned and indicate whether those persons belong to area **1**, **2** or **3** and also if they are $X^2 X^3$ (paragraph 4 above).

†1a. Another break in routine.　　　　　‡1a. A variant; offer of help.

3² I said 'Do it now, not then.' He said 'That's what Kitchener said, "Do it now."' I 'And look what he did.' Spinner 'Yes, he made a boger of it, didn't he?' This spinner is 42 years of age, served in the war, R.A.M.C.

I **11.** 9.20. In the room in which I work we have the mill painter, painting the window frames with white paint. He is employed by the mill and works all the year round, inside in winter, outside in summer. I have, along with others, noticed how he dodges work. He is working very hard when bosses are around, and slacking when he can. This morning I timed him, he came into the room to start painting at 9.20. He is at the mill at 7.45.

I 9.45. The overlooker among his jobs prowls around, to see that everyone is working hard. Talking not allowed. But at 9.45 he came to the painter, who is his crony, out of working hours, for a chat. The overlooker is a spinning overlooker, just that. His work has no connection with that of the painter.

12. 10 a.m. Having no little piecer on this day, the spinner and I had to perform his functions as well as our own. Two men do three men's work.*

The piecer's wage is divided equally. I mixed some bobbins I had cleaned, red-topped ones with white-topped ones. This should not be done. It is a little piecer's job cleaning the bobbins.† A man who carries bobbins from the card room to the spinning room, and who is known as a bobbin carrier, came to me at 10 o'clock in a bad temper, complaining about the mixed bobbins, 'You'll have to separate them, we can't do it,' but he took the bobbins away and no more was heard of it.

At frequent intervals the painter comes down his ladder for a five minute interval. He just stares at the people working. Just stares and speaks not.

*1a. Break in routine.   †1a. Mistake owing to break in routine.

13. 10.45. Much water is drunk in the spinning room. I went for a jug of water (usually a little piecer's job) and noticed a notice above the tap, some piecer had rubbed out 1^2 the word 'not' and so the notice read 'Employees are requested to waste water.'*

10.50. The spinner next to me inquired about my brother, and informed me that for appendicitis the patient must have 21 days in bed.†

On the other side of my pair of mules is a side-piecer who is 1 spinning temporarily. He called to me in bantering tones 'Where shall I see you to-night, and I'll buy you a drink?'‡ He is 32 years old, married, and whilst spinning will get a rise from 32s. whilst piecing to £4 0s. 0d. clear whilst spinning.

11.30 a.m. The wages are brought round by the overlooker, he stays at the end of the room and makes a loud hooting noise. The spinners react visibly, they brighten and become jolly. The spinner receives all the wage, he pays his piecers. It is a well-known fact that spinners are happier and brighter creatures on Friday (pay day).§

14. 11.30 a.m. The painter vanished. This is usual. He had gone to prepare to go home.

12 o'clock. The temporary spinner showed me with glee his notes of cash which he was carrying about with him in his overall's pocket. It is usual to leave it in the outdoor suit.‖

12.15 p.m. Engines stop for dinner hour. There is a general stampede by almost everyone to get out. Rush down eight flights of steps. Some of these people come back well before they need, some at 12.45.

I passed the painter ambling home, smoking a pipe, well dressed, bowler hat and overcoat. The piecers as a rule are without coats or macs. They wear caps mostly. The pies and fish and chips shops did good business with mill folk. Both the people who were going home, and those who were staying

*1a.   †1a. Getting information.   ‡1a.   §1a.   ‖1a.

in the mill for dinner. The weather at this time was dismal and dull, rain threatened.

15. 1.15 p.m. Back in the mill, our little piecer before the
1 engine starts up addresses another boy (16 years) as Sleep. He replies, 'Frank to you.'*

1 1.20 p.m. The side-piecer on the next pair of wheels says by pantomimic gestures, very eloquent 'I am bogered.' The heat is great, it is stuffy, one feels stuffed up. Sleep said it is like the Equator.

3² 1.30 p.m. Our little piecer spoke about a physical culture group he is in. They had their photographs taken and he was
3² full of it. He talked about joining the Navy, and said another
2², 3³ boy in the same mill was going to join the Marines when old enough.

16. 2.20. Painter arrives to start. No incidents worth recording for some time.

3.30. Painter goes out to lavatory for a rest. 15 minutes.

4.20. We start to do a job for which we borrow a piecer. This fellow Sleep came, and was having a word with our piecer, the spinner cursed him, 'I'll smack thi in't bloody earhole.' Sleep sulks.†

4.50. Sleep having finished helping us has not rushed straight back to his own pair of wheels. His own spinner is watching him and startles him into a rush back to work by bawling him out from 40 yards away.‡

Shortly before 5.30 getting our clothes on to go home our little piecer (16 years) said that the 'Flat racing season will soon be here, more money for me!' He runs errands for a bookie.

17. 5.30. Engines stop. Stampede as at dinner. Side-
1 piecer further down the room (32 years) said: 'I've worked bloody hard to-day.' After tea read the *News*. At 6.30. The

*la.   †la.   ‡la.

insurance agent called for the weekly premium. This was a *3*
new agent second week on the job. He had gone to the same
school as I and at the same period. A Catholic. We chatted
for a while.* He was a cyclist. I had been. We had both
toured Ireland last summer. He had landed on a Sunday
morning. He said 'Of course we went to Church, 11 o'clock
mass.' He had formerly worked in a gent's. outfitters at Preston
but it held no prospects of promotion or advance in wages so
he was trying insurance. He would soon be married. Been
courting a long time. Age about 27. My mother who is stone *1*
deaf remarked after, 'He looks religious.'

18. 6 o'clock. A self-denial envelope had been left by the *3, 2*
Salvation Army people during the day, at 6 p.m. an officer,
a man, called for it.

After tea I completed my notes on this subject and then
finished a book I was reading, *The Evolution of Love*, by Emil
Lucka. He treats the subject in a sort of historical-philosophi- *3*
cal manner.

N.B. During the lunch hour I heard (a familiar sound)
coal being pushed, by small boys,† in two wheeled trucks from *2ᵖ*
an adjacent coal-yard to their homes. Pay-day. Dinner-
time. No coal. Get some while we have the money.

7.50 p.m. My mother complained of having to go for our
laundry twice.‡ Taking it on Tuesday, bringing it back on
Friday.

Impressions and Feelings

19. It must be remembered that my impressions were for
the most part conditioned by the fact that I was observing

*Ia. Renewed encounter with old acquaintance.

†When a group is mentioned this is indicated by a small *p*, unless the
number is specified.

‡Ia.

people carefully. Common everyday events were noted and formed impressions on my conscious mind which under normal circumstances would have aroused no interest.*

20. The fact that I had a cold, that the atmosphere was particularly vile, and that the day was dull, were first impressions, which gave rise to feelings of the rottenness of the system under which we live. The general feeling in the spinning room (worse-paid workers) is that work is an evil thing, a thing to be got over as quickly as possible. I thought of the servility of the English people in standing the bad system of working, 8¾ hours a day in a putrid atmosphere for meagre wages and always feeling below par.

I felt the queerness of a system that carefully preserved its property by painting it frequently and thought not at all about the health of its human work-people. Preservation of woodwork. Ruination of employees' health.

The frequent five-minute stares of the painter, allied to the fact that I was constantly on the go working hard, brought a feeling of resentment at the inequality of the distribution of work, and I remembered the poem by W. H. Davies,

> 'A poor life this if full of care.
> We have not time to stand and stare.'

21. I got the impression that the atmosphere, the electric lights burning all day (bad lights), everything combined had an effect on the temper of everyone, spinners, piecers, bobbin carriers, etc. The feeling of futility was a constant one during this day (more so than usual), to see the people wasting their lives (mine in particular) at such an occupation. To know that every piecer dislikes the life he leads at work, and to see how conditioned he has to become, he curses, rails, and dreams, but he comes up every day for more. For more bad air. For more slow painful hours. For meagre wages. After

*The consciousness of the Observer is undoubtedly heightened by the fact that he is observing.

work is over he jumps into a round of pleasure. Pictures, dancing, cards, anything as a reaction against work.

At 11.30 the call of the pay is a marvellous brightening time for spinners. They become jovial human beings for a time. What a power money has. This was an uneventful day.

22. Dancing is a very popular pastime in Bolton. Almost every Sunday school has a dance per week. I enclose some adverts from the *Bolton Evening News*.

I made notes at the lunch hour and at tea-time and have written this account on Sunday, March 14.

23.   *Bank Clerk, Hertford*

(1) Age: 19½. Male. Unmarried. Left inclinations in politics.

(2) On the counter of the London branch of an Australian bank. Normal day.

(3) Quite well, but feeling tired.

(4) Fine sunny morning—rain during the day, but fine in the evening.

(5) The local operatic socy. were doing *The Geisha* at the local cinema—had been on all the week.

24. (6) Got up 8.15, breakfast 8.25 in a hurry. During breakfast it was said* that Ribbentrop had given the King 3, 3 the Nazi salute again. I suggested that our Ambassador did 3 not give Hitler the Nazi salute. I was told that it was quite 3 certain that *we* (England) would do nothing to offend the 3 Nazi court. Left for the station—saw a man in a car whom I 2 thought I knew and waved, but realized that afterwards I didn't know him. He waved back. Amused me at the time.†

*By whom? There is a curious blankness in the home sector of area 1 in this report.

†Confusion of areas 1 and 2.

Got into the train and made notes for this report. Very bad flooding all the way as far as Clapton. Had carriage all to myself on the way up, a rare occurrence.* Started to read *3, 3* George Orwell's *Road to Wigan Pier*—Left Book Club choice for March. Arrived at Liverpool St. punctually at 9.30. Walked to office in Threadneedle St. First greeting was— 'I've got a ticket in the Irish Sweep'†—a fellow of 21, who is intelligent in some ways and clever, was greeted with usual *1* 'Good morning' from nearly everyone, which is a ridiculous convention. Commenting to a friend on the floods, was suddenly filled with joy at remembering having seen a dog-track *2²* under water, owned by a pub keeper, whom I disliked, because we changed at his pub for rugger and he tricked us and charged us an over price for everything. *N.B.* I was not impressed in this manner when I first saw it under water.‡

25. Overnight a shutter to a cupboard had been pulled down, and only the previous evening I had spent half an *1* hour trying to get it up. Got a messenger to open it as it had stuck again.§ He was full of grouses that it was nothing to do with him. I heard that an air mail was in which would *1* mean additional work for me, but I expected it.‖ A junior to *2²* myself, about 18, came and said he had told his father over the week-end banking did not suit him as a career and *3³* wanted a commission bought for him in the army. His father refused. This boy is rather adolescent, and probably thinks it would mean an easy life with not too much work and in a safe position. (What a queer sense of security!!) Another *1* clerk showed me an advertisement for periscopes for use on Coronation Day. I said I was going to keep as far away from London as possible. He said if he could get a seat he would go and see it but not otherwise.** Continued with my work, and got everything up to date by 12.30. Then continued routine

---

*1a.   †1a.   ‡1a, though effect was delayed.   §1a.   ‖1a.
**1a. Discussion tending to result in a shift of social consciousness.

work. Conversation started (with the same man as the Coronation), I think by myself, on athletics and the question of the American superiority in field events.*

26. Went out to lunch at 2 p.m. with the boy who wanted to get a commission in the army. Conversation drifted to Easter rugger and soccer tours. Returned back at 2.45. Continued routine work till 4.30. A member of the bank, *1* about 50, averagely brainless, not even 'bank brains!!' was selling Coronation ties for 2s. which had been planted on him by a friend of his† Argument was going on about Little- *2²* wood's football forecasts and the prospects for to-morrow's games. (Incidentally conversation rarely gets beyond the height of football pools and weather. During the day I endeavoured to get some conversation on interesting subjects, mainly political, but as you see, failed dismally.)‡ Got home at 6. Conversation in the train concerned the floods, and *The Geisha* which was being produced during the week by the local Operatic and Dramatic Socy. Protest was raised by a stockbroker, about 45–50, very well off, about raising the prices for the last night.§

27. When I arrived home I expected to find a ticket waiting for me for *The Geisha*.|| As it wasn't I went and called on the friend I was going with. He said he wasn't going, had a *1* rotten cold, been in bed the day before, and was going to bed early.** I said I didn't mind, because I could go on the next evening. He then thought he would come down into the town with me. While he went to telephone, I posted some letters for him, and arranged to meet him in the local pub. There I met the Capt. and Hon. Sec. of the cricket club to *3, 3* which I belong, and conversation dwelt on the high prices that were being charged by the groundsman who had started *2²* an indoor cricket school one night a week. It appears no one

*1a. Ditto. †1a. Daily routine modified by big events pending in area 3.
‡See Section 7. §2a. Social problem. ||1a. **1a.

is going!* My friend came in and said he would go to *The Geisha* after all. We went and it was rather a dull show. We went out for a drink during the interval and met a Hertford 3 cricketer, about 40. After the show we went behind the scenes 1 to see a friend who had taken part and we got a drink from him!!† I arrived home about 11.30. Packed my clothes for to-morrow's rugger match and went to bed.

28. (7) My feelings were not very strong in any direction— I always feel that banking is a waste of time—that I should like to spend my life doing something that is going to benefit someone who needs help and not adding to the comforts of those who already possess them. I felt a bit annoyed when I arrived home not finding a ticket waiting for me. On reflection I was fed up to think that I could not even start a reasonable conversation‡ on a subject of a slightly higher level than football pools and prospects!!! On occasion I have had one or two interesting conversations, but there are not more than three members of the bank who are sufficiently intellectually interested to even think of talking about something worth-while.

N.B. I made notes at varying times during the day till I got home. After this the rest is from memory which I wrote up on Monday, March 15.

.   .   .

29. I enclose the leading article from the local newspaper on a subject which has been the topic of the town for the last two years, and it does sum up the situation very well. It appeared on the middle page.

HERTFORD BATHS FIASCO

Hertford Corporation's decision to scrap a second Baths' scheme is either a startling instance of the County Town

---

*1a. Discussion on a social problem.   †1a.

‡Another indication that the act of observing has modified an ob server's behaviour during the day.

crying poverty, or a further example of administrative impotence, calling for investigation by the Ministry. . . .

30.   *Housewife, near Birmingham*

(1) Age: 26.
   Politics: None of the political parties are sufficiently altruistic for me. I vote Labour in the elections.
   Religion: I never attend church and am not in the least interested in it. I am a mystic by temperament.

(2) Housewife, *i.e.* Cook-general—nurse—dressmaker—laundress—secretary, etc. Normal day except for details 10.15 to 10.35.

(3) *Health*: Had an attack of lumbago yesterday (after spending nearly two hours shovelling snow). Better today, but back a little 'uneasy'.

(4) Early morning, brilliant sunshine, no clouds. 9 a.m. onwards—fairly strong south wind, driving rain. Yesterday's heavy fall of snow (6 in. or 7 in.) rapidly becoming slush. 1 p.m. to 6.30 fine. Very sunny. 6.30 onwards as at 9 a.m.

31. *Dreams*: I am in B'ham for the purpose of attending a lecture on Psychology to be given by Aldous Huxley. The lecture is due to start at 7.30 p.m. It is now just before 7. I go about five flights of stairs and reach a large classroom which is set out with single desks. At the master's desk sits Aldous *3* Huxley writing. I am the first to arrive. He asks me to take some small text-books out of a cupboard and distribute them. I have some difficulty in finding them in the cupboard, but eventually do so and put one on each desk. I then say 'I have had no tea, I will go out and have some.' A. H. does not speak but smiles. I return downstairs and go through B'ham to Winter's café (here follows a blurred interval). I am back again in classroom which is full of people. Someone tells me

that after the lecture a number of eminent people including
Aldous Huxley, Sir John Reith, the Secretary of State for
Ireland (and many more whom I do not distinctly recollect,
except that they were members of society and foreign royalty—King Carol being one) are giving a comic 'show' on
the stage. I am told that A. H. is to appear as a small boy
in a white satin frilly blouse and short white knickers and
white socks. I say I cannot imagine anything less 'comic' nor
more ugly and that I shall certainly not go to it. I am sitting
near the open door, suddenly great clouds of smoke came
billowing through the door. Huxley and I seem to be the only
people to notice it. It seems as though the place is on fire.
We both go downstairs to investigate. The stairs are in complete darkness. As we go down the smoke decreases. We reach
the bottom and find ourselves in a large, immaculate, perfectly fitted kitchen.

32. 6.30. Awakened by M. pretending to be an alarm
clock and saying 'Time to get up—ting-a-ling-a-ling, etc.'
H. calls to him that it is too early.

7.20. Awakened by H. with morning tea. H. says there is
no post, and that by the garden thermometer the temperature
has remained at the same level since early yesterday evening.
M. gets into H.'s bed.* (In this statement I refer to my husband as H. and my small son, aged 5, as M.)

7.30. M. sings to me *Three little kittens*, *Pop goes the Weasel*,
Old King Cole, etc. I think over my dream, wondering what
on earth made me dream of Aldous Huxley; decide to miss
my bath to-day because of yesterday's lumbago.

7.45. Get up, dress, etc.

*After sending in her report, this observer was asked to confirm
whether certain incidents were of a routine nature, as a partial check-up
on the objectivity of the method of analysis used in this section. Of this
incident she writes 'At the time that this was written M. generally got
into H's empty bed for a few minutes to keep warm.' It is therefore not
1a.

8.5. Send M. off to his bath. H. says 'No breakfast this morning, only toast.'*

8.10. Downstairs prepare toast, write out grocery list while it is cooking.

8.15. H. comes down. Ask him to leave list at grocer's on his way to station. Leave him eating breakfast. Go upstairs, take M. out of bath and into bedroom to dry in front of fire.

8.27. H. leaves for station. Do various odd jobs—put away bath towels, put all M.'s clothes ready for him to put on, put toothbrush and paste ready for him, watch him do his breathing exercises, make up my face.

8.45. Downstairs, give water to bulbs and flowers. Throw out bread for birds.

8.55. Prepare breakfast. M. comes down and tunes in to Radio Normandie.† We dance a jig to the music (?) of 'High o'er the fence leaps Sunny Jim, Force is the food, etc'. 3 3

33. 9.15. Breakfast. Conversation during breakfast.

M.: 'What is he singing? Is it *Does Your Mother come from Ireland?*'

'No, it's *Misty Islands of the Highlands*. You have not been putting on your gramophone lately, M.'

M.: 'No, I'm getting too big now.'

'What is your favourite record?'

M.: *Tannhauser* and the one on the other side.'

'*Coriolan Overture?*'

M.: 'Yes. What is your favourite record?'

'Of all those you have I think I like *Aïda*—the one with the lady singing in Italian.'

Conversation then changes to trains.

*Observer writes: 'No, not normal occurrence. H. admitted to feeling slightly "liverish".' Ia.

†'No. I never listen to Radio Normandie nor to any advertising programmes. M. occasionally switches it on in the morning because he wants to "dance" and because there is no other music on at that time in the morning.'

34. 9.35. Breakfast finished. Make beds. Wash up breakfast crockery. Take a dose of Heath & Heather Kidney Herbs* and give M. his Scott's Emulsion.

I 10.10. Baker calls. Take bread. Say, 'Warmer this morning isn't it?' Baker: 'Yes, it is warmer.'

10.15. Sweep, dust, etc. downstairs rooms and hall. Ad-
3 dress a cutting to *This England* column of *New Statesman*.† Dust bedrooms.

10.30. Butcher arrives. Give order for to-morrow. No conversation.

10.45. Pin together some Coronation cuttings out of local
3 paper. Type out last night's dreams, letter to Mr. Madge, and this survey.

I 11.55. Man calls to read gas meter.

3 12.30. Tune in to Henry Hall for M.

12.50. Stop typing and go to prepare vegetables, etc. for lunch.

1.3. Look out of window and find weather improving.

1.5. Persuaded by M. to do a little work on a rug we are making for the bathroom, while waiting for vegetables to cook.

1.25. Lay table, etc.

1.30. Cut up some raw meat for the cat. Luncheon. Conversation: 'You can't put all that in your mouth, M.'

M.: 'Yes I can, you watch—there—can't I get a lot into my mouth?' etc. etc.

35. 2.0. Clear away crockery. Prepare to go out. Go upstairs, change into costume, change stockings and shoes (after

---

*Not usual routine. 'I occasionally have mild attacks of backache due to slight weakness of the kidneys, and I keep these herbs "in stock" because I find them most efficacious in relieving the pain. On this occasion I took a dose because of my attack of lumbago. (This was also the reason for the Beecham's pill at night.)'

†Not usual. 'I believe I have sent one in before this, and probably shall not do so again. It just happened to occur to me that this particular cutting was worth a wider circulation.'

washing, brushing hair, etc.). Come downstairs, help M. to put on outdoor clothes. Lock doors. Build up fires. Leave laundry on step. Put on own outdoor clothes. Fetch two library books.

2.55. Set out for shops (about 1¾ miles away). Half-way down road it starts to rain. Run back to house for umbrella. Start out again.*

3.25. Arrive shops. M. buys a snow-plough for his Hornby set, for which he has been saving. I buy—1 lb. cod, pkt. envelopes, 1 handkerchief, a small model bear, G.W.R. *Holiday* 3 *Haunts Guide*, a 1½d. stamp, some wooden boats for a small boy whose birthday is approaching, 1 pr. silk stockings, 1 box crayons, a small shrub for the garden (azalea).

At 4.20 we set out for home. Call at grocer's to add some items to order. Remark to grocer 'There is a very strong 1 smell of fish in here.' He replies: 'Yes, we have some friends 2² visiting, they have just arrived, they have come from India. As they had come such a long way my mother thought they 2² would like some haddock for their tea.' Leave library books at small private library.

36. 5.0. Arrive home. Leave parcels in hall and call at next door neighbour's to see if laundry has been left there. Notice on small piece of paper on neighbour's step says 'Please leave grocery at the back door.' Knock door. Neighbour comes to 1 door with eye-glasses in her hand. Gives me laundry. Says 'I can't keep the door open in case the cat gets out. There's the greengrocer at the back-door.'

5.7. Back in own house. Take off M.'s outdoor clothes and own. Give M. the snow-plough and crayons. Put the bear on the mantelpiece with camel and hippopotamus. Look through *Holiday Haunts*.

*There is a break in routine here without any human intervention. Possibly such incidents, involving external physical factors (weather, animals, plaster falling from ceiling, etc.) should form a separate area, 4.

5.25. Go out into kitchen to prepare tea. Lay tea, cut bread and butter, etc.

3 **37.** 5.40. H. arrives. Gives me the *Daily Telegraph* and *New Statesman*, but has forgotten to bring me in the local paper. I **1** give him the shrub and he goes out and plants it. Greengrocer comes to door. I show him some rotten apples he gave me last time he called. He says he will replace them. I order eggs, cauliflower, cabbage, onions, apples, lettuce and watercress. Go into kitchen and make tea. Go back to door **1²ᵛ** and receive greengroceries and pay man. Say: 'How are the children?' He replies: 'They are all keeping pretty well, thank you, except the little one and he has got it on the chest a bit.'

38. 6.0. Call in H. from garden. We have tea.

6.45. I read to M.

7.15. Take M. up and put him to bed.

7.30. Come downstairs and wash up crockery.

7.55. Typing.

8.15. Go into other room. Spend evening deciding where to go for summer holidays. Decide upon Borth-y-Gest.

9.30. Write letter for accommodation. Drink some Ovaltine. Do some work on rug. Play with the cat.

39. 10.15. Suddenly remember I have forgotten to 'lift' M. Go upstairs.* Find he has wet the bed in his sleep. Get clean pyjamas and under blanket. Wake him up and change him. Make him comfortable for night. Tell him a little story. Wash through soiled pyjamas and hang them up to dry. Come downstairs.

10.35. Write an order for the milkman. Carry the laundry upstairs. Put cat to bed. H. comes up. We undress, etc. Both too sleepy for conversation. H. gets into his bed. I take a Beecham's pill and get into mine. We say goodnight. I read

*According to observer this was the only abnormal incident in the day. 1a.

a passage from Sir Thomas Browne's *Religio Medici* and then *3* switch off the light.

40. There seems to be very little to record in the way of 'feelings'. Amusement at the grocer's remark about the haddock. Very mildly annoyed at H.'s forgetting local papers. Annoyed with myself for forgetting to 'lift' M. All these are normal reactions and not in any way outstanding.

Last part of survey from 10.15 typed on 13.3.37 at 8.45 a.m.

41. This day seems to me to be unusual in one particular. Through the whole of the day there were no conversations of any kind. All afternoon I was in and out of shops and walking amongst a large number of people and nowhere were there any conversations taking place. The day seems to be one of flux. My husband tells me that his day has been the same. There were no conversations on the station platform, nor in the carriage on the train both to and from Birmingham. No conversation occurred in his office. I cannot account for this.

42. A heavy shower of rain started as I came up the hill returning from shops. I had been thinking about the difficulties of sending M. to a good prep. school (financial difficulties). I noticed a local tradesman (uneducated type) driving a *2* smart little car in which he had been to fetch his son from a local prep. school, the difference in our financial positions struck me rather forcibly. Immediately after an immaculately dressed, 'permed', manicured, young woman came out of a *2* hairdresser's shop, got into a super-limousine and drove off. My 'feelings' were a momentary feeling of shame at being seen walking along with a heavily laden basket at 4.30 p.m. (I was tired, my arm ached, and it was raining—I walked back to save the 'bus fare), looking (I imagined) rather like a charwoman;* secondly a feeling of resentment

* (I don't resemble a charwoman in any particular.) (Observer's footnote.)

('I'm much better looking than she, and have a much better figure, why shouldn't I be able to afford smart clothes'); thirdly a sense of despair because I am never likely to be in a much better position, not at any rate until M. is grown up. This was all momentary and was all forgotten by the time I reached the grocer's a few hundred yards further.

43. The three foregoing reports are given in full and portray the day's work of three hard-working people. In the third, the family-life sector (area 1) is introduced in detail, since the housewife works at home, not in an office or factory. The other reports are interesting variants of the three typical situations displayed in the first three. That which follows (para. 45), is from an unemployed man—a bare chronicle of existence, the routine of *not* having work. Then comes the record (paras. 46–55) of a day's unemployment of a different kind—for in this case the Observer is a person of comparative leisure. The next observer is another young office worker, but his social horizon is modified by his being an active communist (paras. 56–76). Finally come three short reports, each dominated by a single theme: the first by the weather (paras. 77–82), second by health (paras. 83–86), and the last by sex (paras. 87–92).

44. It is a necessity to emphasize at this point that the analysis and classification which we have given are no more than an experimental and tentative try-out oɪ the sort of methods we think will have to be arrived at. Other persons classifying the reports would almost certainly reach a different set of results. In the course of practical experience over a much longer period, something more definitive may be expected to emerge.

The reports we quote are no more than a handful selected from a growing body of material. Those which are omitted are forming the basis of a more exhaustive index to human activities, starting from the concept of the *social incident*. By collecting, filing and sorting these incidents, in large numbers, we hope to be able to produce a scientific classification for them.

Unemployed Motor Driver, Liverpool

45. Now dear about the 12th an episode in a ordinary man's life.* 7.30 arise breakfast by 8 of toast then out on the never ending round of looking for work 9 o'clock factory time helper, 'I am sorry but all applications for work through the *2* Labour Exchange   good morning.' 10 o'clock. Labour *3* Exchange. The Clerk, 'Yes can you ride a motor cycle, find a *2* fault in any car, have you any long refs. and are they good?' The answer to all this is Yes. 'Here is a card go to R A C *3* Lord St for an interview   arrive by 10.30. in to see the manager 'Well your first job and so on until the present day,' *2* looks at my refs. 'Alright the wages are £2-5-0. hours no limit an easy job passing cars of visitors through the customs. I will have to see other applicants meanwhile you see the chief port officer.' I see the officer in question well it *2* finished with 'We will let you know.' out by 12 noon it is no use looking anywhere now for work so I go home for dinner what was left from Sun. is fried up this is over by 1.30 p.m. I work in my garden until 5.30 p.m. mending rails, turning the ground over, have a cup of tea, rest until 6.30., then I go to Mother's house. Father fell at work and hurt his arm *1, 1* and shoulder so as I have done a little massage I set about massaging him† for an hour, after that I go to a meeting

*This report is taken from a letter to another Observer: it describes Monday, April 12, but is included in this series because it is the first report received from an unemployed man, and therefore represents an important area of existence not covered elsewhere.

†1a.

3 which was called to form a social club   proceedings lasted an hour and half   the president elected and vice president what fee we are to pay 2d. per week and with this the meeting closed   there were just on a hundred members and as this is the end of the day I retire.

46.   *Free-lance, Ayrshire*

Age: 35. Bachelor. Protestant.

4.45 a.m. I cannot recall the dream but into waking consciousness come the images of a reading-lamp with a moderately big shade, and 2 bedroom slippers.

I hear a motor in the distance and listen to the wind. I touch the hot-water bag with my fingers. I lie in a drowsy state—sometimes right or left side, or on back. Some erotic thoughts but not very strong. I urinate into chamber. I think *1²* of an Irish nurse—dark hair—who works in a mental hospital.

5.45. I notice the time. Shortly after I fall asleep.

47. 7.30. I get up and take in paper, rolls and letters. It is cold. Snow on ground.

3   Postcard from Mr. Charles Madge. Booklet (Intourist) on *3* Soviet Russia.

I return to bed. Smoke a Players 'medium' and a De *3* Reszke 'Minor'. I read *Glasgow Herald* ('Bus strike, Britain's *3* new Navy, etc.) and *Ayrshire Post* (Report of Ayrshire Film *2²* Society, Dr. M'Rae's report of Glengall Mental Hospital, letter about —— people—writer of letter doesn't like them— comments on Ayr's poor support of a resident repertory company ('Pelican Players').

I glance at Intourist booklet on Russia, noting girl ath- *3* letes, girl standing on aeroplane, actors and musicians.

3   **48.** 8.10. I get up. Muller's physical exercises—10 minutes. Shave, dress. Blue trousers. Old jacket for house. Stiff turned-up collar.

My mother, 'How's Madrid?'

I reply 'The Government seems to be alright, but I've 3 only glanced at the news.'

My mother is small, rather thin and rheumatic. She feels the cold. She talks about forthcoming competition in *John* 3 *Bull*.

My mother wishes to shut outside door, 'to keep out cold.' I don't mind.

I whistle part of an overture (allegro). Can't remember name. Then hum 'in thought' moderato passage from *Zampa*.

Breakfast. Hard-boiled egg, and gammon. Tea (local grocer's), marmalade. My mother tells me she is writing to 2^2 our lawyers (Glasgow) on a business matter. She asks me to 2^2 post letter in town before 10.0.

I go out to bring in coal. I do not particularly like doing this as a rule, especially when it is very small coal. . . .*

49. 10.5. I leave post-office. Very little traffic. Commercial vans. I go down road towards sea. Usual morning walk. Past railway station, under railway bridge. About 20 work- 2^p men repairing and widening road to sea, in preparation for holiday traffic. (A retired Lieut.-Colonel on Town Council recently wrote to paper saying road had been too narrow.) Road is pretty 'torn'. I do not wish my shoes cut on sharp stones. I take another road to left. I see a religious 'notice' which refers to a saying of Christ's. All I can remember now 3 is 'Verily, verily'. I pass Mr. H., joiner, about 55, stout, 2 'farmery', humorous, full face—a bit of a 'wag', walking fairly quickly. We have a nodding acquaintance. He says 'terrible weather' in a pleasant-humorous way. Head and neck bent slightly forward. I notice a man (upper working class appearance) picking up a shovel (? may have been spade) by the shaft. Raises it with fingers, lightly, does not

*Observer then describes a visit to the Post Office and conversation there, with details of his walk there.

1 grip it. About 45 (?). The young milkman—about 30 or 28, dark hair—who delivers our milk comes along, cigarette in mouth, walking rather quickly. 'Wintry weather,' he says in pleasant voice. His 'car' is near.

There are two aeroplanes (biplanes) from flying school, overhead. Perhaps 2,000 ft. up. (A guess.) Not 'stunting'. Grey sky, I reach sea, having come by route like this:*

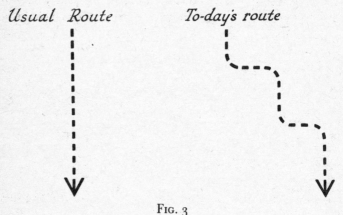

Usual Route   *To-day's route*

FIG. 3

Grey sea. Smoky. Placid. Ashen. The hills of Arran sombre. No one about. Esplanade deserted. A little dog—rough-haired terrier—runs up to me and is friendly.

50. I leave the sea and turn inland up fairly broad road.
2, 2 Two message-boys, one grinning, talking to message-girl who stands between them. I think they all had bicycles.

I turn into Main St. Near church (Established Church of Scotland. It has a tower visible for considerable distance) the
2 stout, senior district nurse (about 50, dark-haired) gets muddy water splashed over her legs and skirt from passing motor. She looks down at her legs, rather annoyed. Just after passing electrician's—on my left—I turn up my coat collar. I have

*This is the only noticeable break in routine recorded in this Observer's day. The incident does not, however, affect anybody but himself.

some difficulty buttoning it. I have woollen gloves on. I
'draw' my brows. Message-girl looks at me in passing. I look   2
back and so does she. Young policeman 'square' cap (talking   2
with assistant cinema-operator inside glas-doored (I am   2
leaving this 'slip of the pen' as I wrote it) glass-door vestibule
of Broadway picture-house (square building with balcony
and 'open' box-office).

It is now about 10.30. Youths and girls sweeping up snow   2ᵖ
in front of shops. One bare-headed working class girl. Mes-   2
sage-boy without coat, on bicycle.   2

I reach home, noting triangles of snow at bottom of win-
dow-panes.*

51. 1 p.m. Lunch. My mother tells me she is going into Ayr
to see my aunt. I am rather sorry, as my aunt is inclined to be   *1*²
depressing.

Paper-girl comes to door with weeklies. We have conversa-   *1*
tion about 'bus strike. Girl says the strikers threaten to burn   2ᵖ
red A. A. buses.

2.0. Sky becoming overcast Another walk. I notice parcel
fixed under door-knocker of house. Boy on roller-skates.   2
Another boy puts toy pistol to his head. Both working-class   2
(appearance). Smoke from 'bus 'exhaust' in my face. Men at   2ᵖ
work on shop for Woolworth's. Shops have Coronation
souvenirs, tea-sets, etc. I get nod from man (working-class
appearance). Don't know him. Crowded A. A. bus. The company must be profiting from the strike. Elderly gentlemen   2ᵖ
with walking-sticks. Many men smoking outside. I return.
Journalistic work.

52. 3.50. Afternoon-tea. Leaking teapot. It is snowing
again. Bearded man with umbrella up. My mother leaves for   2
Ayr. 4.45. I put on gramophone—dance-music. *Take My
Heart, Irish Hits, One Rainy Afternoon, Bird on the Wing*. The

*The report then describes writing a newspaper article, a further visit
to the post office, and two short conversations.

3 shoe-horn is lying on the grate. Read *Spectator*. Keep fires going. Another bowel evacuation. Voice from without—'whoopee' (I think it's that). Wind blowing. Head comes off long poker. I look out of back window and see the electric sign of the Broadway in distance. I am alone in the house. Everything is quiet, save for the wind.

53. 6.7. I make myself some tea. 6.40. I take the *Glasgow*
3, 1 *Herald* into the grocer's. (I always give grocer *Herald* when I have finished with it.) It is snowing. I go down the road. Two
2 upper working-class ladies (they can be described as ladies; they look superior in general appearance) make remarks about something. I don't catch the words but one of the ladies says
2 'like a parachute'. A youngish girl (upper working class appearance) calls to her dog 'Come on, Son.' It is now dark. I am judging appearances by light from street lamps and
1 shops. I meet Mr. W. again. He says 'Don't stand: see you soon.' People in doorways. Quite a stir now, but of course no
2 'buses. Bareheaded youth (working class by general appearance) standing in doorway. Shops have good displays but seem to have few customers. I go home by —— Road—a
2 lane. Time 6.56. I read *Spectator*. Someone outside gives shrill
3 whistle. Evening paper comes—*Glasgow Evening Citizen*. I
3 glance at it and notice photograph of Mary Pickford and advertisement with illustration of woman—'I have lost 38 lbs. of fat.' Also reference to women 'All-in' wrestlers, and 'bus strike. Stop press column very full. Great many items. Back page of paper. My back gets itchy. I notice the time: 7.30 (may have been a minute before or after). Gramophone. Dance records again. From now till 8.50 I read. *Spectator*, *New Statesman*, including book advertisements. Wind howling. Slight itchiness, back of neck. I wind the clock. Gramophone again. I say auto-suggestions.

54. 9.14. Mother returns from Ayr. Snow blows in. I smoke and read. I have been smoking all day.

9.50. Supper. My mother tells me that my aunt had heard that my uncle had been snowed up and his telephone put out 1^2 of order. My aunt is not very cheerful. I am glad my mother does not see her too often. We discuss the 'bus strike.

I brush my teeth with Calvert's Carbolic tooth-powder. Third time to-day. I stand near fire and feel heat on my trousers. I glance at my hair in mirror. Am I loosing more of my hair? I laugh at the thought of old gentlemen with sticks. Gramophone. I listen to 'hot' trumpet in fox-trots. Read and smoke.

10.50. Prepare for bed. Hair lotion, a few of Muller's exercises. I think I fell asleep about 11.35.

55. *Remarks*: Notes taken in pencil continuously throughout the day. I cannot write shorthand.

Notes written up on Tuesday, Wednesday, 16th, 17th March.

Exact conversations not given. Those in inverted commas are fairly accurate. The gist is quite accurate, I think.

Health moderately good. During the evening I felt rather depressed and lonely. Slightly deaf in right ear (cold). Sometimes a little 'absent minded'.

I felt fairly happy during the day, if not exactly cheerful. After 5.30 I was in a rather 'negative' condition, and bored.

A 'mixed' day for me. Not very interesting as far as the emotions are concerned. A few erotic thoughts. I thought a good deal about psycho-analysis and surrealisme.

No outstanding events, except 'bus strike. The emotional tone of —— was 'grey' and everywhere there was an aimless and disappointing 'atmosphere', but I enjoyed the observations.

Clerk, Liverpool

56. (1) Age: 24. Male. Single. Politics: Member C.P., trade union (Shop assistants).

(2) Clerk—particularly: cable clerk and foreign correspondent. Normal day.

(3) Health: good. Slight inflammation of the throat on waking; also slight rheumatism left shoulder. Indigestion after lunch.

(4) Weather—steady rain from 7 to 9 a.m. Sky cleared. Cold with some sun. Wind easterly, dropping. Air humid; streets slimy whole day.

(5) Sport: Wrestling at Stadium. (For other sport, crime; political and club meetings, see cuttings.)
Note: The difficulty with crimes is that they are not discovered as soon as committed; there must have been several committed to-day in Liverpool which will only come to light later.

57. (6) Wakened by alarm at 7 a.m. from dream of which the central feature was that of filling large vats with oil pumped from a distance through a flexible pipe running uphill, I with someone else vague was in charge of keeping the metal end of the pipe in the vat. It was near a factory but the dominant colour seemed to be country green. I dozed until 7.25 when I got up to perform the routine of dressing and getting breakfast at the same time. Put on slippers and dressing gown. Filled kettle and egg pan and lit gas in kitchenette. Cut 4 pieces bread and put them to toast. Banged on *1* K.'s door, the girl in the next room and went to bathroom. When I came out she had laid cloth in her room—she has an electric fire. I watched the toast, etc. while she went to the bathroom.

58. Breakfast ready and finished dressing 7.45. Read *3 Daily Worker*. Conversation about Labour International Con- *3²* ference on Spain. Said I didn't understand how Bevin could resist unity after hearing in conference and conversation experiences of French and Spanish Socialist delegates. She replied that all Labour Parties where she spoke were en-

thusiastic for Spain and perplexed by inaction of leadership. She told a Catholic ward last night that if they wanted to move Bevin it was up to them, and there was applause. K. is a secondary school mathematics teacher. Father an elementary school teacher with large family. She worked her way by scholarships from elementary school to London University. Aged 26. Highly intelligent. I have known her 13 months.

I mentioned relief that the Italians had been checked N.E. 3^2 of Madrid. She said that after November she wouldn't be surprised at anything.

59. I complained of the weather. It was cold and raining steadily. I would get wet going to work on my bicycle, but it was too late to take a tram.

It is downhill nearly all the way to work. I left the house at 8 a.m. Coming down Bold Street I knocked down an old woman.* Probably my fault, but she was crossing the road 2 without looking at the traffic. I saw her plainly, though the rain blurred my glasses (I was not wearing a hat). In wondering whether to go in front of her or behind her, whether there was room behind her between her and the man following her, whether I could get past in front of her before she reached the pavement and how far my back wheel would skid if I braked any harder, I quite forgot to ring my bell, tried to slip in front of her too late, braked and skidded gently into her and the curb. The man behind her—probably 2 an unskilled labourer, rough skin on face; heavy boots and clothes—picked her up and her umbrella and asked me what I thought I was doing not ringing my bell. Why didn't I brake? I should be more careful. I admitted I didn't ring my bell but was too hypnotized to do more than apologize to the old woman. She looked like an office-cleaner. A labourer carrying a 30 m.p.h. speed limit signpost over his 2 sack-protected left shoulder called out as he passed up the

*2a. This whole story is a model description of social incident. Weather was an important causal factor.

hill: 'You have to be very careful, mate, these wet mornings.'
I agreed. The old woman was also dumb—with shock; and
2 as a passer-by was brushing her coat, and asking her if she was
hurt, there didn't seem to be anything to do but get on my
bicycle and ride off. This made me late at the office.*

60. My legs and feet were soaked and the rain was running
down my neck. I put my bike in the cellar and went into the
office and shouted: 'Who the hell would live in bloody England if they could help it?' There were screams from the two
1 cleaners dusting the desks, and laughter from the clerks
1 opening the mail. The clerk in charge didn't say anything—
but I was not so late that I would get him into trouble with
the man above him, so he did not mind my lateness. I de-
ciphered the first ten letters of the cable—in code—and told
3² the clerk in charge the result. In cable No. 37 —— & Co. Inc.
3² U.S.A., offered —— & Co. Ltd., Liverpool, 2000 boxes of
2/28 lb. blocks of refined American lard for 63/9 per cwt.
prompt shipment. Net cost to-day 63/11. Exchange $4.87.

To ease my irritation at the weather I began to cough and
1 snort. Mrs. O. said to Miss D. 'He's in a bad way.'
1 Miss D.: 'But he's got a good pair of lungs has our Donald,
he's got a good pair of lungs anyway.'
Mrs. O.: 'Well, I think he's bad myself.'
1 A clerk: 'Rotten, absolutely.'
Mrs. O.: 'Oh, I mean bad.' (Lancashire for ill.)
There was more banter which I forget.†

61. Mrs. O. is a widow on the P.A.C. drawing her old age
pension. She is kind-hearted, generous, lively and never bad
tempered. Yet her baker son-in-law is out of work; she has an
invalid son at home; and I think the firm gives her 11s. a
week. Her husband was a ships painter, disabled by a fall;

*1a.

†The fact that it was forgotten indicates that it was routine-conversa-
tion, and suggests that the part which was remembered is hardly to be
placed in the 1a category.

spine injury and long illness affected his mind and he hanged himself in the bedroom. His wife was at work when they came to tell her. She told me this without any false emphasis.

Miss D. is Irish, strong-willed, devout Catholic, aggressive, sharp tongued and short tempered.

They both treat me like a favourite nephew.

62. My firm imports provisions from America and the Continent. The Office staff consists of some fifty clerks and typists who are deceived and deluded by the American Company Union Paternally Benevolent manner. Everyone known by Christian name; encouraged to state all grievances but not to join a union. No one knows what anyone else is paid, there being no fixed grades and scales. I am left a good deal to myself, have a desk of my own and a typewriter. I can step out of the office when I like. One of the junior clerks—public *1* school boy, St. Bede's—stopped singing and said to the clerk in charge, Mr. P. 'I think the intermezzo from the *Rusticana* is one of the loveliest things I know.'

Mr. P. agreed. Both sang. Different tunes.

I said: 'I suppose you've been to the Opera.' *3*

Yes, Mr. P. had been to see *Cav.* and *Pag.* at the Empire.

I said: 'Those are the two they always do together, aren't they?'

Mr. P. nodded. A local salesman. Full of 'good stories' and party tricks. Irish. Lower, lower middle-class. He behaves affably to everyone, except when the directors want something.

63. I finished the cable and took the *Daily Worker* and went downstairs to read while drying my trousers at the central heating furnace. Two men from the warehouse were *1, 1* there, doing nothing. Working class. They used to laugh at me and I'm still awkward with them.*

I:'Christ, what a morning.'

A.: 'Come down on your bike?'

* 1a. Social problem due to class distinction.

I: 'Yes, and I want to dry my trousers. How can I get at the fire?'

B: 'Just open the door at the top.'

I did so and held up my leg to dry sock and trouser bottom.

I: 'What's the smell? Have you been putting onions in it?'

B: 'No, it's the wood—pitch-pine.'

As the steam rose from my trousers A said: 'That's bad, you shouldn't do that; all that steam'll rise into your leg.'

I pointed out it was rising away from my leg, and wouldn't harm me, and then someone on our pavement outside kicked the shutter where they shoot the coke through, and the two men moved away. I dried myself, went upstairs at 8.45. Wrote these notes undisturbed.

64. The rest of the staff came in at 9 a.m., but I was too busy to talk to anyone except N. my friend, who said good-morning and put an R.A.C. guide book on my desk. She is an upper middle-class girl. Only working because her father is too mean to give her enough money to use her leisure intelligently. She has unfortunately inherited this meanness and calculates every penny of her money. She pretends to be uninterested in politics but is in her heart fascist.

At about 10.20 I had some discussion with her over hotels in Worcester.

I have known N. since childhood.

65. Mr. A., insurance agent and Labour city councillor, called me up about a note I sent him to put in the press. A description of the film *Defence of Madrid*, which we are organizing. He said it would probably be in to-night's *Echo*. I had put the advert. in yesterday.

Then for two hours I wrote letters connected with the *Defence of Madrid* and the Party of which I am the local treasurer.

At 11.30 the cashier distributed the wages in pay envelopes. I did not speak to him but he has a series of ritual jokes connected with this ceremony. Such as: 'Nothing for you this week,' 'I suppose you don't want any this week,' 'There's a bonus for you—I don't think,' 'There's a nice billy doo (*billet doux*) in there'—meaning an I.O.U. for a sub.

66. By 12.30 the weather was clear and warm so I took some money, a party card and stamps and left the office, to go to the party room which is just along the street about 150 yards.* I ran past Mr. M., a member of the office staff, because I did not want him to see where I went. In the party room which is large and well-lit but rather dilapidated, three men were sitting round a small table near the fire, addressing envelopes from a list, and counting out money.† Standing near was another unshaven, untidy, unemployed man with a glaucoma of the left eye. Of the three sitting, one was the party organizer and the other two unemployed full-time helpers. One used to be a builder's labourer the other a Neon sign fitter.

(margin notes: 1 ; 1, 1, 1 (see footnote †) ; 1)

The organizer asked me for change of a pound, had I brought stamps for him? He gave me 3s.

The man with the glaucoma handed me a printer's bill and said 'Here, I think this is yours. He says he wants it paying.' It was for some handbills and tickets for the group of which I'm a member. B., the organizer, an ex-miner, took the bill and pointed out an error asking P. to take it back.‡ He said he would do so to-morrow, he was going to get some lunch.

67. B.: 'C. (one of his assistants), deduct 2s. 6d. from Mrs. X. and see how she takes it. Tell her that's the first 2s. 6d. of the 30s.'§

(margin note: 2²)

*This Observer's political activities break in on his office routine, and then establish a parallel routine of their own.

†The political allies here mentioned are probably to be placed in area 1, but there appear to be signs that the Observer still finds a certain strangeness in them which suggests area 2; *e.g.* the phrase 'Three men were sitting round a small table.' The disturbance, through politics, of the boundary between areas 1 and 2 is a striking feature of this report.

‡1a.   §1a.

I (bantering) to C.: 'Hey, I notice he gives you the dirty work. "See how she takes it!" '

But B. is a little ponderous and took me seriously. He said: 'Not at all'—and was taken up by C.: 'Yes, it is a piece of dirty work when a woman swears she has nothing and she has the money in the house all the time she's talking to you.'

I: 'God, did she do that?'

I understood they were making up the payments to the dependents of the local comrades fighting in Spain.

C.: 'Aye, and then comes down here and abuses us. She's had more money out of us, man. . . .'

R.—the other assistant interrupted: 'Donald, can you deliver this to S. and have you sent that statement to —— 3² Group?'

I replied that I could and had.

3² **68.** P. as he was going out said that none of his group would be taking part in the poster parade for the Unity Campaign meeting to-morrow; it was too far for them to come; they could give out leaflets at the cinemas. He also suggested that the afternoon meeting on Sunday should start promptly in order to ensure that the evening meeting began promptly also. (The Unity meeting was to take place at the Stadium and we are rather anxious about filling it successfully; if we don't, it will be a political setback for us in Liverpool.) B. agreed and this reminded him to give R. his steward's credentials. I paid B. three £1 notes and stuck the stamps on his card and he said 'You come here to rob me of money', and I laughed and said I would come in about 12 noon to-morrow when he would have a list of expenses ready. I picked up a pile of leaflets advertising the Unity meeting and went back to the office. It was 1 o'clock.

69. At ten minutes past I went out to lunch with N. I said I had to post some letters, get a postal order and buy a hat. Walking to the Post Office we spoke of the weather which was still clear and fine. We decided that first hat shop we looked at was too expensive; the second did not contain anything in my size, the young man said if I cared to wait for three *2* minutes he would get one from another branch. I said I would wait, but presently he returned to say there was nothing in that shop either.

70. Next we went to a ready-made tailor store which I hoped would have cheap hats. It is very vulgarly ornately planned and the attendants are unpleasantly servile. I said I wanted a hat to the first assistant I saw. *2*

'Hat, sir? First floor, sir.' Then shouted 'Lift! lift!'

Another assistant showed me to the lift and a lift boy took *2, 2* us up in the lift. N. noted that the lino. on the floor was the same pattern as that in the sun-parlour at home.* The lift-boy explained that the hats were on the right. I explained to the hat salesman that I wanted something brown, size about *2* 7, and he said would I put this on my head. And without saying what 'this' was he placed a patent hat-fitter on my head and asked me at what angle did I usually wear hats. I adjusted it and he carefully removed it. From the middle he took a sheet of paper which was punctured by hundreds of points, outlining the shape of my head. He cut out this outline. 'This is for the shape, Sir; we'll now try the size.'

'Is this what you want, Sir, try it in front of this mirror; that is a good hard wearing hat and works out at 12/6.' I asked what else he had. He brought one priced 16/6 and I said it wasn't worth paying 4/- for the difference it made. He assured me that he knew exactly what I wanted, and that though the 12/6 hat might be a little bulky in the crown at present, yet when he had moulded it on his hat-fitting machine it would suit me perfectly. If it didn't, I could choose another. I agreed and he retired behind a screen to mould the hat.

*1a. Coincidence.

1   71. While he was waiting, a cutter from the tailoring dept. whom I know quite well as an active but not very militant member of the Shop Assistants Union approached.*

He said: 'Hallo, Mr. T., what are you doing here?'

I said I had come to buy a hat and was now waiting for it to be moulded.

'Did you know I worked here?'

I said yes, he had told me so.

3², 3²   'Have you heard about the NUDAW? I believe H. has been attacking us again. It's awful, it is really! And he's called a meeting of all those in the drapery trade.'

'Oh, yes. But that's at Blackpool.'

2   72. After more gossip which I can't remember, a customer went past and the cutter pursued him. The salesman returned with the hat and placed it carefully on my head. As it was fairly satisfactory I took it and paid for it. Going out, N. noted that they were not nearly as fawning after you had bought something as before. We ate at a Lyons. I related how I had knocked the old woman down and she told me a story

2²   about her mother's ring which I forget. I cannot remember anything else about our conversation during lunch except that the main heads were the Husband Enticement case, the prospect of cruising in the Mediterranean if the Spanish War did not end, the attractions of Vienna as a holiday resort

3²   and the dance organized by the Young Teachers Association which I had promised to go to this evening. As we walked

3   back to the office I saw from the placards outside the *Liverpool*

3   *Post* and *Echo* offices that Madrid was being heavily shelled. N. also related how a friend of her young brother had had

2³   his gloves stolen in a curious manner.†

1   73. As I went through the office the telephone operator remarked on my new hat.‡ I told her I had bought it to

*This incident shows an encounter with a man who belongs to the political section of area 1 in a strange (2) environment.

†An example of the relatively uncommon x³ incident.   ‡1a.

go to a wedding. She said: 'A wedding! Are you getting married?'

I said: 'Yes, on Thursday.' She laughed and said: 'Go on, I couldn't imagine you married. You're too serious. You couldn't let yourself go. Mr. M. can you imagine this man married?'

Mr. M. said: 'Yes,' so she was rather nonplussed and didn't say anything.

Mr. M. said: 'I saw you running along —— Street, and across the old Haymarket and into a door and up the stairs.'

I laughed and told him that I had run because I did not mean him to see where I went.*

74. At 3 p.m. I started writing up these notes.

One of the directors passed my desk and I said: 'Mr. T. *1* I forgot to ask you if you were going to buy any lard to-day.'

'No, I don't want it.'

'Not even after this morning's drop?'

'No, you can keep it. I'm not having any till it gets below 60s. Didn't I tell you?'

'It'll not go that far.'

'Well, we'll see.'†

I wrote two more letters and six postcards to hotels in Worcester for Easter.

At about 4.20 tea was brought round and then I wrote up some more notes.

At 5 I broke off to send out cables and did not finish until 5.45. I could not note and do not remember conversations during this period.

75. At 6.20 I left the office on foot with the Unity leaflets under my arm. At the Stadium I found a friend, L., whom I *1* had arranged to meet here. He stood on one side of the street and I on the other and we handed out leaflets to the passers *2ᵖ* going into the Stadium.‡ After roughly 15 minutes a police-

*Sequel to previous I a incident.   †Possibly I a.   ‡A routine in the 2 area.

2 man approached L. and said something which made L. reluctantly pick up his case and walk across to me.

'What's the matter?'

'He says there's a bye-law against it but I don't bloody well believe it.'*

'A bye-law?   Since when?'

2   While we were wondering what to do next a young man† on a bicycle glided up to us and grinned. He had more yellow leaflets sticking out of the bag behind his saddle. He asked: 'Are you Donald T.?'

'Yes.'

'I'm W. R.   B. told me at the office that you would be here.'

'Well, the bobby's just told us we can't distribute them here.'

'Why not?'

'Says there's a bye-law.'

'Well, that's easy: we just go further down the road.'

But I was uneasy. Neither I nor L. wanted a row with the bobby. We walked away. A hundred yards away.

W. R. said: 'You can do what you like of course but I'm going to stop here and dish 'em out.'

L. said he had an idea. So he and I went back to the bobby, leaving W. R. handing out leaflets as fast as he could.

76. I asked the bobby: 'How long has this bye-law been in force?'

B.: 'About'—deliberately swinging forward on his toes and back on his heels—'two years.'

L.: 'Does it apply all over Liverpool? We've always dished out bills here before.'

B.: 'I don't care whether ye have or not; ye're littering the streets and it's got to be stopped.'

*An interruption to the routine.

†This young man comes from area 2, but after introducing himself as a political ally joins up with area 1.

I: 'And how is it that commercial firms give out leaflets by sandwich men in Lord Street?' 2^{p2}

B.: (flushing and sticking his Irish chin out still further) 'I'm not here to argue. I've told you not to do it. If you go on I'll have to report you and if you want to see anyone above me you know where to go.'

L.: 'Where?'

B.: 'The police station in Dale Street and there'll be an inspector along here any minute.' 2^3

L.: 'But if we stand close to the entrances and hand bills to people as they are going in they can't very well litter the streets even if they do throw them away, can they?'

B.: 'If the management will allow it, I shall not stop you.' 3

L.: 'Oh, bugger the management.'

And we gave out leaflets at the entrances until we had no more.

L. is petty-bourgeois: old public school boy. I have known him well for about 6 years.

At 7.25 I left the Stadium, passing W. R. who had also run out of leaflets. The policeman was right about the litter; the street was a bad mess. It was cold and damp. I took my bike from the office and rode home.*

77.   *Schoolmaster, Northern Ireland*

(1) Age: 26. Male. Single. No orthodox religion; agnostic, perhaps atheist. Politics: none.

(2) Assistant master in a boys' boarding and day school. The day was normal, except that my work consisted in supervising term examinations instead of actual teaching.

*This long report, which has had to be cut here for reasons of space, concludes with two political discussions with friends, a drink in a public house, and an account of the Y.T.A. dance and conversation which took place there.

(3) Health: normal.

(4) Heavy snow had fallen during the night, and it lay thick in the morning. During the day snow fell at frequent intervals, and the air, though cold, was pleasant and invigorating.

(5) Local events: The snow seemed to prevent anything of interest happening. The main roads in all directions were blocked, and traffic was compelled to come by rail. In consequence, papers were late, the distant entries for the Musical Festival (mostly children of elementary school age) were unable to attend.

A meeting of the local Field Naturalists Club was held, the lecturer being a Derry man, the subject being 'The Romance of Donegal'.

Local interest was centred in the snow but beyond typical stories of cars snowed up, of a party at a dance being obliged to spend the night in the dance hall, and of three men delivering bread in County Down who could not be traced, there was no story which seemed in any way significant. The unusual event of a really heavy snow-storm seemed to be taken as a matter of normal unusualness.

Carl Brisson was starring in the film of one of the two local cinemas, and a 'musical' of unknown name at the other.

78. 8.10. While shaving before breakfast, noticed boys *I* snowballing, and saw one boy deliberately throw a snowball *I* at the bedroom window of a member of the staff, and run for it.*

8.15. Said member mentioned that a snowball had been thrown at his window. I told him that I knew who had done it. He said, 'Who?' I told him the name. He said, 'Wait till I get my hands on him.' I said I should ignore it. He replied

*1a. Due to weather.

that he certainly would not. After breakfast, he called up the boy, and fined him sixpence, or half of his weekly pocket-money.* The boy was inclined to be aggrieved, and murmured something to the effect that the other masters knew how to take a joke. On leaving the dining-hall, he slammed the door; the master ignored this.†

Another of the staff said that snowballs had been thrown *1* against his window too, but that when he had looked out and roared, they had scattered; what should he do about it? I and others advised him to do nothing, and he agreed.

Again I watched the snowballing from the bathroom window, and saw the Headmaster walking through the battle *1* from his house, unnoticed, unnoticing, and unscathed.

79. 9.5 to 11.45. Supervised examinations. Once I corrected two small boys for holding their heads too close to their papers, in the fear that they would strain their eyes. I have not felt impelled to do this before.‡

11.45 to 11.55. Break for tea. The matron, in a complaining *1* tone, said: 'The wee boys were out snowballing before breakfast.' I replied, with the thought in my mind that the variety and the experience was good for them, in a cheery tone: 'Yes, I saw them.' She answered, 'They've all got their feet wet.'

11.55 to 1.15. More supervision. The headmaster announced that the singing master was unable to come, since *1* the 'buses were stopped, and so the examination on English Essay would be continued for two periods (of 40 minutes each) instead of one.§

80. 1.15 to 2.10. The same member of the staff who had fined the boy for snowballing in the morning, they had done so without bias; but after a short time they had taken sides, boarders against day-boys. He is himself an old day-boy.‖

*1a.   †1a.

‡1a. Due to weather and the glare of light reflected from snow.

§1a.   ‖1a.

The conversation then turned on the peculiarities of a
2^2 former master, 'Chilly' D——, who had talked through his
nose, and was apparently both vindictive and a fool.

8l. 2.10 to 3.30. Supervision again. I noticed that the
boys whom I had stopped peering too closely at their papers
were back to it again, but forbore to mention it a second
time.

3.30. As the snow was falling and I would be out in the
evening, I lit a fire in my room and spent the afternoon
marking. The fire was unusually hard to light, and I found
the sticks were damp.*

1^p 5.30. Tea. After tea, the boys as usual on Friday asked
whether I or another could give them a lift to the swimming
baths. When I looked out at the snow falling, in an effort to
raise a smile (for the snow has no effect on the baths, which
are indoor), they were slow to grasp my meaning.

On the way to the baths, we found drifts of snow in some
places two or three feet deep; but there was a clear way in
the middle of the road always. The boys were less talkative
than usual, and on the return journey scarcely spoke a word.†

8.0. On return, decided that a fire was preferable to the
3 Field Club's lecture, and marked till 10 p.m. Another mem-
1 ber of the staff, who also had trouble with his fire, made a
loud complaint to the matron about it; she made the maid
lay it again. If it was due to wet sticks, the fault was not the
1, 1 maid's, but the odd-job-man's, but he had gone home.

1, 1 10 to 12 midnight: Played cut-throat with two of the staff.

82. *Feelings*: Anger—with the member of the staff who had
overpunished the boy for throwing the snowball, and with
myself for giving his name. Especially because the master in
question is the newest addition to the staff, and is inclined,
I thought, to interfere.

Anger—with the matron for not realizing that the develop-

*1a. Due to weather. †1a.

ment of the boys' in experience was more important than the chance of their catching colds. Followed by the thought that, had I not been reading Ethel Mannin's *Green Willow*, which gives a vivid description of this development, perhaps I would not have taken sides.

A noticeable disquiet—at the news that —— was suffering badly from snow, —— being my home town, the residence of my family, and the place of work of my fiancée.

Growing realization of monotony and irritating lack of freedom—as the hours of idleness without rest spent in the examination rooms grew longer.

Wonder—that on a day when it seemed that so much of interest might have occurred, so little of significance actually had.

The weather suggested more than once a 'White wedding' of a rather fairy nature. Did it also suggest the thought of 'Chilly' D——.*

Notes of all this were made within a few minutes of occurrence—though there was remarkably little to note. Written up the following Monday.

83.   *Convalescent, South London*

(1) Age: 28. Male. Unmarried. Religion: none. Politics: no firm convictions. Left sympathies.

(2) I have no regular job. The day was normal (apart from one occurrence, see below) in the sense that it did not differ appreciably in routine from other recent days. This routine, however, being imposed by ill-health, is temporary, and, in itself, abnormal.

(3) General ill-health accentuated by the aftermath of tonsillitis. Improving in course of day. (See below.)

*All the incidents in this report seem to be due to the snow.

(4) Cold sunny morning, with gusty wind—a typical March day. Sky of tufted, ravelled clouds, a sense of Spring after several days bad weather. Rain in afternoon, clearing in early evening.

1, 2 84. Breakfast 9 o'clock. My mother, Miss X., a visitor, a plain, dull, repressed, 32, upper middle-class, clergyman's daughter. An argument apropos of nothing about British India, and miscegenation. My mother usually indignant on the subject of British hypocrisy. Miss X. glibly emitting platitudes—'In mixed marriages, you know, it's always the worst *3* qualities of both sides that come out.' I gave her E. M. Forster's *A Passage to India*. She—'I'm not sure, but I believe I've read it. I don't really remember.' Rest of conversation not recorded, above remarks noted an hour later.

85. 10.15. Went to London. Impulse to avoid walking under a ladder on way to station. Walked under it. Suffered from feeling of nervous exhaustion in the train (a common symptom with me in my present state of health). This subsided on arrival at destination.

2 11.0. Appointment with a Doctor, Harley Street. A young man, specialist, of the hearty type, though with a rather stagily genial professional manner, and a B.B.C. voice. A blood-test of mine had proved negative, which gave me a clean sheet, physiologically, after prolonged ill-health.* Tags of general conversation noted half-hour later—asked about the general attitude to the Coronation, among his acquaintances, he said:

'People seem to be divided into two camps—those who make it an excuse for a "blind", and those who want to escape at all costs.'

Returning home, general impressions of a fine day in London—the quicker steps of girls, geniality of ticket-inspectors, etc. Emotive sound of a barrel-organ heard from a taxi—

*This incident dominates the day.

sudden burst of music, as though a door were opened and quickly shut again. On the station platform, a nun with the face, beneath her coif, of some eminent man of letters. 2

Above noted briefly in train.

Lunch at 1.15. No conversation sufficiently continuous or coherent to record. Slept from 2 till 4. Afterwards wrote up some of these notes (longhand) including those below. Dinner 7.30. Bed 9.30.

86. My mood for the day was dominated by the visit to the doctor, which, with its satisfactory result, made the day rather a 'red-letter' one for me. My feeling of ill-health in the morning was probably accentuated not only by a sore throat, but also by apprehension as to the doctor's verdict. This apprehension, acute up to the time of the interview (11 o'clock) gave place to a somewhat confused elation, at the prospect of freedom from a strict regime which had lasted, with few interruptions, for more than 2 years, and had been extremely inhibiting—no alcohol, etc. (I had always been to a great extent dependent on alcohol, being extremely self-conscious, and needing several drinks always before any social contact.) Returning home, this elation persisted, though clouded to some extent by the usual depression and irritation of home associations. The prospect of being 'well' from a strictly physiological point of view, was tempered, too, by the knowledge that I had to adjust myself psychically to normal life, and that this would take a long time probably, as I had been suffering from 'nerves' (to put it briefly!) as much as from anything physical.

87.   *Accountant, Northumberland*

(1) Age: 24. Male. Single. Socialist.
(2) Accountant in Local Government Service. Normal day.

(3) My health was good; a cold which I had caught the previous week-end had not quite disappeared.

(4) The weather was wet and dreary, but less cold than it had been during the preceding week. Patches of snow lay still unmelted in the parks and gardens. In the evening it became colder, there was a strong easterly wind, it started to snow again and the streets were soon covered with an inch of varying intensity continued the remainder of the day.

(5) There were no local events of outstanding importance; the front page of the evening papers was headed with news concerning the freeing of a toll bridge on Coronation Day.

In the sphere of sport the league match between Sunderland and Wolverhampton is the main topic of conversation, there is to be a second replay on Monday, 15th March.

At the local cinemas the following films are showing: *His Brother's Wife*, *The Country Beyond*, *White Angel*, and *Anthony Adverse*.

88. I arose at 7.50 a.m. I did not shave because I was going to a dance in the evening, and as a rule on such occasions I postpone this part of my toilet.*

I arrived at the office unusually early, that is to say, at 8.45 a.m., because it was raining heavily and it was undesirable to take the more circuitous route by the sea.†

The day was spent in preparing the council's estimates of income and expenditure for the ensuing year, on which the rate in the pound will be based. With this work as a background there were many other minor calls upon my time.

At lunch time I oiled my tramping boots; and on my way
3 back to the office I drew some money from the bank.

At 6 p.m., after tea, I made some notes concerning this present matter, then, although I had intended to read until

*1a.   †1a. Due to weather.

it was time to dress for the dance, I felt inclined to go for a walk.* There was a bitter, fierce wind blowing inland, the tide was high and the waves were breaking over the promenades.

In the streets the paving stones were half-dried, there did not seem to be many people about, except in the grocers' 2^T shops where they stood apathetically huddled against the counters.

I returned to my lodgings at 7 p.m., washed, shaved, dressed, fussed unnecessarily with my toilet and caught the 8.15 p.m. train to Newcastle. The streets were deserted then, the snow driving down relentlessly.

89. There were the usual few drably-clothed persons in the 2^T dirty, wicker upholstered carriages. Because the atmosphere in these electric trains is so laden with stale tobacco smoke I almost invariably travel in a non-smoking compartment. The carriages are long and undivided like single deck tramcars. The floors were wet and muddy, the windows were steamy, the passengers had made black smudges and semi-circles with 2 their coat sleeves to gaze out at the dimly lit stations. (I thought it was like wiping the bloom off a plum.)

In my carriage there were six men, three of them wore 2 bowler hats. Two seated near me were talking animatedly; usually the passengers sit looking glumly in front of them, not even reading a newspaper.

90. I had not far to go from the station, through slush covered streets, to the dance hall, a place called the Oxford Galleries, Newcastle's largest and most popular 'Palais de Danse'. It contains two halls, in the smaller a dance organized by the Youth Hostels Association was in progress, while 3 in the larger Roy Fox was playing for the normal Friday 3 night dance.

*Break in routine, probably due to exhilaration at the thought of the dance in the evening.

I was attending the Y.H.A. dance, but from one end of the hall it was possible to look through heavily curtained glass doors into the larger room. With Roy Fox's band there were two vocalists, the greater attraction seemed to be the female dressed in green silk trousers, white silk blouse, and with a green ribbon round her blonde hair.* Whenever she came, tripping affectedly to the microphone the moving sea of dancers coagulated in front of the stage, to watch the sinuous sway of the snake-like body, the lifted arms, the crooked fingers.

The music for the Y.H.A. dance was supplied by a local band who wore frayed and dowdy-looking claret coloured suits.† There were only 140 dancers who, in general, were dressed more attractively and looked happier than the much larger crowd in the other hall.

91. *Feelings*: At the office the time passed rapidly, normally at least some part of the day is inclined to drag. There were possibly two reasons for this; firstly there was a false sense of activity, a continual occupation with petty affairs, and secondly my mind was pervaded with anticipation of the evening's diversion, a dance organized by the Y.H.A., and at which I hoped to meet a young woman of twenty-three who had particularly appealed to me when I had met her a fortnight previously at a youth hostel.‡

My thoughts were reverting all day to the evening's dance and the week-end which I proposed to spend on the snow-covered moors thirty miles inland. At the hostel at which I was to stay I expected to meet the same young woman and other congenial company.

*Roy Fox is clearly a personage from area 3, seen in the flesh. His lady crooner, though not named, also seems to be a figure from area 3.

†The local band, however, can hardly claim a place in area 3.

‡There is mentioned, for the first time, the dominating figure of the Observer's day. He wants to draw her out of his area 2 and into his area 1. In this connection, the social relationships entailed in 'hiking' are important.

When I went for a walk after tea I was abounding with energy, I ran needlessly down on to the lower promenade over which the sea was breaking. The wind freshened my face and made my ears tingle. There was the strong smell of salt in the air, memories of another esplanade surged up within me, where the sea frequently broke wildly over the road and scattered pebbles and seaweed everywhere. (I worked for a year on the South Coast.)

92. The first part of the dance I spent promiscuously, dancing with some of the women I had met on week-ends away, and at the Y.H.A. lectures. I did not immediately attach myself to my particular interest because I was reluctant to run the risk of sacrificing my whole evening to one individual, because also I feared that my exclusive company might not be desirable to her, and because, in any case, it might become less obnoxious if withheld for some time. Yet I felt uneasy when she was appropriated by other men to whom she seemed to be well-known.*

About 10.30 p.m. I took her for some refreshment, we talked of books, she said she was reading *A Guide to Philosophy*, 3 I made some laudatory remarks about *Eyeless in Gaza*; we talked of travel, she told me of places I must visit in Northumberland, I became garrulous about the New Forest, the South Downs and Salisbury Cathedral. We returned to the ballroom, we criticized pretentiously the other dancers. We went to look into the other hall at the seething mass of variously dressed humanity. The room was dimly lit, the coloured spotlight shone alternately on Roy Fox and his lady crooner; he was nonchalantly and unsmilingly signing autograph albums.

I wondered whether my companion would be adverse to my making love to her, her attitude and response to my tentative advances were reassuring.

I glanced at my watch, it was twelve o'clock.

*She seemed to be in area 1 for other men, and he wanted her to be in his area 1.

93. In this section, 28 reports (including those quoted at length) will be analysed briefly. Incidents are only mentioned if x¹; people in areas 1 and 2 are only mentioned if x¹; in area 3 a certain amount of latitude has been allowed, owing to the difficulty of deciding at how many degrees the entries in this area are removed from the Observer. Groups and crowds are not mentioned in areas 1 and 2.

94. A. *Sound-film Engineer, Scotland.*

    Incidents: 1a. None.

    People: 1. Theatre electrician, observer's wife, theatre manager.

             3. Corporation Electricity Inspectors,
Busmen on strike,
Cinema Union,
Bergner,
Shakespeare,
Matheson Lang.

B. *Side-piecer in Cotton Mill, Bolton* (quoted paras. 7–22).

    Incidents: 1a. 21.

               Interruptions to routine: 14,
Discussions: 4,
Co-operation: 3.

    People: 1. Fellow workers in Mill (11),
Insurance agent,
Mother.

             2. Salvation Army officer.

             3. Emil Lucka,
Mr. Blair (founder of local hospital).

C. *Convalescent, South London* (quoted paras. 89–86).

    Incidents: 1a. None.
            2. Appointment with doctor.
    People: 1. Mother,
               Visitor at house.
            2. Doctor,
               Nun.
            3. E. M. Forster.

D. *School Teacher, South London.*

    Incidents: 1a. Discussions at breakfast:
                 with head-mistress,
                 with woman friend.
            3. Reading letter from Hollywood.
    People: 1. Teacher friend,
               Head-mistress,
               Abnormal child,
               Teacher,
               Woman friend.
            3. Aldous Huxley,
               Film stars,
               L.L.C.,
               Queen Mary,
               Daily Express,
               News Chronicle,
               Co-operatives.

E. *In Architect's Office, Oldham.*

    Incidents: 1a. First to arrive at office; unusual.
            3. Attend meeting of Smokers' Defence League.
    People: 1. Wife,
               Postman,
               Fellow staff (6).

2. 2 people in train.
3. *Manchester Guardian,*
   Left Book Club,
   P.R. Society,
   New Statesman.

F. *Woman Novelist, Bloomsbury.*

Incidents: 1a. Unexpected arrival of friend for lunch;
   discussions at dinner party.
2. Fighting for seat in train,
   Dropping glove in train,
   Fascinated watching woman chewing gum
   in train.

People: 1. Charwoman,
   Friends (4).
2. Waitresses (2),
   Clerk at British Museum.
3. 'Esquire,'
   Contributors to socialist monthly.

G. *Civil Servant, Leeds.*

Incidents: 1a. Discussion on snowy weather,
   Worry about new boss.
People: 1. Fellow workers in office (5).
2. Man in train.
3. Grassic Gibbon.

H. *Bank Clerk, London* (quoted paras. 23–29).

Incidents: 1a. Interruptions to routine (8),
   Discussions, etc. (5),
   Free drink (1).
People: 1. Fellow staff (6),
   Friends (2).

  2. Man he thought he knew,
    Stockbroker in train.
  3. Ribbentrop,
    King,
    Ambassador,
    Hitler,
    George Orwell,
    Littlewood's,
    Local operatic society,
    Captain and hon. sec. of cricket club,
    Hertford cricketer.

I. *Housewife, near Birmingham* (quoted paras. 30–42).

 Incidents: 1a. Forgetting to 'lift' small son.
 People: 1. Son,
       Husband,
       Baker,
       Butcher,
       Grocer,
       Neighbour,
       Greengrocer.
      2. Local tradesmen,
       Young woman (with whom she felt indignant).
      3. *In dream:* Aldous Huxley,
          Sir John Reith,
          Secretary of State for Ireland,
          King Carol.
     Waking: Mr. Madge,
         Henry Hall,
         Sir Thomas Browne.

J. *Schoolmaster, Cheshire.*

 Incidents: 1a. Discussion in common room about Spain,
       argument with wife about mathematics.
 People: 1. Wife.

K. *Woman Research Worker, Hampshire.*

Incidents: 1a. Breakdowns in routine (5),
    Late arrival of trombone player at local operatic society.

People: 1. Mother,
   Cook,
   Fellow staff (11),
   Friends (3),
   Trombone player.

   3. *News Chronicle,*
   Technical journal,
   Operatic society.

L. *Farmer, Norfolk.*

Incidents: 1a. Telegram cancelling brother-in-law's visit.

People: 1. Farm foreman,
   Wife,
   Garage manager.

   3. King and Queen.

M. *Undergraduate, Cambridge.*

Incidents: 1a. Surprise at piece of verse seen in friend's room,
    Admiration of photo in another friend's room,
    Third friend's embarrassment with woman nurse.

   2. Problem whether to tip waitress,
   Cheated over bill.

People: 1. Undergraduates (8),
   A don,
   Landlord.

   2. Women on 'bus (2),

          Band leader,
          Waitresses (2),
          Cashiers (2),
          Barmaid,
          Undergraduates (13).
    3.   Dostoievsky,
          Picasso,
          Matisse,
          English faculty,
          Sunday Chronicle,
          Max Baer,
          Queen Marie,
          Arts' Theatre.

N. *Works in Publicity Dept., London.*

    Incidents: 1a. Late for job,
                 Question about insurance,
                 Delay in leaving office,
                 Difficulties with Labour Exchange.
    People: 1. Fellow staff (6).
               2. 'Bus conductor,
                  Labour Exchange clerk.

O. *In bed with gastric inflammation, London.*

    Incidents: 1a. None.
    People: 1. Brother,
                  Wife,
                  Mother,
                  Friend.
               2. Presbyterian minister who comes to call.
               3. *Daily Telegraph*,
                  Daily Express,
                  B.B.C.,
                  Time and Tide,
                  Illustrated London News,

New Statesman,
Alistair Cooke,
Osbert Sitwell,
Duke of Windsor,
George VI.

P. *Clerk in Metal Foundry, London.*

    Incidents: 1a. Breaks in routine (4),
                 Boss's dream.
    People: 1. Director of firm—*Note:* all persons mentioned except the director of the firm are x^2 and all these, except one are introduced in conversation by the director.

Q. *Free-lance, Ayrshire* (quoted paras. 46–55).

    Incidents: 1a. None.
    People: 1. Mother,
           Miss Mac—— at post office,
           Milkman,
           Paper-girl,
           A friend,
           Grocer.
        2. A man and woman,
           A nodding acquaintance,
           A man with a shovel,
           2 message boys,
           Message-girl,
           District nurse,
           Message-girl,
           Policeman,
           Cinema operator,
           Girl,
           Message-boy,
           Gardener,

           Policeman,
           2 workmen,
           Boy on skates,
           Another boy,
           Man who nods,
           Bearded man with umbrella,
           Voice from without,
           Girl,
           Youth,
           Whistle from without,
           2 upper-working-class ladies.

3. *Glasgow Herald*,
    Ayrshire Post,
    Doctor Macrae,
    Pelican Players,
    Intourist—Russian girl athletes,
    Spanish Government,
    John Bull,
    Post Office,
    Church of Scotland,
    Daily Telegraph,
    Ayrshire Film Society,
    Spectator,
    Glasgow Evening Citizen,
    Mary Pickford.

R. *Schoolmaster, Northern Ireland* (quoted paras. 77–82).

Incidents: 1a. Snowball thrown at master's window,
              Singing master who did not come,
              Fire which wouldn't light (all due to snowy weather),
              Boys hold heads too close to papers (also due to snow).

People: 1. Boys,
          Masters,

     Matron,

     The maid,

     The odd-job-man.

   3. Ethel Mannin.

S. *Accountant, Northumberland* (quoted paras. 87–92).

  Incidents: 1a. Did not shave,

     Oiled boots,

     Ran down to sea (on account of Y.H.A. dance and projected hike),

     Arrived early at office,

     Met girl friend at dance.

  People: 1. Girl friend.

    3. Y.H.A.,

     Roy Fox and his woman vocalist (in the flesh).

T. *Dental Mechanic, Herts.*

  Incidents: 1a. 7 discussions with various people on various topics.

    2. Gave man lift in car,

     Visited lady socialist candidate.

    3. Took part in chorus of local operatic society.

  People: 1. Proprietor of lodgings,

     Boy assistant,

     Friend.

    2. *See* Incidents.

    3. Freud,

     Giles and Esmond Romilly,

     Radio Times,

     Aldous Huxley,

     The Government,

     The Church,

     Left Book Club,

> County council,
> Rowing club,
> Operatic society,
> Royal Family,
> Duke of Windsor and Mrs. Simpson.

U. *Woman Undergraduate, Oxford.*

    Incidents: 1a. Birthday of May,
              Routine interrupted (3),
              Incidents with dons (2),
              Bottle party.

    People: 1. Friend,
              Maid,
              Landlady,
              2 Dons,
              4 Undergraduates,
              A small boy.

V. *Shorthand-Typist, London.*

    Incidents: 1a. Commissionaire comments on Observer's
                paleness.
           2. Conversation with chemist,
              Man upsets glass in restaurant,
              Conversation in Underground, and buy-
              ing a hat.

    People: 1. Son,
              Sister,
              Girl friend,
              Fellow staff (9).
           2. Chemist,
               Man in restaurant,
              Office workers on train,
              Shop-girl,
              Husband and wife in restaurant.

3. Radio announcer,
Daily Telegraph,
Daily Express,
A trade union,
Daily Worker,
News Chronicle.

W. *Shorthand-Typist, London.*

Incidents: 1a. Friend's laughter at long strides,
Meeting with young man frustrated,
Flowers for sick member of staff.

3. Attend meeting of group of Christian women.

People: 1. Friend,
Newspaper man,
Fellow staff (5).

3. A. P. Herbert,
Freud,
Group of Christian women.

X. *Commercial Clerk, Birmingham.*

Incidents: 1a. At home, minor troubles (4),
Office minor troubles (8),
Boys outside office on account of snow,
Laughing at a poor joke, conversations (3 or more).

People: 1. Postman,
Daughter,
Wife,
Fellow staff and customers (10),
Mother,
Sister,
Same pay-desk girl at cinema as many many years before.

410

2. Seen in streets: 24 people mentioned indi-
vidually, also haulier and odd-job man
at office.

3. W. H. Auden,
Dali,
Oscar Homolka,
Conrad,
Frank Vosper,
Queen Mary,
Dick Whittington,
Mother Goose.

Y. *Welfare Supervisor in Edinburgh during Day.*

Incidents: 1a. None, because travelling.

2. Minor troubles of travel (5),
Tepid bath,
Minor troubles in connection with job (2),
Failing to accept a biscuit,
Failing to buy sweets.

People: 2. At hotel (15),
On railway journey (13),
At shops inspected (9),
In cafés and on other journeys (24),
61 *in all.*

3. *Scotsman,*
Daily Telegraph,
Tatler,
H. G. Wells.

Z. *Unemployed, London.*

Incidents: 1a. Looking for jobs in paper,
4 incidents in connection with moving
house.

2. 5 incidents in connection with moving
house.

People: 1. Landlady,
Fruiterer friend.

2. Neighbour,
Gas Co. employee,
Seen in course of day's wanderings (5).

3. *Dalton's Weekly,*
Daily Telegraph,
New Statesman,
Disney,
Police.

AA. *Clerk, Liverpool* (quoted paras. 56–76).

Incidents: 1a. Due directly or indirectly to bad weather (5),
Conversations with friends,
Political encounters.

2. Knocking down an old woman,
Stopped by policeman from handing out leaflets,
And buying a new hat.

People: 1. Girl friend,
Fellow staff (11),
Friends and political allies (13).

2. Old woman knocked down by observer,
Passers-by (3),
Shop assistants (6),
Policeman,
Barmaid,
Friend's father.

3. Bevin,
NUDAW,
NUWM,
Trades' council,
LNU.

AB. *Psychiatric Social Worker, London*

    Incidents: Ia. Forget handkerchief,
                     Attend party.
    People: I. Charwoman,
                 German doctor friend.
            2. Seen in course of visiting patients' relatives (15),
                 Mrs. E. for lunch date,
                 Guests at party (10).
            3. *News Review*,
                 LCC,
                 Mrs. Simpson,
                 The King,
                 Baldwin,
                 The Archbishop.

95. In concluding this section, it is fitting to point out that any explanations or hypotheses put forward in the course of analysis are the first tentative approach to a new set of scientific problems. To the scientist who may feel that in that case it is premature to publish results, we may say by way of reminder that MASS-OBSERVATION has to attempt more than other sciences (which is not to say that it is better than other sciences). Briefly, it has to attempt more because more people are involved; because the research is not being done by one worker, or group of workers, but by a very large number of Observers. The numbers are part of the project; and the numbers cannot be obtained without a public exposition of results at the earliest possible stage.

In addition to the ordinary difficulties of scientific presentation, the editors of this volume have had to consider difficulties of other kinds—difficulties comparable to those which the film industry and the newspaper industry have been built up to overcome. These are the difficulties of appealing to a public of unknown size and of every kind, and the elementary financial problems arising out of this. But again, MASS-OBSERVATION is more than journalism or film documentary, because it has the aim in view not only of presenting, but of classifying and analysing, the immediate human world. By publishing this book at this stage we are fulfilling another of the tasks of MASS-OBSERVATION, that of inviting observers and potential observers to contribute both to the analysis of material here presented and also to the future construction of MASS-OBSERVATION on a truly democratic basis.

Afterword

by David Pocock
Director of the Tom Harrisson Mass-Observation Archive

I was about fifteen when I first read *May the Twelfth*. Pretty much at random, I had grabbed it from the school library shelves to read during some predictably boring lesson. Under the shelter of my desk I opened it, and still remember the initial puzzlement and then the tingle of delight that comes with real discovery. And no doubt my own covert reading was suited to what I took to be a magnificent subversion of authority. The Coronation of George VI was 'history' as far as I was concerned but it had never occurred to me before that 'history' could be written in this way. If I derived anything more permanent than this first pleasure it was a critical sense that precisely such details as those that Mass-Observation had recorded were at least to be borne in mind whenever later I was to be faced with an 'official record'.

I hope that some of the people who have been reading this book will have been as ignorant of Mass-Observation and its development as I was, and so been able to share my adolescent experience. If they do, they will be responding as at least one of the authors, Humphrey Jennings, would have wished. For him the book was to carry on in prose the experiments being made with the documentary film. The material was to speak for itself, guided minimally by the hand of the producer. 'The unity of the material . . . is due to all the social life of that day being hinged on a single ceremony of national importance.' (p. 347) But what that unity *was*, what significant comment the complex montage was to make, and the kind of national importance to be attached to that ceremony was ultimately to be made in the mind of the reader; it was to be a serious aesthetic and moral experience.

The co-author, Charles Madge, would not, as a poet, have been out of sympathy with this aim, but as a journalist, Communist, and later Professor of Sociology, he had also some scientific and political purpose: '*Mass-Observation* is more than journalism or film-documentary, because it has the aim not only of presenting but also classifying and analysing the immediate human world.' (p. 414) He regarded himself as combining anthropology and social psychology in his handling of the material and, writing for *The Left Review* while *May the Twelfth* must have been still in preparation, he described these two sciences as 'potentially the foremost allies of revolution'. (*The Left Review*, 1 July, 1937.)

Whatever their purpose: aesthetic, political or 'scientific', the founders of the Mass-Observation 'movement', as it was called, all shared a belief that whether the observation was *of* the masses or *by* the masses (it was in fact a combination of both) it was certainly *for* the masses. The original intention was to publish quickly and so feed into the public mind the truth about contemporary Britain. The ideas of Freud had been quickly popularized in the 1930s and there is no doubt that the publications of Mass-Observation were somehow to work in the collective mind like the insights of the psychoanalyst, dissolving repressions, disentangling complexes and would, by extending consciousness, bring freedom – of some sort.

Publication on this grand scale was never achieved for various reasons but even this first venture was, in

one respect at least, not aimed with any precision at the
intended target. A contemporary letter from someone
describing himself as 'a working man' complained at
the price. How could he be expected to afford a book
costing 12/6 when a miner's wage was about £2 a week?
His point takes on more general force when we remind
ourselves that in 1936 it was calculated that 30 per cent
of the population 'were able to devote less than 6s a
week to food' (John Burnett, *A History of the Cost of Living*
(Pelican, 1969), pp. 287–8). A cheaper edition in October 1938, priced at 6s, did not improve the relatively
low sales and anyhow by then the possibility, likelihood
or certainty of war – according to your point of view –
had made the Coronation seem a very distant event
indeed.

The reactions of reviewers of the time reflect something of the difference between the conceptions of the
two authors. The harshest comment was that of the
Reader in Sociology at the University of London. T. H.
Marshall wrote in *The Highway*:

> A four hundred page volume . . . which is so completely
> devoid of interest that even the most well-intentioned
> reviewer is at a loss to find anything to say about its
> contents.

It was a difficulty which Marshall then proceeded to
overcome to the tune of some two thousand words.

More charitably, a reviewer in *The New English
Weekly*, commented that it would be surprising if Mass-
Observation, founded only that year, had developed
any 'theoretical basis worth discussing . . . in so very
short a time'. He went on to say that it was the 'best
book on the Coronation so far', and its republication
fifty years later can only endorse that judgement.

The non-academic reviewers were more sympathetic
to the book as a narrative: as, quite simply, 'full of
human interest', as having 'something of interest to
teach us about our fellow men', as an 'admirable guide

to historians of our present times, to the social worker,
and the realistic novelist'. All of which judgements,
banal as they may seem, remain true.

Tom Harrisson, the third of the founding triumvirate
of Mass-Observation, had no hand in the compilation
of *May the Twelfth*. Writing to Madge in 1940 he
reminded him that he had had no opportunity to see the
book until it was in page proof and that even then his
criticisms had been ignored, 'naturally enough', he
added. The letter continues:

> This book did not attempt to be anthropology, if by
> anthropology we mean not only the description but also
> the integration and explanation of a whole phenom-
> enon in its cultural context; it was rather a detailed
> piece of documentation, having much in common with
> the documentary film.

He had been a good deal more frank in a letter written
in 1938 to Geoffrey Gorer: 'it was a crazy idea to have it
edited by a whole bunch of intellectual poets'. Nevertheless, he made a point, which is I think a wise one,
that at that stage he would prefer to see 'the movement
wallowing around in a maze of fact' rather than 'bee-
lining' for a premature conclusion. The book was
valuable as history 'not of course as sociology' and did
demonstrate better than any other kind of commentary
the extraordinary way in which a sense of 'common
bond and focus' overwhelmed the many social
differences. And his remarks would apply with equal
force to more recent work on a royal occasion by Mass-
Observation.

May the Twelfth is unique among the publications of
Mass-Observation. As Tom Harrisson increasingly
dominated the investigations through the war period,
so the writing up of the material reflected his influence
even when he was not the sole author. They are more
conventionally organized and concerned to present an
argument, and, despite his scientific pretensions, they

are alive with the pleasure he had in writing about his material, his enjoyment of the facts themselves. Talking to him, I had the lively impression that he relished his 'observations' as a painter might relish his pigments – in themselves, independently and regardless of what later might be made of them.

When I read the book again I found that it still had the power to do more than just evoke memories of my first reaction. The abiding interest lies in the actors themselves. The very lack of analytic commentary has the effect of putting the reader there, as though he or she were watching from the top of a slow-moving bus, sitting in the corner of the public bar, strolling through the street. And even the commentary itself has, in 1987, an interest of its own. It is fascinating to discover that in 1937 even on Coronation Day, it was possible, at Hyde Park Corner, to see a girl lying on the ground in the arms of a policeman. (p. 144) The piquancy of the scene is heightened by the solemn comment in the accompanying footnote. Again, the misanthropic 'Platonist' who was hoping for rain to spoil the occasion, had to be there, one feels, and his comments, as he looks out of the window, have worn better over the years than the footnoted analysis of the hidden symbolism of his hair-oil, which has an effect, now, quite other than that intended. (p. 317)

It is, I think, in the nature of Mass-Observation material that it should be abundantly quoted; it is intrinsically interesting even in its 'raw' state, as anyone who has, in any capacity, worked in the Mass-Observation Archive at the University of Sussex can testify. Researchers seeking evidence on their chosen topic report the need for near superhuman discipline if they are not constantly to be distracted by the invitations at every turn of the page to charge off in pursuit of some 'by-the-way'. I think that there are two related and rather obvious reasons for this.

The first is that, with the exception of the very few

whose business takes them into the many cultures of which Britain is made up, the majority of the population live in their familiar circles, move along their habitual lines, and speak to people who 'speak the same language'. Understandably, we assume, without examining the assumption, that, minor differences apart, everyone else (apart from those whom we 'simply cannot understand') is much the same as ourselves. It comes as a surprise then, and often a fascinating one, to discover that within a few miles of oneself, or sitting next to one on the bus for all one knows, there are others, no less ordinary than oneself and to all appearances normal, who are living in a radically different world and viewing a shared world with very different eyes.

The second reason is that we complement the discovery of difference, which can even be a little unsettling, by deriving comfort from unexpected similarities. Our fantasies, quirks and fads, particular problems with our children or the electric toaster, seem peculiarly ours and yet it is a pleasant surprise to discover that this one is shared by some unknown five hundred miles away and that one by a woman recording her thoughts fifty years ago.

Some such explanation must account for my continuing interest in *May the Twelfth* because I am still surprised every time it occurs to note not just similarities but apparently identical features in the reactions on that Coronation Day and those reported in the Day Diaries written for Mass-Observation on 29 July 1981, the wedding day of Their Royal Highnesses, the Prince and Princess of Wales. Part of the surprise springs no doubt from our sense that so much has happened over fifty years, so much has changed. Notably, we might instance the popularization of television. There were only 60,000 viewers in 1937. Even at the Coronation of Queen Elizabeth II the owner of a television set was a rarity in many streets, and an invitation to watch with them was a privilege. Nevertheless, I have only to substitute 'television' for 'wireless' and very many of the reports in *May the Twelfth* might have been written in 1981. It is perhaps important to remember that the wireless of 1937 was a fixed element in the living room, not a small object to be carted all over the house, and listening to it had become a family occasion as 'loudspeakers [had] replaced earphones'. (p. 270)

Then, as more recently, we find people hurrying to complete domestic chores in time, debating the propriety of eating during 'a religious ceremony', sitting down to follow the commentary with a printed Order of Service, rising from their armchairs to sing the National Anthem. We have the same reports of people being drawn reluctantly into the proceedings, of tears and the same explanations of tears, similar attempts to escape the whole thing, some successful, some not. In 1937 there was the 'Platonist', more interested in the daddy-long-legs on the windowsill than in kings and crowns; in 1981 the major event on 29 July for a man in Peterborough was that he cycled out into the countryside to release an injured hedgehog that he had nursed to health.

For 1981 we have the diary of a young man who sedulously and even ostentatiously avoided anything to do with the Royal Wedding until the small hours of the next day when he listened to a programme about it on the BBC's World Service. He 'was unexpectedly moved by it. Realized all of a sudden that the real point of the day was the British celebrating themselves . . . Felt absurdly, nicely, English. Slept.' Not very different from the mood of the typist whose thoughts are recorded on pp. 303–4 of *May the Twelfth*, although she may have been a little more aggressive in expressing her indifference. Her feelings also changed as she was seduced by the public celebration and if, at thirty-nine, she was more suspicious of these awakened emotions, it is not surprising. We would find in the 1981 records, also, just such doubts as the more self-conscious analyzed in their diaries the spontaneous feelings of the day.

In the last fifty years and with increasing pace during the present reign, the royal family is more exposed than it was then, but the stereotypes do not change. Queen Mary, who to my childish eyes was a swathed ramrod surmounted by a toque, an awesome, remote figure, clearly received her special applause from the crowd watching the Coronation Procession, just as her daughter-in-law, the Queen Mother Elizabeth, is reported in 1981 to have received particular and affectionate attention. We find the same expression of an almost possessive sympathy, and anecdotes suggesting a privileged knowledge of the feelings, sentiments and preferences of members of the royal family.

The commonest theme in this sympathy is the apparent fatigue of the central figures; 'he sounds tired', 'she looks tired', 'they must be tired'. And I believe that this is a very mild expression of the sense that the central figure, usually of course the monarch, is on these occasions peculiarly vulnerable. The mistaking of a broadcast about the delay of Edward VII's Coronation for a news bulletin on page 47 excellently illustrates this anxiety, and the incident was fed by the rumours along similar lines in the preceding weeks. In 1981, there was a man whose exclusive interest, apparently, was in the safety of the bridal couple, once he was assured that they were safely inside St Paul's, he switched off, figuratively and literally.

Once the ceremony or climax of the occasion is over, the monarch is relatively safe. This quite illogical shift from anxiety to relief has deep roots in the human psyche. In those rituals that confer status, that transform an ordinary mortal into something more, and identify it with an exalted role, the contrast between the mortal human and the eternal role is most marked in the phase preceding the moment of transformation; the greater the office, the greater the contrast: the crown is never so heavy as when it is first imposed.

Kingship is an institution much older and more complex than constitutional monarchy and more primitive, in the sense that it is an expression of a powerful human need. For evidence of this we have only to contrast the rational demands of constitutional monarchy with the popular insistence on royalty. There is no constitutional requirement for the monarch's family, other than her immediate successor perhaps, to play any part, let alone be invested with the distinctive glamour of royalty; no presidential figure could evoke the insatiable curiosity about its private life that the Queen evokes – all this is the creation of the public, it is what we wish to be so.

Sometimes one reads the comment that the British Royal Family is to be likened to one or other of the unending television serials about some wealthy family. The judgement could not be more superficial: it is rather the reality of royalty and the distinctive complex of emotions which royalty alone can evoke, that accounts for the popularity of coloured shadows.

INDEX

(Numbers in italic refer to Part Two)

I. General

Index

Index

Index

Index

II. London

Index

436

III. Newspapers and Periodicals

IV. Popular Songs

Index

V. Index to Observers' Reports

CM: Mobile Squad.   CO: Observers.   CL: Answers to questionnaire.